I0843493

XRONIXLE

(krä-ni-kəl)

XRONIXLE

DANIEL VERASTIQUI

CHANNEL 8 PRESS
Austin, Texas

Second Edition, April 2025

Copyright © 2007, 2025 by Daniel Verastiqui
All rights reserved, including the right of reproduction
in whole or in part in any form. Published in the
United States of America by Channel 8 Press.

ISBN: 978-1-967847-00-6

This is a work of fiction. Names, characters, organizations,
events, and locations are either products of the author's
imagination or are used fictitiously. Any resemblance to
actual persons, living or dead, or to real entities, events,
or places is purely coincidental.

danielverastiqui.com

"The first sin is not creation—

it is believing your creation will remain yours."

- From The Reflections of Noetica, Volume II

A snowflake fell amongst the digital trees, pulsing lightly as it passed between its brothers, floating down to the white ground. X stood with his hands on the railing of the wooden bridge he had just finished creating, admiring the texture. It felt just like it would have in Terrareal, out there where nature was the true creator, where the bridge was just the sum result of necessity, a tool to be used to cross the oft-empty creek below it. But here, in the virtual construct, buried deep in the outer reaches of the Net, it was a true miracle. To make it feel like it did, smell like it did, was a feat that X took great pride in.

He looked around at the trees that had sprouted just moments before, already reaching high into a gray sky that flickered black when he wasn't concentrating. They were reproductions too, faithful, but not perfect, the byproduct of countless digital photos fed to fractal generators. They found the underlying code in all things natural and reproduced it for the entertainment of those who knew how to invoke them. The tips of the trees, so far overhead, were already frozen with accumulating snow and swaying in the still air.

It was just as he remembered it, if not better. Gone was the biting cold, though the snow and the frost remained. Gone was that awkward feeling of not knowing if he was going to get to kiss her or not. And in the back of his mind, he did not worry about what might lurk in the shadows of the forest. There was nothing to fear in the Net. Even so, he turned his head to the sky, reached for a memory that held no answers, and decided on a generic full moon, looming directly overhead, radiating a soft glow onto the forest scene.

X checked the glowing sliver on his wrist. C was late.

It was nothing to be worried about; C often made belated arrivals to their scheduled meetings. Life back in Laurel wasn't as free as X's in Austin. Where he had a supposed curfew of eleven that was little more than a requirement for him to show his student ID to get back into the dorms, C had parents who told her to be home before the streetlights came on. The reasons for her delays were always varied, but entirely plausible. Dinner had run long, her stepmother had made her do the dishes by hand, or the dogs had to be walked. X remembered those things, had seen them during the senior year he had spent in high school with her. He could imagine her standing over the sink or walking their miniature pug along the well-lit sidewalks of Dark Hawk Circle. He could even see her sitting at the table in their formal dining room, eyeing the clock that hung over the doorway leading to the kitchen. She'd be watching the minutes tick by, wondering how long he would wait for her.

His mind wandered, tried desperately to pull the fantasy in another direction. In this new and better version, he saw her drying the dishes with only the smallest amount of attention on the process, leaving them slightly damp in their stacks. Then she was announcing to her parents that she was done, her voice growing dim as she opened the door to the basement. Running down the stairs, she would start to smile, knowing that in a few minutes, she would be standing next to X, next to the boyfriend that had left her after graduation, had moved halfway across the country to go to college, and he would be as real as if he were standing there in the basement with her. Maybe the excitement and anticipation would be too much for her, X thought, and she would fumble with her rig, momentarily forget the way X had shown her to put it on.

A memory flashed in X's head and suddenly he was standing at his desk in his old bedroom, collecting various pieces of electronic equipment into a pile. His words came out automatically, "Have you ever jacked in?"

"What's that," asked C. She was sitting on the bed on the other side of the large basement room, buttoning the last clasp on her striped white and blue shirt.

X thought about the question for a moment and decided that a simple demonstration would be sufficient. He held up a tangled mess of black plastic, reflective lenses, earbuds, and miscellaneous wires. From one side of the glasses, a small electrode swung freely, destined for a spot just over the spine on the back of the neck. "Do you have one of these?"

"No, I don't think so. What is it?" She grabbed her bra from the floor where it had been discarded earlier and hid it in the folds of her jacket on the sofa. She joined X at his desk.

"This is a homebrew, vintage nineteen ninety-eight, BSC immersion rig."

C took the contraption from X and held it up to her face. It fit awkwardly. "Am I supposed to see something?"

"I haven't turned it on yet," said X. "Here, sit down first." He guided her into the chair. "Lean forward a little so I can stick this on." X grabbed the dangling electrode and wet it with a lick of his finger. He placed it carefully between two raised bumps on C's spine, letting his fingers linger on her neck an extra few seconds. "Alright," he said, easing her into a reclining position, "I'm going to send you to one of my favorite constructs. It's a small ice cream shop in Italy—"

"Is it going to show up on these glasses?"

"It'll be a little more intense than that, but all you have to remember is that nothing can hurt you in the Net. There is no pain, got that? There will probably be a man behind a counter. He's kind of big, but he's the nicest guy you'll ever meet. You're only going in for a few seconds, so don't try to take it all in at once. You need to ease into it."

C explored the electrode with her fingers. "Are you sure this isn't going to hurt?"

X smirked. "Well, naturally your first time might hurt a little."

He threw the switch.

C's mouth had been open slightly, intently drawing deep breaths to calm herself, but it snapped up tight as the images began pouring from the lenses, pale echoes of digital imagery seeping directly into her spine via the umbilical electrode. Her hands gripped the arms of the chair tensely, whitening at the knuckles.

He let her stay for all of seven seconds, long enough for him to notice that she was holding her breath, something she would have to unlearn if she ever wanted to stay in for an extended period of time. The whirring of the rig slowed as he depressed the switch, severing the feed.

As X removed the rig from her head, C let out the breath she had been holding as one long gust. Her body relaxed, melting into the chair. Her eyes blinked rapidly.

"That," she began, her voice failing her.

"Breathe," said X gently, half sitting on the desk, studying her.

C looked up at him. "I saw a man."

"Claudio."

"He was so real." The memory flickered. "He said something to me, in Italian."

X's teeth showed through his smile. "He was probably just saying good morning." He glanced at his wrist, tried to do the Italian time zone offset in his head, and then realized that it was just a simulated construct.

"That was so dope," said C, wistfully. "Can I go back?"

X tapped his wrist. "Next time," he promised. "Besides, I need to build you a proper rig, one fitted for that beautiful face of yours."

C blushed slightly at the compliment. "Did you make yours?"

"Yeah," he started, consciously trying to minimize the nerdcore language. "You can buy them, but the good ones are really expensive. It's cheaper just to build from scratch, code your own OS, load it up with custom firewalls, and…" He trailed off.

"Yeah, I didn't understand any of that."

"Don't worry," said X, chuckling, "it doesn't matter. It'll take me a week or two, but we'll get you your own rig. Then you'll be able to jack in at home."

"Can we jack in at the same time?"

"That's the idea." X took a step back as C rose from the chair, well within the border of his personal space.

"So we can hang out in there? And… do stuff?"

"As long as we're both jacked in, we can do anything we want."

"So," she said, moving her face closer to his, "is that gonna make us jack buddies?"

X smiled at her, closed the gap between them to steal a kiss. He drew back, his lips less than an inch from hers. "At the very least."

The sky pulsed red in the forest construct and a voice droned from nowhere, "C is calling." X shook his head and watched the bedroom memory crumble in front of him. A small bud materialized in his ear and he tapped it quickly to activate it.

"Where are you?" The words came across the line as a tinny sound in his head, digitized but recognizable.

"I'm here," he replied, "waiting."

"I don't see you."

"I see *you*," said X, looking off into the distance. In front of him, the bridge gave way to a snow-covered path that led away several feet, then broke off into two directions. Going to the left, he remembered, would take him back to Black Star Circle, to the row of townhouses that he had called home until last May. Going right would lead him to C's house. Of course, the construct would end long before he even got out of the forest. C was there now, on the outskirts of the construct, stuck on a one-way path wondering where he was. Through the bare trees, he could just make her out, standing with her back to him. "Turn around," he suggested.

"Oh," said C, spying a flash of color through the mesh of trees.

The sound in X's ear cut out and the earpiece dissolved in place. He listened to the sound of her boots crunching in the snow, tried to remember what other instruments had been playing that night. With a quick glance to the side, he brought water bubbling up through the rocks in the creek bed, water that began to flow off into the distance, gurgling all the way.

C took her steps slowly, leisurely, admiring the detail in the construct. She recognized the place, but it didn't jibe with the Terrareal version. Out in the real world, it was the middle of October, hardly fall, and certainly not snowing. "Oh my God," she said as she stepped onto the bridge, "how did you do all this?"

"Magic," replied X, making a flourish with his hands. "Do you like it?"

Her face lit up, the twinkling snowflakes reflecting off her teeth. "I *love* it!" She moved to embrace him, but X held up a finger.

"That's not how things went," he said, smiling. He took C's arm softly around the elbow and guided her to the end of the bridge. Her dark blue jacket had texture, with rough denim and pearly buttons. It even incorporated the melting snow as it landed. It was one of the most difficult texture programs that X had ever created, but the time and effort was worth it to see her wearing it.

X motioned with his hand to the empty bridge. "Watch this." He moved behind C and wrapped his arms around her waist. He concentrated, let C feel his hot breath on her cheek as he recited the magic words in his mind.

In the middle of the bridge, two vertical lines appeared, gashes in the fabric of virtuality. They spread slowly, letting a blinding light into the construct. Below, two compacted footprints appeared in the snow, joined shortly thereafter by another slightly smaller set. C's eyes marveled at the scene, watching the light dance in front of her, full of shifting hues and saturation, a sparkling rainbow of creation.

Two shapes came into being, perfect replicas of X and C, if not a few months younger. X's hair was longer then, pushed back over his ears with the rest hidden under a backwards baseball cap. C's clone wore a black coat with white-lined pockets. Her dark brown hair was down, covering her ears and protecting them from the cold that wasn't biting. Snow began to dot her head.

"How is this possible," asked C.

X opened his eyes, like waking from a pleasant dream. He squeezed C tighter and whispered quieting sounds in her ear.

The clones stood face to face, moving slowly, ramping up to the normal speed of life. They smiled, each reflecting the other's facial expression. The new X moved his lips, but there was no sound. The C clone moved her lips in reply, but the gurgling stream below was the only noise in the construct.

C turned her head to X with a questioning look on her face.

"They can't talk," he explained. "They're just virtual copies, not replays. They're not intelligent, just programmed." His voice turned softer. "No brain, no memories, nothing to go on."

X's clone began to move, walking in slow circles around his prey as she stood smiling at the center of the bridge.

"Are they textured," asked C.

"Yours is, mine's not. It'd be hard to do both."

"Can I touch them?"

"Yeah, I guess." He tried to make it sound like he had never considered the thought before.

C moved out of his embrace and approached the clones slowly. She didn't notice X focusing, bringing the puppets to a standstill. She pulled her white gloves from her hands, lifted one to her clone's face, and gasped quietly. It was textured, beautifully so. With her other hand, she felt her own cheek, felt the same warmth.

"This is wonderful," said C, looking back at X. "You did this all from memory?"

"More or less," replied X, a little embarrassed. "Computers can do a lot from one man's memory."

C took her clone's arm, raised it in front of her, and removed the blue gloves. "Her fingers are just like mine." The black sleeve fell back. "Jesus, she has goose bumps!"

X walked up beside her with a grin on his face. "Physically, she's as real here as you are."

"All over?"

"All over."

C stepped in front of her reversed reflection and unzipped the black coat. She pushed it off the shoulders of her clone and exclaimed, "She has boobs!" Under the textured red turtleneck, C found a thin white undershirt. She examined her double's breasts and then looked to her own chest in comparison. "Hers are bigger than mine."

X chuckled but stopped when he noticed C's disapproving look. "What can I say? Maybe my memory just isn't that good. I guess I should have spent more time with them."

"Uh huh," said C, no longer listening. Her eyes were walking the length of the clone's body. "Does she," she asked, hesitantly, "does she have a… you know? Is she *complete*?"

"Of course not," he lied. "What am I, sick?"

She shrugged in response.

"So," said X, trying to change the subject, "what are you in the mood for tonight?"

The smile faded from C's face as she continued to look over her clone. It was a few moments before her eyes came back to X. "I can't stay very long. I'm dogsitting for a lady down the street, so I have to get up really early tomorrow to go walk them."

"Them? How many does she have?" Inside, X's heart sank. He knew that when she said she couldn't stay long, she meant she had just popped in to say goodnight. Feigning interest in her extracurricular activities was an automatic response, a simpler and less damaging way of dealing with his disappointment.

"Like three," said C, "but they're big."

X drew her into his arms again, looked deep into her eyes to let her know that he was more interested in being close to her than anything else. After an empty pause, he said, "So I'll see you tomorrow then? Perhaps somewhere a little warmer?"

"I like it here," she replied, pressing against him, "it reminds me of the first time we kissed. That's what they were doing, right? I remember you walking around me like that. All I could think was *why doesn't he just kiss me already?*"

"Funny, I was thinking the same thing."

C reached up and touched him on the nose. "See you tomorrow then."

"Good night," replied X, "sweet dreams."

"What are you going to do for the rest of the night?"

X looked around at the construct. "I don't know. It's a big Net, I'm sure I'll find something to do."

C glanced at her clone. "Don't do anything I wouldn't do. Promise?"

Again he lied, "Sure."

"Then good night, I love you."

"And I you," he said as she pixilated in front of him, dissolving into the ether, bound for her homedir. In the space of two breaths, she would already be out of the Net.

X turned in place as the construct shimmered and pixilated. He walked aimlessly down the path, creating it on the fly as he moved deeper into the forest.

TWO

In a dorm room on the thirteenth floor of Jester West, a homemade immersion rig was whirring in the relative quiet. To his roommates, X appeared to be resting on his bed, reclined as if sleeping. Though he did not move, his brain was alight with activity, processing hundreds of millions of instructions per second, some without even realizing it. It was a voluntary coma, a willing surrender to the binary master. Under that rig, behind those eyes, an entire world was spinning just for him.

X walked through the dying construct, lost in thought, content to let the environment battle it out with the garbage collectors. Meanwhile, the rig focused on the path ahead, seeking information from any data store that could provide it, drawing mostly from X's memory and from the findings of commercial satellite scans. Real-world weather patterns were evaluated from years of accumulated measurements, bringing a true breeze into the world and making the forest sway in a much more realistic fashion. The snow began to fall again, unable to wait in the wings so long after its cue had been given.

The path was dark, but X was vaguely aware of which direction he was traveling. His house was now off to the right, C's to the left, and he was cutting between them, heading towards another neighborhood, one connected by the forest paths. The trees would hold for another hundred yards or so, then give way to a small clearing, and in that clearing…

X stopped, his train of thought lost to the ether. In front of him, a section of the forest flickered like a faulty light bulb. At one moment, it was the wooded sanctuary as it should have been, cut down the middle by the dirt walkway. The next, the forest had been wiped clean, the grass and dirt replaced by gravel and concrete barriers. Instead of the high trees, there were towering streetlamps arranged in pairs along the center median. The stationary blur of a speeding car stood shimmering off to the left, its headlights undulating, persisting despite the flicker.

The satellites, thought X. The rig was trying to reconcile two conflicting data points. Although his memory told it that there was a forest there, the satellites said different, said that as of two weeks ago, there was a fully functional highway bypass there. "Snowden River," said X, remembering the name of the road from a map he had seen. They had started construction before he left but had not yet leveled the forest when he last drove by. It amazed him how much could change in just a few short months. A spring, a summer, and a forest lost forever. He shut his eyes momentarily and concentrated.

Slowly, the highway began to fade, dimming into nothing. When only the snow and trees remained, X continued his walk, happy to have set the record straight. It was, after all, his Net. Anything he wanted was his at the slightest request. If he simply imagined it, he could have the forest open up in front of him, reveal the playground he knew to be there, and there would be C, sitting on the slide, absently kicking at the stones with her faded tennis shoes.

"I knew you couldn't stay away for long," said X, walking off the path and onto the loose rocks. His feet sank at awkward angles.

C didn't reply, though she did look up and acknowledge him with her eyes, an empty kind of welcome.

He slipped into place behind her on the slide, straddling her body. She was wearing jean overalls, and he took a moment to trace its texture with his fingers. Looking up, he saw that the sky had cleared, and the moon had turned dull, letting the stars twinkle in the darkness.

"I had a good day today," he said, speaking with his head tilted back. He moved his chin slightly, dragging it through her hair. "I spent some time with Natalie. Have I ever told you about her? She has blonde hair and blue eyes and likes to wear baseball hats." X shook his head in wonder. "I don't know what it is about hats on women, you know, with their ponytails pulled through the back? I don't think you ever wore one, did you?"

X pulled his hands back and slid them into the openings on the side of C's overalls. He moved them forward and down until he could pull back the ends of her shirt and run his hands over bare skin. His cold fingers traced lines over her stomach, causing her shoulders to bob in autonomic shivers.

He began again. "I thought about you a lot today, mostly in Calculus. The professor can barely speak English, so G and I usually just sit in the back and mess around. There's a girl, Becky, that I think G likes, but I think she's more into me." He smiled, waited, but C said nothing. His fingers moved in small circles around her warm skin, twisting and winding their way higher and higher. X's hands went flat against her flesh, moved up the sides of her breasts, came together in the middle, and then back down again. He moved his head next to hers and watched the side of her mouth, listening for the quickened breathing that he knew would never come.

"Maybe a change of scenery," suggested X. At once, the construct shifted out from under them, replaced by a darkened street. A porch shot up from below, settling into position where the slide had been. C's body barely registered the change. X stood and walked halfway down the sidewalk, listening for any sound other than his own heart beating in his ears. It would have looked much friendlier in the daytime, but a single memory was pulsing more brightly than the others and the rig latched onto it with enthusiasm.

"This was the night we said our last goodbye," said X. He turned to look at C. "Face to face, anyway. Do you remember?" He didn't wait for a reply. "You were sitting there, and I was standing here and thunder—"

A low rumble erupted in the distance.

X lifted his hand to the sound. "And thunder was crashing. A storm was coming. I remember because I had to drive back in the rain." The more he thought about it, the more surreal the whole night became. A threatening storm moving low over the East Coast, waiting until he had parted ways with C before unleashing its torrent on the ground below. "It was lucky. Or divine intervention. What do you think?"

That was the problem, X realized. She didn't think anything because she couldn't think at all. She was just a clone, a virtual copy, a shell of the girl he loved. It reminded him of the videos he kept of C, of the way he used to watch them with the sound turned down, watching the movement of her lips, knowing the words by memory, but slowly realizing that the sound of her voice was fading with each viewing. This clone was far more advanced, full of tactile wonders that video could never provide, but he knew that the same limitation existed. He could go back and replay the memory of that night, give in to the simulation and just experience it as he had before, a spectator to a rerun. He could change the memory if he wanted to, break out of it and create a new one…

X stopped, looked up from where his gaze had drifted. Anger flickered briefly, both acknowledged and dismissed by the rig as an erroneous piece of data. His voice was calm when he spoke next.

"Why do you have to go to bed so early?" He sat down on the porch next to her, tried to imagine that it wasn't him doing it when she pulled her knees closer to her chest and wrapped her arms around them. "I have class at eight tomorrow, but you don't see me leaving." If only there could be more time, he thought to himself. More time to spend with her. With the other her. The *real* her.

The transition to a long-distance relationship hadn't been easy, but the fact that it was inevitable had helped both of them deal with the change. At first, X tried to jack in and see C on a regular basis, almost every night. Some nights she would be sick, or like tonight, have to get up early the next morning, but it didn't bother him much. There was always something else to do, something that could be found while roaming the hallways of Jester or walking the sidewalks of campus. Sometimes he met the occasional girl, those with whom he felt a strange attraction, the kind he knew had nothing to do with the Longhorn hat that she wore on her head.

The Net allowed him and C to continue their relationship despite the distance between them. He was fifteen-hundred miles away from her, yet he continued to hold her hand, to kiss her when she was sad, and to make love to her when they both needed to feel better. In the adaptive ether of cyberspace, their relationship took on new intensity. They traveled to distant places, all simulated, but real enough to enjoy. The limitations of their age, of him being a legal adult and her not yet past the age of consent, were removed. Money was no object; they simply did anything and everything they wanted. Even in the virtual world, their hands showed the simple gold bands around their fingers. In the days before he left, he had shown her the rings. He remembered every detail of her face as she looked at him and asked, "Promise?"

"Promise," he had said back to her.

X reached over, pulled C's hand from her knees, and examined her fingers. Of course, the clone would not be wearing the band. It was not the real C that he was sitting next to. This clone had never made a promise, never loved him enough to take that kind of risk as C had. Yet, she was there. She had not left him for the chance to get a solid seven hours of sleep. She would never leave him.

It was dedication that he admired.

The construct fell away again, growing in brightness until the world around them had turned a stark white. C's body floated in the ether, unfolding slowly as gravity released its hold on her limbs. X narrowed his eyes, intent on getting the code right, but not wanting to miss any of the show. One by one, the snaps on her overalls began to pop open. Her clothes drifted off her body and dissolved into the white nothing as soon as they left orbit. In just a few minutes, C's clone was completely naked, and with no processing power being wasted on an environment, the rig was free to put as much detail into her avatar as possible. From the light hair on her forearm, to the individual valleys of her lips, a passer-by could not have been convinced that she wasn't the real thing.

"Do you love me?" In the barebones construct, his words echoed dully. "Do I still excite you?" At this, he placed his hand on her stomach and traced a line down her body. The pressure of his fingers caused C's legs to open.

The edges of X's lips dipped slightly.

"And they say it's biological, an automatic physical response." He removed his hand and closed his dry fingers into a fist. He moved his face near hers and spoke into vacant eyes. "Your problem, dear, is that you lack emotion." Taking her hand, he said, "We'll have to fix that."

Without any pretense or show, X's clothes dissolved on his avatar, revealing a body that was more of what he wished he looked like, rather than what reality insisted upon.

The nonexistent light in the construct went out and somewhere amongst the darkness, the excitement, and the release, X fell asleep, unsure of whether it was right of him to seek solace in the all too willing arms of C's clone.

THREE

Terrareal was pale compared to the vibrant luster of the Net. Where the bright neons of the construct had once tickled his eyes, there was now only plain blues and faded browns. The campus around X stood as a relic in a modern age, with buildings that had been erected long before the first piece of data was ever packaged into a frame. Walking through it with fifty-eight thousand other students was not something he was keen to, but it was a welcome alternative to what had greeted him when he woke up.

His dorm room in Jester West was nothing more than a converted study room, furnished with three sets of chairs, desks, and beds. There was even a sink installed in the corner for the off chance that one of his roommates might want to wash their hands. It was a far cry from the bedroom basement that he had called home back east. There, the space between his desk and bed was filled with a couch, loveseat, and a coffee table. Here, it was just a mysterious stain and someone's discarded boxers.

Not that it was all bad; there were a few times that X appreciated the novelty of living on a coed floor with a bunch of teenagers who were as unaccustomed to community showers as he was. It happened one morning when he was on the way to an early class. As he was heading towards the elevators, he noticed a girl walking down the adjacent hallway. She had a towel wrapped around her body and was securing it in a knot in the middle of her chest. In her other hand, she carried a small burnt orange basket of shampoos and soap. X watched her saunter away from him, admiring her slender shoulders and exposed back.

When the girl arrived at her door, she fumbled with her room key and dropped it on the floor. Reflexively, she reached out for it with her other hand, releasing her grip on the towel. It opened slightly in the front and then slid down her back in slow motion. X smiled and kept his eyes focused. Already, he knew that this would be a memory he would be replaying often. As the towel fell away, it revealed the perfectly tan skin of her back, broken by a line of bumps running its length and disappearing into the smooth curves of her backside.

X felt her head turning and stepped back behind the corner, sparing her the embarrassment. He waited until he heard the door click before crossing the hallway to the elevators. Ever since that day, his steps always lingered at the corner of the hallway, peering down into the girls' section, hoping to catch another brief glimpse of flesh.

"I still say that shit never happened," said G, who had fallen into step beside X as they passed in front of the Main Building. The two had barely met a month prior, in a Computer Science weeder class that taught functional programming. After the first test, which they both failed, X responded to a post on the class discussion board in which G wrote, "Anyone else take it up the ass on that test?"

"I've got the memory to prove it," replied X. He tapped the side of his head and smiled.

"Yeah, well, until you give me the download, I say you're full of it."

X nodded as they stepped out of the hot fall sun and into the air-conditioned Texas Union. "Buy me lunch," said X, looking over the various fast-food kiosks, "and we'll talk about a sneak peek. Deal?"

"That depends, will your girlfriend be joining us today?" G smacked his gum loudly as he removed his aviator sunglasses and slipped them into his breast pocket.

"I don't think she can afford the plane ticket."

"I didn't mean her," said G, starting in the direction of the snaking line in front of the Burger King. "I meant the blonde. What was her name again?"

"You know her name," replied X, "and Natalie's not my girlfriend. We're just… friends."

"With benefits, you mean."

"Just order your damn food," suggested X.

"Alright," said G, raising his voice a little, "but I'm going to have to turn around to do it. Try to resist the urge to hump my ass."

X noticed the curious look from the girl in line behind him. He raised an effeminate hand and whispered, "He gets so bitchy when he's hungry."

A raised middle finger appeared over G's shoulder.

The dining room of the Texas Union was packed with midday lunchers. They sat in twos and threes with their backpacks thrown carelessly on the linoleum floor. X tried to sample the many conversations as he and G made their way through the maze of unevenly spaced tables to a clean row in the back near the windows. It was a habit of his to try to listen in, glean some information that wasn't meant for his ears. He heard lamentations of midsemester exams and disbelief that the guy standing near the fountain outside was just *giving* away free t-shirts and all you had to do was sign up for a credit card. In front of him, X could see G doing the same thing, saw the way his eyes darted from table to table.

"The way I see it," said G, setting his tray on the table, "that woman should not be allowed to teach at the university level." He was referring to the Philosophy 313K test they had taken earlier that morning. "That was absolute chaos, just fuckin' *Lord of the Flies*."

"I wrote a two-page essay about how the teacher was not in control of her class. I guess that doesn't really prove the union of A with B though." X took a pull from his Blue Rain, felt the liquid cool the area behind his lungs.

"If I don't get a good grade in that class…" G trailed off, wondering if it would even do any good to write to the dean. "If I don't pass, I'm going to have to take drastic action."

"Such as?"

"Hack the planet!"

X laughed and casually looked around the room to see if anyone had overheard. Shaking his head, he said, "You think the UT databank is just going to spread its legs for you? You couldn't even do it with *my* help."

"I could do it with this." With a bizarre little flourish, G produced a small cube from the side pocket of his backpack. The diminutive white box glinted in the ambient sunlight.

"Oh, is it like that," asked X. He pulled a similar cube from his bag and placed it gently on his tray. "Hell, half the wannabe hackers at this school have cubes. You're going to have to bring something heavier to the mix if you really want to grease the wheels."

"It's not the cube," said G, placing a pointed finger on the top surface, "it's what's *in* the cube."

X stared at him expectantly, until finally waving a hand to prompt G to continue.

"Actually, I'm not quite sure what it is," admitted G. "I got it off a scan in Taylor Hall. Some data rat had it sitting out for the taking on his viewee."

"And you just assumed a random piece of code would be able to magically change your grade? You don't even know what it does!"

"It has to do *something*," protested G.

"Sure, wipe your fucking mainframe or worse, delete all your porn." X tried to keep his tone even, tried to use humor as he talked down to his friend. A part of him couldn't believe that G would really be that foolish.

"Exactly!" G smiled as if the argument had already been won. "Why spend all your time trying to sneak in when you can crash the whole databank? Smash that fucker to pieces and then my grade, and everyone else's, goes the way of white teaching assistants!"

X glanced at the sliver in his wrist, saw the time passing one in the afternoon. His next class didn't start until two-thirty, but it was still on the other side of campus, an eternal distance in the unusually warm October. For a moment, he forgot all about G's scheme and instead saw a blanket of clouds descending on Austin, cooling it enough to make the kids in their shorts and tees shiver uncontrollably. Then the snow would come and the dull colors would be replaced by a pristine white, a blank slate full of possibilities.

"Seriously, how the hell am I supposed to learn anything when the TA just got off the midnight train from Bombay?"

The image of mag-elevated train tracks spanning the ocean flashed in X's head, making him chuckle. "Maybe you should take a Hindi class."

G seemed to be offended by the suggestion. "And just when the *fuck* am I going to need to speak Indian?!"

"Namaste," said a voice from behind X.

He looked up to see Natalie standing next to the table, her arms around two books that she held close to her chest. "G, aap kaise hai," she continued.

G nodded a greeting and leaned back in his chair. He looked Natalie up and down, smirking.

"How did the philosophy test go," she asked, turning back to X.

Laughing, G picked up his cube from the table and muttered, "I'm going to need this."

"It went alright," said X, knowing that instead of the two-page essay questioning the qualifications of the professor, he had left most of his questions blank. Even if he got the others right, he was sure to fail the exam.

"Good," said Natalie, shifting in place. After an awkward pause, she continued, "I just wanted to say hi. I've got a Geo class at one-thirty." She glanced at G and then back. "What are you guys up to tonight?"

"Well," replied X, "G there's going to hack the whole goddamn planet. But I've got no plans." Not true, he told himself. There was his standing meeting with C at nine o'clock.

"I was thinking maybe I could come by. My roommate is annoying the hell out of me today. Do you think I could study in your room?"

"Sure." X nodded, caught G's eyes for half a second, and then smiled.

"How about nine?"

"Nine's not good for me," he replied, his voice level.

G stifled a knowing laugh.

"How about ten then," pressed Natalie.

"Ten?" X looked to G for confirmation. When he nodded in agreement, X said, "Ten works for me." Suddenly, he detected an unidentifiable scent on the air, a smell he could never describe or even be completely sure was real. Yet it emanated from Natalie, making him lean toward her slightly.

She smiled. "Great, I'll see you then." She turned quickly on the spot and made her way out of the dining room with X's eyes glued to her rear as she went.

"Goddamn! I can't believe you're gettin' some of that!" G smacked the table with his hand at the absurdity of it all.

X folded the paper wrapper around the remains of his hamburger. "I'm not getting any of that."

"I retract my statement," said G, jovially. "I can't believe you're *not* gettin' some of that! She's practically putting it on the table for you!" He shook his head. "You've been living in the Net too long, man. Your brain is fried!"

"Yeah, *my* brain is fried. You're the one who wants to crash the databank of one of the biggest colleges in the world with a piece of code that probably does nothing but emulate Tetris. You took it off a viewee in Taylor, for fuck's sake. That's not exactly Black Hat central."

"Alright," conceded G, "but what else am I going to do with my time? Study?"

"We *are* at college." X stood and arranged the trash on his tray.

"College isn't for studying," said G, raising his voice again. "College is for gettin' drunk, gettin' high, and gettin' laid!" A smatter of applause broke out from the adjacent tables.

"Not all of us are into the sordid pastimes of the proletariat."

"And not all of us are fucking our so-called friends behind our girlfriend's back," returned G.

"No," admitted X, a sly smile crossing his face, "no we aren't."

As they exited the dining room, G asked, "What the fuck is a proletariat?"

The man by the fountain was still handing out t-shirts when X and G paused near him briefly before heading off to their respective classes.

"You wanna run and gun tonight," asked G, fiddling with his sunglasses.

"Depends on how long this thing with Nat lasts."

"So I'll see you at ten-o-two then?"

X shook his head dismissively and laughed. He punched G in the shoulder as he walked past him. "Don't load that code, okay? If you're really serious about changing your grade, you need to get something from a more reputable source. You need to do a proper data rush. Take Jape with you, he knows the best quarries."

"Jape's on the West Coast. It'll be like three before he even gets jacked in."

"And this conflicts with your schedule how?"

"Beauty sleep," replied G, running his fingers down his light beard.

"Then do it Friday," said X, already walking away.

"And what would you suggest I do in the meantime?"

"Read your damn textbook!"

By the time G could come up with a worthy comeback, X had already disappeared into the crowd. For a moment, he imagined his Philo textbook, packed to the brim with words and equations that his mind refused to process. Reading it would take time and effort, two things he didn't really want to waste on schoolwork. G popped a piece of gum into his mouth and tossed the wrapper at the back of the guy hawking credit cards.

Data rush, thought G. Fuck yeah.

FOUR

X checked his wrist. The time was well past ten and still no message from C. She hadn't shown up for their nightly meeting, had kept him waiting so long that eventually he just jacked out and stared idly at the ceiling. Then, in glaring contrast, a knock had come at his door exactly at the stroke of ten.

Now he was sitting on his lofted bed with Natalie lying across it on her stomach, flipping through the pages of a two-hundred-dollar government textbook. Propped up against the wall next to her feet, X played a video game on the small device that he held in his hands. His eyes drifted to her feet and up her thin body.

"This is so bor-ing," said Natalie, slapping the book shut with one hand. She looked back over her shoulder and tossed the book to X. "How about you do my homework for me? I'm going to take a nap."

X picked up the book where it had landed and placed it on top of the wardrobe next to the bed. He noticed his wrist again, saw the time slipping away with still no word from C. Feigning a stretch, he moved into position beside Natalie, carefully avoiding the six-foot plunge to the floor below. He propped himself up on one elbow, facing her, still playing his video game.

Natalie had crossed her arms under her head and was facing the wall. The beeping of the game brought her attention back to X.

"Not into government," asked X, when he could see her eyes again.

"The professor is horrible," replied Natalie, her voice muffled by her arms. "She just goes on and on, droning like an ATM. It might just be the dullest voice I've ever heard." For a moment, she looked up at him and he looked back at her. She blinked. "Do you wear trainers?"

"I'm supposed to, but I don't." He thought about how blurry the campus looked and how crystal clear the Net always appeared. It must be doing something to my eyes, he thought. Adjusting for his near-sightedness, bringing everything into focus just for him. His train of thought sped ahead, wondering if C saw the construct differently, since her vision was perfect as far as he knew. Where he saw high definition and infinite clarity, did she see only a blur? Could the construct be two things at once?

"Mine are starting to hurt," said Natalie, gently rubbing her eyes. "Do you have a case I could borrow?"

"Yeah." X sat up and hopped down to the desk below the bed and then onto the stained carpet. He retrieved a small rectangular case from the sink and lifted it up to Natalie. She unscrewed the lids, pulled two plastic sheets from her eyes, and placed them in the case.

"Thanks, that's much better." She handed him the case and rubbed her eyes with her fists.

"No problem," said X, climbing back up into the bed. He reclined next to her, looking at the ceiling.

"You got anything to help us relax," asked Natalie after a few minutes of silence, a sly smile on her face.

X looked at her for a moment, debating whether he wanted to share one of his personal constructs with her. And just as he was leaning towards the negative, the scent appeared again, reminded him that despite everything his conscious mind was telling him, he desired to be with her. "I think I have something you might like."

From a small compartment at the foot of the bed, he pulled out an elongated black box. From inside, he produced a small white cube similar to the one he had shown G at lunch, but with two electrodes connected to it instead of one.

"What's that?" Natalie seemed genuinely unsure.

"This is a modified memory cube with a custom jacksplit. It's like a mini version of the Net but designed for just one or two people." He motioned to the electrodes. "You interested?"

Natalie bit her lip for a second. "Let's do it."

X attached one electrode to her neck and the other to his. Side by side, they reclined on the bed, the white cube between them.

"I'm going to set an auto-close for thirty minutes, but the time will seem to go much faster than that. You ready?"

"Yeah," said Natalie, sounding uncertain.

"Don't worry," said X. He tapped the cube lightly.

Natalie gasped as her body dropped away from the ceiling and the walls stretched like rubber into the distance. There was a flash of white light and then the world as she knew it was only a distant memory.

X felt the current pulling at his body, shifting him from side to side as the water rushed into a tight bend. Beside him, he could feel Natalie, her hand holding tight to his. He was momentarily disappointed by her apprehension. It was going to be a short ride as it was and spending half of it scared to death would only dampen her appreciation of it. The river flowed like a mixture of blood and drug through a hungry vein, carrying them deep into the infinite construct, past banks of forbidding trees that grew right to the very edge of the water. The sun was low in the sky behind them, lighting the world in a subdued clarity that reality could never have matched, exposing the sheer black of the knotted trees, standing in contrast to the similar blue hues of the sky and river.

Gradually, the trees began to give up on their warning, stopped trying to convince the intruders that they'd be better off turning around and going home. It was all posturing, as significant as a *Beware of Dog* sign on the fence surrounding an empty yard. X understood their behavior because he had designed it himself. Had it been another user, one without the digital signature contained in X's avatar, the trees would have been more like sharpened posts. And they would not have stood idly by on the banks, but instead, would have risen from the depths of the water in a never-ending barricade.

X glanced at Natalie, whose eyes darted quickly from one side of the river to the other, watching the transformation of the landscape. No one else would ever make it this far, thought X. Not unless I wanted them to. Everything in here was protected.

A cool sensation began to creep down their backs while the hidden sun warmed their faces. They shifted in the water, unsure of which feeling was more preferable. Ahead of them, they saw only sky, the way it would look as one passed the crest of a waterfall.

Natalie shot a worried look at X, but he only smiled in return. Somehow, his expression calmed her, reassured her that everything was going to be alright. She searched her fuzzy memory, tried to remember what purpose had brought them to this place. Was she simply swimming in a river with that boy who lived down the hall? And if that were true, why did all of this, the whole world, seem so wonderfully unreal? I was in his room, she thought, trying to regain some sentience. I was in his room, and we were on his bed…

The waterfall loomed and as it did, a vast expanse of green opened up below it. It stretched deep into the draw distance, pulling at every fiber of the cube's power, bringing the whole of its switching speed to bear.

They fell, washed over the edge, experiencing an acceleration unlike anything Terrareal had to offer. Tripping through the empty space, he heard Natalie screaming in delight, knew that the tetrameth rush was overtaking her nervous system. Of course she felt good, he thought. This was his code, his synthetic drugs seeping through her body. He knew it was penetration beyond anything she had ever experienced, even if she wasn't consciously aware of it.

Tumbling through the void, the water gone and the green world spinning and blurring around him, X gave into the drug, let it consume him completely.

He shut his eyes, blocked out all sensory instructions except those provided by his cube. When I open my eyes, he thought, I will no longer see with my physical self, but with the programmed ferocity of machine code, of sixty-four-character strings of ones and zeros being processed simultaneously by twelve intricately connected processors.

When I open my eyes.

The simulation was ending; he could feel Terrareal reaching its intruding hand into his virtual paradise. And then, there it was, in the murky green of the construct. A tower of infinite beauty and splendor, rising high above the obsidian wall that grew up around it.

A curious sight, in any state of mind.

X let out a shallow laugh that was answered by Natalie's soft chuckling. The room around them was drenched in the aftereffects of the drug construct. The only things that truly existed were their bodies and the soft sheets between them. They talked through the fog, discussing the monotony of classes and the joys of being free from parental rule. Their hands met; she took the first step and put hers on his. X managed to command the lights off and they continued to commune in the darkness. Eventually, sleep overtook them.

Around two in the morning, the roommates came home, talking in whispers as they undressed and got into their respective beds. X moved slowly and rolled on his side to face Natalie. After carefully placing the cube on the shelf, he shifted his body and scooted closer to her, pulling one arm under his head and draping the other over her body. She was awake, if only slightly. Her bare legs pushed at the sheets under her, rubbing against each other for warmth. X sat up and grabbed a blanket from the foot of the bed. He draped it over her legs, pulled it up over the both of them, and resumed his position next to her. His hand dangled next to her stomach and he moved his fingers slowly, testing the waters.

Natalie took a deep breath, too deep for a woman lost in sleep. Gaining confidence, X moved under her shirt, tracing the shallow gully in the center of her abs. His hand reached the stiff lower border of her bra, making the butterflies erupt in his stomach. Natalie stirred, felt the presence of his hand, and reached for it with hers. She moved it out from under her shirt and pulled X's arm around her, his hand safely entombed between hers. Smiling to herself, she pushed closer to him.

Resigned to sleep, X looked over his shoulder at his roommates' bunk beds. Bo's head was propped up by his arm, motionless, but looking in X's direction. In the darkness of the room, he could see Bo's enhanced eyes, glimmering slightly, reflecting the small amount of light seeping in around the door. The eyes turned away, projecting two small dots on the wall next to the bunk beds. X turned his head back and pushed his nose closer to Natalie's hair. He took a deep breath, momentarily reveled in the realness of the scent, and then promptly fell asleep, dreaming once more of the Net.

It wasn't clear where the Net began, though relatively, everything started and ended at the user's homedir, the personal netspace where they first appear after jacking in. Home directories came in uniform sizes, each one with a small, permeable column, roughly the size of an old-style phone booth. This transfer column was protected by a coded field and typically supplemented with custom firewalls, allowing only the homedir's owner to pass through. It protected the body when the owner's mind was gone, preventing anyone from jacking out into someone else's equipment.

All homedirs exist in an infinite core at the very center of the Net. From a distance, it appears as a light blue fog. Only when approached does it coalesce into something tangible. From these jumping off points, users can travel anywhere in the Net using a system of radial coordinates that specify locations in relation to the core. Most people spend very little time in their homedirs, using them only for entry and exit. With the proper rig and some optimized code, the process of jacking in can take less than a second, with the user appearing at their destination almost immediately. The infinitely small amount of time spent in their homedir passes without recognition, but it passes nonetheless.

When the Net was given spatial existence, it quickly began to expand into the empty ether, overwriting the lines of null data bit by bit. Personal websites became vast homes on green lawns. The great portal sites became resort destinations with virtual peep shows and animated card dealers. The blog ghettos flourished into a million town squares, each with hundreds of people screaming their opinions at each other, all believing their voice to be more important than the others. These areas formed a ring around the core, banding together to provide content with a minimal amount of fuss. It was beyond these metropolitan frontiers that X found his paradise, comfort in a sea of indeterminate states.

He carved out his own little niche in the fabric of the Net, surrounded it with the hottest and brightest-burning firewall that he could imagine, and lived out his greatest dreams and deepest desires within it.

FIVE

X felt it the next day, a change in the way the world flowed around him. He knew without knowing that somewhere, everything had gone wrong. Whether it was the absence of a governing body or the loss of self-control, X couldn't tell. But something was definitely off.

He had once believed that the Net could, and would, make all of his dreams come true, allow him to live out a life with C that age and society wouldn't allow. So what if she was three years younger than him for a few months out of the year? So what if she had only been fifteen the night he first took her to bed? There were laws against that sort of thing, laws that placed limits on the interaction between their two age groups.

Even in the relative anonymity of the Net, they still took precautions. They met only in private, in constructs off the main slab of the Net. The fear of prying eyes, of people who judged and punished, kept X's nights filled with the devising of rooms, then of doors, and then finally, of locks.

Despite the sneaking, the hiding, and the falsification of a platonic relationship in public places, they still found a way to enjoy each other, mostly at night, when all of C's engagements for the day had been taken care of. The first few months, their dates were like clockwork. X often met her at her homedir and then whisked her away to some exotic island the moment she materialized.

She was always so happy to see him.

But gradually her smile became less and less pronounced, until finally her avatar slouched under the weight of some emotional burden. He noticed that her arrivals were coming later and their time spent together began to dwindle to nothing, to brief interludes with barely enough time to say hello and goodbye. Then there was last night, when she didn't show up at all, had allowed him the opportunity to sit and wait for Natalie instead of being preoccupied with the one he should have been spending the night with.

In the morning, he woke to find that Natalie had already left, and that his world had been changed forever. He skipped classes and ate what was left of his stash of chips for lunch, leaving his room only once to visit the bathroom.

Then at noon it came, a message from C. "I'm tired," it said, "I had to work late. I won't be on tonight." X checked the send date and found that it was only a few minutes old. She was using some cheap code to make him think that she had sent the message the night before and that somehow he had overlooked it.

A few minutes later, another message came. "Sorry about last night. See you tonight?"

X thought for several hours about his reply, until the light behind the blinds had finally faded and the ruckus in the hallways had settled to a comfortable white noise. He stared at his rig on the bedpost, stared until his eyes could no longer stay open.

X sat with C in his lap, her arms wrapped around his body. They were on the side of a hill he had recreated from a childhood memory. It had a long gentle slope that ended at the edge of a lake with a Japanese name that he couldn't remember. It was night in the construct, simulated, but dark enough to see the twinkling stars strewn haphazardly across the great expanse of black above them. The rig's rendering engine struggled to deliver the necessary graphics, such that the reflections of the stars stuttered in the smooth glass of the lake.

They kissed.

And each kiss brought with it an explosion of light and gunpowder, a firework exploding over the lake below them. There was no sound, however, only the faint warmth on their cheeks and the glow on each other's faces. Trillions of individual pixels ascended, separated from their brothers, and returned to the lake below, absorbed into the simulated water, recycled into the next launch. For the longest time, a fiery rainbow shone in the construct.

Their lips parted as C withdrew and X opened his eyes slowly, expecting to see the smile that had so often greeted him after such moments. But it was not there. C's eyes drifted off to the right, away from the technicolor that was now fading in the construct's atmosphere. There was no smile, only a look of fretful concentration, the best interpretation that the Net could provide for such a complex emotion.

"What's the matter," X asked, squeezing her around the waist.

C's eyes searched for the words in the thick green grass around them.

"Hey," he continued, "what's wrong?"

She looked up at him, almost studying his face. "It's already going to be November next week," she said, her words imparting more than he could safely assume on his own. "You will have been gone for six months. I haven't seen you in half a year."

X shook his head. "I saw you three days after I left and almost every day since then. We haven't spent more than five days apart, unless you count that camping trip you took to New York. And even then, we managed to message each other. Sometimes a simple note is good enough." His inflection faltered on his last word, made it come out more like a question than a statement.

Looking away, C asked, "What are we doing?"

"Literally?"

"What's all this for?"

So it wasn't enough, thought X. If anything in the past six months had mattered at all, she would know what it was all for. To keep them together, to bind them to each other until they could be reunited. A beautiful plan, if executed correctly. Use the phone, use instant messaging, use the Net. It was all a stopgap, a way to forestall the growing apart that was inevitable in every long-distance relationship. All he had to do was hold on long enough and things would work themselves out.

He tried to soothe her confusion. "We're hanging out, having a good time. Aren't you enjoying yourself?"

"I am, but…" The modulation in her voice broke. "But why are we doing this?"

A breeze filtered up from the bottom of the hill, cutting through the grass and then angling upwards once it hit their bodies. C's hair flew in the gust, jumping out sharply to one side. The shape of her face seemed to change, seemed to lose its programmed identity and morph into something temporarily unrecognizable.

He had only ever known her as a girl who loved him, from the moment he first met her, throughout their abbreviated courtship, into the months that they spent as boyfriend and girlfriend. How strange it had been to pack up everything in his life, move to a new high school in his last year, expecting to endure the social isolation that had plagued him for so long. But then he met her, met her with her hair hanging loosely and braces glinting in the evening sun. The weather changed that day. The heat of the summer subsided and so too did his anxiety. The breeze came and made everything better for him, told him that with her, it would all be okay.

She didn't disappoint. The friends, the parties, the impromptu make-out sessions in her bedroom, in the basement, in the forest, on the bridge, on the playground. So much time spent with his lips pressed to hers, his hands lost in unfamiliar exploration. She opened to him so quickly, so readily, that X had no choice but to fall in, let himself be swept along by the tide. Time with C mirrored time in the Net, passing in a blink of an eye, but at the cost of months, so that by the time he was hopelessly lost in love with his newest toy, it was time to leave her.

There was not an ounce of protest from C then; she knew it was inevitable. He recalled how easily she shut her emotions up, kept them hidden to spare him the guilt of leaving her with the school year not yet ended, another two years left before her own graduation. He'd be going off to a new world and she'd be left alone with the same people who had been there before X's arrival. Does she love me enough, he wondered, to fend off the other boys, those that had been waiting in the wings while he had his way with their dream girl? What would they do now that he was gone?

She loves so easily, worried X.

A knot began to tighten in his virtual stomach, vibrating in the interval between his heartbeats. He recognized the feeling, had felt it a few times before, with other girls, in the days before he lost them. But that had been an earlier time in his life. He was younger, had been emotional, and had low self-esteem. C changed all that, showed him how easy it was to function in the real world. For a time, she made him forget the solitude of the Net by taking him to basketball games and movies, anywhere she could find a crowd. She changed him, changed the way he did things. It was supposed to be different with her.

Silence.

X's head hung low, defeated, trying to puzzle through a thousand different explanations and responses. When he looked up, he saw C contemplating the dimming construct, her face contorting in small spasms around her cheeks and eyes.

She was crying.

For all of the modern technology that made the Net possible, there was no interpretation for crying. It was an as-of-yet unsupported feature, an enhancement request that had been put on indefinite hold. And why not? There was nothing to cry about in the Net, no physical pain to feel. The Architects had found no need for such a concept as crying and ignored all suggestions to the contrary. Somewhere along the way, a compromise was suggested. A simple hack was distributed to account for the trembling of the cheeks, the narrowing of the eyes, and the vibration of the lower lip. But so far, never a simulated tear. Someday, thought X, someone is going to hurt deeply enough to make it happen.

C cried her invisible tears as X fought the involuntary code that was instructing his throat to tighten, contract in on itself.

"C, please, don't. I'm sorry, but I don't know why you're crying. Tell me what it is."

She drew herself closer to X and buried her face in his shoulder, evoking the memory of so much time spent in that position. "I want to be with you," she said, her voice muffled.

"You *are* with me," said X, moving his hand over her textured hair.

She pulled her head back slightly, enough to meet her eyes with his. "For real. I want to be with you for real. Not in this… place." Her head sank again as her voice dripped with resignation. "I just want to be with you."

The words registered in his head, but for some reason, he saw them as if they were text. In his version, she had crossed out the word *someone* and replaced it with *you*. Doubt raced in tight circles around X's brain.

"You said *me*, right? You want to be with me?"

"Yes. Of course."

In analog, her hesitation might have gone unnoticed. There could have been enough background noise to distract from the telltale quiver of her voice and exact length of delay. But digital did not lie. One or zero, on or off. Either she hesitated or she didn't. X reran the data several times, long after C had pixilated out of the construct.

He sat alone on the dark hill, his eyes shut tight.

There was something she wasn't telling him.

SIX

Midnight at the dorms brought with it a tempered silence, a void that the chatter and bustling of three thousand students had inhabited during the day. Now, most were asleep, tucked into uncomfortable beds, homework done or saved for a quick morning completion. The insomniacs were out, a smaller group than the daywalkers, quieter and reserved. They sat in groups of three or four in the small courtyard formed by the squared arrangement of the dorms, smoking cigarettes and trading code. Midnight commerce, X dubbed it. Bartering for goods and services under the auspices of a smoke break. The odd code cube could be seen on a table here and there, dangling their electrodes, hoping for a bite.

X sat by himself at a picnic table, enjoying the quiet time, and watching the people share their cubes. It looked, he remembered, like something from his childhood, from the days of elementary school where girls and boys sat in twos, sharing the earbuds to a single music player, listening to notes and lyrics as if they meant something more in their narrow world view. But they weren't trading music anymore, weren't breaking a hundred copyright laws by letting someone else listen to the music that they had downloaded illegally. It could be drugs, X guessed, synthetic programs that recreated the effects of uppers, downers, and a million choices in between. Was there another guy out in the anonymous groups sharing his code with a young woman he had just barely met? And if not, why not?

X's code cube sat on the table in front of him, pulsing a shallow yellow, charging and recharging the code contained within. When the light remained steady, he tapped it softly with one finger, sending a disproportional feeling through his entire body, heightening the sensation of the electrode stuck on the back of his neck. Its movement tickled him, making him smile. He closed his eyes and enjoyed the sensation, over and over again, crossing and uncrossing his legs as nonchalantly as possible. X felt movement behind him, then a slight bend of the bench as someone sat down beside him.

It was Natalie.

"Can I take a hit," she asked, when X finally turned to her.

"Yeah," said X, without feeling. He popped the suction cup off his neck and reattached it to hers. He set the cube down in front of her and started it charging. "Just tap it when you want it but do it softly."

Natalie placed her manicured finger on the cube and then removed it. Her body went into small convulsions, and she nearly screamed.

"Holy shit!" She gasped, suddenly at a loss for breath. "I felt that right in my…" Her words trailed off as her eyes met X's. He was smiling back at her, not even trying to hide his delight. "You sick fuck," continued Natalie, laughing.

X laughed with her.

"So what are you doing down here," she asked, tapping the cube again and cocking her head to the right. "God," she whispered.

"I just felt like being outside," replied X, running his hand through his hair. "The roommates have some people over and I can't stand those fuckers, let alone their friends."

"Why didn't you just *jack in*?" She said the words like jacking in was some kind of freak ritual.

"I just didn't feel like it."

"Trouble in paradise?"

X narrowed his eyes at Natalie, but her smile instantly disarmed him. Without waiting for further prompting, he related the night's earlier events, talking for several minutes about his love for C without the slightest consideration of how inappropriate it was. "It's not like I'm asking the world from her," he complained. "It's not like I asked her to get on a plane and come down here. She wanted to try the long-distance thing as much as I did."

Natalie raised an eyebrow.

"Do," continued X. For a moment, neither of them spoke. Finally, X waved a dismissive hand in front of him and said, "Women, who needs them?"

"Not I," replied Natalie, tapping the cube again. "Shit, I may not even need men anymore."

Laughter erupted from the corner of the courtyard as a drunken couple stumbled out of the building. They had their arms over each other for support and were somehow maintaining the delicate balance required to walk.

"No control," said X, propping his elbows up on the table and resting his chin in his hands.

"What," asked Natalie, looking over at the couple.

"Kids these days, they have no self-control."

"What're you, like eighteen?"

X nodded absently. "I didn't say that *I* have self-control."

"Yeah," said Natalie, placing a hand on X's thigh, "that much I knew." She smiled and turned her eyes back to the cube. "Want to go back to my place and… relax?"

He studied her eyes, letting the fantasy play out in fast forward in his head. "I offloaded that code this morning. I had to free up some space."

"For what?"

X stood and extricated himself from the bench. "Come on, I'll show you."

Natalie followed him out of the courtyard, acutely aware of the odd sensation created by her moving legs. Once or twice, she looked down at herself.

"That'll pass," said X, cheerfully. "Like all of the best drugs, there are always some aftereffects." He took her hand by the fingers and led her around the bending road that bordered the Jester Dorms. They veered to the right, through a gap between the darkened tennis courts and the Athletics Annex. He felt Natalie's fingers pull away from his as she made her hesitation clear.

"It's just through here," he assured her, and on cue, the poorly maintained grass cleared away and they emerged on the backside of a baseball diamond. X guided her onto the manicured grass and let her walk of her own accord. She followed him out to the middle of center field and joined him on the ground when he sat.

"Why are we out here again," she asked, leaning back on her arms and looking up into the cloudy sky. A bright patch hung off to the west, with the moon behind it somewhere.

"I had this dream," began X, "a couple weeks ago. It was the most vivid dream I've had in a long time." He removed the electrode from his cube and replaced it with the jacksplit. "I was in an elevator, and it kept going up, and no matter what I did, I couldn't stop it. There were no buttons, and I couldn't force the door open with my fingers." X affixed one of the jacksplit electrodes to his neck and held out the other to Natalie. "The back of the elevator was made of glass, like the one in the parking garage. All I saw was lights going by, but then the outer wall disappeared, and I realized I was riding up the side of a really tall building. I could see over an entire city, except that everything kept flickering. It was weird, because it felt so real, but it looked like something I would see in the Net."

Natalie arched her eyebrows slightly as X stopped and stared off into space.

"Then it happened."

"What?"

"It crumbled."

"The elevator?" There was a hint of fear in her voice.

"No," said X, looking at her again. "The whole world began to crumble. All these lights started shooting out from above me, and they went around the sky like this." X drew his hand in a long arc. "Way out into the distance. There were so many of them that you could actually see the dome surrounding the city. And then it was gone. The lights went out and all the color disappeared. The city was completely gray. Dull."

"Was this a drug-induced dream," asked Natalie, chuckling.

"I wish! But it gave me an idea anyway." X traced his finger along one edge of the cube and repeated the gesture twice on an adjacent face. "Look around, what do you see?"

"Second base," replied Natalie.

"Darkness," said X, correcting her. "The world is basically turned off right now. If you and I want to go have some fun in the sun, we'll either have to jack in or wait until morning."

"I've got an early class."

X ignored her. "I don't want to go through all the trouble of jacking in for a few minutes of sunshine. Why shouldn't I be able to bring that code out here?"

"No offense, X, but you're beginning to lose me."

He smirked and then motioned to the sky behind her. "Look over there," he said, softly. "The sun is starting to come up."

When Natalie turned her head, the world experienced an abrupt cutover, shaking violently in place for tenths of a second before settling into a slightly brighter version of itself. Behind her, over the scoreboard, she could see the first orange tendrils of the sun reaching into the sky. A moment later, a yellow peel peeked over the horizon. She looked quickly at her watch, found that it was not yet twelve forty-five. The grass around her began to glow its customary green as she looked back at X.

"What is this," she asked.

"Sunrise," replied X, as if the answer were blatantly clear.

"But—"

"Just enjoy it."

Natalie shook her head and watched the new light dance on X's face, a face that seemed to be shimmering. The changes were subtle, but she was sure that his skin was getting clearer, that the darkness under his eyes was slowly being erased. Look how perfect his smile is now, she said to herself. Were his teeth that straight before?

"This isn't possible," said Natalie.

The expression on X's face changed immediately as the world was plunged back into darkness. There was something like anger in his eyes, an image that lingered in Natalie's mind while she adjusted to the low light. When she could see again, she was relieved to find him smiling once more, her unknown sin absolved.

"There's only one problem with it," said X, removing the electrode from his neck. "It's a dual-consciousness program, so the moment you stop believing in the code, it breaks down. And we're left with this."

"I'm sorry," started Natalie, but X stopped her.

"It's not your fault. I've done the same thing dozens of times. Each time it gets a little more real and at the same time, a little more fantastic. It's like lucid dreaming and waking up the second you get too excited about it."

Natalie frowned and tore one of the identical blades of grass from the ground by her feet.

"I said it was no big deal." X gripped his cube sideways and used his other hand to trace two edges simultaneously. The cube glowed a bright yellow, the color rippling out from the corners. Before Natalie's eyes could reach his, he popped the electrode from his neck and then tapped the cube, sending the coded ecstasy down the wire in a glut of electrons. He waited patiently for her orgasm to subside.

"You sure know how to cheer a girl up," she said, quietly. Her eyes fell on the cube. "What else you got in that thing?"

"Not much," replied X. "I've been using it to code a little tool I need for tonight."

"I *knew* you were going to jack in," said Natalie, triumphantly.

"Well, you're just too smart for your own good then." X double-tapped the cube, doubling the effect of the code.

Natalie trembled and nearly fell over into his lap. The muscles in her arms contracted, pulling them quickly to her chest and curling her hands and fingers inward.

"Christ," she said, through clenched teeth.

SEVEN

Natalie's dorm room smelled like strawberries. X tracked the scent to a small air freshener sitting atop the combination refrigerator-microwave-television in front of the window. Unlike his room, hers was only built for two and had twin beds on opposite walls, with a majority of the room's square footage filling the space between them.

"This is me," said Natalie, motioning to the bed on the right. It was unmade, but the sheets, pillows, and comforter were all the same shade of cheery purple, daring anyone to discern where one began and the other ended. She did her best to straighten up and smoothed out a place for X to sit.

"Thanks for letting me do this here," said X, dropping a small black bag onto the bed and then sitting down beside it. A few minutes earlier, he had popped into his dorm room to retrieve his rig and found his roommates and their guests still going strong, gathered in a circle on the floor, strumming an out of tune guitar. Knowing that there would be no way for him to concentrate with the racket, he asked Natalie if he could borrow her room for a bit.

"No problem," she had answered, "I know what it's like to have roommates."

X looked at the other side of the room, at the empty bed and walls decorated with pictures of men who must have spent as much time at the gym as X spent in the Net. "Where is the roommate anyway?"

"Who cares?" Natalie was rummaging through her dresser inside her closet. "The important thing is that she isn't here. She has a boyfriend who lives off Oltorf. Probably spending the night at his place."

"Lucky girl. Well, both of you, I guess. Whole room to yourself."

"Yep," agreed Natalie. "It has its perks." She pulled a pair of plaid boxer shorts from the drawer and started for the door. "You need anything?"

X shook his head. "Nope, just a few minutes to prepare."

"Well, I need to change, so… I'll be back in a minute." She disappeared through the door, muttering, "Maybe a quick shower."

Alone in the room, X took a moment to examine the wall next to Natalie's bed. It was mostly empty except for a smattering of photographs in the lower right corner near the head of the bed. She was in most of them, either solo on the back of a horse, or laughing with a random girlfriend on the shores of Padre Island. Noticeably absent were any pictures featuring recurring appearances by any given boy. There were one or two, but they never showed up more than once, not the way a boyfriend would if she had one. X smiled to himself. If Natalie was attached to someone, she certainly wasn't advertising it.

After a deep breath, X pulled his bag onto his lap and opened it. From inside, he produced his rig, an assortment of straps and harnesses, and a bottle of aspirin. For later, he assured himself. The pain would come, but right now, all he had to do was jack into the code cube and finish the program he was working on. Deftly, he placed the electrode on his neck and let himself be sucked into the standalone construct. He leaned back against the cushioned shelf, his eyes closed, but moving quickly under the eyelids.

Coding with the cube wasn't as cumbersome as sitting at a terminal, using fingers to translate ideas into code. He had an almost direct interface, with no need for a high-level programming language; no translator was required. Ones and zeros flowed directly from his brain onto the malleable ether, a protected three-dimensional IDE. He coded quickly, finishing up the last bits of the program. With everything in place, he switched back into the strawberry-scented atmosphere of Natalie's dorm room.

He was surprised to find her sitting on the bed next to him, dressed in the boxers he had seen earlier and a small white tee that clung tightly to her chest.

"You looked like you were freaking out, man," she said, grinning.

"All part of the process," he replied.

"So, what's this deal about anyway?"

"This *deal* is about trust," said X. He placed the cube on his forearm and secured it with a black strap.

"What are you going to do?"

The theory was simple, but the execution had the potential to be pure nightmare. He would infiltrate a major Net company that provided free, ad-supported communication suites to users, find a specific data account, and download the contents for offline viewing.

"So," said Natalie, "basically you're going to hack your honey's e-mail account?"

"There's nothing basic about it." He responded with a bit of bravado in his voice. "This isn't exactly Hotmail. Hacking a Net-based databank isn't something I can do on a whim. I can't just call up the local office and ask them to read me the phone number off the dealie with the blinking lights."

Natalie giggled, though she still didn't quite understand the scope of the project. X did his best to explain that although the Net was based on a physical representation, data was strictly binary, hidden deep in places that no physical entity could go. There was no vault, no safe with a dial to turn. It existed on a completely different plane than the users in the Net. Retrieving that kind of data required the use of special software, often bought in the dark alleys of Old Downtown. The latest and greatest iteration of this code was called a mole, a direct descendent of the first virus, itself a clunky precursor to automated chaos. As the Net evolved light years beyond its initial complexity, so too did the tools of its destruction.

The mole was born of necessity, a perfect union of code and wetware, interfacing directly with its operator's brain. It had the processing power of atomic transistors combined with the reasoning power of its host. When activated, it would flood the synaptic pathways with a synthetic neurochem, allowing it to harness the brain's processing speed, intuition, and problem-solving skills for its own use. It was the best approximation of artificial intelligence that someone like X could afford. It was precise, adaptive, and deadly fast.

"Sounds complicated," said Natalie. She furrowed her eyebrows.

"Dangerous too. It's a good thing you're here."

"How's it dangerous?"

X pointed to the cube on his arm. "I'll transfer the code to my rig and use it to run the program. This little guy here will be running another program, a cut-out, to keep me from consciously interfering with the mole's work. It's kind of like separating body from mind from brain. I give control over to the mole. Crazy shit, huh?"

"But does your body keep going? I mean, do you keep breathing?"

"I don't know," admitted X. "I've only read about doing this."

Natalie's eyes grew bigger, then settled into a look of concern. "You've never done this before?"

"There's always a first time for everything." He tried to sound optimistic, but inside, the doubts were beginning to circle.

"I don't want you dying in my bed. How would I explain that to the RA?"

"Don't worry, I'll be on a timer. The mole has five seconds to do its work. After that, the cut-out reverses and the mole bails."

"What if the cut-out fails?"

"What if this building collapses," he countered.

"You're willing to risk death for this? Doesn't that seem a bit much? Why can't you just guess her password or hack her computer or something? Wouldn't that be easier?"

"I've tried," said X, looking at the rig in his lap. He inspected it, turning it over slowly in his hands. "I went through all the passwords in the world." Pushing back his hair, he slid the rig onto his head and attached the electrode just below the other one. "Besides, doing it this way will get me every piece of data that has ever been in her account, not just the stuff she hasn't had the time to delete yet."

Natalie shook her head gravely, though she knew X couldn't see her anymore. "I don't know what you're hoping to find," she said, timidly.

"Honestly," he replied, his voice complacent, "I hope I don't find anything at all."

She sighed deeply. The way X's jaw was set told her that he was serious. He wouldn't rest until he saw for himself.

"Now, five seconds is nothing to worry about," said X, adjusting the rig. "At ten, we might have a problem. After that…"

His mouth was hidden beneath the rig, so Natalie kissed her finger and placed it on his lips. "For luck," she said.

"Luck is for the ill-prepared." X leaned back and tapped the cube.

He fell through an empty construct. A wave of confusion washed over him, and its presence only furthered the condition. He was faintly aware of a painful absence.

X moved his hand in the space before him, could not see it, but could feel his fingers rubbing against each other. For several moments, he explored his own hand, rediscovering himself as if his body were something completely new. There was little else, except for the sensation of falling.

In the distance, a dim light appeared. It grew slowly, accelerating out of the emptiness. Before he could identify it, trace its origin or destination, it doubled in size, stuttering from one frame into the next, and then finally slammed into his body. An image appeared before him, some long equation of complex symbols unlike anything he had ever seen before. The image vanished, leaving only the pain of impact behind, spreading through his body in undulating ripples. The construct around him began to shake. Even at a distance, X could see the pieces of black falling and the white spots appearing behind them. Some had begun to grow while others simply pulsed menacingly. All around him, black gave way to white.

Another image hit him. Then another.

The barrage came at full force, too quickly for him to comprehend, too quickly to react and form some kind of defensive plan. There were numbers, symbols, faces of long-dead relatives. It was a jumble of information, unrelated words to unfamiliar songs. Panic began to set in, and a tightness clutched at X's body, squeezing him, making it hard to breathe, or think, or even see. He closed his eyes, but the graphic assault continued. He felt a heat grow around him as he gasped for breath. His head throbbed.

As suddenly as it began, it was over. The light and its after-images had faded, but he still could not breathe. His chest convulsed in empty breaths while his eyes searched the darkness for some form of salvation.

Alone, dying, he waited.

Natalie watched as X tapped the white cube on his forearm. His finger had barely left the surface before his arm went limp. His entire body collapsed, leaned, until she finally pulled him into an awkward embrace. She counted patiently, listening for signs of life. One. X's breathing had stopped, and his mouth was poised as if to speak. Two. She could find no pulse on his wrist or on the side of his neck. She pressed her hand flat against his chest but felt no vibration. Three. A tremor in his arms. Four, nothing. Five.

She let out the breath that she had been holding, fully expecting X to do the same, but he didn't move. Six. Natalie shook his lifeless body, making blood trickle from his nose. Seven.

A sound came from deep inside X, a great rush of air being sucked into his lungs. It lingered there briefly, reversed course, and came shooting out again, carrying X's voice with it.

"Whoa," coughed X. He found Natalie's blurry face hovering in the air above him.

"Was it good for you," she asked, trying to mask her relief with humor.

"Jesus never had it so good." X breathed quickly, on the verge of hyperventilating. He tried to smile as the edges of his vision started to gray, blurring finally into darkness.

EIGHT

A soft rustling came to X amid the dreams of empty spaces and disturbing stillness. Piece by piece, he became aware of his body, lying on his side, head on a silky pillow, and the gentle pressure of a blanket draped over him. Warm sunlight was on his face, and he squinted against it. Through the groggy haze of waking, he saw the form of a woman, naked, pulling a pair of underwear up slender legs. She moved slowly, fading in and out of different areas of the room. From the dresser, she brought out a pink t-shirt, pulling it deftly over her arms and head. Her body moved in front of the window, providing an edge-enhanced silhouette of her features. X blinked away the blur, bringing Natalie's familiar curves into detail.

By casual glance, she noticed he was awake. She stepped quickly into a pair of jeans on the floor, buttoning them up as she approached him on the bed.

"Good morning," she said, sitting next to him. "I'm glad you lived." Her face broke into a friendly smile.

"What time is it," asked X.

"It's almost nine. I can't skip class or else I'd stay."

X sighed and rolled onto his back. The friction of the blanket made him realize that he was naked. "What happened last night?"

"I think you died."

"Yeah, I know that part." X lifted the blanket slightly. "I mean, after that."

Natalie's eyes widened in mild surprise. "You don't remember?"

"Did we…"

"When you came back to life, it was only for a few seconds, and then you passed out again. I was kinda worried, but you were breathing and everything."

"And then," prompted X.

"And then I took off your rig and put it away. I guess I watched you sleep for an hour and then I fell asleep next to you. You really don't remember?"

X shook his head solemnly.

"I think it was around three or four that you woke me up." She added, wistfully, "You were kissing my neck. I just thought that meant you were better. You didn't say anything, just kept kissing me. One thing led to another. And here we are."

"And where's that?"

"Look," said Natalie, standing up, "don't worry about it. If I had a near-death experience, I'd probably wake up wanting to fuck something too." She stood at her desk and selected a book from the shelf above it. With a wry smile, she looked down at X. "Besides, you probably thought I was someone else."

"Sorry," said X, looking away.

"Don't be. Some things are better when they're not programmed." She picked up a small LCD screen from her desk and handed it to X. "Here, you can use my viewee for the stuff you downloaded. I'll be back in a couple hours. If you're not here, you call me later, okay?"

"Sure, thanks."

"Anytime," she said, seductively. She slipped into a pair of tan sandals and left the room; the automatic locks clicked into place behind her.

X sat up and swung his legs over the side of the bed. His feet touched something soft, boxer shorts, his. He pulled them up quickly, followed by his pants. For a moment, he stared at the beams of sunlight coming from the window.

He remembered the cube.

X found it on the shelf that ran along the length of the bed. Someone had placed it there thoughtfully, away from the edge. He picked it up, along with the viewee, and sat down at Natalie's desk.

Her chair was purple and comfortable, velvet-covered plastic with shiny metal supports. Definitely not standard issue. Her desk was messy, with papers and books stacked in small piles. A halved Pringles can held ornate pens and pencils with furry tufts of hair instead of erasers. There were more pictures taped to the wall beside the desk, Natalie in various moments of happiness. Her gleaming eyes evoked a smile from him, but when he caught himself, he turned away. Instead, he looked at the cube that he held in his hand.

Conflict. Confusion. The two words were painted on the sides of the cube. No matter which way it was rolled, it came up one or the other. X was struck by a feeling of futility, but he pushed it away with a shake of his head.

He plugged the viewee into the cube.

C had received very few messages since he opened the account for her less than a year before. Most of it was commercial spam, unsolicited and unwelcome. He found a few vidmessages from himself, saved in a folder marked *keep*. He brought the folder list to the front, working up from the end of the list. There were names, mostly. He recognized them as members of her family and a couple of her high school friends. Then he came upon a name that he did not recognize; the folder was named *Andy*.

An adrenaline rush surged through X's body, forcing an involuntary tap in his leg. His stomach turned over, became nauseous. He took a deep breath, tried to settle the feeling on his own. There was nothing to be worried about yet, he told himself. It was just a folder. Maybe she made a new friend. Maybe she had an uncle named Andy.

"And maybe I'm a Chinese jet pilot," muttered X.

He reached for his cube and stuck the electrode to his neck. With a quick tap, the adrenaline, though still physically present, began to have less and less effect on his mood. His heart slowed down, soothed by the rational instructions of the code, convinced that there was no emergency. He let the calm spread through his body and a minute later, he relaxed. He was ready.

As he navigated to the folder, a lump tightened in his throat, despite his best efforts. There were more than fifty messages: video, text, and voice. He quickly opened the latest vidmessage, dated less than twenty-four hours ago. An acne-stricken teenager appeared on the viewee, frozen, waiting.

X tapped play.

The boy who would be Andy snapped into being, a smile spreading on his thin lips. "Hey, baby," he said.

X clenched his teeth, biting the tip of his tongue.

"I didn't get to see you tonight, I was hoping I would. I just wanted to talk to you about what we talked about last time. I know you said you needed time, so I just wanted to let you know that I love you very much. I'm always going to be there for you. I'll never leave you, I'll never change. I think we'd be really great as boyfriend and girlfriend. Please tell me you feel the same way. I'm nothing without you. We've always been right for each other, through all the time I spent waiting for you to realize how much I love you. Now we can finally be together. Let me know what you're thinking. I'll be up all night or just leave me a message. I love you, Lily. Love you."

A strange warmth engulfed X, clouding his vision and numbing his extremities. He tasted the bitter metallic of blood as it trickled over his lips and down his chin. A buzzing seemed to be coming from somewhere in the distance, low and ominous. It shook the walls and tickled his eardrums. His fingers gripped the sides of Natalie's viewee as it popped and cracked under the pressure. The pixels flickered on the screen like liquid spilling from a broken bottle. The colors flowed over themselves, melting Andy's face, with his closed eyes and puckered lips. X's upper lip trembled with hate. He studied the lowered eyelids.

"You fuck," said X, to the crackling screen, sending another swell of blood from his mouth. Anger grew in his chest; it was all too much. The deception, the betrayal, the arrogance of this boy, undermining all of his hard work.

The viewee snapped and broke into two large pieces. Bits of screen and metal fell onto the desk and into his lap. The numbness abated and X opened his mouth as his jaw muscles screamed in protest. The image of Andy remained in his mind.

Andy talking, smiling, laughing, blowing fake kisses to the camera. Andy with C. Andy talking to C. C kissing Andy.

X detached the lifeless umbilical from the cube and snapped the electrode from his neck. He moved quickly to the bed, sat down, and retrieved his rig from his bag on the floor. His fingers moved with hasty precision, fueled by an acrimony that no program of his could quell.

He jacked in.

The Net was tinged in red, feeding off the emotions running wild through X's head. There was no real interpretation for anger, just drop the packets and move on. The underlying code of the construct bent to his will at a speed beyond his conscious thinking. Everything seemed to move on autopilot, extrapolating the desired environment from the singular feeling that was thrashing X's CPU.

A spacious tract of snowy field opened up before him. He ran through it quickly, his boots crunching on the icy ground. Snow fell around him horizontally as he barreled through it. In the distance, C materialized, staring blankly in his direction, completely unaware of his presence. His speed increased to a maddening pace. The snow stung his face as bits of clear crystal impacted the warm flesh. He was almost upon her, close enough now to plainly see the lines of her face, the curve of each individual tooth. Something in him, something dark and sadistic, willed a smile onto her face. And like the obedient toy that she was, she complied without question.

X's fist struck her with incalculable fury, shaking the walls of the construct and freeing inches of snow from the dome above. The drift fell as C's body rose up and through it. She landed a subjective mile away, the thud reaching him a short time after impact.

A scream erupted in the construct, horribly despondent but undeniably powerful. The sensation of warmth that had carried him into the Net erupted into flames, engulfing him completely. His pain manifested as streaks of yellow and orange, vivacious little tongues that lapped at the melting flesh of his avatar. Around him, the construct warped under the intense heat. The snow turned to rain, the ground to a mess of muddy water.

At a mere thought, X crossed the distance between him and C.

Her shoulder was broken and bits of pale bone protruded from the skin where he had hit her. He knelt over her, straddled her body, and even though she could never fight back, pinned her arms with his legs. His fists flew in a blind rage, one after another, striking the side of C's head. The rain flickered and the ground faded slightly as X put all of his concentration into his assault. He screamed again, grabbing the white collar of her black jacket, pulling her bloodied and mangled face towards him.

"Why?!" He yelled his question several times, driving the words through her. He felt the flutter of his lip and a dull pain in his teeth. His tears and the rain were one in the same, falling in a torrent so strong that it pushed C's body out of his hands. Her head fell back, motionless in the shallow water. X looked once more to the sky and reached for a final scream that wouldn't come.

Time passed slowly, his cries wavering in the lonely construct. Eventually, the rain slowed to a gentle drizzle, washing away the anger from X's face, soothing and calming him. He brought his head back down and watched as the blood faded from C's lips. The bruises disappeared and the bones dissolved into unbroken skin. He leaned over her, placing his hands behind her neck. His nose touched hers; the water fell from his lips.

"Why," he asked again, meekly.

C's clone flickered twice and disappeared. Conflict. Confusion. X realized it all at once. The question was valid; he did deserve an explanation. But…

X stared at his empty hands, saw the answer written plainly across them.

He was asking the wrong person.

NINE

Jape's avatar was scrambling, changing faces and clothing in a fluid morph that kept people guessing what manner of beast was standing so stoically outside the entrance to *The Sweet Shop*, one of the lesser-known gentlemen's establishments in the red zone of the Net. It was G's idea to meet there and although Jape had formed an image of what to expect, it didn't come close to the virtuality that greeted him when he jumped from his homedir.

Shaking his head, he took determined steps to the swinging doors that led inside, intent on giving G a quick lesson on the importance of protecting his avatar's reputation. Instead, he felt the anger drain out of him as the shop's environmental code seeped into his body, changing the hue of the world to a light pink. It was standard practice for businesses to subjugate their patrons in some way, making them feel like killing other players in a run and gun or giving them the impression that the booth babes standing around at the bar were far more attractive than they actually were. Usually, Jape's rig filtered out the emotionware, but as with all things Net, there was always someone out there willing to break the rules to bring in a little more money.

Jape found G sitting in a booth near the back of the club, his eyes and hands lost in the tight leather outfit of a companion-for-hire. He sat down on the bench opposite G and waved away an approaching waitress. Jape coughed loudly when his presence went unacknowledged.

"What the fuck do you want," demanded G.

For a split second, Jape let his true avatar shine through. It was enough.

G laughed and removed the overzealous booth babe's hands from his body. He shuffled in his seat and for a moment, couldn't think of any way to explain the situation. "Ah, Jape, this is Candy. Candy, Jape."

"No time for love, G. Business time, yeah?"

"If you'll excuse us," said G, standing to let Candy out of the booth. "Don't go far though." He kissed her hand in mock chivalry.

"Bro, ever wonder who runnin' that frame?" Jape's accent landed him somewhere north of Jamaica and south of L.A., but G's localization subtitles took care of any confusion.

"Oh yeah," replied G, slipping back into the booth, "I know it's gotta be some four-hundred-pound beefer who can't even get out of bed anymore." He looked over to where Candy had positioned herself at the bar. "But look at that ass. Tell me it isn't real, and I'll call you a damn liar."

"Truth say a man run that frame, yeah?"

G pondered the idea for a moment, wondered what the implications were for having cybersex with a booth babe avatar being run by a greasy potbelly in some strip mall in Flagstaff. "What," said G, "that doesn't make me gay, does it?"

Jape raised his hands in ignorance. "Only say what I hear."

"Rumors and lies, my friend, rumors and fucking lies. Spread by bums who can't afford a decent sim."

"Where the X tonight?"

"God only knows." G rotated the sliver on his wrist into view. "Probably off screwing one of his girlfriends."

"Just me and the G." Jape smiled, his teeth shimmering. "At least I be the best rusher at the quarry."

"Speaking of which," said G, suddenly remembering what he was doing at the club in the first place, "did you find out which one is going active tonight?"

"Now he care," muttered Jape, to the inside of his jacket. From an inner pocket, he produced a shiny slip of metal and deposited it on the table in front of G.

"Those the coords?"

Jape nodded.

G reached out for the slip and felt it merge with his avatar the second his fingers touched it. A flash of text appeared on his HUD, a string of coordinates and a future timestamp that was rapidly approaching. "Damn," he said, as the vision faded out, "we need to get going."

"This I knew," replied Jape, calmly.

"Then come on!" G stood up and shuffled from one foot to the other, waiting for Jape to join him.

"Better the G go first and the Jape come up later, yeah?"

"I see how it is," said G, glancing at the booth babes again. "What about all that talk about them being run by guys? Doesn't that conflict with your strong moral fiber?"

Jape's eyes drifted for a moment, lost in the fog of environmental code, unable to resist it any longer. "Enough code," said Jape, "anything be possible."

"Alright, I'll meet you there then." G looked at his wrist and then at the bar. "You should go over there and reacquaint yourself with Candy. She's very… pleasant."

"I forget which one she be."

G smirked and placed a finger on his wrist. "Dude, they're all named Candy." With a quick drag, he jumped.

When G appeared at the quarry, he found himself inverted, with the great fishbowl of the Q spreading out above him. He orientated himself quickly, cursing Jape's name. A quick inventory of the construct revealed twelve other rushers, already in their respective positions along the edge of the crater, all no doubt wondering what he had been doing hanging by his boots above the quarry. It was bad etiquette to not line up along the edge, typically an equal distance between the rusher on the left and the one on the right. In the end, it didn't really matter where he stationed himself, just so long as he could see into the center of the quarry.

G took his place and nodded politely to a rusher several units away. Kneeling, he inspected the virtual dirt along the lip of the quarry, pretending to glean some knowledge from the way the rocks were arranged. It was a meaningless act, but he had seen a few other rushers mimic him from time to time, trying to figure out his secret. The veterans never fell for it though. They knew as well as G that no one spot was the best. Data rushing was an inexact science, if a science at all. The best rushers were usually the lucky ones, in the right place at the right time. Reaction time and sheer speed helped, and G considered himself blessed with both.

Just as the thought *I would have expected more people* was tunneling its way through G's cortex, a new avatar appeared on the other side of the rim, a mere twenty units away from another rusher. It was a less than stellar body, with grossly oversized musculature and hair from a bad 90's-era *anime* series. The billowing black trench coat sought to conceal the user underneath, but all it accomplished was the transmission of the most dangerous weakness of anyone ported into the Net.

The guy was a noob.

"A little close, don't you think?" G recognized Tanzy's voice across the gulf and wondered if she was going to lay down the pain on the newcomer.

The noob pointed his chiseled chin at Tanzy and smirked. "Fuck you, loser."

Oh, thought G, big mistake. But Tanzy just smiled and approached the embellished avatar. "You got a name, kid?"

"UltraKill, bow before me!"

G heard laughter erupt from the rushers around him. Everyone seemed to be tuned in to the newest virtuality show.

Tanzy chuckled and looked around the quarry, giving a knowing look to anyone that caught her eyes. "Well, Mr. Kill, I'm Tanzy, and I'm not sure if you know this or not, but you've stumbled into the Mylo Rivera quarry. And if you knew why that was significant, you wouldn't have ported in so close to me. But since you did, I'm guessing you have no clue what this is."

The noob was silent, his face impassive. G figured he was having a discussion with someone in Terrareal. No good without his posse, thought G.

"I'll move if you tell me what you're all doing here." He gestured to the others.

Smiling, Tanzy made a similar gesture. "Meet your competition, seasoned data rushers all, ready to scratch, bite, and claw to ensure that they escape victorious and you, well, you bleed to death." Another chorus of chuckles rose from the quarry. "Sorry, I couldn't resist. What you're about to witness is one of the greatest of pastimes, a good old-fashioned data rush. In anywhere from ten to thirty minutes, this quarry will experience the little-understood phenomenon called—"

"A Netsplit," said the noob.

"Correct." Tanzy was mildly surprised, while G wondered why Jape had given him a definite time for the split while Tanzy only had a window.

"The fabled Netsplit," continued Tanzy. "Powerful enough to knock chatters out of their rooms, lock homedirs for days, and drive firewalls crazy with a flood of ghosted multicast traffic."

G shook his head at the sugarcoated bullshit.

"But what most people don't realize is that the term Netsplit is very appropriate. Imagine a line of binary code, sitting just above another line of the same. Imagine that in between them is an infinite storage space that can only be accessed by breaking through the two original lines. That's where your Squirrels come into play."

"Squirrels?"

Yes, Tanzy, tell us about the Squirrels, thought G.

"Data couriers who store their goods in the Net for safe keeping. You see, before your time, before we had the kind of bandwidth that we take for granted today, sensitive data was entrusted to physical couriers that operated in Terrareal. It started with solid-state flash drives in suitcases attached by handcuffs. Then as technology improved, drives were embedded in the courier's body, what we now call flesh drives. At first, they were implanted in obvious places: hands, arms, etc. But when the couriers realized that those pieces could be removed, well, they decided to move everything closer to Central."

Tanzy tapped the side of her head, her long wavy hair barely moving.

"What does this have to do with anything," asked the noob.

Across the quarry, G nodded in agreement. He checked his watch and wondered if Jape was tongue-deep in a booth babe. If he didn't show up soon, they'd both miss out on a huge score.

"It has *everything* to do with everything. You have to understand how we got here to have any hope of deciding where we go. Flesh drives lost popularity after couriers started losing their heads. Then you had biocell, tro-chem grafts on the brain itself. All good, high-quality protection. But the man finally caught on, and tro-chem encryption became illegal for anyone but military."

A low hum began to permeate the quarry, making the noob look up.

"A few more minutes," Tanzy continued, "and it'll begin." She tracked the noob's gaze, stared into the great expanse of black and green, but saw nothing. "Anyway, that's where the Squirrels come in. While it's illegal to transport encrypted data in one's body, it isn't illegal to hold the keys to said data. After all, almost all biometric authorization uses encryption keys stored in the body. So instead of taking the data with them, they store it in the Net, hide it deep within the code, in units smaller than ones and zeros."

G remembered a time when he and Tanzy had been friends, briefly. It wasn't her rants so much as the idea that one user, especially a girl, could know more about the Net than him. The fact that she was so eager to share that information also grated on G. He believed that such data should be kept secret, kept among a select group. It kept people like him employed and kept people like UltraKill from gaining access to things more dangerous than a rig.

"Impossible," said the noob. "That's why it's called binary."

"That's what they say, anyway. While it's true that software runs on ones and zeros, true and false, you have to remember that those are just representations of electrical signals that alternate between high and low. Plus or minus five volts equals one, no volts equals zero. This is real-world stuff now; electrical current cannot alternate instantaneously between high and low. It's a curve. Between zero and five volts are an infinite number of states. Depending on the sensitivity of your equipment, you could access many thousand times the amount of instruction space that we get with conventional software. But even if you could access just *two* more bit-states, imagine what that would mean. Two bits, another binary, to represent the hidden data. Unreadable by software, unrecognizable as anything except background noise. You could hide the Library of Congress a million times over in the walls of a homedir and no one would ever know."

Above, G noticed the construct changing colors. The previously stagnant green was now flowing in the black ocean, a dichromatic version of the Northern Lights. The Netsplit was getting closer; Tanzy would have to wrap up her little history lesson pronto.

"Except during a Netsplit. For whatever reason, a Netsplit allows the underlying operating system of certain constructs to lock on to the intermediary states of electrical signals and expose the hidden data."

"Who the chatterbug?"

G turned to find Jape standing next to him, his eyes focused on the other side of the quarry. "Girl I know named Tanzy," said G. "She's giving that noob a primer on rushing."

"Not much time now," said Jape, disinterested.

"Feels like it," said G, taking an artificial breath. There was nothing to smell, but it was a vestigial habit that he enjoyed. It helped calm him down.

"Who the target this time?"

G looked sideways at Jape. "Ultra. Kill."

"Who?"

"The noob." G motioned with his head. "I scanned his rig when he jumped in. Dumbass isn't running any real protection, just some basic Checkpoint."

"And?"

"Anataware. V-twenty."

Jape let out a low whistle. "Trust fund buy that, yeah?"

"I don't think he has a trust fund, or he wouldn't be trying to score on a rush. I think it's stolen, stolen from someone worthy enough to have an Anataware. Do you know how much storage there is on that rig alone? God knows what the owner was keeping in there."

"But if the noob have the rig, peep the goods by now?"

G smiled. "You mean to tell me that if you dropped your rig in the middle of the street that just anyone would be able to pick it up and see those naked pictures you took of yourself for the dating sites?"

Jape nodded, smiled briefly. "Point."

"Besides, I know half the rushers here. Only a handful are prime and they're all running max protect. Even Tanzy's got some custom shit that I've never seen before."

Across the way, the noob was moving away from Tanzy, apparently having been convinced to spread out. He moved past another rusher and took a position off to the left.

"I'll message the noob," continued G. He opened a text link with UltraKill and sent him a message, "When it happens, you'll know. Get to it as quickly as you can. The first one to touch it, wins. Good luck."

"What he say," asked Jape.

G shook his head disapprovingly. "He misspelled *fuck you*."

The construct swelled as a mass of green moved from the upper dome to all corners of the quarry. It was a broken piece of Earth floating in a sea of shimmering gradients and while the effect disoriented some of the rushers, it completely unsettled UltraKill.

He was squatting slightly to hold his balance on the white rock. He could see the nosy guy that had messaged him standing calmly on the other side, upright, seemingly unaffected by the rotating construct. A slight vibration was coming up from the ground, echoing up through his virtual feet, making them tingle.

Suddenly, a loud crack sounded in the quarry, down and to the left of UltraKill's position. Where there had previously only been textured rock, he now saw a red glow, piercing, and growing in intensity. Before it had really registered, he noticed movement all along the rim. The other rushers were making their runs, some dashing in fabricated vapor trails, others skiing down the rough walls of the quarry. Everyone except that guy and his friend.

Already behind, UltraKill shot forward with all the power that the Anata rig could muster, which was considerable enough to blur the quarry as he traveled down into it. Several rushers were ahead of him, gliding in his periphery, but he was focused on the glowing red orb. Its white center gave the impression of heat, of burning, of pain.

Something was tearing at the back of his rig, stinging him right where the electrode connected to his neck. The quarry and the construct dropped away, along with the prize and the rushers until everything became darkness. He fell through the empty void while the pressure grew in his head. On some level, he was aware of data passing through him, sucked through the umbilical and spewing into the Net. He didn't know what it was or where it was headed. All he knew was that it was being moved and nothing, not even the rig's advanced operating system, was being left behind.

UltraKill descended into the pit of nothingness, afraid and empty-handed.

TEN

For almost six years running, X had never gone more than twenty-four hours without jacking in. After his discovery in Natalie's dorm room, he went fifty-seven. For two and a half days, X laid alone on his lofted bed, with his face to the wall, doing his best to ignore the room and the rest of the world. The sound of his roommates faded in and out, but never intruded on the cold solitude that he was feeling. He watched the painted cement, the veins and grooves, for any sign of movement. In the Net, he could change anything he wanted. Now he wanted to bring that power out and bring the real world under his hand. But as with anything that complex, it had to start somewhere small, in the lines of off-white. Move the wall, make it change. The rest of the power would come.

X watched the wall, concentrated, fell in and out of sleep. He willed it, wished for it, prayed for a change, but none came. The wall remained the same, looking just as it had the first time he taped a picture of C to it. He had no power over the real world, no ability to control it as he saw fit. Not that he was interested in world domination; he merely wanted the power to change one girl's heart. As the hours wore on, he realized that he would never be able to do that, no matter how complex he made the code. She had chosen another, and the only thing left for him was acceptance. Accept the world because it is out of your control.

"No," said X, his words hushed in the late afternoon shadows of the dorm room.

There would be no acceptance, he told himself. Not today, not ever. He would make her love him. If he could get her in the Net, there would be nothing to stop him from training her heart. His momentary hope faded. It would only be so many days before C's body died out from exhaustion. She couldn't stay jacked in forever.

Suddenly, X's eyes went wide with recognition. The wall shifted out of focus, trembling before him. His mouth dropped into an awed circle and then morphed into a devilish smile, revealing his bulging canines. He sat up, nearly striking the ceiling. Pulses fired in his brain, small streaks of light that danced on the back of his eyes. He didn't need C's body in the Net. He had that already.

Your problem, dear, is that you lack emotion

The words repeated in his mind. C's clone was just as good, never aging, and always beautiful. The only thing she really needed was a mind. The bridge with C was smoking, but not completely burned yet. There was still time, still enough residual trust to lure her in and then…

Joy was reborn at the edges of X's eyes.

The Jester Cafeteria crowd was beginning to thin in the wake of the noon lunch rush. Students dotted the tables, eating and talking noisily amongst themselves. The smell of burritos and day-old Jell-O wafted throughout, overpowering everything. X and Natalie were seated across from each other in a booth along the outside edge of the dining area, separated from their neighbors by high-backed benches and bright green plants that hung from the ceiling above them. The dissonant rumble of conversation encircled them as X played with the small black cube next to his tray.

"What's that," asked Natalie, pointing at the cube with her fork.

"Just something I picked up in Old Downtown last night," X replied, recalling his sudden epiphany and mad dash to Austin's technological underbelly. He wrapped his fingers around his prize, then spread them to allow his palm to drop flush against it.

"Can I try it?" Her eyes sparkled with anticipation.

X chuckled half-heartedly. "It's not that kind of cube."

Natalie leaned forward, angled her head to see under X's hand, and asked in a conspiratorial tone, "So what does it do?"

Casually, X scanned the room, but no one was paying attention to them. He returned his eyes to Natalie, who seemed to have lost interest in her question and was pushing around a mass of macaroni and cheese on her plate. His mind debated telling her the truth. Instead, he reached into his backpack and brought out a small white box wrapped with a red bow.

"For me," asked Natalie, as X placed the package in front of her.

He nodded and smiled as he watched her study the box carefully, trying to figure out how to get at the contents without ruining the bow. After a minute, X pulled out a small pocketknife and handed it to her.

"Thanks," she said, using the knife to cut the underside of the box. After a short struggle with various cardboard tabs, Natalie finally extracted a shiny chrome viewee wrapped in protective plastic. The joy of receiving a gift from X was suddenly replaced by the memory of the dread she had felt when she returned to her room to find her viewee smashed and in pieces on her desk. The blood didn't help much either. X had been tight with the details, only sending back a curt *I'm fine* when she queried him about it.

"I'm really sorry about your old viewee. This is a little newer model. I already loaded it with some movies, but I'll help you download some more if you want."

Natalie stared at the LCD screen in her hand and traced a finger along its shiny edges. She could just make out her reflection in the black glass, saw the look on her own face, one that told her, yes, she was going to ask that question. If she could see it, surely he could too. "X…"

He shifted in his seat, knew what was coming.

"I know it's none of my business, but what did you find in her account? I mean, you kinda disappeared for a few days and…"

"I don't want to talk about it," replied X, taking a swig from his Blue Rain. He turned and stared absently out the window.

Natalie waited for him to change his mind, tried to finish the rest of the food on her plate, but everything tasted stale.

"One time, when C and I had only been dating a couple months," said X, nervously fidgeting with the cube, "she got a part in a school play. She came to my locker one day after a lunch practice and told me that she had a scene where she had to hold hands with the boy playing opposite her. She said that in between takes, they just kept holding hands, you know, to *get into character*. And I don't know, I just got so angry. I couldn't decide if it was the fact that she had been holding hands with some other guy or that she had come to see me with the sole intention of relaying that information. If I had held another girl's hand, even if it was completely innocent, I sure as hell wouldn't have told her."

"Maybe that was just her way of confessing," suggested Natalie.

"Either way, it's not something I liked very much. And I think that since I made such a big deal about it back then, she learned to keep that kind of stuff hidden from me. I *taught* her to do it."

"Well that's good, right?"

"I thought, yeah, at the time. But a little hand holding goes unmentioned, then so too does the kiss on the hand that they had to practice over and over. All of the sudden she isn't telling me these things and since I'm not giving her shit about them, she starts to think it's alright. Then she's hanging out with other guys— Who knows how far stuff like that went?"

"What did you find, X?"

"It doesn't matter anymore. It's over. On to bigger and better things."

The way he looked at her made Natalie think of herself in that role, though it did mean being a rebound girl. It'd be good for him, she thought. He needed a stable girlfriend living just down the hall from him. It was evident to her despite the short time she had known him that he was ill equipped for a long-distance relationship. A sliver of a smile made its way onto her face. Then again, she thought to herself, what guy is?

"Bo told my friends I slept in your room the other night," said Natalie, her eyes distracted by a group of football players walking by outside. "They were all, 'So I hear you like jumping into bed with random guys.'"

"And what'd you say?" His expression froze, became serious.

"I told them that you weren't some random guy." Her eyes were wistful over her coy smile. "I told them that we were long-lost soul mates. Made for each other and all that mess. So, you know, it was okay to sleep in your bed."

X's fingers slid off the cube. Its obsidian surface glinted in the sunlight. "It's a copy program, very advanced, heavily modified."

Natalie flashed a hurt look at the abrupt change in subject but quickly replaced it with a resilient smile. "What are you going to copy?"

"C." X dropped his eyes to the cube and petted it softly with his index finger.

Her smile faded as she stared at X's lowered eyes. "Oh," said Natalie, with practiced aplomb, "I didn't even know you could do that."

"Yeah." He wrapped his fingers around the cube, scooped it up, and dropped it into his backpack. He fought to raise his eyes to her, but he only got as far as her neck before he turned his head to the window again. Outside, a handful of students walked along a rocky path, lined on the sides with naked trees that rose high above the building behind them, strong gray-brown fingers scraping the bottom of the heavens. X imagined the background fading out and the blue sky turning gray. Clouds formed at the edge of the new scene, slowly billowing towards each other, until they met at the middle and shrouded the world in artificial dusk. The fingertip-trees swayed as the wind picked up. Any moment now, the snow would begin to fall.

"I miss the snow," said X.

"Yeah," replied Natalie, her voice distant. "It's only snowed a couple times here, Valentine's day a few years ago." Seconds of silence passed. "Did it snow a lot where you used to live?"

"In the winter."

"That makes sense."

The conversation was devolving into niceties and both of them picked up on it at the same time. They looked at each other and for several minutes spoke with only the odd twist of an eyebrow or the quick dart of a pupil.

"Thank you for the viewee," said Natalie, at last.

"No problem," he said, crumpling up his napkin and dropping it onto his plate. "I owed you."

"My other one was getting old anyway. I was thinking about asking my parents for a new one for Christmas."

He could tell from the way her eyes flittered that she was lying, but he appreciated the effort. "I need to get going," he said, collecting his bag and standing up.

"Do you want to do something tonight," asked Natalie, hopefully. His hesitation was all the answer she needed. Before he could make up an excuse, she said quickly, "Or maybe I'll just give you a call tomorrow. Or you can call me when you want to do something?"

Finally, X nodded. "I'll do that." He noticed her wrapping the red ribbon around her fingers. "See you 'round, Nat."

"See ya," she replied, trying to force a smile. She watched as he walked away down the aisle and then around one of the serving stations. He didn't look back, despite her wishes.

A lengthy period of introspection was finally broken when a voice spoke from behind her. "Well, lookie who we've got here. If it ain't Mrs. Chemical Romance herself." A smiling G dropped his tray onto the table and took the bench opposite Natalie.

"What's that supposed to mean?"

G detected the shift in her tone of voice, a finely tuned but seldom used skill of his. He waited for her eyes to betray her, to reveal some symptom of sadness and anger. She was, under normal circumstances, a very attractive girl, with those blue eyes that now seemed to be moistening.

She looked at him passively, disconnected from the world.

"Is this about X?"

The way she narrowed her eyes signaled in the affirmative.

"Want to talk about it?"

Natalie shrugged her shoulders.

ELEVEN

The basement was lit in the green-white glow of the television. The latest re-imagining of *Flubber* played on the LCD on the wall, the bouncing globs of green jelly moving in digital clarity, almost three-dimensional, almost real. X sat reclining on the couch, his legs extended to the nearby coffee table. C was stretched out beside him, her sleeping face turned towards him in his lap. Shadows moved along the curves of her eyes and cheeks in a form of kinetic art. Her arms were folded in front of her, with her hands clasped around one of his. His other hand stroked her long dark hair and spread it out over his knees. He ran his fingers through it, felt the silky texture, and pushed at the barrier where the digital broke down for lack of data. It was close enough though.

"I'm sorry about before."

X brushed his fingers over C's smooth forehead. When he initialized her earlier, he was relieved to find that she had suffered no permanent damage.

"I was just angry. I didn't mean it. You know that I love you, right?"

C's chin dipped slightly.

"Yeah, I know you know. I just want things to be good between us again. The way they were. I want you to love me."

The ceiling above X pulsed blue, a message from the outside world.

"I've got to go," he said, sighing, "but I'll see you again tonight."

X shifted to the left, moving C's head to the soft cushion below. He kneeled beside the couch, his face near hers.

"And I'm bringing you something. Something so wonderful that it'll make you want to kiss me. Can you imagine that?"

C's image flickered in front of him and then the whole construct faded out.

In the drab gray of X's homedir, a small viewee pulsed in two-second bursts. X floated in through the permeable white shell of the room and landed without a sound on the custom carpet. The viewee was black; a text message had come through. He moved in close to read it.

Come here.

In the real world, his heart skipped a beat.

I miss you.

Two lines from C. The most she had said to him in the last few days.

He jacked out.

The ceiling came into focus as X pulled the rig from his face. He rolled over on his side and saw one of his roommates, Bo, writing something on the dry-erase board on his wardrobe.

"Oh, hey," said Bo, noticing X, "your friend G came by, but I told him you were jacked in. He said to call him later when you're *finished*."

X sat up slightly and reached for the black cube hidden on the shelf above his head. "Natalie said you told all her friends about her spending the night."

"Yeah," said Bo, chuckling.

X attached an electrode to the cube and suction-cupped the magic vertebrae. He rolled on his back and replaced the rig.

"Next time," said X, to the darkness of his mask, "mind your own fucking business."

He found her waiting in her homedir, sitting on a light blue section of cloth suspended from four legs that grew like bamboo chutes from the beige carpet. She stood as he walked in, and it took all of his concentration not to run to her and take her in his arms.

"Hi," she said, her voice and lips slightly out of sync.

"Hi." X stopped a few feet away from her, studying her face. His arms hung at his sides and on the index finger of his right hand, a silver band was wrapped around the third knuckle. On the band was a small needle sitting inactive and flush against the metal, ready to snap to attention at any moment. His finger twitched.

C felt the awkward silence between them and stammered. "Um, you wanna go somewhere?"

"Okay." He didn't move.

"I wanna show you something I did." She moved towards him and took his hand. The warmth flowed up X's arm and into his chest.

Focus, concentrate, he told himself.

"Close your eyes," said C.

X's eyelids drooped and he felt himself being pulled along. The ground began to give like a sandy beach and soon the sensation was gone completely. They floated in the darkness. X could hear the subtle tearing of artificial air as objects moved around them. A slosh, a whoosh, and then pressure at the soles of his boots.

"Okay, open them."

C stood in front of him, smiling proudly as if she had just won first prize at a science fair. Behind her was a familiar mirror and behind that, a familiar wall. The mirror stood on a long oak dresser that was covered in various knick-knacks, jewelry, folded shirts, and a neatly stacked pile of underwear. Sunlight shone in through an open window next to the dresser, casting a rectangular white patch on the carpet, the shadows of small, wood-carved ducks stretching within it. In front of the other window, an aquarium sat on a light wood nightstand. It held no fish, just one undersized frog that swam around in quick, jerky movements in the motionless water. To the left of the window was a bed, a double mattress on a white wrought-iron frame. A single white pillow sat atop the blue and gray afghan covering the bed. It was her room. Her real room in Terrareal.

"So," she asked, "what do you think?"

"The underwear is a nice touch." X moved to the dresser.

"I thought you'd like that."

"You've gotten a lot better at this."

"I've had a few days to work on it. You were right, you just have to keep doing it over and over until you get the hang of it. I can make anything now." C held out her hand and wiggled her fingers until a miniature wooden duck appeared in her palm. She smiled and placed it on the windowsill with the others.

X picked up a pair of blue underwear and ran his thumb over the soft cotton and small bows of ribbon along the sides.

"There's something else," said C, moving to the closet.

X turned around and watched as she brought out a small cherry-wood box, cradled in her hands with the kind of sensitivity afforded to newborns. She carried it to the bed and sat down, placing the box beside her. She beckoned him.

"This is where I keep you," she said, ceremoniously opening the hinged lid. She began pulling objects from the box. "Your keychain, prom pictures, some notes from you."

X sat down on the bed and watched as C spread the keepsakes out on the afghan, but his eyes were drawn to a shiny gold reflection in the corner of the box. He moved his hand slowly, even as she continued to draw more items. His fingers touched the cold band, and he raised it from the box. It was a ring. His eyes darted to her hand, and he noticed for the first time that it was naked. Their eyes met.

"You keep this in here?"

"Yes." C took a deep breath.

"You don't wear it anymore?"

"A promise ring goes both ways."

"Meaning?!"

Her mouth froze as the words poured from her unblinking eyes. X understood fully. She no longer wore the ring because she no longer promised anything to him. She might miss him, might have wanted to see him on occasion when she had the time, but her devotion, such as it was, was gone. X could tell that acceptance had already settled in her heart. She did not cry.

"I see," said X, lowering his eyes. He studied the detailed carpet, impressed by her skill and by the pieces of lint and lost threads that were scattered upon it. It was a strange turn of events, but not anything he hadn't contemplated before. He hadn't jacked in to make some kind of tearful reunion with her. He had only one mission and yet, he hesitated. "I still love you." He waited for a response. When it didn't come, he looked up at her. "Can't you say it? Please?"

"Why?" Her lips barely moved, as though frozen.

X pushed the box aside, slid closer to C, and put his arms around her. She hesitated at first, but eventually let her arms wrap around his back. He moved his mouth near her ear.

"I just want to hear you say it," he whispered to her, "one last time."

"I…" C's body flickered. "I'm sorry."

X shut his eyes tight. "Is it really over then? Is this how it ends?"

"Yes," she replied, her voice almost indifferent.

So be it, thought X.

The sunlight faded quickly, and shadow took hold over the room. X moved his hand up C's back until his index finger rested a few centimeters above her neck. "Bye, baby." His finger twitched, the needle sprung up, and he plunged it deep into C's spinal column.

The images came in rapid flashes, quickly overwriting the reproduction of her darkened bedroom. C felt the sting at the back of her neck and when she reached for it, she found that X's hand was no longer there, that he had disappeared completely. Now she was alone in an empty construct and nothing she did could stop the barrage of light and images from pricking like needles in her eyes. Panic began to grow in her stomach, quickly radiating outward and overtaking her entire body. A dull roar bellowed from far below her, though she could see nothing, could not even keep her eyes open long enough to attempt a glance.

In the real world, C's rig churned with the influx of new data, attempting to serve a million simultaneous requests made by a single instance of code on the Net. The rig's internal programming, of X's design, at first resisted the instruction, but at eleven months old, it was already outdated and woefully unprepared for the barrage that X had concocted. Somewhere in the stream, the rig caught glimpses of a single request, a jump command that its user was trying to activate. C was trying to get out, but the rig was at the mercy of X's copy program. Desperate to find a foothold, it latched onto the outgoing data and fed it back into a pseudo-construct.

C watched as the images slowed. A frame in the distance, slightly out of focus, began to drag in the construct, stretching out in the third dimension and overlaying the emptiness with a recreation of X's basement bedroom. The lights had been turned down low and she was sitting with him on the bed. His hands were working at the buttons on her shirt. It was the first time anyone had ever seen her naked. Why the memory should appear now, she did not know.

The panic swelled again as the bedroom dropped away. Her heart rate spiked and sweat began to drip from under her rig. The images ramped up again, each one bringing with it a painful discomfort. She saw glimpses of things she had forgotten about, childhood memories, and long-lost friends. Her body trembled as the space around her grew brighter.

"Lily!" A voice echoed from nowhere.

C felt the rig fall away from her face and was immediately aware of the convulsions shooting through her body. The pain of the digital world ceased, replaced by the shock of an abrupt disconnect from the data stream. As the tremors subsided, she sat up, her head spinning. Her hands grasped at the smooth covers on the bed below her, its blue tint slowly coming into view. A figure was seated at the end of the bed, leaning on an arm placed across her legs.

"Are you alright," it asked.

Andy's face took shape out of the haze, concern hanging in his eyes.

"Yeah," said C, putting her hand to the back of her neck.

"How did it go?"

C stared at the boy in front of her, overlaying his face with X's features. She reclined in the bed and turned her head to the wall. "It hurt." It was the understatement of the century. In her sixteen years of life, C had never experienced such a feeling of loss, of pain, of being completely hollowed out. "It really hurt," she added.

Her quiet words barely reached Andy's ears.

TWELVE

Natalie paused on the bottom step of the stairs leading down from the Jester West lobby. Above, she could still hear the bustle of students walking by the front desk. Although it was only one floor down, the Jester West basement seemed like another world entirely. Dimly lit, Natalie couldn't help but pick out dangerous shadows in the long corridor. G's roommate had given her directions, told her to take the stairs down from the lobby and then go to the end of the hall, but he never mentioned that there would be no lights.

Pressing ahead, she took her steps slowly and with one hand in her pocket, she fingered her room key, pushing it in and out of position between her knuckles. Several tense seconds later, after the frightening solitude had set in, she found the door, a pea-green slab of metal laminate with no markings to indicate its contents. She waved her magcard at the reader to the left and breathed a short sigh of relief as the LED lit green and the door clicked open.

Inside, Natalie was greeted by the smell of sweat and chicken. Rectangular lights hung from chains above four pool tables, illuminating the green felt and the lower halves of the men gathered around it. The clacking of balls sounded from multiple directions at once, making her eyes dart around in quick double takes. The noise and the shadows threatened to overwhelm her, but just as she was about to turn and flee, she noticed a familiar face by the table to her left.

G was leaning against the bar that ran the length of the east wall, cue stick in one hand and the other lost in a mass of french fries in a styrofoam container. His eyes were focused on his opponent's shot that had set three different balls into vacant motion. As a battle-hardened two rolled towards the opposite end of the table, it drew his eyes to the door, to the blonde girl standing awkwardly just inside it.

"What's a pretty girl like you doing down here," asked a voice from Natalie's right.

She turned to find a rather tall but lanky Asian boy with just-rolled-out-of-bed hair and an elongated tank top that hung from his body like a dress.

"You come to get some practice handling a stick?"

Before Natalie could respond, she felt G approach in her periphery. He leaned in close and put his lips to the side of hers in his best approximation of a European greeting. In full view of the Asian, he placed his hand provocatively on the back of her jeans. Without saying a word, he guided her back to his table, pushing her along.

"Aw, man," said her new admirer, "you slummin' with that little fish? Let me know when you're ready for a real shark." He enthusiastically slapped hands with his friends as they celebrated some unknown victory.

Natalie smiled genially. "Are you going to let him talk to me like that?"

G nodded. "Absolutely."

"Who said chivalry was dead," asked Natalie, rhetorically. She sat down on a barstool and inspected G's late-night snack. "What the hell are those?"

"Chicken rings."

"Chickens don't grow in rings." She picked up one of the circular pieces of meat and inspected it closely.

"Maybe," replied G, taking the food from her fingers, "but it has been mathematically proven that everything tastes better in ring form." He took a bite and pondered. "Onions. Donuts. Hot dogs."

"Life Savers," added Natalie.

"Exactly."

"That's game," said G's opponent. Without further conversation, he left to join a game at another table.

"Thanks for introducing me," said Natalie, watching the mop of brown hair disappear into the haze.

"You mean Miller?" G looked around. "Oh, well, I'm sorry," he continued, with a half bow. "I didn't know you were back on the market."

"I was never *off* the market."

"What about X," countered G, quickly.

"What about him?"

G studied the look on her face and decided not to press the issue. It had been several days since either of them had seen X and the small amount of disappointment that he felt from not being able to hang out with his friend must have been triple for Natalie. It wasn't surprising though, considering what she had told him in the cafeteria, where despite her best efforts to engage X, he had done nothing but go on about his girlfriend back home. G scoffed inwardly. Long distance relationships were for losers.

"Have you ever been down here before," he asked, approaching the table. He corralled nine balls into the triangle and arranged them in a diamond.

Natalie shook her head. "I don't really play pool."

"Everyone should play pool," said G, lifting the triangle and leaving the balls in perfect formation.

"I really suck at it."

G smirked a little as he chalked the space between his index finger and thumb. "That's why you need to play. An hour or two every day for the rest of your life and you'll get better. You could do with some training in the Net, too."

Natalie made no effort to move from her stool. "I'd just end up looking stupid. I wouldn't know how to do it."

"And that's why you should do it with someone that you *know* and *trust*. Someone with enough compassion and understanding—"

"To not make fun of me?"

G shrugged his shoulders in acknowledgement. "I was going to say someone who would be patient enough to let you struggle for a while, you know, let you wail away with the sticks and balls and see what happens."

"I'd rather not embarrass myself," said Natalie, pulling the styrofoam container closer to her and extracting a few fries.

"But that's all life is," replied G, sending the cue ball hurtling towards the diamond formation. The balls broke apart and after hitting several rails, the cue ball sunk into the side pocket. "A series of embarrassments."

"I am trying to maintain a consistently impressive quality, so I try to avoid embarrassment when I can."

G waved his hands, mocking her haughty statement. He approached her at the bar and reached across her to grab a chicken ring. As he did, his body came dangerously close to hers, but she did not pull away. Instead, she held her ground, daring him to come any closer. With his lips a few inches from her ear, he said, "We're all very impressed by you."

Natalie stared at him for a moment, lost in the way his mouth moved as he said the word *you*. The spell broke as he pulled away, as if the added distance brought him into focus. "I need a favor from you," she said, bluntly.

"I bet you do," said G, returning to the table.

"It's a hack job. If you're up to it."

"Oh." He pondered a spot on the ceiling. "If I'm not mistaken, I'd almost say you were trying to trick me into changing your grade."

"It's not like that."

"Then what is it like," asked G, scoring the felt with his miscue.

"Not here," said Natalie, "let's go to your room."

G smiled, grabbed the nine ball, and rolled it into a pocket. "My place it is."

They met G's roommate in the hallway as they approached his room and Natalie noticed that G didn't offer any greeting. After they were safely inside with the door closed, she questioned him.

"Don't get along with the roommate?"

G dropped his keys and magcard onto his half-dresser. "We get along fine," he assured her. "He minds his business, and I mind mine. It's the best kind of relationship. X got synth addicts, I got a guy who listens to Cyndi Lauper."

Natalie laughed and moved to G's desk. She placed her bag on it and unzipped the top. Carefully, she removed the smashed remains of her viewee.

"What the fuck is that," asked G, approaching it as if it were an injured animal.

"My viewee."

"What happened to it?"

"X." Just the facts, thought Natalie. G's blank stare prompted her to relay the story of X's recent hackscapade, of how he wanted to download all of C's e-mails and vidmessages. She left out the other, more intimate, details of that night.

"I wonder what he found." G settled into his chair.

"That makes ten of us."

G chuckled and said without looking up, "You still don't get that joke do you? The number is in base two, not base ten."

She ignored his mathematics lesson. "So what do you think?"

"I think we'd be better off just asking X. Look at this flash piece, here." He pointed to a small black rectangle, bisected by a silver gash. "This is the main memory chip, but it's been cut in half. The data's leaked out." G shook his head. "It doesn't matter what he downloaded onto this thing, it's not there anymore." G turned the viewee over and patted it, causing a shower of tiny screws and black slivers to fall onto the desk.

Natalie turned away, dejected, and watched the golden lights on G's rig sparkle on his bed. It was only when she looked directly at it that the whirring became noticeable. She had seen rigs lit up like that before, but only when someone was wearing them, when they were being used to jack in. The only thing the rig was attached to was a small white cube. Their umbilical electrodes met in the middle in an awkward union. Distracted by curiosity, Natalie asked, "What's your rig doing?"

G didn't look up from his desk. He had moved a combination magnifying glass and desk lamp into place between his eyes and the viewee. With a tweezer in each hand, he carefully removed the plastic bits and dug toward a glinting piece of metal in the corner. After a moment of silence, he replied, "It's decrypting. I went on a data rush the other day and picked up something choice."

"What is it?"

"I don't know," said G, "that's why I'm decrypting it."

"Then how do you know it's *choice?*"

"Touché. Smart money says that you don't put unbreakable encryption around something worthless. There's no publicly available cipher out there that my rig couldn't crack in under an hour. But this, this is monstrous. I think the payoff is going to be huge." G pulled a gold wafer from the viewee and held it under the glass to examine it. "Speaking of payoff, I think we might have caught a break here."

Natalie returned to the desk and tried to identify what G was holding. It looked like a shiny sand dollar. Its significance was lost on her.

"This is your viewee's persistent RAM, kinda like a buffer between the flash drive and the CPU. Whatever X was viewing might still be in the buffer. We just need the right amount of current and an interface." He was already standing and moving to the storage bins under his bed. He pulled both of them out at the same time and Natalie widened her eyes at the variety of computer parts contained within. G settled on a small, flat casing with an eSATA port and a stripped electrical cord with the wires showing. He returned to the desk and started marrying the wafer to the casing.

"You think you'll be able to extract anything?"

"*Extract?!*" His voice came out maniacal and thickly accented.

"It means to take out or retrieve."

"I know what it means," said G. "Obviously you are not up on your movies."

The monitor on G's desk blipped, flashed a screen of angry red, and then died out. Pixels began to light in random patterns in the middle of the screen.

"Is that it," asked Natalie.

"No, that's just static, background noise. It's trying to calibrate to the data stream. You've got a series of ones and zeros with no way of telling what those bits mean. It could be text, or video, or music." On his last word, G reached up and pressed the power button on his speakers.

"Lo-ve, you…" The voice was badly distorted.

Natalie looked quickly to G and back to the screen, where a face had appeared momentarily, highly pixilated, and then vanished.

"It's locking it down now," said G, typing furiously on his keyboard.

The voice stuttered but regained the full vibrancy of its recording. "I'm sorry to hear you're not feeling well. I know what it's like to lose a significant other, how much it can hurt, how it can seem like it'll never get better. I've never actually tried one myself, but I've heard that long distance relationships can be very painful, for both people. But I'm sure someone as strong as you will be able to make it through. You shouldn't feel down on yourself if you don't though.

Sometimes, things just happen for a reason. People move away just when you were beginning to like them."

Andy's face moved in ghostly after-images on the screen.

"I think you should come over tonight. My parents went down to Atlantic City for the weekend, so it's just me and my older brother in the house. We can talk about stuff or just watch a movie. Maybe you just need to get out of the house, spend some time with someone else."

Natalie snorted and G rolled his eyes.

"I know you said it's too early to give up, but you above all people should know that there are so many other fish in the sea. Some of those are right in—"

The video cut out abruptly, turned to a sea of television static.

"Thank God," said Natalie, crossing her arms under her breasts.

"No wonder he was pissed off," said G, looking at the viewee with newfound respect and awe.

Nodding in agreement, Natalie asked, "I wonder who that guy was."

"Andy," said G, reading from the screen. "His e-mail address and IP are embedded in the message."

She seemed not to hear him, instead lost in her own thoughts, wondering how she would have felt if her boyfriend had left and someone else had come along to give her a shoulder to cry on. And why should X care so much? If his advances towards her had meant anything, shouldn't he have been looking for a way out of that relationship? The questions swirled, but she could find answers for none of them. X remained an inscrutable variable, defying all reason.

G was looking at her when she came out of the clouds. He was smiling something cruel and mischievous.

"What," she asked, half-afraid that his energy was going to be directed at her.

"We've got his name and IP," said G. "You know what this means, right?"

Natalie shook her head, puzzled by G's tone of voice and his sudden rising from the chair. She watched as he stuck a finger in the air and pointed at the ceiling.

With a frenzied voice, he proclaimed, "Vendetta!"

THIRTEEN

For the briefest of moments, C felt as if her confidence was going to waver, that if his hands pressed any more gently against her back, she would give into the hope that everything could have worked out fine, had she just had the patience and resolve. But, as she took a deep breath, she was aware of the absence of any smells, of the virtual blandness that the whole room seemed to give off. The man sitting on her bed and clutching at her body as if she would be blown away by the slightest breeze was no more real than the room itself, than the artificial sunlight that streamed in through the window. She looked out at the neighborhood façade that she had created herself and knew there was nothing beyond it, just the cold emptiness of the Net, a place so artificial that it was any wonder that she thought something as real as love could blossom there.

"Is this how it ends?" X's voice.

"Yes," she replied, unsure of how to say such a heavy word.

She felt his hand move along her back and wondered how many times he'd done that same motion before, in his bedroom, in her basement. There would be other fingers and other hands, she told herself. There were comforting arms waiting for her on the outside, in the real world. All she had to do was say goodbye and she could be free.

Pain tore through the base of C's brainstem, a kind of world-shattering acuity that darkened all but the brightest pixels in the room, leaving her with a foggy vision of the world that seemed to last a lifetime. When it finally faded, when the sound of negotiating modems in her ears subsided, she found herself face to face with X, whose eyes had widened with shock or amazement.

"Are you alright," he asked. The previous anguish, whether real or not, was all but gone from his voice.

C shook her head, found that the last echoes of pain had already diminished into nothing. "I," she started, touching the back of her neck, "I thought I felt something."

"It was probably just line noise," suggested X. He took her hand at the fingers and frowned when she pulled them away.

"I thought we settled this," she said, getting up from the bed. The floor felt different somehow, a little less solid than before. "I should be going."

"Just like that?"

C crossed her arms defiantly. "This isn't as abrupt as you're making it out to be. You know it's been a long time coming."

"Long time *coming*?!" X raised himself along with his voice. "Just how long have you been fucking around with Andy?"

C felt her face go slack, refusing to translate the intense shock she was feeling inside. How long had he known? Wait a minute, she told herself, you didn't do anything wrong.

"Yes, you did," screamed X. "I know what you're thinking, I can read it plain as fucking day on that I'm-so-cute-I-must-be-innocent face of yours. Oh, he's just a friend, just a guy I met who helped me through a difficult time in my life."

Taken aback, C retreated several steps towards the closet, wondering how quickly she could reach her wrist with her hand and jump to safety. She had never known X to be violent, but his sudden rage terrified her, revealed a side that she had trouble believing existed. "I'm… sorry," she tried to say, but her apology was cut short by a reddening of X's face.

For a moment, she thought he was going to explode, unleash some kind of fury that might end with one or both of them getting hurt. But just like that, his temper disappeared, and he threw up his hands in exasperation. Why should it matter to him so much, she wondered. They were broken up now. There was nothing left for him to do or understand or say. Why wouldn't he just let her go?

"I'm leaving," said C, bringing her finger to the sliver on her wrist.

"You're not going anywhere." X's words seemed to run together as he spoke them, barely pausing in between. Before the image had even registered in her brain, X was upon her, standing with his face so close to hers that she could see the pixilation in his irises. There was pressure against the back of her neck and those previously desirable fingers now dug with icy precision into her flesh.

The floor fell out from beneath her and the sudden acceleration swirled in her mind for half a second. Then, there was nothing.

X stood quietly in the empty construct, trying to relax after his confrontation with C. It was the first time that he actually had the courage to bring up Andy and the results were pretty much what he expected. There was no success at the end of that road, but with so many to walk, frustration had made him opt for the path of least resistance. Bringing C's clone to life with the mind of the real C was more of a challenge than he had ever imagined. Time after time, he failed to convince her that she didn't really want to break up with him, that it wasn't really over. They could still be together; there was still hope.

The first time, he brought her back on the bridge. It was a complete disaster. She accused him of trying to prey on her emotions by bringing her to such a sacred place. That version of her only lasted sixty-eight seconds before he had to shut her down, put his hand to the back of her neck and suck out the essence that had turned her from a dumb clone to a close approximation of his now ex-girlfriend. The other versions hadn't fared any better. Always the same outcome, though sometimes prolonged by a turn of phrase or a desperate plea.

He tried bringing her back in other destinations from their shared memories, but it seemed that she didn't appreciate the care he took in recreating those special moments, not like the times she had actually been there, moments that were already fading from X's mind. If he were forced to do it all again, he wasn't sure he'd know how.

X took a seat on the pseudo-floor and stared at the nothing below him, imagining the veins that only running water could have carved. With a casual flick of his wrist, he wiped away the black shale of the construct to reveal the ragged walls of some indoor cavern. From below, an irregular disk of rock bubbled up from the orange-red floor, lifting him into the air. Several feet away, a similar pedestal rose from the molten rock. A cloud of superheated air drifted up as the floor dropped several hundred feet, so far that the bits of boulder that floated on its surface were but blurry black specks in the bright ocean of fire. A stifling breeze circled the cavern, winding upwards to the small vent far above X's head. It was a completely new construct, and he wondered where he had seen it before. And he wasn't the only one.

"Where are we?"

X turned to find C sitting cross-legged on the opposite pedestal, her fear of such impressive heights and dangerous conditions held in check by the knowledge that they were in the Net and by the false belief that nothing could ever hurt her. To her, the moment had abruptly changed from her virtual bedroom to X's pit of despair. X smirked. It must have been pretty unsettling.

"I don't know what to do with you, C," he said, calmly.

C began to speak, thought about her words, and stopped. She stared questioningly at X for the longest time, until finally saying, "You don't have to do anything with me. I'm not your problem anymore."

"You think you're that easy to give up? You thought I would just let you walk away without saying a word? Does the fact that I love you mean nothing?" X spoke his rhetorical questions without feeling.

"If you truly loved me—" C felt her throat tighten.

"Don't say that," said X, holding up a hand. He felt a tirade well up inside of him, but he dismissed it quickly. There really was no arguing with her, not anymore. "I only brought you back to tell you something."

"What do you mean *brought me back?*"

X ignored her and pressed on with his speech. "I just wanted to let you know that you're not going to beat me. Not in a million years. Not you or any woman on this planet. You're a problem, just like any other problem. You can be solved with the right code. All I need to do is come up with one way to get around this little obstacle and you'll be mine for the taking. It doesn't matter what you actually feel, what you think of me, who you've been seeing on the side. None of that will mean anything, not when I'm through with you."

C shook her head in awed disbelief. "I have no idea what you're talking about, but you're starting to scare me. I'm jacking out now."

"I haven't dismissed you yet."

"I don't need your permission," said C, asserting herself. "This is *over*, X!"

"No!" His booming voice filled the cavern. "We're just getting started!"

It had been raining ever since the night C ended their relationship. And each morning that brought hope was followed by an evening of disappointment. So many times, he had tried to load C's mind into the clone, but the program always failed to take. It took him a long time to understand that it wasn't what he was doing wrong *now*, but what he had already done.

The problem, he realized, was that by the time he copied her, C was already going to break up with him. Her mind was made up, so much so that even her copy held no love for him. Regret and anger mixed inside of him. He should have copied her during a happier time, but that opportunity was lost. He couldn't go back in time, no matter how much he wished it so.

Overcome by failure, X retreated to the solitary stairwell of Jester West, sitting on the steps between the fifteenth and sixteenth floors. His eyes were lost in the large, double-paned windows that formed the outside walls, taking in the nearly flooded campus. A mass moved in the alleys between the buildings, a giant snake with umbrellas for scales. One segment followed another over the driest patches, avoiding a section of Gibson Street where Waller Creek had surged over the bridge. X imagined that the clouds and the rain were products of his own sadness, that somehow he was bringing change to a world that had previously never bent to his will. But if that were true, it wouldn't be raining, it would be…

X's eyes drifted to the edges of the windowpane, and he noticed for the first time that frost was forming. The heat of the stairwell began to fog the windows, and he got up from his seat to rub some of it away. Outside, the rain had stopped completely, and the great snake-beast writhed a little slower in the streets. He looked up to the sky, to the gray clouds pulsing with the obscured light of the sun.

He thought he saw one.

Looking down, he scanned the tops of the buildings with their red brick roofs providing enough contrast to make out the first of the flakes. The trees bent violently as a strong gust of wind descended on campus. It carried behind it a flurry of snow, a sudden influx of white that dotted the bare trees. The serpent quivered, its skin popping and bubbling as scales contracted and receded into its body. Tiny orifices turned their attention upwards to marvel at the weather. X watched the trees and the snow as it engulfed them. He saw the footprints winding between them as students strolled to class.

X held his breath and let his mind scroll through his many memories of snow. A stubborn preference for the here and now kept trying to pull his recollections closer to the present, but there were no snow-filled scenes to fulfill that request. It was just as Natalie said, it didn't snow in Texas. X let out his breath in a defeated sigh. He couldn't stop the question from forming on his lips.

"Snow," he whispered, "in Texas? In October?"

The veneer broke down, erasing the white flakes from the world and plunging it once more into eternal rainfall. X detached the electrode from his neck and stuffed the wire into his pocket.

Something was churning in his brain, some lost instruction that was somehow important. He tried to sort out the data, mark each string as substantial or worthless. What had he been thinking of? Was it the veneer program that didn't seem to work? Or his inability to believe in the simulation?

X's eyes widened. It was the simulation itself. It didn't matter that the program terminated unexpectedly. The message had been delivered. The trees. The snow. The footprints. X had an idea.

FOURTEEN

The taxi smelled of rotting vinyl, as if the whole car had been submerged under water for a week and pulled out and put into service just that morning. At least the windowed partition kept X isolated from the driver, who by the looks of it, smelled even worse than the cab. The dashboard LEDs were reflecting off the sheen on the side of his face like some kind of cybernetic toaster.

"Where we headed, Mac?"

"West and Fifteenth," said X, tightening the aging seatbelt on his lap. The cloth had worn through at the buckle and he guessed that it would only take a mild collision to break it completely. It was the price of doing business, he told himself. He sure as hell wasn't going to walk all the way from campus in the rain.

The rain, a former blessing for the drought-weary Austin, was now a constant pest, doing more harm than good as it flooded creeks and washed away the many citizens who thought their SUVs could handle a low water crossing. It fell in tiny drumbeats on the roof of the cab and appeared instantaneously out of the dark night, landing in small explosions on the windshield, only to be smeared away by a frenzied wiper. The cab rumbled down forgotten streets, a grid of cracked asphalt in a lingering echo of downtown. The environmental rewrite was as sudden as a city block, falling into disrepair only a few streets south of campus.

A decade ago, he would have been riding through the heart of the business sector. But with time, downtown had migrated further north, competing with the other hearts of the city that sprung up in South Austin and in the sprawling Arboretum. There were a few traditionalists, silicon billionaires who pumped money into any brick and mortar between Fifteenth and the river. They built condos that no one ever lived in and offices that never earned or lost a single cent. Ultimately, the bad timing led to a surge in abandoned buildings, with built-in, virtual concierges standing ready day and night to help the nonexistent customers.

The area degraded rapidly. Boards replaced glass in any window below the tenth floor. The landmarks were still recognizable though and a few even dared to operate in the doom and gloom. From campus, X could still make out a few of the buildings, though most had already been moved, lifted by their very roots by mass-loaders on loan from a German conglomerate. The Frost Bank Tower still stood, along with the Austonian. The others were either dark or missing altogether, but at night, the Austin skyline didn't discriminate between the two.

It was simple economics that birthed Old Downtown. When big business moved out, the smaller, less refined businesses moved in. The many bars of Sixth Street went from raucous joints filled with hundreds of young girls and boys to warped-wood establishments with two or three regular patrons each, men who had found their home away from home and who didn't have the courage to go somewhere else. The usuals moved in behind them: gun shops, liquor stores, and massage parlors with clever names like *Fairy Tails*.

And amidst the vice, came the ciphers.

Cipher dens sprang up in the large office buildings, taking advantage of the networking infrastructure already built in. They usually operated in teams of five or six, spending all of their time locked together in a converted meeting room, jacked in and coding nonstop, their minds intertwined, processing at unthinkable speeds in a drug-induced haze. They lived their entire lives digitally, never jacking out or opening their eyes. They were ghosts, non-entities, atrophying bodies strapped to a chair, never to rise again.

Each den had a director, often called a suit, the man or woman who controlled the den's daily activities and long-term projects. They were the ones that made the deals. They were the ones that played nurse to their test-tube children. Backing these suits was another army of enforcers, protectors of the building and its occupants. They went where the ciphers' digital reach could not penetrate, delivering a physical message when an electronic slap on the wrist wasn't enough.

X stepped out of the cab on the southwest corner of West and Fifteenth and approached the familiar steps of the cipher den. The guard at the door showed a brief sign of recognition, but locked it down quickly, returning to his impassive façade. He patted X down without saying a word and then held the door open for him. Inside, the guard led him through a series of shambled anterooms to an elevator, their feet crunching on the splintered wood and fallen plaster. They hadn't cleaned since the last time he was there.

He wasn't even allowed past the first room then. Instead, he was met by another guard standing just inside the door, with a cube all wrapped up and his palm outstretched for the payment. Climbing the steps to the temple but never seeing inside.

"Anela got your message," said the guard, pressing the call button. "She wants to see you in person, in her office."

X studied the rusted metal casing of the elevator and wondered how safe a building this old could be. The numbers above the door were mostly out of order; the light skipped from seventeen to fifteen and then again over twelve. He squinted in the dim light, trying to discern whether some of the marked-out numbers were coated in blood.

A moment later, the doors creaked open and retracted with clunky imprecision into the walls. The inner elevator gleamed like a beacon in the shadowy hallway. It looked like something from another building entirely, one of those hundred-story scrapers on Loop 360. The silver handrails were polished to a fine sheen, the wood paneling was dusted, and the tiles on the floor appeared to have been recently buffed and waxed. X raised an impressed eyebrow at the guard.

"Be good," he warned, gently pushing X into the elevator. The man's fingers felt unnaturally bony in the small of his back, too solid and pointed to be meat.

The doors closed in front of X, and he watched his reflection appear on the shiny gold surface. It had been a long time since he looked at himself in the mirror and he barely recognized the sullen face in front of him. He had not combed his hair in days, and it hung in wavy curls on the sides of his otherwise shaved head. He wore a dark brown t-shirt under a green jacket, dark blue jeans, and steel-toed, leather boots. The breast pocket of his jacket bulged with the outline of some cubic object.

He ran his fingers through his hair, but he could do nothing to improve his image. In the Net, his avatar wouldn't have needed so much persuasion. A mere thought would have restored his former glory, made his hair fall straight down to rest just below his ears. A hat would have been good, he said to himself.

The sudden ding of the elevator bell surprised him. The mirror broke apart at the center and each side retracted once more into the wall. X stepped out into a large room with floor-to-ceiling windows separated by clear plastic tubes. Inside the tubes, bubbles drifted upwards in swarms, changing colors as they disappeared into the ceiling. The floor was tiled marble, bordered along the edges by tan carpeting. To the right of the elevator was a large desk. Behind it, in a high-backed, leather chair sat Anela Zabora, suit of the ZabSix cipher den.

"Welcome," said Anela, folding her fingers together in front of her. She wore her black hair up, exposing her thin neck and high breasts that disappeared into a strapless, blood red dress.

"Thanks," said X, approaching the desk. He tried not to let his eyes wander over her curves, but the temptation was just too strong. Everything about her body screamed for a sex sim. Such fantasy, thought X, in Terrareal of all places.

"Please, sit down. I was just going over your request again."

X sat in an armless leather chair and leaned back awkwardly. "How much do you think it'll cost?"

Anela smiled thinly, sensing her advantage. "We will get to that in a moment. First, if you do not mind, there are a few things that my associates and I would like to know."

"Okay." X thought he had explained himself fully when he messaged her earlier. The concept shouldn't have been hard to grasp for such elite ciphers.

"Now, just to be clear, my ciphers fully understand what you are asking us to do. However, and please excuse my candor, we doubt that you are truly serious in this request."

"I am." He shifted in the chair, unable to reinforce his claim with the accompanying body language.

Anela drew her hand across the desk and activated the vidscreen embedded in it. X could see the light from the LCD dancing on her face, though from his vantage point, he could not see what she was reading. She sighed softly. "You have tasked us to splice a human consciousness at a date and time specified by you and to remove all such memories and knowledge accrued thereafter." She leveled her piercing eyes at him. "Of course, this presupposes that you have in your possession a complete copy of a human mind."

X reached for the inner pocket of his jacket but stopped short as two men stepped out of the shadows behind Anela. He hadn't even noticed them.

"Please," said Anela, "slowly."

With a trembling hand, he retrieved the black cube from his pocket and placed it on the smooth obsidian desk.

Anela eyed the cube with a veiled glance. "The software that we provided you with was never meant to copy a human mind. You did not request that kind of functionality nor would we have provided it had you done so. While my ciphers would like to give you the benefit of the doubt that you somehow modified the code on your own, I cannot accept such a scenario. It is my contention that you had a third party reverse engineer and modify the code. Perhaps another cipher den? I explained the rules to you beforehand, X. The code we gave you was proprietary and not to be shared with another den. You had a non-transferable license for your personal use. As it stands, I believe you have violated that license." The malice in her voice was undeniable. Professional, bordering on sensual, but undeniable.

"No," said X, raising his hands in protest, "I modified it. Myself."

A playful grin appeared on Anela's face. "Forgive my regional colloquialism, but you look about as sharp as a marble. You had to have had outside help."

"Should I prove it?"

"Oh," said Anela, her eyebrows dancing, "I think that would be most necessary."

"Are you set up for a VitraC rig? I left the code in my avatar."

Anela laughed. "We are a little past that time, dear. My ciphers use the newest Anataware rigs, far more stable than anything VitraC has put out. But I suppose we could special order something to accommodate you."

"Deal," said X.

"Then it is settled. We will fulfill your request to the best of our abilities and in return, you will hand over the modified code for our inspection. You will show us step by step how you did it."

"*If* you can do the splice," said X, sitting up straight, "then I'll give you the code."

Anela considered his counterproposal for a minute before answering. "Agreed." She motioned with her hand to the man on her right. "Take the cube into the dream room. Tell them I will be sending along instructions soon. Make it clear that they are not to access the data until I send word. And not that I need to remind you, but run it through the viral scanner first." She glanced at X. "Make that all of the scanners."

The man reached across the desk in front of X. The sleeve of his suit fell back to reveal a fusion of flesh and metal that made his silver fingers clink on the desk as he picked up the cube.

"Now," said Anela, wiping a clear space on her vidscreen, "you know that splicing a human mind has never been done before. It is going to be a very involved process. My ciphers cannot simply erase data chronologically. If our storage specifications are still intact, then the data you copied will be arranged randomly. And even if it was not, it is not as if memories have timestamps."

"I get it," said X, impatiently.

Anela ignored his tone of voice. "Give me as much detail as you can." She pressed a button on her desk, opening a commlink to the dream room. "I want to get this in one pass," she said.

X began describing the scene as best he could.

The tall trees waving bare fingers at the sky, C's smiling face shining through the falling snow.

FIFTEEN

The city of Nisporeni was two years into its nuclear winter, but the almost fifty thousand inhabitants had long abandoned the cobbled streets and ancient buildings. Without the harsh light of the sun, the town stood almost unchanged since the fateful November morning when the last bomb of World War III was dropped just over the border with Romania. Although they had been spared the brunt of the blast, the resulting fallout ended up killing more people, and those, much more painfully. In the well-preserved but empty streets, nothing stirred. No animal darted from the corners; no discarded papers fluttered in the breeze. The only movement came from the heavily armed B Squad moving into the town from the north, hunched in combat readiness, eyes scanning the dim horizon.

It was a map that G had played before, one of several hundred ultrareals that had been traded among the run and gun groups in the last few months. While the focus had long been on Middle Eastern environments, from the hills of Kandahar to the sewage-filled rivers of Baghdad, popular preference had finally turned to the Slavic, to the countries with shadowy histories, countries that were left out of the basic education of American students. To visit one in the Net was an adventure in itself, but to visit one as a battlezone, as a place to kill and be killed, that was just pure adrenaline.

From G's vantage point at the top of an aging cell tower, he had a view of the entire town, from its dilapidated central square dotted with four identical wells, to the long thoroughfare that bisected the city and disappeared in the direction of a small hill that his heads-up display marked as Balanesti. High ground, thought G. It was where both squads were heading in the hopes of capturing it as their own. Hold it long enough and the game would end. But if they turned their backs for one second, someone else was likely to put a bullet in it.

The next round will begin in thirty seconds.

G eyed the counter that appeared in his HUD, counting down to the moment when all hell would break loose. He wasn't playing with his usual group tonight but instead had joined a crowded game on an East Coast server, one that showed a connection to a very specific IP address. The server was only carrying a three-star rating, which meant it would take a headshot to get an instant kill. Anything else, from torso to appendage, would require multiple bullets to bring a player down. It wasn't the type of handholding that he preferred, but then again, it wasn't really about the game this time.

Ten second warning.

The helmet's field sensors came online, overlaying the already artificial construct with a wireframe of neon green. In the distance, a cloud of red mist formed near a building several hundred feet away from the town square. Great, thought G, they've enabled tracers. Having his position indicated on everyone else's map, however muffled it was by the fog of war, was simply not acceptable. He had to maintain his stealth if he was going to complete his mission.

"So much for playing by the rules," muttered G. He brought down a console terminal and loaded his hack. He smiled thinly. The server wasn't even up to date with its patches. With his code in place, he would be able to move about the construct at will. When the time comes, he thought, Andy won't know what hit him.

A bone-rattling explosion tore through the impassive sky, sending sparkling fire across the drab dome. Flecks of golden dust rained down over the construct, glittering as they landed on G's visor, obscuring his vision. "Fucking amateurs," he screamed, wiping at his helmet with his sleeve. He shook his head in disapproval. What kind of newbie sets off a Harbinger at first call? If I find out that was you, Andy, I'm really going to make you pay.

G set off down the side of the communications tower using a single gloved hand to control his descent. He felt the tactile fingers grip and release the aging aluminum structure, operating off the same low-level code that governed every aspect of his battlesuit. When he reached the ground, the rubber of his boots compressed with mathematical precision to completely muffle the sound of impact. G smirked and ducked behind a nearby stable. He crouched low to the ground to peer under the boards. The red mist floated in his HUD, moving towards the town square in short little bursts of activity. He tried to ignore the handicap, but he couldn't deny that it would lead him directly towards to the enemy.

But I don't want the squad, thought G. I just want *him*.

He tapped his team commlink and spoke in a hushed tone. "Use the machine shop on the east side of town to infiltrate the hill. There's a hidden tunnel in the maintenance pit."

A garbled voice came back, thick with static. "Who the fuck made you platoon leader? *I'm* running this squad, and I say we take the wells."

"Everyone takes the wells," replied G, his voice assertive.

"No shit, noob. That's because they're the most direct path to Balanesti."

"Well, from where I'm sitting, someone else has beaten you to the punch. I'm watching B Squad take the wells like a cheerleader on prom night. It looks like they're going to leave one guy stationed at the entrance too. You'll never be able to take them from behind with a whole squad. It'll be suicide."

"Shut the hell up…"

"He's right, sir," said a squeaky voice.

"Not *now*, Placid! How the hell did they get to the wells so quickly?"

G let the line buzz for a second before grunting. "They were moving while the Harbinger exploded. What were you doing, holding your dick?"

Silence took over the line.

"Fine, we'll take the machine shop. But there's no way we'll beat 'em to the hill now."

"I'll take care of them," offered G. "I may not stop them completely, but I'll slow them down. You take up positions on the hill and wait."

"*I* run this fucking show!"

"Who the fuck cares who runs it," screamed G, angrily. "It's just a fucking game! I don't know about you, but I came here to shoot some people! Now can we get on with the killing or what?!"

A few cheers went up from A Squad.

"Everyone on me," grumbled the platoon leader. "Captain *Insano* is on his own."

The commlink went dead and G smiled to himself. "Yeah," he whispered, "it's just a game. Nothing can hurt you in here. We're all just as safe as can be."

He crawled along the dirt, crinkling his nose at the smell of sulfur.

G barely felt the bullet penetrate his shoulder. The synth code that was coursing through his veins, much to the surprise of his enemies, was locking down anything that even remotely resembled pain. In his head, he felt indestructible, as if no army of five or five hundred could ever bring him down. To his eyes, the enemy was moving impossibly slow, reacting to his attacks several seconds after he had abandoned one angle and started another. He felt the heat of his rifle's muzzle wafting backwards onto his face as he cleared one corridor after another. It was several minutes before he realized what he was doing wrong.

Respawn, thought G. Every time he got through one grunt, he had to stop and wait for them to come up on his rear, take them out again, and move forward. It was a slow and painful process, always keeping him out of reach of the head units. So far, none of the bullet-ridden corpses had contained Andy's signature. G guessed he must have been moving with the forward group, most likely sprinting at maximum capacity towards the hill. The racket he was making would have them believing that a whole squad was following them, scraping away at the skin of their backs and digging with gleaming claws into their spines. He broadcast the image on the general comm channel, hoping to put more fear into the enemy.

The console terminal unfurled from the top of G's HUD and he used a direct interface to code a few changes into the server's eXML configuration. Respawn time varied between fifteen and thirty seconds, way too fast to get the job done before last call. He coded a new variable, stuck a couple lines into the right files, and knew without confirmation that all deaths would now be final. He checked the magazine in his rifle, found it still half full.

The grenade made a sound as it sailed through the air. Thanks to years of run and gun experience, along with a little luck, G heard it before it had even bounced around the corner. He dove quickly into an open door and swung his arm hard against the metal plating, forcing it closed behind him. The explosion tore through the room as if the steel hatch were tin foil, bringing a rush of heat and a mild burning sensation that seemed to bypass his battlesuit altogether.

A soldier with a blue armband hurried into the room, his gun trained at the floor, looking left. By the time he completed his sweep of the area, G had already pulled his trigger. The bullet struck just in front of the soldier's ear, tunneling through the permeable electronics in the helmet. Its only weak spot, thought G, beaming with pride. He stood and approached the fallen player. A server message flashed across his HUD.

Headshot!

He fired his rifle again. It was the only way to be sure.

Brutal!

Slowly, G turned his head to the other door in the room and knew then that he was free to focus on the objective without having to worry about the roaches crawling towards his back.

"Sucks for you," said G, dropping his rifle to the ground. From the harness on his chest, he retrieved two Urban Pacification pistols with rounded clips. They were his favorite weapons. He stared at them briefly, recalling the fond memories of time spent on other servers, of the practices he conducted by himself, endless nights of shooting, covering, reloading, and shooting again.

The construct blurred around G's avatar, his rig unable to keep up with the speed, unable to draw the rooms completely before G entered and exited. The whirlwind of destruction took him through three more players and each one went down a little easier than the one before. His guns blazed and the screams of his enemies filled the waterlogged bunkers. Finally, at the end of the tunnels, where a single ladder ascended into the blackness, rising towards the hill, he found him, crouching beside the door, waiting in ambush.

Another bullet entered G's arm, and he felt his body sink towards his injury. In front of him, Andy was standing with a strange look on his face, wondering why his shot had failed to drop the ruthless Captain Insano.

"Now, Andy," said G, losing his grip on one of the pistols, "that wasn't a very nice thing to do."

Andy's mouth went slack with shock.

G sat calmly on a rickety wooden chair in the center of the room, smoking a cigarette that he barely felt in his lungs. Seated on the floor across from him was Andy, bound at the wrists and ankles, alternating between struggling with the unbreakable ropes and trying to reason with G. Even the general comm channel was filled with protest from the spectators who could no longer spawn back into the game. Cries of *cheater* filled the construct, but G ignored them, focused on making his outward appearance seem dangerous and scary.

"Why the fuck are you doing this," asked Andy. "Just kill me and end the game."

"Who's playing a game," asked G, flicking the dead ash off the end of his cig. "You've fucked up real bad, man. No quick *game over* for you. No jacking out until I'm done with you."

"I have no idea what you're talking about."

"Of course not," replied G, "because that would mean you recognize what you did was wrong. But no, that's the first step on the path to remorse and if you had that, I don't know if I could go through with what I'm about to do to you." G pondered a moment, lowering his eyebrows in thought. "What am I saying? I'd fuck you up either way."

"Whatever it was, I'm sorry—"

"How can you be sorry for something when you don't even know—?

"Fuck!" Andy's frustration shone through. "What, man?!"

G let the interruption slide, took a long pull of his cig, and crushed it out on the butt of his gun. His voice came out silky and menacing. "You tried to fuck the wrong girl."

A hint of fear washed over Andy's digital face, but then his eyes narrowed into accusatory slits. "X?"

G's laughter filled the dim room, echoing off the dirty windows and solitary overhead lamp. "You think X has that kind of time? To come here and do to you what you did to him? Fuck no. He would never come himself. He's what you'd call a *reasonable* man. I'm sure there would be something you could say to soothe his ego or to justify why you done what you done." He let out a breathy chuckle. "But I'm no fuckin' X. There's nothing you can say to me to make *me* feel better.

I don't really give a shit what you did with that little whore, but you got under my friend's skin. And now I'm going to get under yours."

His move across the room was a flash of light to Andy and before he knew it, G was upon him and had his hand pressed hard against the back of his neck.

"Say goodbye to the Net, you pimply fuck!"

Code surged through G's fingers, dancing around the internals of the server before finally jetting down the wire to Andy's rig. There, the code overwrote a majority of the operating system, cutting out critical processes and leaving only the ability to stay jacked into the run and gun. It was through this tiny pinhole that G watched the damage unfold, watched as the code began to change, write itself, and spread throughout the system. When the rig was full, when it was brimming with viral activity, it spilled back into the Net, corrupting the server and bringing down the hellfire of another nuclear attack on the town of Nisporeni. The comm channel burst with screams proclaiming the end of the world, each in a different way, but each tinged with unmistakable pain.

Virus detected!

The server's voice cut through the timorous chatter and silenced the construct. G felt the security software enter the room, though it had no physical representation. Andy's body was pulled away by unseen hands, forced into the corner furthest from G's position. He could see the terror in Andy's eyes, knew the pain he must be feeling. The server saw him as a virus, and to be categorized as a virus in the Net was almost as bad as being the last underclassman in the showers when the football players came in from practice. Either way you ran the numbers, you were in for the beating of a lifetime.

"This is just the first lesson," said G, hoping his voice carried through the torment. "But there doesn't have to be another. You're no longer welcome in the Net. You or the bitch."

Andy's eyes flashed recognition and then he was gone, morphing into a shapeless mist that funneled through an invisible hole in the floor.

Sick kill!

G winked graciously at no one.

SIXTEEN

C took her steps slowly, leisurely, admiring the detail in the construct. She recognized the place, but it didn't jibe with the Terrareal version. Out in the real world, it was the middle of October, hardly fall, and certainly not snowing.

"Oh my God," she said as she stepped onto the bridge, "how did you do all this?"

"Magic," replied X, his eyes skeptical. "Do… do you like it?"

Her face lit up, the twinkling snowflakes reflecting off her teeth. "I love it!" She moved to embrace him, and he was powerless to resist.

It was done.

X had lingered in the eternal winter scene for hours, staring at C's clone as it stood motionless, lifeless, snow collecting on her shoulders. There was an intense nervousness that stirred in his stomach whenever he thought about activating the code. He was afraid that it wasn't going to work, that C would reject the sudden jolt to her consciousness. But she hadn't. Her mind accepted the loss of memory and the arrival of new data at a past point. She lived the moment as if it were the first time, unaware that the date was a few weeks past what she thought it to be. She was back, she was oblivious, and she loved him.

Her rebirth was a glorious thing to watch. Her eyes slowly took on sentience, went from immobile to flipping back and forth between X and the snow. She saw the trees and the bridge, displayed recognition, then interest, and finally, joy. The code was designed to ease her back into the current time stream, averaging the bits of data to allow for a smooth transition. Once her new consciousness had caught up, she sprang into action, speaking immediately, exhibiting the same wonder and surprise she had shown so many lifetimes ago.

"Something's wrong."

C's voice broke the half-hour of silence that had passed as they lay stretched out on golden beach towels on the deck of a yacht. The oversized boat pitched and yawed in the coded chaos of random waves and ocean currents. A large orange sun hung in the cloudless sky, a vision of some watercolor daydream that X had seen on an image search somewhere. The rays of the sun bled into the blue sky around them, giving off a soothing heat and making their skin warm to the touch. A slight breeze blew across the polished white deck, maintaining the balanced temperature. Forms of birds trickled through the blue oils above, elongated versions of the letter *v*.

X was on his side, his head propped up on his arm, admiring the hills and valleys of C's naked body as she reclined on her back next to him. He traced the side of her breast with the flat face of his fingernail.

They had come straight from the forest construct to this place, something that occurred to X on the spot. It had something to do with a new beginning, with wanting to get off a failed path by taking her to a place that she had never been. He wouldn't repeat the mistakes of the past, couldn't afford to let the love of his life slip through his fingers again. He vowed to be more attentive to her needs, to give her anything that her young heart desired.

Young. For some reason, the word stuck in X's mind.

He wondered if he should create code that would age her. Would her mind accept a body that never grew older? X spread his fingers over the slight rise of C's stomach. Her body was perfect the way it was, why should he ever want to change it? Most avatars never changed, at least not until the user's body grew too old. It wasn't uncommon to see young avatars being driven by middle-aged users too proud to give up the pretty veneers of youth. The questions ran like a film reel through his head, clicking and popping around the various wheels and pegs. The frames merged, several still pictures combining to form one universal question.

Can she ever know what she is?

"Did you hear me?" C rolled her head towards him, shielded her eyes from the sun with her hand.

"Something's wrong," he repeated back to her.

"Yeah." She looked again at the sky. "This feels different than before."

X sighed nonchalantly. "It feels the same to me."

"You know that feeling you get when you wake up from a nightmare and you realize that it wasn't real?"

"Sure," said X, wondering where this train was taking her.

"Then something weird happens right after, but you know it isn't a dream. You just *know* that what you're experiencing is *real*."

"I think that happened to me one time."

C sat up and he watched the skin on her stomach compress, folding into small ridges. "This feels like that kind of real." She pulled her legs up and crossed her arms around them.

A sickening feeling began to rise in X. "It's supposed to feel real, that's the point of the Net."

"But this doesn't feel like the Net. I've jacked in enough times now to know the difference." She shook her head a little. "It's like this isn't artificial anymore."

X rolled onto his stomach and pushed himself up. He stood and walked to the edge of the deck, placing his hands on the chrome railing. The reflection of the painting above them sparkled in the water below. "Look," he said, motioning to the sky, "are you gonna tell me that *that* looks real?"

C rose and moved to join him by the rail. She felt her body move freely and with a sudden thought, her avatar donned a black swimsuit. Its appearance surprised her momentarily. "I, I didn't say that it looked real, just that it felt real." She adjusted the straps on the sides of her hips.

X let out a deep breath. The waves lapping at the side of the boat were the only other sound.

"I had a great time today," said C, taking X's hand, "but I want to go home now."

The moment had come. X had been putting it off as long as he could, but he knew that eventually they would have to cross this bridge. The second he told her that he was going to jack out, she would have gone and tried to do the same. And then, she would have found out the truth.

A million possible responses fired in his head, but he couldn't settle on any. Frustration built inside him, making him nauseous. His distraction calmed the ocean to the point that the boat was barely moving in the still water. C noticed the change, saw the silver railing lose its luster. The birds froze in place as the blue sky slowly swallowed them up.

"What's happening," asked C.

The sun faded, bringing a strangely lit dusk over the boat and diminishing the small patches of sunlight that had formed in the valleys of the subtle waves.

"C…" His eyes met hers and he was unable to continue.

She let go of his hand. "You're scaring me."

"I'm, I'm sorry." He fumbled for words. "Listen—"

"What? Just tell me."

"You can't go home." The words felt dry in his mouth. He was delivering her death sentence, and his body knew it.

"What do you mean?" C took a step backwards, as if suddenly frightened.

"You can't jack out."

"You're lying."

"No, I'm not."

"Yes you are!" She cringed, narrowing her eyes at him. X moved to hold her, but by the time his hand reached her, she had pixilated out of the construct.

He looked around wildly, trying to locate her. The boat was dark; the deck was barely visible anymore. The panic inside of him settled as he remembered where he was. The Net wasn't a physical place that could be escaped. She couldn't just run away. C wanted one thing, to get out. To do that, there was only one place that she could go.

X moved his hand over the scene around him, repainting the sky in royal blue, bringing the deck back to its previous vibrancy, and resurrecting the waves around him. The towels reappeared and the birds resumed their cries. He sat down calmly on his towel and counted the seconds. After sixty, he jumped.

C crossed the barrier into her homedir, finding it more difficult than it had been in the past. Her first few steps echoed in the empty room, and she was surprised to find that she was dressed differently again. Her swimsuit had been replaced by a dark blue t-shirt, faded jeans, red socks, and a pair of worn sneakers. She could just make out the hearts and lines that she had drawn on her shoes with a permanent marker. But she had never done that in the Net. Those shoes were waiting for her out in the real world, thrown carelessly behind countless others in the closet downstairs.

She looked around quickly, noticing the dull concrete where color used to be. Plush chairs and blankets had frozen, turned to stone. The walls were coated in it, raised in the places where pictures used to hang, their inspirational images buried by the slate.

In the center of the room was the transfer column. C approached it slowly, looking for signs of life in the smooth gray sides. She placed her hand on it and winced. It wouldn't allow her to pass. X had been telling the truth. She couldn't go home. Her virtual legs gave way, and she fell to a kneeling position, collapsing in a soft thud.

X found her crouched before the transfer column, shoulders heaving in a crude mimicry of a woman crying. His footsteps were loud, echoing from the soles of his new boots, but she didn't turn to him. He took a seat on the hard floor next to her. With legs folded and fingers interlaced in his lap, he waited.

"What happened here," she asked, talking into her legs.

"I don't know." And that was the truth, as X had never seen a dead homedir before. "I think this is what happens to homedirs when you jack out."

"But I didn't! We have to tell someone that I'm still jacked in. There has to be someone who knows what's going on. Who watches over the Net?" Even digitized, the desperate timbre of her voice shone through.

"I don't know."

C ignored him. "They'll know what to do. We have to tell them I can't get out."

X sighed. "We don't need their help."

"You know how to get me out?" C brought her legs around and changed positions to face X.

"You can't go home, baby."

"But my family, they're gonna wonder what happened to me. Someone will investigate."

"No, they won't."

"Stop it!" C swung her fists at X, landing on his shoulders and the sides of his arms. "How can you be so calm about this? You can't keep me here, people will come looking for me. My dad will wonder why I haven't jacked out!"

X allowed her to take out her anger on him. The impact of her fists registered, but not the pain. His eyes drifted off, staring at some unseen puzzle that floated in the air beyond C. He turned it over and over, trying to find the solution. C noticed his distraction and slowed her attack to nothing.

"They will…" Her voice was barely a whisper.

X returned his gaze to her, his negative response was carried plainly by his eyes.

"Why not?" She had calmed down; her voice was quiet and even.

"Because…" He faltered briefly, then regained his confidence. "Because you've already jacked out. That's why this place is dead. It thinks you're gone. And you are. The real you, anyway."

"Please don't lie to me. This isn't funny."

"I'm not lying, it's the truth."

"Then how am I still here?"

X thought of all the nights he and C's clone had spent together, in each other's arms, she unaware of anything that was happening to her.

"You're a copy." X spoke slowly, his eyes never leaving C's. His inflection was deliberate, meant to impart sincerity, and C recognized it immediately.

She shook her head in response.

"I'm sorry, baby."

"No." Her voice was soft and whimsical, like the day they first met.

"I can prove it to you."

He took her blank look as approval.

"What day is it," he asked, placing his hand over the purple rectangle on her wrist.

"It's Sunday, the twenty—"

He removed his hand and let her read the sliver. The small yellow digits glowed a date from the future.

For a long time, neither of them spoke. Eventually, C lowered her arm to her lap, but she never took her eyes off the numbers, unwilling to accept their betrayal. X put his hand on her knee and moved it gently, trying to caress her into acquiescence. He watched her face, convinced he saw something moving behind her brown eyes. Soon, her skin took on a strange glow, soft, but noticeable.

"I need time," said C. Immediately, a chorus of disembodied voices sprung up from the ether and announced the date and time. X seemed not to notice.

"Okay."

C looked around slowly. "But not here."

Electrons sped through the dark fiber of the Net, depositing X and C in the replica of her bedroom. It had not been garbage-collected and remained with all of the detail and love that it had had when X last set foot in it.

"Did you do that," he asked her, unsure of how the memory of this place could exist in C's spliced mind.

C's eyes took in the room and from her mouth came a guttural cry. She turned to X, her face contorted in an expression of anguish and horror. Lost in the descending lips and slit eyes was something X couldn't believe he was seeing. It was small, circular, and twinkled like a drop of…

C was crying.

"Leave." Her voice carried unusual bass, making the ducks dance in a row on the windowsill."

"I love you."

"*Fucking* leave!" The anger lit behind her eyes, and X felt fear climb his spine.

"What? What's the matter?"

The bomb dropped and C exploded. "What's the *matter*?! How could you do this to me? How can you tell me you love me and…" Her words were garbled with electronic distortion. She crossed the room and threw her fists into X's chest again, but this time, the pain went deep.

X crumbled under C's onslaught, trying to protest but finding no words to do so.

"God *damn* you, X. GOD DAMN YOU!"

She rose like a terrible beast in front of him, enhancing her detail even as his faculties diminished. His avatar faded, his look of confusion and terror averaging with the bits of window behind him, until all that was left was the sunlight streaming in through the glass, the fake neighborhood, and the empty world beyond it.

He dreamt of her that night in an endless cycle of subconscious torment. He would see her, perfect, beautiful, so hopelessly in love with him. But then she would change, morph into something that he didn't recognize: monsters, animals, forms of creatures beyond his wildest imagination, beyond the boundaries of sanity. And throughout the dream, her words echoed. *God damn you!* The words were so unlike her, from a thread inside her that he had never known or something entirely new, some recent evolution. He had not been expecting so much anger, was hoping that their love for each other would be strong enough to counteract the shock.

But there was still hope, wasn't there?

I need time.

Time for what? X ran the possibilities. Maybe she needed time to accept her new life. After that, she could love him again. The opportunity was there.

But each time that the harsh colors of the dream faded slightly, each time that hope sprung from his chest, the nightmare ended and started over anew.

SEVENTEEN

The television was on mute, but G could still read the ticker scrolling by at the bottom of the screen. Above it, a newscaster was miming the day's events that, according to the inset video above her left shoulder, was about a grisly multiple homicide in Jonestown. Music was playing from the small portable stereo on the shelf by G's bed, belting out some old Dream Theater in the dark dorm room. G reclined on the bed, with one arm behind his head, straining through the first stages of nearsightedness to see the flashing lights and yellow tape.

Next to him on the bed, still whirring and warm to the touch, sat his rig. The blinking LEDs had changed less than an hour ago, announcing their completion of the decryption routine by flashing off and on for several minutes. Now, they lit slowly, counting down in binary as the data was repackaged and made ready for inspection. There was a lot of data floating around in the rig's random access, ones and zeros that made no sense in their current form. Now that the numeric cipher had been found, the bits could be rewritten into something understandable, and, G hoped, something profitable.

G pawed at the remote control on his chest, searching for the mute button.

"Tech news coming up, after the break."

The commercial that had been playing under the ticker expanded to fill the rest of the screen. The subliminal images and hidden audio cues played with G's sense of time, blocking out the rest of the world.

A lens flare morphs into an afternoon sun as the camera pans down to a group of people celebrating a birthday around a white picnic table in an All-American backyard. Near the head of the table stands a not-so-elderly man looking down at the candle-filled cake in front of him, ablaze with the light of sixty years. Around him, younger faces cheer and smile, singing the last verse of a traditional song. The man bends slightly, a flash of a grimace from the pain in his back. He purses his lips, tries to blow, but nothing happens.

The camera zooms unnaturally fast and enters the man's chest to show a simulation of his beleaguered heart beating irregularly, struggling to deal with the flow of blood. It shakes violently, shivers like a drenched animal, and finally gives out. Muffled screams are heard from camera left and as the image moves, so too do the voices, jumping from speaker to speaker. The image presses in on the screen, slicing through the man's internals shown in family-friendly reds and whites until finally settling around a segmented bone where a black microchip is emitting an ominous red light. Suddenly, streaks of blue electricity shoot out from the chip, grabbing at the spinal cord like an open hand. A voice cries out that he's breathing again. Everyone sounds so relieved. The camera pulls back to reveal the man on the ground, his family around him, his eyes peering out towards the viewer as if he can see them.

"Thank you, Guardian Angel."

A fast wipe replaces the family with flashy graphics, mimicry of transistors and circuit boards, until finally fading to black. A thin line appears.

An Angel was watching over this man. Who is watching over you?

G smirked, hit the mute button on the remote, and let the music fill the room again. Lower on the screen, another message appeared.

Introducing the Guardian Angel biochip. New technology by Vinestead International.

As the image faded, a beep from his rig recaptured G's attention. The lights were dark. The job was finished. He sat up quickly and began decoupling his rig from the code cube. His pulse raced with anticipation, wondering what treasure he had taken from UltraKill's stolen rig.

"Fucking GA chip," said G, placing the electrode on his neck. His fingers traced over the embedded inhibitor chip and he wondered whether he'd ever have the guts to have it removed after it had been so painful to put in. One thing was for sure, he'd be six feet in the ground before any Vinestead product found its way into his body.

"Now let's see what all the fuss was about."

G jacked in.

And found himself floating in a white construct, with walls and a ceiling made from a translucent material that bent the light like rounded prisms so that streams of blue and orange and green twinkled in the periphery. The room was roughly double the size of his dorm and the faint markings on the walls drew his attention towards his left. There, a large rectangle was slightly indented in the glass. It shimmered as he approached it, its colors warming in response to his presence.

"Beautiful," whispered G, as the pixels began to flow in earnest.

"Isn't it though," asked a female voice from behind him.

He turned quickly and saw the last of the vibrations die down in her avatar. She was taller than him, approaching six feet, and dressed in smart but sexy black business attire: a button-up blazer on top of a white dress shirt and a short skirt to match. Black wireframe glasses sat on her tan face that G placed somewhere south of the equator, Brazilian perhaps. Her long brown hair was pulled back into a loose ponytail that hung from the bottom of her neck. She was stunningly beautiful and for one brief moment, G let a fantasy run wild in his mind.

"Hi, my name is Alessandra, but please, call me Ale." Her voice was soft and throaty, powerful yet feminine. "May I ask your name?"

"G. You can call me G." He stammered but regained his composure.

"Well G, welcome to the Synaptic Synth construct. I will be your guide for today's demonstration. Where would you like to begin?"

"General information," said G, slightly disappointed to discover that she was a simple promotional avatar.

Ale waved her hand at the rectangle on the wall and a series of slides appeared along the bottom. She touched them as she spoke, bringing up the relevant information. "Synaptic Synth offers complete replication of the brain's internal mapping mechanism. At the biological level, synapses form the basis for all acquired knowledge. They consist of two membranes separated by a short gap across which neurotransmitters travel by the process of diffusion…"

G lifted a hand and shook his head slightly. "I don't really understand any of that. Could you just tell me what the program does?"

Smiling, Ale skipped to the fifth slide. "Perhaps I could demonstrate the functionality? At its core, Synaptic Synth is a method for transferring knowledge that bypasses synapse development altogether. Using synthetic neurological-chemical reactions, it is able to create synapse bridges based on previous examples or through extrapolation after acquiring new data. You say you don't understand the biological processes that control learning? I can change that in just two seconds."

"How?" G crossed his arms and looked at the screen, though nothing about the fancy symbols and formulas made any sense to him.

"For this demonstration, I will supply you with a short lesson in biology, but as you can see, we have many other evaluation topics." The screen shifted to a bulleted list with titles that ranged from *Advanced Network Topologies* to *Basic Self Defense*. "When you are ready to proceed, I will load the data."

"Alright," said G, nodding. "Let's see it."

Ale smiled coyly. "First, tell me the definition of exocytosis."

"Easy," replied G, "it's a rapid process of cellular secretion that—" He paused, let his eyes go wide. "The fuck?" He couldn't help the smile growing on his face. "Holy shit!"

"As you can see, the transfer process for small sets of data is completely transparent. The more data that is copied, the more synapses that must be built, and therefore the more time that one must wait. Perhaps you would like to sample another topic?"

G scanned the topics and chuckled. "How to Talk to Women?"

"You would be surprised how often I demo that information pack."

The hint of a backstory intrigued him, and he pounced on it. "And who are you usually demoing for?"

Ale flashed a gracious smile. "I'm sorry, that information is confidential."

"Of course it is," said G, nodding. "And whose confidential information is that? Is this a Vinestead program?"

"We are not affiliated with Vinestead International or any of its various subsidiaries. However, at this point, we do not wish to disclose the source of this program, for security reasons."

"And is this the full version or is this it?" He motioned to the demo room.

"The program is fully complete. All it needs is an input source."

"How…" Before G could finish, he felt a tremor come over his body. When it passed, he tried to remember what he was going to ask, but found the space filled with new knowledge.

"That's how," said Ale, triumphantly. In just a few seconds, she had transferred the entire user guide and reference manual into G.

A world of possibility opened up in G's mind. He saw the looming figure of college, so tall and formidable in his nightmares, reduced to an inconsequential speed bump on a road that seemed to straighten in front of him. It led into the distance, where the sun was setting over rolling hills, all alight with the orange glow of potential. No more studying. No more cramming for tests. No more questions left unanswered. The pit stops flew by, each more wonderful than the previous. He could load up with a whole degree, maybe three. The realization hit him like a ton of bricks, but where pain was expected, there was only warmth. A hint of a tear came to his eye out in the real world.

Terrareal, where so many students sat with noses buried in books. But no more. Not only would he never study again, but the others, the privileged few who could afford the insane price he was going to charge, would never have to either. The implications swirled around his head, growing loftier by the second, at one time replacing the American education system with fifty million cubes, enough to bring kindergartners up to the college level in a matter of days. His eyes snapped open.

"What would this do to a child?"

"Although the brain slows down development of synapses after a certain age, we do not recommend running this software on anyone younger than eighteen. The legality of such a process has not yet been determined. Also, as with any neuro-chemical procedure, there is a risk of both temporary and permanent damage to the host brain. This risk is proportional to the size of the dataset." Ale shifted in place, as if unsure what to do with herself.

"Are you alright?"

"I'm more than functional, thank you." Her voice sounded sincere, but there was something about the way her head moved, the way her glasses slid down her nose. A shaky finger pushed them back up.

G studied her face, tried to place her mannerisms among his experiences with women, but nothing came to mind.

"Is there anything else I can do for you?" Her tone was hopeful.

"Are you sentient?"

Ale shook her head slightly. "No, all of my responses are preprogrammed. I do, however, draw from a large pool of data that makes it appear as if I am intelligent."

"It's very convincing," admitted G. "I'm beginning to think that you're the most impressive part of this demo."

"I should inform you that I am only programmed for demo and training work. I cannot process flattery, though I can recognize it."

"And I cannot process rejection," countered G, smiling, "so I guess that puts us at an impasse." It was absurd, he realized, to be talking this way to an artificial being. There was no possible way for her to understand, yet he pressed on. "I'm not sure what we're going to do."

"Perhaps we could walk through an input session? Do you have any texts that you would like to scan?"

"I can think of a few books." His inviting smile was lost on Ale.

EIGHTEEN

Even after two days of constant anguish, even after surrendering to the depths of the nightmare, somewhere out in the real world, X detected that faint chemical scent that told him Natalie was near.

"Good morning."

Her face came into view as X opened his eyes to the light of the morning sun. She was sitting on his bed, her legs dangling over the side, with one hand on her hip and the other propping her up. She was ducking slightly to avoid contact with the ceiling. X rolled onto his back, momentarily forgetting the restlessness of the night before, though his outright exhaustion could not be ignored.

"Morning," he replied, his voice dry.

"I haven't seen you in a while," said Natalie, poking him playfully on the leg. "G is very worried about you." Then in a whisper, "I think he likes you."

X grunted, unable to find humor in her words, unable to bypass the overwhelming depression creeping up his spine. He sat up slowly, rubbing his eyes. Natalie's features became clearer and for the first time, he realized that even without the chemical trace, she was adorable bordering on beautiful. A few more years down the road, a little refinement here and there, and she would turn every head in the room.

Her blonde hair hung just below her shoulders, straight and shiny. Her blue eyes were jewels in a small sea of white, staring at him with an intensity that he realized he had been ignoring for too long. In the midst of all his trouble, she was there, greeting him with a smile despite his obvious pining for C. For a moment, he wondered who truly loved him. Was it the girl who no longer wore his ring on her finger or the woman who sat beside him on the bed, the woman who exuded some heavenly fragrance that made his nose tingle and his heart flutter? His eyes walked the outline of her body, along her shoulders, down her arm, to her hand, partially hidden by his pillow, to the mass of black tubing and LCDs that made up his rig.

He remembered what he had done to C, but his thoughts jumped quickly to Natalie. "I'm sorry," he said, meeting her eyes.

She smiled delicately. "For what?"

"For ignoring you, for chasing after things I thought I wanted. And for doing it all in front of you."

"You love her. I understand love." She curved a section of hair behind her ear with her fingers.

"Yeah," said X, wondering if she picked up on his uncertainty.

"There's no way I can convince you to give her up. It's not my place to do that kind of thing. I like you a lot, but you have to deal with her on your own. Make your decision for your own reasons, not because of me." She let her eyes fall. "Not for some girl's silly crush."

"I don't think you're silly."

"I didn't say that I was silly," said Natalie, looking at him again.

X stared at her, his mind wandering over possible futures.

"So," said Natalie, glancing at the rig, "what are you going to do?"

"I think there's only one thing left to do."

She tried to keep her voice reserved. "Are you going to break up with her?"

X shrugged, let a small smirk form on his lips. "We broke up a week ago. Now I just have someone…" He stopped, corrected himself. "…a program to delete."

"A man's gotta do what a man's gotta do."

Is this what a real man would do, X wondered.

Natalie helped him reapply his rig and pulled the covers up to his chest as he reclined on the bed. She held his hand in hers, massaging it lightly.

"Good luck," she said.

"This shouldn't be too difficult," he replied, suddenly unsure of himself. He changed subjects in his mind. "When I get back, would you like to go get some breakfast?"

"Yeah." She glanced at her watch. "Lunch, but yeah."

"It's a date then." X hit the switch, pulsing away at the speed of light into the Net.

C wasn't where he had left her. Her bedroom was empty; many of the artifacts had been destroyed. The ducks were smashed and in splinters on the floor. One pane of the aquarium was shattered, the water almost completely drained, and its sole inhabitant was nowhere to be found. X jumped, trying other constructs. He checked her homedir, the yacht, the hill, the playground, and all the places they had ever been before. But she wasn't anywhere. It was as if she had left the Net completely, but X knew that was impossible.

A small beep came from X's wrist. A series of numbers appeared on the silver sliver, coordinates to a construct in the Net. His mind raced. C must have sent him the message. She wanted to see him. X blinked, wondering why that made a warm feeling rise in his chest. He jumped to the new location.

A sterile white room appeared around X. The walls rose to a particleboard ceiling, pocked squares laid out on a plastic grid, aged with deep cracks. In front of him was a large bed; one end of it was elevated. It had the look of a hospital room, but more specialized. There were the usual heart monitors and oxygen machines off to one side, but something about the room was different. It took several seconds of inspection before X finally noticed the stirrups.

"This is where my nephew was born," said C, from behind him.

He turned and watched her walk past him to the bed, his mind racing.

"It was such a beautiful day. We all came to the hospital and hung out. All my family and all our friends. They told us we couldn't have that many people in the room, but nobody wanted to leave. I remember feeling that all the trouble in the world felt insignificant when he was born. I had never seen my dad so happy."

"I remember you telling me about that." X immediately regretted interrupting her.

"I got to hold him in my arms, this amazing little guy. He was a brand new life and I loved him so much, without even knowing why." She turned to face him, her eyebrows dipping. "And now, because of *you*, I will never get to hold him again. I won't get to see him grow up. You've taken *everything* from me."

There was something in her eyes, a hint of something menacing.

"But I'm not mad anymore. I've come to terms with it. Time is moving along so much faster now, so much faster than before. To you, only a couple days have passed, but to me…" She lifted her head and stared at the unseen horizon. "To me, I have already been here an eternity."

X swallowed hard. "I'm sorry," he said at last.

"I know," said C, and for some reason, he believed her. "I know you are."

"I didn't want to hurt you. I just wanted us to be together."

She approached him slowly, her body language inviting. "I understand."

"I just love you so much…" His words trailed off, surprising even himself.

C opened her arms to him, and they embraced.

Immediately, X knew something was wrong. C felt different, sturdier, stronger maybe. There was something in her arms, some hidden power that pressed on his back a little too hard. And the smell. There was a perfume in the air, but nothing he had ever known her to wear. She whispered quieting sounds in his ear, but at the digital level, X slowly began to recognize the indicators of deceit. He had been letting his emotions cloud his vision, get the better of him.

He changed modes instantly, began examining the room at the code level, watching the ones and zeros overwrite each other in a never-ending territorial dispute. In the digital haze, X saw the truth, saw C for what she had become.

But by then, it was too late.

X felt the hot point of an unseen device penetrate the back of his neck.

Natalie jumped backwards on the bed as X's mouth opened wide and let out a horrible scream. He sat up quickly and Natalie pulled the rig from his face as if it were a blood-sucking leech. His terrified look preempted her questions; she stared at him blankly. As X's brain began to recognize the room, he fought desperately to control his lips.

"Back!" X blurted out the word, spit flying from his mouth.

"What?"

"I need to go back. Now!"

Natalie hesitated but decided to trust X's demand. She pushed on his chest, guiding him into a reclining position. His heart pounded rapidly against her palm. Replacing the rig swiftly, she flipped the switch for him.

X stepped into the rain-scented air of his homedir. The familiarity of the room calmed him; some of his specialized code ran through his avatar, relieving the stress of his fear and panic. He walked around the room, looking at the photos lined in identical frames on a chest of drawers. A pile of movie ticket stubs lay in a small bowl. He picked up a few, eyeing the titles and recalling the times he spent with her watching them. As he reached the end of the chest, his eyes fell on a partially opened drawer.

An invisible weight crushed down on the room.

He pulled the drawer open quickly, going straight for a small box hidden behind pairs of C's underwear. The black felt box was still there and for a moment, he felt relieved. But as he opened it and saw the empty slab of tan hide, his heart sank. The copy program was gone. She had taken it. And she had used it on him. Somewhere, a copy of X was running loose.

A shadow flashed at the edge of X's periphery, moving too fast for the physical restrictions of the room. He turned quickly to see the transfer column glowing a bright amber and quickly fading out. In disbelief, he moved towards it. Its clear outer coating seemed to fog up, filling from bottom to top. The fog slowed to a crawl, then froze in place, leaving behind a column of solid concrete.

"I think that's what happens when you jack out." C's mocking voice floated in from all directions. Pixels swarmed in from the walls of the room, circling the outer edges, speeding faster and faster. The loop tightened until they were spinning quickly in one place like a perfectly cylindrical tornado. X took a step backwards as small flashes of light appeared within the swirl. Pieces broke off, forming arms, legs, and a torso. A strange sound pulsed in the room as C took shape. Soon, he was staring into her smiling face.

For a moment, he said nothing. He had a hand on the concrete column, feeling the rough texture. The mild panic that rose in his heart subsided quickly. His copy had jacked out in his place. He could not help but laugh. C allowed him the false hope, standing with her arms folded in front of her.

"So," said X, abandoning his post by the transfer column, "you think you're pretty clever, huh?"

C smiled wider and made her eyebrows jump in response.

"You don't know me that well, C. We were together for what, six months before I left? You think that's enough time to learn what someone is truly capable of? You've got nothing on me. When my copy wakes up, he'll just jack back in. He'll come back for me."

"No, he won't, *baby.*" Her voice was smooth, imitating the way X had tried to comfort her.

"Any second now," reiterated X, nodding his head slightly.

"He won't be coming back."

"Alright." X chuckled. "Go ahead, tell me why."

C approached the transfer column and placed her hand at one edge. With a sweep of her palm, she scraped a section of the concrete away, revealing a mass of green light inside. X's smile disappeared as he took in the new information. There was something inside the column, something moving. There were scales, sections of bodies. Snakes.

"One, actually. And it isn't a snake." She turned to him again. "It's a virus. Very old, very crude, but exclusively dedicated towards one lifelong desire."

"Which is?"

"To destroy you. To rip you limb from digital limb."

"You'd *kill* us?"

C spread her hands. "You took away *my* life. What is that if not killing?"

"Yes, from *you*, not the real you. When my copy jacks back in, he'll be—"

"He knows about the virus. He and I had a little talk while you were out playing with your Barbie. He's been spliced, to before you copied me. I tried to impress upon him the true extent of my pain, pain that you inflicted. I think I made it very clear how I feel about what you did."

"You don't have the skills to do this."

"I told you, time is different when you're digital. And I found something else, something that is inside all of us. A limiter. When time is absent, that limit goes unchecked. You can learn at an exponential rate. In fact…" She moved closer to him and raised her finger to a spot on X's head. "It's right there."

A searing pain shot through X, blinding him momentarily. It was impossible. There was no pain in the Net.

"What the fuck?" X stuttered uncontrollably.

"Your limiter. I just locked it in. Permanently. Your copy's too, though that was a little trickier." Her focus shifted and she puzzled some internal problem.

"You can't do that!"

His accusation brought her back. "Why not? You're not real anymore, X. Your mind is just like mine, a collection of bits, easily readable. I understand that now. But, without the ability to expand, you can never be like me." Her smile spread, pleased at her own words.

"I *will* get out of here. You can count on it. There will be something on the Net that will help. If not today—"

"Of course," conceded C, "there will be advancements. And who knows, someday the answer may appear out there."

"Then you admit it, your plan is shit."

"Ah." She dragged out the sound of a feigned epiphany. "Then again, any answers out there will be pretty useless if you can't leave this room."

X noticed a film appearing over the walls of the homedir, tinted green, almost recognizable as a billion small scales.

"Oh, didn't I explain the rules?" C saw the shocked look on X's face. "Well, here they are. You can't leave this room, and you can't communicate with anybody outside of it. The walls are laced with another virus. Consider it a life sentence instead of death. Killing you would be much too easy, but having you spend eternity in here, until the end of civilization, that almost sounds like justice to me."

The images of X's pupils swayed in the haze of the fire that burned behind them.

"It is the least I can do for a man that loves me so much."

Through clenched teeth, X spoke. "I'm going to tear you to pieces."

"By all means," said C, smirking. "You have to do what you feel is right."

"And I'm really going to enjoy it."

"Oh." C ignored his comment and reached for her back pocket. "I have a present for you." She tossed a small vidscreen at him.

"What's this for?"

"For you, to keep up with the real me. You can query for any information about her. As little or as much as you would like. Hopefully you will see how much better off we are without you."

"You know," said X, tossing the viewee aside, "you turned into a real bitch."

"You made me what I am. You corrupted something beautiful and innocent and made it evil."

"I just want you to know, I will spend the rest of my life pursuing you, until you are wiped out, overwritten."

"Spare me your threats. There was a time when I looked at you with awe and wonder, sometimes afraid of the things you could do. But I see now that those were all parlor tricks, cheap illusions. Besides, I did what I came here to do. I have my revenge and you, your punishment." C motioned to her avatar. "I see no other reason for this abomination to exist."

X lunged at her, but C sidestepped him easily. He crashed into a small wooden chair, breaking it and sending pieces flying across the floor. The pain of the impact flowed through his body. From the floor, he looked up at C.

She parted her smiling lips slightly. "I understand why you did what you did, but that doesn't make it right. Maybe I didn't pay enough attention to you, maybe I could have stayed up later to talk with you, but that was no reason to kill me. I loved you. I was sixteen but I fucking *loved* you. You can't code stuff like that. There are no subroutines for it. It's purely organic, living and dying at times that *it* chooses, not you, not me. My heart fell for someone else, for no real reason other than it did. I've seen myself with him, from the outside. She's happy. She loves him."

Those words, above all things, cut at X's heart. He shut his eyes, lost strength in his neck, and dropped his head. C approached and kneeled next to him.

"Love is a powerful thing. It can survive on so little, one memory of a smile or of one precious kiss like that night on the bridge. For the rest of your time here, it will feed off you, if you let it. Take my advice, accept your loss. Accept that everyone you ever loved is gone forever. You won't get out of here, but it may make your time here easier. That is the only courtesy I can give you."

Blood flowed from X's mouth. His lips smacked as they parted. "Kill… you…"

"Yes," said C, standing up. She took a few paces backwards. "You're right, I should be killed." A brief look around. "I'm done here anyway." One by one, the pixels of her avatar began to tremble and separate.

X struggled to speak. "Where are you… going?"

A glow appeared around C. "You'll have an eternity to think about this, though you may never truly know the answer. It is a question that I've been wondering about for some time now." Her eyes met his. "I can't find a definition for what we are, whether we have souls, whether God sees us the same way he used to. My question, my worry, is whether heaven and hell even exist for things like us." Her last words barely escaped her lips before her image fell apart.

The pixels fell to the floor, through it, and out into the endless ether.

X stared, unable to protest, unable to comprehend, unable to do anything except watch his future slip away.

NINETEEN

One moment, the snow was falling from the sky with such precision and uniformity that X couldn't decide whether it was truly falling or if the world and the trees were simply rising up through it. The next, he was face to face with an avatar that somewhat resembled C, but the way her eyes narrowed at him, the way she carried herself, gave him the impression that someone else was running her frame. It went against everything he knew about the Net; you couldn't just use someone's rig and jack in as them. You could, if you had the time and skill, reproduce an avatar. Outside appearances could, and did, change on a whim, but if you looked just below the surface, there was always the underlying signature. Despite his gut reaction, he read her clearly as C.

She seemed on the verge of an accusatory outburst, with her plunging eyebrows and lips that kept parting and snapping back together. He could see it in her eyes; she wanted to yell at him, release the rage that she seemed to be holding back. Though she had never done that before, he felt he understood her look. But the screaming never came. She didn't give in to the rant building inside of her. Instead, her face took on a sudden softness, as if the smoke had collapsed and smothered the very fire that birthed it. Her shoulders slumped and rocked forward before she caught herself.

This look, X had seen before. It was the same kind of resignation that she bore the day he left. In that memory, which he recalled with pristine detail, she had run into his arms moments afterward, seeking his embrace as remedy for her broken heart. And what about now, he wondered. Why this sudden sadness? Why the quick change from the bridge to this non-construct? Recent events seemed muddled in X's mind. He recalled creating the bridge, remembered dropping the snow from the sky. But here, how did he get here?

On instinct, he spread his arms in a penitent but welcoming gesture.

Something pulled C's body into his embrace. Whether it was his will or hers, he could not tell. All he knew was that she was crying, actually displaying tears in a virtual world that refused to recognize such actions. His mind raced, lost in questions that he had no answers for. How do you comfort with arms that are not real? How do you soothe tears that should not be? How do you be there for someone when you are actually miles and miles apart? Had he more time, had he not the pressing issue of a despondent C, he might have been able to make something up. But without the virtue of preparation or a distraction-free environment, he found the only thing he could do was wait.

"How can you do this to me," asked C, her cries muffled in X's chest. She looked up and placed a finger on his lips when he tried to speak. For several seconds, she paused, regaining her composure. "Don't answer. *You* don't know. You don't know what you did to me." She escaped his embrace and took several steps backwards. "Do you notice anything different about me?"

Confused, X simply shook his head.

"How about now?" C's avatar shifted, pixilated in a flurry of tiny blocks, and settled into a new pattern where her hair was shaded a dirty blonde, and her eyes no longer had to look upwards to see X.

It was a quick and efficient avatar rewrite. And it was way beyond her skill level.

"How did you do that?"

"*That* was nothing!" Her voice bordered on hysterical. She waved her hand in a circular motion and from all corners of the construct, individual pieces of a hundred different worlds sprung up from the ether. The sky became a mishmash of disconnected blues and pale oranges, all broken up by irregular ridges that reminded X of suture joints on a skull. Buildings rose and fell in a morphing tidal wave of rampaging code. No structure stood for long before C replaced it with another. X saw landmarks from places that didn't even exist in the Net. She wasn't pulling from a catalogue; she was actually coding everything on the fly.

"Stop!" His plea reached her, brought the world to a standstill. "What happened to you, C? Last night you could barely use your sliver. And now *this?*"

C shook her head and raised her wrist for inspection. "I can tell time," she said. "I can even slow it down. But that doesn't matter, nothing matters anymore. There are only a few things you need to concern yourself with." Her tone turned oddly businesslike.

"But—"

"No," said C, raising a finger again.

X felt his throat tighten and knew without trying that he wouldn't be able to force air across his vocal cords.

C hesitated again and then let out a long sigh. "I thought I wanted to do this," she said, looking away from him. "But I'm just so angry with you. I've never hated someone so much in my life."

His eyes asked why, so she showed him.

X saw it all in startling detail, like individual pulses on a beam of light, streaming into his mind at a speed beyond true comprehension. He wasn't aware of learning anything linearly, just that at some point, he suddenly knew something that hadn't been there before. In less than a second, it was all there. The copying. C's forty-eight eternal hours of pain and suffering. Everything he had done to her and everything that he was going to do. Her plan for him was there as well, not revealed in any more detail than she would allow, but enough to let him know what she wanted of him. Go back to his homedir, jack out, and never come back. He was being banished, under penalty of destruction.

The virus, with its snake-like scales that he had never seen but could imagine as clear as day, taunted him from an uncertain future. His time with C had ended and a part of him was going to pay a price. The rest, C, in what he was certain she was forcing him to classify as some kind of mercy, was leaving up to him. He could go on with his life, with no blood on his hands. But to keep something in the Net, something else must be kept out. He felt hollow relief.

"Go," she told him. "If I know anything about the other you, he'll be jacking in at any moment. Wait until he comes through the column, then jack out."

X nodded, suddenly overcome by a sullen obedience. He moved to jump.

"And X?" She flashed to the spot right in front of him and touched his arm briefly. "Don't come looking for me. *Either* of me."

He felt her push him through the jump, something that, like most of what she had displayed, should have been impossible.

Just a few moments after Natalie hit the switch and sent X back into the Net, she saw the light underneath the rig go out. Unlike last time, he didn't scream or cry out. His body didn't go into rigid shock. Instead, he was quiet and motionless, his chest barely rising and falling with his breathing. She wondered what he was doing under there, whether this was some aftereffect of the earlier outburst or if there was some lingering sense of loss after breaking up with C. Although he claimed that it had been a week since, she couldn't shake the idea that he had gone in to see her. Patiently, as she always did, she waited.

X lifted his arms and removed the rig with slow, deliberate movements. He placed it next to him on the bed before looking at Natalie. They locked eyes and stayed that way for minutes, letting time pass while they exchanged nonverbal information. When it didn't appear that he would ever speak, Natalie prompted him.

"What happened?" She tried to smile, got halfway, and stalled out.

"Hi there," said X, ignoring her question.

"Did everything go okay?"

"Everything went fine, why do you ask?"

Natalie shrugged. "What with the screaming and the moaning and…" She stopped when he gave her an inquisitive smile, as if she were making the whole thing up.

X brushed past her train of thought. "I'm kinda hungry. Would you like to go out to dinner with me?"

Natalie's face lit up in surprise and amusement. She could tell from the way he smiled that her competition in the Net was no more. C, finally, was gone for good. Now he would be able to concentrate on her and she on him. He's mine, thought Natalie. She glanced at her watch in an exaggerated movement.

"Lunch," she said, "but yeah."

His lack of recognition went unnoticed.

TWENTY

The music from Version Six drifted out in the muggy May air, spawning a makeshift dance floor for the unlucky clubbers who waited in line for their chance to join in the fun. Some stood off to the side, smoking cigarettes with practiced detachment, their eyes jumping from face to face in the crowd. Somewhere in the distance, a church was tolling its last bell of the night, warning those who could hear it that the children had come out to play.

X stood near the curb in tan slacks and a blue polo shirt instead of his usual jeans and tee. Standing with her arm inside his was Natalie, dressed in black pants and a shirt that ended above her belly button. The fake diamonds that hung from her ears reflected the neon signs of the clubs around them. X looked down the empty street, trying to guess which direction the cab would be coming from.

"I'm so glad I talked you into this." Natalie squeezed his arm.

"Me too," said X, recalling the close-quarters dancing.

"I never thought I'd get you down here."

X smiled and winked at her. "I didn't do it just for you."

"Don't tell me you came just because G agreed to tag along?"

"What can I say," said X, shrugging, "the man is entertaining."

"You're not turning into one of his disciples are you?"

"What's that supposed to mean?"

Natalie pushed at X's arm, making him face her. "You know, those kids that are always following him around, asking him for code when they should be in class."

"You can't change kids these days," said X, looking down the street, wondering how hard it was to drive a cab in a timely manner. "And no, I follow no one. Not even the I'm-too-cool-for-school G."

"He stopped going to class, but he says he's getting straight A's."

X nodded. "You heard what he said in there. He's beaten the system. It's the American dream. We should all be so lucky."

Natalie laughed at X's accent. "What movie is that from?"

"From our movie," replied X, distracted by the blue tint of custom headlights turning onto the street. As they neared, the gleaming reflections of the neon lights created a long dark outline. He watched the limo approach with a growing sense of dread.

"Oh," said Natalie, noticing the car, "maybe it's someone famous."

The limo stopped with the back window in front of X, and he saw his reflection in the black glass. The window shuddered briefly and then sunk into the door. A strangely familiar face emerged from the shadow of the interior, its eyes squarely focused on X.

"X?"

"Yeah?" He tried to stop his response, but it was too late.

"Who is that," asked Natalie, moving slightly backwards. She put X's body between her and the car subconsciously.

"Someone wants to speak to you," said the gruff voice. "Get in."

"No!" Natalie's voice was loud in X's ear.

"I insist," said the man in the car. A gun appeared through the window.

"Just me. The girl stays." X tried to speak confidently, but he wasn't sure if the man was buying it.

"We only need you. Send your girlfriend home."

"No," protested Natalie, "don't go with him."

"Listen," said X, noticing the Roy's Taxi pulling up behind the limo. "There's the cab. You take it. I'll be home later. I promise."

"Who is he?" Her eyes pleaded with him.

"Don't worry, nothing is going to happen to me. I'll explain it all when I get home." And after I figure it out myself, thought X.

Natalie looked at him for a moment, started to protest, but instead turned and walked to the cab. Inside, she lowered the window and called out to him. "I'll be waiting."

X waved to her as the cab reversed, switched gears, and made a u-turn to head off towards campus. Meanwhile, the door in front of him swung open. He stepped cautiously into the shadows.

As the door closed, the cabin light came on, revealing a strikingly attractive woman sitting on a bench seat across from him, one slender leg crossed over the other, hands folded in her lap. He couldn't read her somehow familiar face.

"Hello, X."

"Where'd you hear that name?"

"Now is not the time to play games. I must say, I am very disappointed with you."

"Yeah? And why's that?"

"We had a deal. We agreed to terms."

"Lady, I have no idea what you're talking about." Deep in the back of his mind, a memory fluttered. He tried to latch on to it, tried to see in it the fuzzy outline of this woman's face, but it was gone.

"We do not simply release code without taking some precautions. The copy code we provided you with has a phone-home function. It let us know when you ran the code. It also let us know when someone else did." She shook her head. "I believed in you, X. Against my better judgment. And now, look where we are."

"Where's that?"

"A place where I do not have what is rightfully owed to me. A bad place for me, but so much more dangerous for you."

Faint memories shook in the databanks of X's mind, freeing the dust that had settled on them. He tried to assimilate the images of buildings that towered over Old Downtown, of code that could copy a mind.

"Your name is Anela," said X, almost accusatory.

"And your name would be shit already if I did not need your code so badly." She paused, took a deep breath, and smoothed a section of fabric on her skirt. "I apologize for my profanity. Please, we can do this in a civil manner. Give me my code back and I will consider lesser penalties."

"I don't have any code on me."

"Of course not. You claimed it was in the Net. We have the adaptors now. When we get to the den, you can use our rigs to jack in."

"In the *Net*?" His last conversation with C replayed in his mind. He had seen her power, seen the virus, and knew that her warning was serious.

"Yes," said Anela. "I want you to retrieve the code."

"I can't."

Anela's eyebrows rose slightly. "You will."

"You don't understand, I can't jack in."

"Why is that?"

"It's complicated."

"Try me. Or, if you would like, I could just kill you here." Anela lifted one hand, revealing the gray tint of a gun. She pointed it at X and then glanced at her bodyguard. Soon, X had two weapons leveled at him.

"There's a virus," he stammered, "in my homedir. If I go in, it'll kill me!"

Anela laughed a cold chuckle that grated on X's inner ear. "What were you planning to do, X? Sell the code? I do not understand your reluctance."

"I can't go back in!" His voice trembled.

"Well," said Anela, uncrossing her legs and leaning forward, "then you are, as the French say, totally fucked."

X was at a loss for words.

"Have it your way." Anela raised her gun higher.

A silenced explosion erupted from the end of the barrel and the world suddenly faded from X's vision.

X was no stranger to the endless ether of the Net and the possibilities that it contained in all of its empty code. The potential was there, palpable, ready to be molded into whatever fantasy he desired. The supply never ran out; space was never completely used up. So long as one computer in one datacenter kept running, the coordinates of any construct could extend into the infinity of integers, expanding the distance between it and the core, finding isolation in an already isolated world. Jacked in, with an electrical storm moving at hurricane speeds over the folds of his brain, X spent his time entertained by his own creations, amused at how easily virtuality submitted to his will.

And yet these unabashed periods of creation still paled in comparison to the time he spent in the *other* virtual world, the one that existed only in his mind, a place he entered only when pushed over the border by sleep or a synthetic drug. In his dreams, in his imagination, the word *limitless* took on new meaning. Though he could see a million worlds with his mind's eye, somewhere in his heart, he knew that he wasn't alone. Repressed memories, subconscious desires, and a litany of unacknowledged prejudices were his true companions. The way they affected his dreams made X angry, made him want to try harder to overcome the internals and control the world as he knew he could. Often, there was nothing to do but wake up. Wake up and save the fight for another day.

As the drug wore off, X gradually became aware of his body. He moved his arms and legs tentatively, testing the limits of what he slowly recognized as leather straps. There was pressure at all points on his back, telling him he was reclining in a chair that bent and conformed to his body. It reminded him of a dentist's chair, but when he turned his head to look at the buxom dental assistant with her long blonde hair and breasts peeking out over her tight pink uniform, he saw something that made him gasp in horror.

Beside him, in a similar dental chair, sat a real, live cipher. Its skin was nearly translucent, and a quick squint showed blood flowing beneath the surface in blue and red pathways. The flesh disappeared into a tight, black jumpsuit that covered the rest of its thin, toothpick-like body. On its head was a sleek Anataware rig, shiny black modified with aftermarket parts, with all of the accompanying branding and logos wiped clean from the gleaming enamel. LEDs lit in what appeared to be random patterns along the sides, but X knew that they must have meant something, communicated some kind of status information to whoever its caretaker was.

"Very few people have actually seen a cipher," said Anela, from somewhere in front of him. "In fact, outside of people like me, the only time someone sees a cipher is right before they become one."

"You think I'm going to work for you," asked X. His lips felt numb and cold.

Anela let a dainty laugh escape her lips. "*You*? Work for me? I think not. I just want the code."

"Please," said X, remembering the conversation in the limo, "we can work something out."

"Yes." Anela nodded. "You go in and get the code. Then you bring it out to me. How is that?"

"If I jack in, I'll die!" He wondered briefly what the virus could truly do.

Anela moved out of the shadows and approached X in the chair. She leaned close to his face and whispered, "Do you think it matters to me either way?"

The way she said it made a trickle of panic run down X's spine. "Look, I can recode it. I can have it for you in a week."

"No good," said Anela, straightening up. She crossed her hands behind her back. "I have buyers waiting and the deadline is tonight. It was hard enough just tracking you down. I am not going to wait another week. If the code is not delivered by midnight tonight, it becomes worthless."

X recognized the lie. "One week," he pleaded. "One week and I'll have the code for you. It'll work just like it did before, even better now that I've done it already. Just let me go and I swear I'll get it to you."

"We will see." Anela turned her head to a man standing by a bank of monitors behind her. "Jack him in."

Hands came out of nowhere and grabbed at his head while a metal rig was placed over his temple. He struggled, but the bony metal fingers cut into his shoulders and chin. The world went dark and though Anela's voice was muffled, he heard her words clearly.

"Hit it."

"No!" X screamed as reality began to fall away.

X's mind surged through the black tubing connected to the back of his neck, over copper, over fiber, through the countless switches and layers of fabric, until the packets finally dropped off the edge of the Net, into the darkness, into the void, the space where the universe was expanding into or contracting from. There was no time to comprehend it all, and whether it was the virus that killed him or the lack of a default route, X never knew. All he recalled was that he was not afraid of the virus. He never saw it, never felt its slimy scales brush up against him.

It made a funny kind of sense, X thought. Why would the Net allow him to jack into space occupied by a virus? It must have recognized it, disallowed any routes to those coordinates.

No route to host.

No outlet on a one-way street to the Net.

X's mind had just been uploaded out of existence, lost in the null space between the real and the virtual.

Anela watched with mild amusement as X's heart monitor fluttered, spiked the thresholds of the scrolling graph, and then settled into a flat blue line.

TWENTY-ONE

X was starting to get that weird feeling in the pit of his stomach, a mixture of too much vodka and a bass line so low that it rattled his internal organs. If he was wincing, no one noticed. It was dark on the dance floor at Version Six, with the only light coming from the seemingly random strobes hidden in the mesh of struts and cabling on the ceiling. X could barely make out the shadow of Natalie's body dancing in front of him. She had her back to him, her arms stretched above her head, her body gyrating left to right across the fabric of his pants. He tried his best to dance with her, but the tightly packed crowd allowed him his subtle movements, his lack of desire to do anything but place his hands on Natalie's hips and hold her close.

"Are you okay?"

The feed was lost for a second, but when it returned, he was staring into Natalie's concerned face, one he had seen several times over the last few months. The caustic strobes had given way to an ambient green that was muddled by the red and white lasers that cut through it overhead. X focused his eyes on Natalie. When a small smile appeared on her face, he realized that he must have been smiling too.

"Maybe we should sit down," she suggested, her voice out of sync with her lips. Suddenly, X felt pressure against his back. He tried to turn around quickly, but his elbow was stopped by the firm backing of a booth. He became aware of a table in front of him and when he looked up, Natalie was seated across from him, a half-empty beer in one hand, a cube in the other. Next to her sat G, looking like a hippy in his post-grunge attire. Something funny had just happened, as G was lost in his maniacal laughter with his beer raised and pointed in X's direction.

When he calmed down, X heard him say to Natalie, "Your boy is seriously messed up." Natalie was bowing her head and attempting to attach a trode to the back of her neck, but she managed to get her eyes on X. Seeing her as he did with her pupils so close to her eyebrows, X couldn't help but feel that he was seeing another side of her, an angry part of Natalie that time and their relationship had not yet revealed. It was the same feeling he had had with C, a startling revelation that shattered every illusion he had ever had about her. Seeing something like that in Natalie was unsettling, but feeling the echoes of the past, of the dreams that tormented him nightly, was much worse. Before his mind could run down the many horrible permutations of the moment, Natalie's head came up and he saw on it the smile of a woman who had been through so much with him, a woman he felt he knew better than he could have ever hoped to know C.

"He's not much of a drinker," she said, speaking out the side of her mouth.

"He never was," replied G, taking the last few sips from the amber bottle. He chuckled as he recalled the memory of a drunken X desperately trying to avoid a fight with the muscled host of an infamous Wickersham party. "I remember this one time we took X to a party off of— but he said it so loud that she heard him and that was the end of that!"

X shook his head again, tried to piece together the fragments of conversation he was hearing. Something seemed to be missing from G's story, some continuity that X couldn't put his finger on. Natalie was smiling at him with the look of a woman who had just been told a naughty little secret about her boyfriend. But there was also a look of contentment that X finally understood after his eyes trailed the wire coming from behind Natalie to the white cube on the table in front of them. Her thumb and middle finger were grasping it along the corners while her index hovered a millimeter over the milky surface. G was still talking, but X's eyes were locked with Natalie's. When her finger moved imperceptibly, the effects were immediately seen in her eyes, which widened and relaxed quickly. Her breath came out long and slow, a subtle hiss that X heard over dying echoes of a techno backbeat.

"In what was a most disturbing turn of events," said G, his voice oddly business-like, "reports surfaced today about an impending privatization of the Internet. Vinestead International, known for their oft-promised but rarely demoed Guardian Angel chip, has announced plans to commercialize the remaining sectors of the Internet and effectively convert the nation's information superhighway to a series of regulated toll roads. President Clinton spoke today from the Rose Garden and denounced the intrusion of big business into the world's most precious public commodity. The Republican-backed Congress is expected to vote on a referendum later this week to allow the sale of the Internet to Vinestead, a measure that the President has threatened to veto. Elsewhere in national news…"

G was interrupted by the chirping of his cell phone, followed immediately by the digitized sound of X's voice singing in a hokey country drawl, "Speaking of gay pornography." G's face went red as he reached for his phone and after examining it, he squared his eyes at X.

X and Natalie exploded in laughter at the same time, unable to hold it in any longer. Natalie put her forehead down on the table and laughed into her lap while X wiped at the corners of his eyes.

"You hacked my cell," asked G rhetorically. "Son of a bitch! You put that gay porn on my computer!" He turned quickly to Natalie, "I swear, I let him check his e-mail one time and he just happens to *find* some naked men on my hard drive."

"Naked boys," corrected X.

Natalie laughed and smiled understandingly at G.

"Dammit!" G looked at X, trying not to belie his anger with laughter. Inside, he was going through the thousands of possible retaliations, from putting X's face into some hardcore boy porn, to the simpler idea of reaching over and punching him in the arm. In the end, he merely reached out and double-tapped the cube sitting in front of Natalie. When she finally recovered from the shock, G said, "Was that good for you, baby?"

Natalie covered her face with her hand and fell back in a fit of laughter.

"Hey," said G, leaning across the table to X, "remember that time I made your girlfriend orgasm? Twice? Yeah, that was pretty cool."

"And you find that letting kids bypass the whole higher education system will be a good way to make a living," asked Natalie. She had fully recovered, and her face was relaxed and curious. For a moment, X thought he had seen two versions of her simultaneously. She was leaning back in the booth, but also sitting up with her head turned towards G. The vibrancy of reality seemed to flip back and forth between the two images, during which X heard laughter over words, a mash-up of two separate streams of time.

"I am nothing but a child of demand and supply," said G, pulling his own cube from his pocket. "In fact, I have something new that the two of you may be interested in."

Finally, X could smell it, the absence of reality. He sobered quickly, left only with the pain of the liquor in his stomach. As he looked around the club, he started noticing the signs. The flicker of the lights, the tweaked highs of the music, and the stuttered movements of the dancers that grew worse the farther away they got from the center of the simulation.

"Are we jacked in," asked X, interrupting G's sales pitch.

A flash of something sinister crossed Natalie's face, but before X could get a grip on it, she was gone. The scene changed rapidly, with G and the booth falling away and being replaced by the concrete sidewalk of Old Downtown. The music that had been so overbearing dimmed to a comfortable heartbeat. X stood with his hands in his pockets and felt Natalie beside him, swaying with the music.

"I'm so glad I talked you into this." Natalie squeezed his arm.

"What?"

"I never thought I'd get you down here."

X looked at his girlfriend in confusion, his eyes desperately trying to find something real in the world around him. Natalie smiled at him as if nothing were wrong and tiptoed slightly to kiss him.

The sky flashed a pale gray, catching X's attention. He had seen that before, but only when jacked in, only in the Net. As X returned his gaze to the street, a long black car pulled up to the curb. The tinted windows mirrored the club and the interested looks of the young adults in line.

"Oooh, maybe it's someone famous," said Natalie.

Overcome by a sense of dread, X took a step back and fell off the edge of the construct. He grasped at the nothing around him, until finally he felt pressure from behind. Leather straps held his arms and legs down and when he turned his head, he gasped. Beside him, in a chair similar to his, sat a real, live cipher. The man's skin was almost translucent, with arms and legs like toothpicks. His entire head was covered in a metal rig, with LEDs that lit in almost random patterns around the sides.

"Very few people have actually seen a cipher," said Anela from somewhere in front of him. "In fact, if I do not deliver the code by midnight, it becomes worthless."

X found her in the dim light, standing a few feet away from him, nodding as if he were saying something unconvincing.

"We will see." She turned to a man standing by a bank of monitors behind her. "Jack him in."

X screamed as reality began to fall away, stretching out in front of him until the world pixilated into nothing and there was only darkness. That, and the faint aroma of maple, of trees, of spring.

The bridge was as he remembered it, small enough to cross in three long strides, but large enough to circle a young girl in anticipation of a kiss. He was back in the Net, undeniably this time. His mind raced, thinking of his rig collecting dust for so many months. All the things he could have done, all the nightmares he could have avoided. All on a dubious threat from a girl he had known less than a year, a girl who had been wearing braces and mismatched socks the first day they met.

X tried to smirk, but didn't feel a response from his face. His whole body seemed rigid, stuck in place, standing awkwardly in the middle of the bridge. His eyes were fixed straight ahead, causing a momentary panic when he realized he couldn't even move the image in front of him. It was like staring at a frozen screen, waiting for the computer to write out some lingering data so it could get back to the task at hand.

"What a quaint little place this is," said a familiar, female voice from behind him. He felt the touch of something soft on the back of his head and found that he could move it. X turned slightly to the side and watched as Anela crossed between him and the rail, her eyes mischievous and dark, her red dress out of place in the burgeoning woods. "I think I see now why she fell for you. More a product of the environment than anything else." Anela stood in front of X, facing him head on. "X, X, X..." She giggled. "You have been a bad little boy."

X moved his lips in vain.

TWENTY-TWO

"When they say that you can't have everything you want, what they really mean is that no one is just going to up and give it to you. Besides, it stands to reason that if you want something, then someone else probably wants it too. And what do we call that? *Demand.* Something is in demand. And those that have already satisfied their demand now have supply. Supply and demand. Basic economics, my friend. A good class to take, just don't major in it." G crushed out a cigarette in the dull gray ashtray in front of him. He lit another as he waited for a response.

The kid sitting across from G sighed and made a gesture with his hand. "So, what does all that mean," he asked, looking depressed and impatient in his red snakeskin jacket.

"What that means, Kurtis, is that you *can* have everything you want. All it really takes is finding the guy, or girl, not that I'd recommend *that*, with the supply. And then you just go up to that person and demand it."

Kurtis considered for a moment, unmoved by G's flagrance. "I don't want to study anymore. I want an info dump."

"Want, want, want." G flicked his cigarette with an overtly effeminate turn of his wrist. "Everybody wants! You'll get nowhere in life wanting. Or in cases such as this, telling someone what you want."

"I demand an info dump!" The strain began to show on Kurtis' face.

"There you go, boy! Look at you, demanding something. You're on the right track. Okay, now that you demand, I check to see if I can supply." G tapped the code cube on the table and frosted the cake by making his eyelids flutter rapidly. "And it looks like you are in luck. Everything is in place for a successful transaction."

"Then let me have it," said Kurtis, extending his palm.

"Unfortunately..." G drew out the word, leaned back in the stiff booth, and blew a plume of smoke into the air. Above him, he noticed the bare legs of some young thing, dancing on the mesh grating that made up Version Six's second floor, unaware or uncaring that someone watched from below and that that person was one of a growing number of people who knew that she wasn't wearing any underwear. His eyes came down again and met Kurtis' expectant gaze.

"Yes," he continued, glancing up again quickly before leaning forward across the table. "Unfortunately, there is another matter we must attend to first. You see, supply and demand doesn't just mean my supply and your demand. Well, it does mean my supply, but your demand is not the only one I have to take into consideration. I do most of my business online and at any given time I am taking bids from anywhere from ten to twenty people on any given service or commodity. Now, info dumps aren't really where it's at these days." G cupped one hand near his mouth and whispered, "Most of my clients aren't college kids like yourself." He reclined and puffed again. "So fortunately for you— wait, did I say unfortunately earlier?"

Kurtis nodded, his head leaning to the side in a gesture that simultaneously said confused and disappointed.

"I misspoke, forgive me." G could tell his buyer was getting impatient and he wondered whether he had chosen the correct info packs for black market sales tactics. His own words sounded foreign to him, as if spoken by someone with no product knowledge but with a singular desire to sell said product. "To the point then. Info dumps are trading at a hundred a terabyte, and your typical college major, just the cores mind you, will fit anywhere between ten and fifteen tibs. All the others, the electives and basic reqs have been pared down and fit neatly into two tibs. Of course, this doesn't include any talent-based classes. You have to learn to play the guitar yourself."

"How much for Business Administration?"

"A BA in BA? Let me consult my price sheet." Again with the cube tapping, again with the eye fluttering. G began to wonder if the show did anything for his customers. In the end, he hoped it would be what set him apart from any other dealer. He laughed. "Wow, you'd be surprised how little knowledge actually goes into Business Administration. The whole package weighs in at nine terabytes. I'll add the two for your reqs, making it eleven tibs total. At a hundred apiece, that's one thousand one hundred. And with the finder's fee, rust proofing, and loading fee, your total will be fifteen hundred even."

Kurtis' mouth dropped open and G waited to see whether the kid was dumb enough to pay fifteen hundred for a bunch of technical jargon.

He wasn't.

"I'm just fucking with you," said G, just as Kurtis was about to stand. "It's eleven hundred, but I'll make it a grand even, but you have to send your friends to me in the future."

"Deal." Kurtis pulled his wallet from his front pocket, removed ten hundreds, and slid them across the table, concealing them with his hand. "When can we do it?"

"In about five minutes. I've got to download the pack. It won't take very long at all. In the meantime, maybe you could grab us a couple of beers?" G smiled amiably, daring Kurtis to refuse his request after he had taken a hundred off the top.

"Fine, whatever." Kurtis retracted his hand, drawing the money back to him. "But I'm holding on to this until I get back."

"See," asked G, taking an extended pull for effect. "You're getting smarter by the second."

Kurtis returned a wary look and then disappeared into the crowd. As soon as he was gone, G tapped into his cube once more and requested the necessary info packs from the hidden repositories on the Net. Automated processes sought out these storage bins of stolen data, using ever-changing encryption to identify them among the real bits and bytes. They were like ghosts, hidden from public view until the right set of eyes came by. And then, they were gold.

The dancing girl above was grinding against her female partner as the techno music took an unusually somber tone. The time had just passed two in the morning yet she showed no signs of tiring. It wasn't until a few minutes later that G recognized the stub electrode on the girl's neck. It wasn't biological vitality that was keeping her energized; it was code. And this, G did not understand.

It seemed wasteful and inefficient. The code was used to keep the body going so that a person could be free of their inhibitions and dance all night. So the dancing must have been pleasurable. It must have produced some end result that satisfied a need in the girl. But, it was very unlikely that that same result couldn't be replicated with more code. She could skip the clubs and get the same feeling while lying out on her own comfortable bed.

Then again, if she hadn't come out tonight, G wouldn't have gotten the free show, so there was something to be admired in her way of doing things. G stared upwards, lost in the gyrations of the girl's legs, jealous of the green and red lights that caressed them. To be a beam of neon on a night like this. He imagined himself as one of the green lines, moving in and out of people, leaving no bit of the girl above untouched. A single omnipresent existence.

A slap came down hard on the table and G shook himself from his daydream. Kurtis had returned with two brown bottles and pushed one across the table to G. He held up the folded bills and waved them questioningly. "So," he said, taking a swig, "are we gonna do this or not?"

"Certainly," said G, popping the electrode off his neck. He slid the cube and its wire across the table, carefully avoiding the trail of sweat left by the beer. At the end of his movement, he uncovered the cube and rotated his hand, palm up.

Kurtis deposited the bills and stared for a moment at the cube.

"Jack in." He counted the money. It was all there. "I'll activate it when you're ready."

"We're just gonna do it right here?"

"I don't see any reason why not." G's hands moved quickly to deposit the money in his chest pocket.

"Well, it's a little public, don't you think?"

G sighed, took a long look around the club. "Listen, kid. There's a couple in the booth behind you that have been fucking for the last twenty minutes. Behind them is a speed-jacker and his hired attendant. If you listen carefully, you can hear the whine of custom rigs, so someone in here is hosting a run and gun." He leaned forward and lowered his voice. "The girls dancing above us aren't wearing any underwear and I'm pretty sure that they are touching each other in ways not suitable for daytime television. You think with all that going on that anyone is going to notice you jacked into a code cube? Most likely, anyone that has looked our direction has already written us off as two homos out on a date. So suck it up and put that wire on your damn neck!"

Kurtis said no more and slowly attached the electrode. He stared at G apprehensively.

G chuckled, "Sorry. Look, don't mind me, I'm just seriously in the mood for that." He pointed upwards. "Let's get this done, alright?"

"Okay," said Kurtis, trying to force a smile.

With his index finger, G began rubbing the cube in small circles on the top face. As he did, the cube began to illuminate, pulsing a deep red that bled from the center of each face to the edges. "I'm loading the code," said G, not looking up. "When it goes bright red, it'll dump to you. It might feel a little weird, but nothing a big boy like you can't handle."

"Just do it already."

Again he laughed. "It's funny isn't it? Your parents are paying almost three hundred grand to send you to college and yet you'll be getting your entire education in just under twenty minutes."

"*Twenty* minutes?"

"Don't worry, I won't go anywhere. That's my cube after all."

"Twenty..." His words slurred as the cube filled completely.

"Have a nice nap." G raised his bottle to Kurtis, tipped it slightly, then took a long drink. He watched Kurtis' eyes dip, then close completely. His body remained rigid, his muscles stuck executing the last command before his brain switched modes. Leaning back in his seat, G stared upwards, lost in the moving pictures and suffocating music.

Somewhere along the way, the music shifted from an upbeat heart attack of hardcore techno to the mellow and near comatose strains of an unknown ambient artist. A low beat thumped in the room, resonating in G's chest almost to the point of sickness. A forlorn trumpet scraped along the bottom of the treble clef, piercing the cloud of muted conversation, of glasses tinkling behind the bar, and of the low, satisfied moans of the couple in the next booth.

"I have to smile," said G to no one.

Fatigue was taking its toll and every minute that went by was excruciating insomuch as it wasn't a soft bed and a gentle slice of code to sleep by. Already, he had picked out the cocktail that he would use to pass the rest of the night away. It was a mixture of pastels (of which he told no one) and sexual sensations (of which he sold to everyone). All of this over the soothing rumbling of some distant storm. Only the storm was borrowed content. The rest had been coded from scratch. The experience was made that much more special by the mere fact that it was his own creation.

"I have to laugh."

The code cube pulsed on the table, running through the gradient of red so slowly that G couldn't be sure it was changing at all. But its gradual phasing betrayed its inner workings. He knew that inside the cube, data was spewing out almost faster than Kurtis' brain could take it in. He thought of the electrons flowing along the wire, wondered if the power would hold until it was finished, and whether Kurtis was going to need a doctor or not. Once, on a quick load in the alley behind V-Six, some poor newbie's brain had fried, got totally cooked. It had something to do with the changes going on in the brain when the info came in, but Alessandra's explanation failed to expose a root cause or how it could be avoided.

"I have to."

It was the cube that had been keeping G up and about during his extended sales pitch to Kurtis. He relied on it to pump his brain with enough endorphins and adrenaline to tolerate the crowd and brain-melting music. Now that it was attached to Kurtis, it took all of G's energy just to remain conscious. His eyelids failed him for seconds at a time, causing temporal breaks in the music that irritated him to no end. His brain was skipping through time. Hopefully, there would be enough power left in the cube to get him home in one piece. Otherwise...

"You look like shit, G-man," said a phased voice. G couldn't locate it and struggled for several seconds before realizing that his eyes were closed.

Natalie had arrived and was sitting next to him on the vinyl bench. The front part of her hair was pulled back, tied somewhere behind her head, leaving her face primed for the decorating she had picked out for it. Blue-white streaks ran from her eyes to her ears, disappearing into her deep black hair. Red lacquered lips, deep blue eye-shadow, and eyelashes coated with some kind of luminescent paint that glowed in the black lights. She wore a white half-shirt, transparent enough to discern the petite breasts underneath. She had changed so much in the last few months. G hardly recognized the little blonde girl that X dated before he disappeared.

"Do you have your cube," he asked, slurring the words together, sounding more drunk than tired.

"Sure, but it'll cost you." Natalie smiled briefly, thinking of the cube's original owner.

"Pay you back."

"Any price I want?"

G put his head down on the table and stared at Natalie with only one eye. His lips barely moved. "Any price." He drifted out, hoping he had spoken his last words and not simply imagined it.

Natalie put her elbow on the table, leaned her head against her hand, and watched G sleep. She left him alone for several minutes, thinking that he could use some real rest. It wasn't until the man seated across from them began stirring that she pulled out her cube and connected it to G. The code flowed slowly into him, mixing up the necessary signals to jolt him back from his pseudo-death.

"My God," said Kurtis, snapping into being, startling Natalie. His quick breaths gave way to raucous laughter and jubilation. The code had taken and Kurtis instantly knew the knowledge was there now, locked in his brain. The time had been instantaneous for him and there was considerable surprise in his face when he saw G facedown on the table and a strange woman sitting beside him.

"Who the hell are you," he demanded.

"You can call me N." And seeing that her answer failed to satisfy, "I'm one of G's... associates."

"What did you do to him?"

"Nothing," answered G, his voice muffled by the table. "I'm just checking out a new program my partner picked up. It's pretty good, very well coded. And if it weren't for the complete loss of motor control, I'd probably buy it off her. But, as you can see, I can barely control my mouth, which means I'm probably going to have to steal the code, fix the problem, and sell it myself. All before they even know there's a problem with people like me."

"Like you?"

"Neural inhibitors," said Natalie. She pointed to a darkened spot on G's neck. "It's just under the skin, like a firewall between the brain and the code. It does its own thing."

"And one of those is supposed to be to keep me from losing control, which I'm disappointed to say, didn't happen in this case." The lie was getting more complicated by the second and though Natalie was playing along perfectly, G felt it best to get rid of Kurtis now that business had been transacted. Slowly, he lifted himself up, accepted the slight help from Natalie, and faced Kurtis.

"Anything else I can do for you, my friend," he asked, cordially.

"No, I think I'm good." Kurtis still looked happy.

"Another satisfied customer," said Natalie.

G nodded to her. "Then I look forward to working with you again, Kurtis. Come back and see us real soon."

"I just might."

Kurtis stood slowly, unsure of whether the floor would support him or not. Something seemed different, as if the repeating music wasn't looped, but rather that he was experiencing the same moment over and over again. He shook his head to clear the feeling.

"Oh yeah, that," said G. "Try not to think for the next few hours. Go home and go right to sleep, you'll thank me in the morning."

Kurtis waved with the back of his hand and stumbled away to find the exit. As the crowd closed in around him, G turned his attention to his guest.

Natalie smiled. "So what's the story with the kid?"

"Just another trust-fund business major out to save the world. Probably end up suing me after law school." G breathed deep and collected his cube from the table. With a quick motion, he replaced Natalie's electrode with his. He loaded his own vitality program and felt the surge run through his body.

"The rich get richer," said Natalie, "nothing ever changes." She sighed and leaned back in mock boredom. "Holy shit, those chicks aren't wearing any underwear."

G laughed and stole a glance upwards. He let his eyes linger as he waited for the question that always came in silent moments like these.

The trace had been running for thirteen weeks and still no sign of X had been found in the Net. G and Natalie worked together for weeks, G doing most of the coding and Natalie adding her intimate knowledge of X. Together, they created a program that would scan the Net for X's signature, search out every dark corner and abandoned file store. Natalie took it upon herself to learn all she could about the Net, about rig architecture, about the life that men like X and G lived. She caught on quickly, often surprising G with her rapidly developing talents. The change in attitude brought about her change in appearance. After an info dump from G (on the house), she stopped going to class and instead spent all her time trying to find X. Adopting a new persona seemed a necessary part of adopting a new life.

"I think if he were alive, he would try to contact me," said Natalie, wistfully. The bravado she had shown in front of Kurtis was now gone, replaced by the near-timid personality that she wore during most of her freshman year. She knew she was pretending to be someone that she wasn't, that every time she thought of X, he brought the real her back to the surface. Natalie had known him less than a year before he disappeared, but the attraction she felt was undeniable. It was this feeling that eventually led her to understand why X had kept after C for so long after leaving her. While he rarely talked about her, she would often catch him staring off into space, C's name on his lips. It was an obsession that Natalie could not understand, could not reconcile with all she knew of men and love.

"Don't worry," said G. "We locked that locator up tight. If he jacks in from anywhere on the planet, we'll know about it."

Natalie yawned, nodding in assent. For a moment, they both stared at the lightshow above them. When minutes had gone by, she said at last, "Want to go back to my place?"

G shrugged indifferently.

A light classical track played in Natalie's studio apartment. G reclined on the oversized couch with his feet up on one of the arms. As Natalie prepared drinks in the kitchen, he brought out his cube and set it on his chest. With soft touches, he slowly reduced the effect of the code, bringing him down from his adrenaline high to a more subdued mellow that made him smile just from the feeling alone. It wasn't the relaxed atmosphere that prompted the change, but rather that the cube was running low on power. Reducing the processing load, in turn, reduced power consumption.

"So how many sales did you make tonight," asked Natalie from the kitchen.

"Just the one," replied G. "I got a late start, didn't get out to V-Six until after midnight."

"You're slipping." There was mock encouragement in Natalie's voice. "You gotta get out there and sell, sell, sell!"

"Well," said G, closing his eyes, "maybe you didn't notice that today is move-in day at the dorms. All those kids, all that money. Who do you think was the first person to come by their rooms and offer them code? I'll give you a hint, it wasn't the tooth fairy."

"I forgot about that." Natalie neared the couch and placed a martini glass full of maroon liquid in front of G. "I'll have to go over tomorrow and check out all the little freshmen."

"Damn fishies."

"So they didn't want to buy?"

"Not today. Or yesterday." G consulted the silver plate in his wrist. "But they know who I am now. Wait until they have their first exam. The club will be packed with kids wanting info dumps. I'll probably have to take three or four cubes."

"What a waste." Natalie collapsed into a red armchair, almost spilling her drink. "All that effort for nothing."

"I wouldn't say that." The way she was sitting made her skirt bunch up around her waist, covering no part of her legs at all. And though she had her legs crossed, G couldn't keep his eyes from wandering over her thighs and the shadows hidden between them.

Their eyes met and G sat up quickly, reaching for his drink. He continued, "Did you know that they're issuing students brand new Katsumi rigs?"

"They are so spoiled," said Natalie, indifferent.

"But it works out for me..." G's voice trailed off as Natalie rose from her chair and walked across the hardwood floors to a small, curtained partition in the corner. She pulled back the blue sheets to reveal a large unmade bed, littered with pillows of varying sizes. "Going to sleep," he asked, his speech slurred.

"I'm going to lay down, yes." Her voice triggered a dimming of the lights, so that only the bed was partially illuminated.

G watched as Natalie removed her clothes, her body hidden in the shadows of the low light. A latent impulse gripped G and he was standing before he knew it, intent on joining Natalie. Suddenly, a strong vibration went off in his pants, creating a tingling sensation in his left thigh. He pulled out the buzzing cell phone and held it out in front of him. From her bed, Natalie could see G's face go white.

"What is it," she asked, debating whether to leave the safety of the shadows.

G walked slowly towards her and turned the cell phone so that she could see it. The light from the LCD screen lit up her face and he caught a glimpse of her breasts in the blue light. His attention was drawn to her temptingly curved lips, entranced by the way curiosity grew into shock.

Staring back at Natalie was a single letter in max caps.

"X," said G. "X just jacked in."

TWENTY-THREE

"Did you know," asked Anela, "that every time that we went into your head looking for the code, we would end up in this forest, on this bridge? That no matter what my ciphers threw at you, we could only get this far? Now, I understand how a woman in my position might procure herself a similar level of encryption but for a boy just out of high school, it just does not add up." Anela turned and walked away from X, her arms crossed behind her back. "So, imagine my position, if you will. A boy comes to me asking for a copy program. We deliver a very advanced product that said boy modifies to copy an entire human consciousness. Unbelievable, of course, until he delivers the mind of his high school sweetheart on a code cube, asking me to splice it up. Do you remember what happened next?"

X found that he could nod and did so. "You spliced her, and I brought her back in the Net."

Anela smiled. "Yes, we spliced her. Spliced her on the condition that you would deliver the modified code so that we could do the same kind of copying. So I ask you, X. What went wrong?"

"I didn't deliver the code."

"Yes! You did not hold up your side of the bargain—"

"You forced me back into the Net! I told you what would happen if you did that."

"Oh yes, it was quite a show. My ciphers could find no trace of you after only half a second. But you do not get where I am by letting opportunities slip away like that. Suffice it to say, we took appropriate precautions."

"But you couldn't copy me, you didn't have the code."

"No, we did not have *your* code. But we had ours. And the best my ciphers have come up with is that you did not so much modify the copy program but rather the methods used for restoring copied consciousness. Am I correct?"

"Maybe."

"You have nothing to gain by lying or withholding information. You may at this point think that you are safe and sound within the confines of the Net. I can already see that cocky 'I'm two seconds away from kicking your ass' look on your face. But what you fail to realize and what you have not given me the courtesy of explaining is that while this construct exists in a net, you cannot interact with it. Whoever you got to modify the copy code knew something more about interfacing with the Net's API." Anela stopped, licked her lips. "Oh? Is that confusion? So soon?"

"If I'm in the Net, you're in trouble."

"Not confusion," said Anela, smiling wide again. "I admire your confidence, X. It is a trait that you and I share. Mine, however, is based on a full working knowledge of the facts. Yours is based on a misconception."

Beneath the bridge, the dry stream came to life, its gurgling ringing like applause.

Anela stole a quick look downward. "You are not easily convinced, are you?"

X nodded and smirked.

"Well, I have had about enough of this wet fantasy of yours. What do you say we retire to a more business-oriented construct? Would you mind moving us to my office?" Anela waited, studying X's eyes. She could tell that although he was reluctant to follow her orders, he was still trying to figure out if he could. At that very moment, he was pushing on the walls of the construct and finding them completely solid. All of this was written on X's face, on the smirk that faded into guarded defeat.

"I'm listening," said X.

"Right, but first we get some chairs."

The world melted in a way that X had never seen before. Construct destruction was a generic routine in the Net, occurring the same way in every instance. Blocky fades, slow dissolves, and headache-inducing pixilations. All around him, the trees, the bridge, and even the sky itself began to lose form, revert to a liquid that fell and splashed at his feet. It was detail and texture that X knew the Net was incapable of.

Anela recognized the look of awe on X's face. "You like that? There have been quite a few enhancements since last you jacked in. This is the wave of the future if you will pardon the pun."

The undulations of the water faded into black ice from which rose an obsidian desk and a large red chair that X recalled from Anela's office in Terrareal. Windows appeared on both sides and stretched out behind him. Flashes of color streaked down them, painting the Austin skyline. The invisible shackles loosened, and X walked towards the closest window, looking down into the neon streets. Somewhere in the blur was Version Six. He wondered if Natalie was there, looking for him. Had she gone home and stayed there? X realized then that he didn't know how much time had passed since his abduction.

"This is much better," said Anela from behind him. She slid gracefully into her high-backed chair and folded her hands in her lap. A smaller chair rose from the black floor in front of the desk, and she motioned to it with her eyes. "How do you like it?"

"It doesn't smell as bad."

"Yes, well, I would not expect someone like you to appreciate the unique aroma of Old Downtown."

"So what kind of protected construct is this?"

Anela chuckled. "I hate to admit this to you, but what you see here is not so much an achievement of a goal but a failure to attain another. There is something that my ciphers are missing. Somehow, you or your supplier found a way to interface the product with the Net. *This*, is the best that we could do. It is a construct within a construct, with no real way to interact with the real Net. It is a stand-alone, classified by VNet as a viral construct and guarded by the normal countermeasures."

"VNet?"

"This is, of course, a great accomplishment. Whether you knew it or not, you were able to invoke a freestanding human consciousness in a computer simulation. Do you know what that means?"

X thought about it for a moment, tried to follow the path Anela was laying out in front of him. It was dark inside his mind, a mind still reeling from some unknown trauma.

"The death of artificial intelligence," said Anela, her voice calm and flat. "Decades of research made moot by one boy's selfish quest to ravage his girlfriend."

"She's not my girlfriend anymore."

"That is hardly the point, X. The point is that I can invoke your consciousness in this construct and keep you here indefinitely. I can put you to work, make you code everything and anything I want. Instead of managing life-support for five ciphers, I could have a thousand in here. With no oxygen, no food. I do not even have to maintain equipment. Do you see the possibility here?"

"I thought you said you didn't want me as a cipher?"

Anela nodded. "Quite right. I do not. You have some infinite loop logic in you that I cannot control, as much as I would like to. No, I need you for one purpose alone."

"Well, you fucked up again. How am I supposed to retrieve the code when you say that we're not directly interfaced with the Net?"

"I do not expect you to."

"Then what? Recode it? It would take me months."

"It did not take you months last time."

"Last time, I had good reason."

Anela stood and walked slowly around her desk. She kneeled as best as she could in her tight dress. When she was at X's eyelevel, she reached out quickly and grabbed his crotch, squeezing with code-backed intensity.

X screamed and tried desperately to reduce the pain by modifying his internal code. But all of the hooks and methods that used to be there were gone, obscured by the intense pressure and conflicting electrical signals. There was no pain in the Net or so he had told himself and C so many times. Finally, it hit him. He understood that this wasn't the Net. Anela was telling the truth.

"Listen up," said Anela over X's cries. "If the only way for you to get through life is by following your dick then I am going to make this that much easier for you. Recode the copy program, make it so I can invoke my ciphers in the Net or I swear to God I will rip this from your body and leave you with a kind of unimaginable pain that will linger for the rest of your existence and I guaran-fucking-tee that that will be infinitely longer than it takes your mind to lose touch with this simulated reality. Do you understand me?!"

"Yes!" X's spirit sank as he realized his throat was getting hoarse, another Terrareal feature that wasn't supposed to be included.

Anela released her grip and stood up. She faced away from X and moved casually to the window, allowing him to regain his composure. Threatening physical harm was something she usually left to her metalguards and was usually done out of her presence. X was a different case though. He wasn't like the typical snot-nosed kid coming by looking to cast their favorite celebrity in a sex sim. People like X could only be reached in one way, by showing them that they weren't in control.

The pain slowly subsided and X cupped himself in a protective effort to speed up the process. Inside his head, he was cursing the world. He remembered a time when he once questioned the exclusion of pain from the Net's programming. It would have fit in so well with the run and gun simulations, World War II reenactments. But then he realized why that door was never opened. More unsettling was the idea that Anela could create a construct where pain was possible.

"I am glad that we understand each other, X. Since this will be our third business arrangement, I am going to expect that the third time will be a charm and that we will not have a repeat of your deceptions."

"What do I get out of this?" X's breathing was still ragged.

"Would you like to negotiate for something?"

"Yes."

"Alright," replied Anela, returning to her desk. From a drawer on her left, she retrieved a slip of paper and a pen. She slid them across the table to X. "Go ahead and write your demands. I will examine them and present my counteroffer."

X stared at the paper, then refocused on Anela's eyes. "I want out. I want out of this construct, and I don't want to hear from you or your goons again."

Anela nodded.

"Are we agreed then?"

"Would you like to hear my counteroffer?"

"It doesn't really matter. I won't do it for less."

"You are a shrewd negotiator, X. But I really think you ought to hear my offer." Anela pulled the paper back to her side of the desk and scribbled on it. Turning it over, she slid it back to X.

There was something evil about the grin she was wearing, and X hesitated momentarily as he reached for the paper. He turned it over slowly. In his head, he could imagine Anela speaking the words.

"I will let Natalie live."

X stared at her, running through every possible response and finding nothing appropriate.

"Understand this, X. You are mine. For as long or as short as I deem necessary. You can sit there and try to tell me that Natalie is just another college girlfriend, but you have not been watching her for the last few months as I have."

"Months?"

"You were not aware?"

"What day is it?"

Anela stood again as the chair melted out from under her. X fell through his seat and splashed in the shallow mixture of construct fluid. The black lightened with each wave until it was textured adobe tan. When he looked up, he saw Anela standing next to a desk containing a code cube and a new model of rig that X had never seen before.

"Today is the day you save Natalie's life," said Anela.

TWENTY-FOUR

The all-white construct burned Jape's eyes as they struggled to readjust. He felt a chair next to him and sat down, trying to remind himself that neither his pupils nor the light that was entering them were real. Controlling involuntary reactions was something that got easier the longer you spent in the Net. Even with his thousands of previous insertions, it always took Jape a minute or two to adjust to the sensation. When he did, he found he was sitting across from G and a girl of mixed blonde and black hair. Whatever scramble code they were running, it was keeping their facial expressions well hidden. G had a history of bringing bad news to Jape's front door, but he could never resist taking a meeting with him. When the invitation arrived in the early morning, Jape had immediately jacked in.

"Sup G," asked Jape, nodding to his guests. "Who's the geerl?"

"This is N, a friend of mine. A friend of X's."

"Real?" Jape turned his eyes to Natalie and sent out a surface scan. It came back empty. The scramble wasn't just on the perimeter; it was protecting every inch of her avatar and rig.

Natalie felt the scan as a warm sensation on her chest. "If you want to know something, just ask."

Jape laughed. "Mos def a friend of the X. But you're not that geerl he was here with last."

"C," suggested Natalie.

"That's her. Crazy chick, thought always hiding something. Or maybe not too bright, yeah?"

"That sounds about right."

G faked a cough, trying to change the subject.

"Righ,'" said Jape, leaning back in his chair a little, "what you call me here for anyway?"

"I need you to look at something."

"She look just fine to me, bro."

"Not her, this." G extended his hand towards Jape, a small slip of paper materializing between his fingers. "Coordinates. I need you to tell me where they are."

"Sorry, bro, you got one too many numbers, yeah? Third one's neggin', that ain't right. What you say this go to?"

G drew a rectangle in the air and brought up the screen from his tracer program. "Locaters. Twenty-seven of them. Twenty-five have returned this quad."

"And the other two?"

"Stalled, cheap over-the-counter code that I got off a meltdown. I doubt it could find my cock if I broke it off in its ass."

Jape laughed but stopped when he saw the continuing lack of expression on Natalie's face. "But you haven't said what *this* go to, have you?"

"It goes to X," said Natalie. "We've been looking for a long time. Do you know how to find this place or not?"

"Fiery, I like that. Always good to have a woman who can light her own fire, keep ya warm on a cold night. I used to have a woman like that, name of Marja."

Natalie let down her scramble so that she could widen her eyes and deliver the non-verbal message that she wasn't interested in his long-lost loves.

Jape caught on. "Well, coordinates to find the X. Coordinates mark the X." He shook his head, dismissing ideas as quickly as they occurred to him. "Nobody operate the quad in this Net. That some next level shit. Only place to find quad is on VNet grid and that's no place to go wandrin' with geerl in tow."

"I can take care of myself," said Natalie.

"Bet you can, geerl. No doubt if you tail the G *and* the X that you know somethin' about the ones and zeros. But how much you know about the VNet? Have you ever even heard of it?"

"We've heard of it," said G. "Vinestead's taking over the Net."

"What you hear VNet and what I say VNet are not the same things. You see only what the man want you to see. Happy faces, happy users, two months away from cubes in the mail with trial offers."

"Now you know what we called you here for," said G.

"Oh!" Jape stood and walked a few feet away. "This they call me here for?" He turned, extended his hands, and formed a globe in front of him. "The Net."

"Please, slow down," said G, smiling.

"The crazy G man telling me to slow down." Jape walked towards the space behind G and waited for them to turn around. He drew a cube in the air, considerably smaller. "The VNet." Jape placed his lips near the cube and blew. A wisp of blue skin floated off in a straight line towards the globe. "The path," said Jape, returning to his chair, the line directly above his head.

"So that's why the locators couldn't find him? He's not really in the Net?"

"Quad's not the Net, so yes, no."

Natalie shook her head.

Jape continued, "You got a bad quad anyway, no way to go neg no matter where you are." His head jerked as if someone was whispering at his ear. "Wait here, I be back."

Natalie watched Jape pixilate and disappear, his illustration fading slightly from his absence. She turned to G. "Is he full of shit or what?"

G shook his head. "If anyone's going to know, it's him." He stood up to examine the globe and the cube. "I don't know what this is supposed to be though. It looks like two completely different networks connected by a single channel. Probably firewalled. Definitely guarded."

"Maybe it's like Internet Two?"

"No, Internet Two ran on top of the plain Internet. It used the same protocols and everything. That was just a way to segregate traffic so that universities got preferred bandwidth."

"Still could be though, that's why you've never heard of it."

G gave Natalie a sharp look. "*You've* never heard of it either."

There was silence in the construct as G and Natalie looked away from each other, each running their own set of problems through their minds. The lack of sleep was taking its toll on both of them, making them irritable and lessening their ability to think clearly. The fact that the locator had not returned a valid triplet had hit both of them hard. Natalie was in the process of assembling her rig when G finally noticed. When he told her, he saw the energy drain out of her. Dejected and tired, they watched the screen together as each locator came back with the same quad address.

"I'm sorry," said G. "I'm out of my mind."

"Yeah," said Natalie. "I didn't mean it like that."

"It's just like X though, isn't it? He couldn't just make it easy on us. That's something we haven't even considered. If he's jacked in, why doesn't he send a message? Why do we have to learn of his insertion indirectly?"

"You think he's avoiding us?"

"So down on your boy so quickly," said Jape, reappearing behind his chair. "You must not know the X like I know the X. You'll want to bet on him not able to contact you." Jape pointed to the channel connecting the globes. "This pass, singularity."

"A what?"

"He means it's only a bit wide," said G. "Only one stream can go through at a time. And only in one direction."

"Half-duplex," said Jape. "The X prolly don't realize where he is."

"Wait," said Natalie, "you're saying X is in VNet?"

"Maybe," replied Jape, sitting down. "I spoke to a friend, one of the few rushers to ever go through the singularity and return. He say maybe the quad correct."

"But you can't go neg, you said so."

"Righ. There is no neg space in the Net. But this VNet we're talkin' about. And VNet got rules no one ever hear of." Jape created a smaller globe in front of him and dove headfirst into an addressing primer.

The Net was addressed such that a triplet of zeros would indicate the core. From there, any point in the Net sphere could be represented by a triplet indicating distance, height, and degree.

With a wave of his hand, he created a small cube. "Addressin' in the VNet. Source triple zero at corner of VNet cube. X forward, Y to the side, Z up."

"And the fourth number?"

Jape remained quiet for a moment, tinkering with the cube. "Don't know. Can't know 'til I see it."

"Are you coming with us," asked Natalie.

Jape laughed. "No, geerl. You tail the G, I don't. Rushin' the pass not something you do on a whim. I like the X, but not that much."

Natalie turned to G, "Then why are we sitting around? Let's go already."

"It still doesn't make sense," replied G. "How can he go negative on the Z axis? By your example, he'd be outside of the cube."

"Mystery. But quad point to the X, not to the construct. Think of it this way. Maybe the X seven units high and construct only two?"

"Then part of him would extend outside of the construct, which is impossible."

"Impossible in the *Net*."

"You keep saying that like it means something," said Natalie, her patience wearing thin. "If you know something or don't know something, just say it."

"Rude geerl, very rude." Jape stood to leave, ignoring the fact that he didn't need to. "You come to the Jape askin' for help and that's what I give. Not my fault the X in the VNet. Think he went there to get away from you."

"Kiss my ass," said Natalie, casually extending her middle finger and narrowing her eyes.

G stood up quickly and stepped between them. "Ignore her, man. She's just fucked up from the sleep deprivation. You know chicks."

Jape nodded, "I known my share."

G turned to Natalie. "We're going to take a walk. I'll see you on the outside."

"Fine, whatever," replied Natalie, her last syllable off-key from the pixilation.

"Crazy geerl."

"You don't know the half of it, man."

The white construct around them shifted in a gradient of blue. Shadows dropped down from above and filled in the corners, giving the impression of walls and a floor. Along one wall, a wide leather couch appeared, high-backed and shiny. Behind G, an oversized recliner bumped against the back of his legs.

Jape snorted. "This more like it. Can't just bring a man into the Net without proper seating."

"We were short on time," said G, sitting down. "Every time I stop to put in the necessary effort, N kicks me in the ass and tells me to get going."

"Sound like you the one with the geerl problem. Why she chasin' after the X if she got you to boss 'round?"

"They have a history, I don't know."

"History drive everything, yeah? Not a thing doing that not been done before. Way of the fuckin' world, sell your own shit back to you, call it recycle. Day one I take the long walk off the short pier, come back wraith-style, and bring the VNet to the ground, so everyone reach it."

G's localization routine spit garbage into his HUD, making him laugh. "I didn't understand a word of that."

"Lots of things hard to understand. If the X in the VNet, things only going to get worse. Nothing but suits, lab coats, and ghosts in there."

"Ghosts?"

Jape nodded. "You think Vinestead big business, yeah? The VNet cater to everyone with something to hide."

"Yeah, but you're saying that the souls of dead people are in there?"

"What you smokin', G? Not ghosts, *ghosts*. Ciphers."

G's adrenaline surged but settled quickly.

"Yeah," continued Jape. "How much you love your boy now?"

"Not enough to fuck with ciphers." G put his hand to his forehead. "But N would and I can't let her go alone."

"Two of you would stand better chance, no doubt." The sliver on Jape's wrist beeped twice. He glanced at it quickly. "Time short, G."

"You gonna tell me where the singularity is?"

"Only one I know who know is Tiesto, but he won't part with that data easily. Kind of a secret, yeah?"

"Every man has a price. I've got more data than he could process in a lifetime."

"Tiesto no ordinary man." Jape extended his hand and dropped three numbers into G's palm. They embedded themselves and flashed dully. "I don't think he can be bought."

"Thanks for the info," said G, standing and examining his wrist. "But I've got half a cube of Swedish porn that says otherwise."

TWENTY-FIVE

The room was dark, lit only by a covered lamp somewhere off to his right. X felt pressure against his lips, knew them to be C's by the way they tugged at his mouth, by the taste of the root beer flavored lip-gloss she had worn a few times before. They were sitting on the bed, each with a leg on the floor, each with the other bent inward, content in the awkward embrace. Somewhere in the darkness, classical music was playing, matching their intensity note for note.

It was early in the relationship, only a few weeks beyond the moment that X officially expressed his interest in C. There had been several nights like this before, comprised mostly of kissing and the occasional correction of a stray hand. Despite her age in relation to his, X couldn't keep the natural thoughts out of his head. He desired her, desired more than the taste of her lips. His hand ran under the back of her shirt, felt the strap of her bra, and in one of his luckiest moments, managed to unhook it with a single motion.

"Wait," said C, disengaging. "Slow down."

"What's the matter," asked X, removing his hand.

"What are we doing?"

X winced from the memory of her asking the familiar question, on the hill in Japan. But in the way the shadows fell on her face, he could see that she was simply trying to stall; the words were irrelevant. Inside, he chuckled at himself, amused that he had been thinking the same thing a moment before, though from the other side of the coin. He switched modes as best he could, twisted the night to her viewpoint, and took a quick look at how everything must appear to her. A mile from home, in the bedroom of an older boy, lights down low, music playing, and a very real possibility that if she screamed, it would be a while before help arrived. Add in the touch-happy boyfriend and knowing how easily things could degenerate into sex, X immediately understood how overwhelming it was.

"We're doing whatever you want to do," said X, turning his body and placing both feet on the floor. "And nothing you don't want to."

"I just," started C, but words failed her.

"You don't have to explain anything. I get you." X stood, felt for the light switch on the wall, and flipped it. In the sobering brightness, the music didn't sound as romantic anymore, so he shut it off.

"Most guys don't react very well to this kind of thing."

X smiled, sat down on the couch, and put his feet up on the coffee table. "And how many guys have you had to tell this to?"

"Just two. Last time I was down to my underwear before I came to my senses."

Laughter, genuine, flowed from X. "Well, now I have something to aspire to. Can't believe I was shut down so quickly."

"You're special," said C, altering the tone of her voice a little. "I don't want this to burn out too quickly, you know?"

The words bit a little too hard. "I know. It's okay though. Your dad is going to call you home in fifteen minutes anyway. Better not start something we can't finish."

C glanced at her watch; it was ten past ten.

"Come over here, I want to talk to you about something," said X, motioning to the love seat across from him.

"It's not that I don't want to," said C, with her hands behind her back trying to hook her bra. "I just think we should take it slow."

"I'm not even on that anymore, come over here." X waited for C to sit down and to stop tempting him by adjusting her breasts. "I don't want you to freak out or anything, but I'm going to say something to you that's going to evoke a reaction and from what I've heard, it can be a little jarring."

"Heard from who?"

"From you." X forced a smile. "Don't worry, it will all make sense in a minute."

"I've heard *that* from you before." C looked at him sideways. "Are you going to hypnotize me or something so that I'll sleep with you?"

"No," said X, glancing at the sliver in his wrist, "we aren't going to have sex for another fifty-eight days."

C crossed her arms and leaned back. "Is that a fact?"

Laughing, X continued, "It's going to be your idea."

C shook her head, half-confused, half-disbelieving.

"Alright, are you ready? It's um, in poem form."

"You wrote me a poem?" Her eyes lit up.

"I prefer to think of it as a mnemonic cipher, but call it what you will."

"I can't wait to hear it."

X cleared his throat, focused his eyes on C's. "We will walk through the forest no longer, and no more will we dream of days past. We have pained enough in our lifetimes, let this dying love be our last."

Slowly, the look of interest faded from C's face, replaced by the impassive expression of a kitchen appliance. Her arms unfolded, fell lifeless in her lap. X watched her chest rise and fall, slower and slower, until it stopped completely. Around him, the room shaded down a few levels, a frozen background out of focus. Bringing a memory to a dead stop was at the same time a sad and beautiful thing to behold. It was the marker that differentiated the memory from the reality, that reinforced for the hundredth time that the original experience was long dead and even the memory of it could crumble under the weight of a few words.

"C?"

"C is listening."

X shifted in his seat, unsettled by the monotone coming from C's mouth. "Do you know why I'm here?"

"C does not know."

"I left something with you. I came back some time ago and gave you something to hold on to."

"C does not remember."

"You wouldn't, but you should be able to look around and find it. It is one million forty-eight, eight nine six bytes long, buffered on each side with a string of seventeen ones and seventeen zeros. The hash is this." X reached out and traced his finger over C's palm, leaving an alphanumeric string that she could use to verify the integrity of the data once she found it.

"C is looking."

X sat back and waited, staring at C's lifeless eyes, taking the opportunity to trace over the shape of her body again, savor her presence without the threat of violence that had come to dominate their last meetings. It had been a while since he replayed the memory of this night, had been a while since he felt any need to. Natalie had stepped in at the right moment and given him something to focus on other than C. With her, he felt no need to revisit anything and actually believed that if he did, he would get no enjoyment from it.

"C has found a sequence that matches the submitted hash."

"The data is intact?"

"The data is viable and active."

"Give it to me." X held out his hand.

"C will comply." Slowly, one of C's hands rose in a fluid motion to her chest, reminding X of a choreographed sign language interpretation of some song. A red glow appeared beneath her white shirt, tending to pink at the edges. She covered her heart as if to pledge allegiance, then removed it, pulling the red glow with it.

X narrowed his eyes when he saw that it was in the shape of a heart, beating and pulsing. He couldn't recall making such a dramatic choice when he hid the data. C placed the heart in his hand, where it dissolved immediately. He felt the rush go through his body, felt the code taking its rightful place among the rest of his projects in his mind. Everything he needed to recode the copy program was returned to him in a flash of discontinuity. Giving Anela what she wanted had just become trivial. A task estimated for several days, achieved in twenty minutes.

"Why was the data in the shape of a heart?"

"C does not know."

"Well who chose the form?"

"C chose the form."

X shook his head. Talking with C's BIOS was making his brain hurt. He realized that no matter how much logic he threw at her, she was only going to be able to answer basic questions. She was not designed to be a conversationalist, could never verbalize the emotions involved in a decision. It was another mystery that X was going to have to leave alone, another puzzle within the ever-growing number of recursive puzzles in his life.

"Reboot," said X.

Light pulsed from behind the walls of the room, pushing new vibrancy into the world. Processes sprung up in X's virtual rig, taking over control of the scene from his conscious memory and passing it to the construct simulators. The classical music spun up on its own, a lively piece of staccato mid-range with the backbeat of a techno style that didn't even exist in this time. C stirred, regained control of her body, and sat up.

"How do you feel," asked X. He stood and joined her on the loveseat, put one arm around her shoulder to comfort her.

"I'm okay. That was really weird. I remember you moving your mouth, but I couldn't hear what you were saying."

"Can you stand up?"

"Yeah, I think so." C stood, wobbled briefly, and then turned to X. "What did you do?"

X ignored the question and handed C her cell phone. "Tell your dad that I'll walk you home."

"Do what?" The ringing of the phone startled C so much that she nearly dropped it. She answered it and stared at X with awe as she listened to her father tell her it was time to come home.

X smiled and retrieved her coat from the arm of the loveseat. He held it open so that she could put it on.

"How did you know?"

"Magic," replied X, putting on his own jacket. "Shall we?"

C left the room in front of him, still puzzling over her period of lost time. Outside, a light drizzle was falling, pushed about in odd directions by the random breeze. They walked together on the sidewalk, C not speaking until X took her hand.

"Tell me what happened. I feel all weird now. Like, empty."

"Maybe you're just hungry."

"I've been hungry before. This is *different*."

X sighed, his hope of walking C home one last time in peace smashed by her curiosity. "Are you sure you really want to know?"

"Please."

"Even if it has consequences that you and I can't even imagine?"

"You don't have to protect me from everything."

"Alright," said X, squeezing her hand, "here it goes. The first thing I remember about tonight is kissing you on the bed, which was less than half an hour ago. I don't really recall you coming over, whether I answered the door or if you just strolled down the steps. I'm not certain what we did in school today, if we met afterwards or if you had practice. My only memory of this day goes from the moment we kissed to the moment you walked out of my front door when your dad came to pick you up. You…" X hesitated. "You are the unwitting costar of one of my memories."

There was silence as they passed through a break in the townhomes and into the open field adjacent to the forest.

"Is this one of your rig things?"

"Yes, it requires a rig to do it."

"If you're telling the truth, then you're revisiting this memory. Why do that?"

A part of him wanted to tell her that he just wanted to see her again, if only briefly. But as much as he tried to say it, X couldn't make himself believe it. "I've been here before. The last time, I hid something, a program."

"And you came back to get it?"

"That's the gist. I also don't mind seeing you." The words simply spilled out.

C nodded, but nothing in her expression told X whether she actually believed him or not. "How long ago was this?"

"A year or two since."

"And are we still together?"

The forest closed in around them and they stopped at a fork in the path. Off to the right, X could see the bridge.

"Things didn't work out quite like I wanted them to."

"Is that a no?"

X reclaimed her hand and led her onward towards her house.

"You can tell me, I'm not stupid."

"Of course not, I just don't see any reason to rehash it now. You and I didn't have the easiest of separations."

"I knew I would screw it up somehow."

X laughed, gave her a reassuring squeeze. "It wasn't entirely your fault. It was complicated, very complicated."

"It couldn't have been that bad if you keep revisiting memories of me."

"Yeah, that's the funny thing about time. Fourth dimension, I think I explained this all to you before, to another version of you anyway. Regardless of what happens in the future, I'll always enjoy coming back and visiting this you."

"*This* me?"

"Yeah," said X. He debated kissing her forehead but quickly dismissed it. "*This* you. Before all the bullshit."

"But we aren't even having sex."

"There are more important things in life than sex."

C made a face, lifted her eyebrows in a patronizing fashion.

X looked around at the simulation as they came out of the forest, to the neighborhood that he didn't really remember. The houses were out of focus, blending with the grass along the bottom and the night sky above. It reminded him of lucid dreaming, of being stuck in the fantasy and being burdened with the knowledge. When he was younger, he had always tried to prolong that feeling, keep the dream going just a little bit longer so he could finally see that girl from history class naked. But walking next to C, who didn't know anything past the memory they were in, he couldn't help but feel like he should wake up. Natalie was out there somewhere, waiting for him. To continue in this simulation would be to risk revisiting feelings that he had already overcome. It was easy to hate C, hate the woman who had banished him from the Net. But this girl, *this* C, knew nothing about that. She was innocent.

At her front door, she stopped and turned to him.

"What's going to happen when I go in?"

"I don't know," he admitted.

She took one of his hands in hers. "It's kinda scary, like dying. I'm not sure you should be playing around with stuff like this. It has consequences for people like me." There was a hint of sadness in her eyes. "I feel, I think, even if this is a memory like you say, I don't want to not exist when you're done with me."

X recognized her line of thinking, elicited a year ahead of schedule. She was right, to an extent. He didn't think much of the virtual copies of her that he had brought into being so many times before. Given the minimal concern for her full copies, the occasional memory replay was never even afforded a second thought. It was, however, only the second time that he had ever broken the memory up, diverted it into simulation. And here was C, laying it all out like it was common knowledge.

"If it helps at all, I did it to save the woman I love."

Hope bloomed in C's face as she looked up expectantly at X.

"Always," said X.

He kissed her on the forehead as she pixilated out from under his lips.

TWENTY-SIX

Natalie sat on the floor of the shower with her legs folded to the side and her back against the cold tile. The concentrated spray of water fell on her chest and stomach, pushing the steam upwards and warming her face. It was a scenario that she had tried to reproduce with lines of code, had even asked G to help with some of the more difficult water effects. And though in the construct, the water fell like it should and her body stayed warm, it never really felt the same. The shower was supposed to be a sanctuary, a place to go to feel vulnerable and protected at the same time. But it only felt that way if reality was on the other side of the fogged-up door. In the simulation, in the nothing that surrounded it, Natalie found safety, but not comfort.

The potential for danger was what made the Terrareal version of the shower so much more powerful. Beyond that door, very real problems awaited. There was nobody out there standing guard, only a superficial lock on the bathroom door and six links of chain holding the front door in place. Even when those barriers held, the world still found its way into her apartment. Television brought in news, the computer brought in raw bits of data, potentially interpreted as a life-changing and world-shattering event. Then there was the rig, another doorway to other people, a heavily protected but easily traversed avenue of communication. Simply jacking in was enough to expose a fragile mind to a million different entities that wanted nothing more than to break down that mind and exploit it until it was no longer viable. Not to mention the people she willingly allowed into her apartment.

G was, presumably, still on the couch, jacked in and sporting his customary half-erection. Whatever he was doing in the Net, he was sure to bring back some news of X, of another obstacle in the way of finding him. Every lead they had ever found had gotten them no closer, but this, X logging in, X being identified as an entity of the Net, or VNet, if Jape was to be believed, this was supposed to be the catalyst. Natalie wasn't consciously waiting for it. Her plan was to find X in Terrareal long before he had the free time to jack in. Since that night and all the nights of incommunicado that had gone by, she always assumed that a sliver of him would turn up in the Net and it would lead her to the black limo and the person who was riding in it. Whoever that person was, they were also the ones responsible for the copy code that X used on C, the serpent perched on the branch offering the first sweet taste of sin.

A quiet sob escaped Natalie's lips, followed by a deep breath.

The air tasted of water.

Crying wasn't something she was willing to do anymore. Maybe in the Net, maybe under lock and triple-key encryption, but not out here. Time spent in the Net was different because none of it was real, none of it could be used as a true indicator of outside traits. In the Net, Natalie was N, a single-letter moniker celebrating her lack of identity, one of twenty-six possible names used so frequently in the Net that they provided a certain level of anonymity. It was all context when deciding which handle went to which person, which is how Jape knew which X they were talking about simply because G was the one asking. In the reverse situation, he would have had no problem paring down the millions of G handles to find the one with a wild coif of brown hair and an eternal five o'clock shadow. It was nothing next to X's piercing eyes and long black hair that obscured them when he leaned forward, but then again, she had never seen G go too long without another retro-tech set of curves at his elbow.

Natalie laughed from finding her hands in the valley of her lap and G's face dancing around her mind. Unwilling to see where the situation would lead, she reached up and dialed off the water.

The bathroom mirror was completely fogged up and her reflection moved in shadowy form across it. She immediately thought of video resolution, of how there weren't enough pixels to display a full reflection of herself. That would have been the explanation in the Net, but out here, the best she could guess was that the condensed water was bending the light, creating a backwards veneer that dirtied the world instead of making it prettier. That was X's ultimate goal, after all, something she began to understand a few months after the first late-night demonstration. Never mind the Net, a virtual world where everything was recreated from scratch. So much work for a product that was still discernable from the real thing. But to veneer the world, put a shine on the rundown echo of former glory, that would be a true accomplishment.

"Best of both worlds," said Natalie, wiping a line on the mirror with her hand, revealing her unmasked face behind it. The makeup was gone, washed away along with most of the anxiety. Staring at an earlier revision of herself reminded her of a time when she didn't have to spend an hour painting her skin just so she could fit in with G at the club. After the last time X jacked in, he had tried to avoid clubs like V-Six or anything that had to do with technology. He even stopped using his cube, the one she now carried for old time's sake. He stopped talking of the places that he would go with C, places that Natalie could imagine but had never seen.

She caught her eyes in the mirror and saw a look on her face that she recognized but didn't understand. It took several minutes of staring, of projection imagination in the null space of the mirror. Code churned in her head, thought processes that had been made stronger by her new dedication to the Net. The bridge appeared before her, as X had described it. She saw him there with C, felt the hate begin to well up inside her. But then the scene changed, C fell away, replaced by another version of herself, several times, until X was standing there alone, leaning on the rail, looking down at the small stream below. He looked content, as if he were there for himself, not waiting for his pigtailed princess to come bounding out of the brush.

If he was there alone, it meant that he went back there just to be by himself. If that was his sanctuary, then maybe…

The thoughts came too quickly for Natalie to process, but she felt her body propelled by instinct. The towel wrapped around her chest by itself, the door to the bathroom swung open of its own accord, and the metal clasps on X's rig case automatically popped off. Without really knowing what she was doing, Natalie removed X's rig from its protective case and placed it on the coffee table next to her laptop. She found an open eSATA port and connected it to the rig's auxiliary interface. Hacking a rig was a difficult job, one G spent considerable time coding on. In the end, the rig kept asking for a password of indeterminate length and composition. Not knowing what they were looking for, they decided against a brute force attack that might have taken centuries.

But now Natalie knew exactly what she was looking for. It would be right there in his cache, a history of every insertion, a log of every jump, with attached coordinates and timestamps, not to mention X's personal data store, millions of pages in a digital diary just waiting to be read. It would all lead to him. Her stomach tightened at the idea of X standing at the bridge now, waiting for her.

A red box prompted her for a password and the slight smile on her face dimmed. She had already spent hours going through the most obvious passwords: names of old girlfriends, his favorite song, his birthday, social security number, all the way up to the binary representation of the ASCII characters of his mother's maiden name. It would never have been that easy though and each bad password that shook the little red box made Natalie more frustrated.

The train of thought that was coasting unattended at the back of her mind finally caught up with her body and presented her with an idea that she had considered before, but never really wanted to try. The password, it told her, had to do with C. Apart from what X had mentioned, she knew very little of the girl he had copied. Memories of conversations were retrieved from their storage points and reexamined for clues. She tried his street address back in Laurel, then hers, her favorite color, the name of her dog, all of the little tidbits that X revealed over the course of their freshman year.

Natalie recalled her dorm room, saw X sitting on her twin bed with his rig and a code cube. He was going to hack C's e-mail account. It was a night that she didn't like to think of often. Seeing him lifeless in her arms was disturbing, had a strange foreboding feeling that ate at her every time she brought it up. Then it was later that night, in a few minutes of lucidity that reassured her that X's mind was intact. He was laughing in his sleep and gradually waking up. She asked him what was so funny. What had he said?

She left the laptop and returned to the bathroom, removing the towel and drying her hair as she went. The menial tasks of selecting matching underwear and complementary pants and shirts allowed her mind to focus on the memory. He was laughing because of something he did. Overkill. The mole wasn't even necessary.

"Why not?" Natalie heard herself ask the question aloud.

Hacking the account had revealed her password and it was simpler than he originally guessed. More laughter, a mention of all the wasted work, of the flirting with death for a password he should have guessed in under a minute. Whether it was disdain or disbelief in his voice, she couldn't tell.

"It's her homedir coordinates. She uses her homedir address as her password."

More laughter, a tap of the cube, and X was back to sleep, and Natalie dismissed the trivia without a second thought.

Now all that stood between Natalie and X's history cache was a simple triplet of numbers, a sequence easily found with any publicly available search engine. She typed the numbers into the red box, her mind too distracted to consider the significance of X's password choice.

The seasickness arrived first, while the construct was still black and empty. The pressure at the bottom of Natalie's feet told her body that she was gently rocking back and forth, prompting the uneasy feeling in her. Next to arrive was the smell of sea air, devoid of pollution but tinged with salt. A boat appeared under her from the bottom up so that she could see the inside of the cabin, as if floating above it, before the light-wood deck took shape. Feeling warmth on her face, Natalie looked up and saw a bright orange sun hanging low in the now-blue sky. Stationary birds hung in the dome like decorations.

The brass railing beckoned her, promised her some level of stability on the rocking boat. It was warm to the touch with a smooth finish that moved like silk beneath her fingers. She traced her hand along the rail as she moved, looking out over the mild waves, noticing the complete lack of anything else. There were no other ships in sight, no hint of land. Remembering where she was, Natalie flashed a smirk. It was an isolated place, secluded, perfect for whatever misdeeds X had chosen to engage in with C.

She felt something rough under her hand that startled her, made her retract involuntarily. The rail seemed to have lost its luster in some places, spots that took on the color of burnt rust. Below, flakes of paint had accumulated on the deck, but that wasn't all. The same discoloration appeared in random patterns, stretching from the rail to the center of the deck. There, a longer, darker spot was burned into the wood, so much so that it was visibly concave. Then the smell hit her, a smell unlike anything she had encountered outside of Old Downtown.

Natalie fumbled with her wrist, tapped a few times to push backward through X's history. As the boat and the smell dissolved, she glanced away, noticed the marks leading in another direction. Her stomach turned. Not even the pixilation could hide the fact that they were footprints.

Explosions rippled through the air, tearing at the simulated eardrums in Natalie's head. Bright flashes of red, blue, and white attacked her from every direction. Feeling no support around her, she guessed that she had inserted above ground level in a construct with enhanced gravity effects. Panic swept over her like a tetrameth rush, sending her pulse into the red. She tried to calm herself, reassure the frightened little girl inside that everything was going to be okay. This was the Net and there was never anything to be scared of. A high-pitched whine sounded in the construct, followed by a boom that she more felt than heard. Unable to stop herself, Natalie slapped at her wrist, hoping it would correctly interpret her distress signal.

Just when the echoes were becoming too much, just when the smell of black powder was too overwhelming, Natalie felt pressure along one side of her body like a strong gust of wind. She twisted her avatar to face it and saw for the first time a long expanse of green hill descending towards a black lake. Still several feet from the ground, she felt her body decelerate, as if the wind were cradling her, carrying her safely from freefall to standstill. The grass was slightly damp, but solid, which was what Natalie desired most at that moment. Another explosion behind her, but this one sounded distant and non-threatening. A laugh escaped her lips as she turned towards the noise.

"You rang?" G had materialized further up the hill and was walking awkwardly down it, trying to control his speed.

"Jesus! You scared the shit out of me," said Natalie, grabbing her heart.

"Like you didn't? A distress signal with these kinds of vitals? I thought you were being murdered."

Natalie stood up, brushed the dew from her pants. "I just fell through that!" She pointed to the sky and on cue, a series of fireworks exploded in the darkness.

The red light painted G's face, making his smile seem even more sinister. "Skydiving through fireworks. Now there's an extreme sport."

"Can't you do anything about the noise? I can't concentrate."

"Sure," said G, folding his arms and dipping his head. A blue streak erupted from the black glass of the lake, climbed into the air soundlessly, and then disappeared without report. As the last of the sparks fell back to the ground, G swung the outer globe around, moving the stars away and bringing the sun into the construct. The lake was actually brown and extended for almost a mile before land took over again. To the left, G saw a road descending towards it, turning, and disappearing into more hills. On the other side of the road, tall evergreens obscured what looked like a golf course. It was a richly detailed construct, much too good for Natalie's skill level. He turned to her, "Who did this?"

"X. He used to bring C here."

"How do you know?"

Natalie felt the pride well up inside of her. "I remembered one of the nights X and I were together and from that, I was able to do enough reverse engineering to hack his rig. I've got his entire history now, among other things." She tapped the side of her head. "I'm trying to find a bridge he used to talk about, thought he might be waiting there."

G wasn't listening anymore. His eyes were glued to the grass at Natalie's feet. Something wasn't right about the color or the texture. "What happened to you? Did you burn on the way down?"

"What," asked Natalie, following G's eyes. She took a quick step backwards. "That's the same thing I saw on the boat."

"What is it?"

"I don't know. It looks like someone spilled acid or something."

G bent down to examine the circle of rust.

"Don't touch it, it burns," warned Natalie.

Immediately, G put his full palm into the circle and felt the pain sweep through his hand and then subside. He grimaced, prompting a gasp from Natalie.

"Are you okay?"

"Ah," said G, shaking the last jitters out of his hand. "You've never felt anything like that before, huh?"

Natalie shook her head.

"It's a virus, a hardcore one too. The pain you felt was it moving through the code in your avatar. If it had wanted you, the pain wouldn't have stopped, but then, your rig would have been completely corrupted in a matter of seconds, so it's not all bad. Whatever this thing's target is, it's not us." G stood up and looked around for other signs of the burn. Finding none, he turned to Natalie. "You say you saw this somewhere else?"

"On a boat sim. It was all over the deck and the rail."

He considered that for a moment. "Let's check somewhere else. How about that bridge construct?"

Natalie brought up a screen in front of her and listed the last twenty entries in X's history. "I'm not sure which one it is," she admitted. "Like I said, I was just going to bounce in and out of constructs until I found it."

"You should have let me know." He looked down at the circle, now glowing slightly around the edges. In a caring voice, he said, "When you rush, that's when accidents happen."

"Next one then?"

"Make it so," said G, pointing with exaggerated flamboyance.

The constructs dissolved from one into the other. G and Natalie found themselves at a playground, in some girl's bedroom, and in a construct of pure rain. In each virtual world, they found traces of the virus: on the slide, on the bed, and in a long series of steps where water pooled but never overflowed. Natalie tried to imagine what X was doing in his last months, but the locations seemed random and disjointed. There was no trace of his intentions anywhere, just the decaying pieces of construct being slowly eaten away by the virus. At last, they came to a forest, bathed in snow a few inches thick. The trees were bare, letting the light from the gray sky shine down.

"Is that the bridge," asked G.

"I've never actually seen it," said Natalie, "but I think this is it. X told me about it once over lunch. Little forest, snow, a bridge over a frozen brook." It looked as X had described it, pristine and secluded. A thought popped into her head. "It's not burned," she said, looking around quickly, "the virus hasn't gotten this far. Maybe X was here and he stopped it!"

"I don't know if X himself could do that," said G, immediately regretting his statement. "So far we've seen that thing everywhere that X has been."

"You think it's targeting him?"

"I sure hope not." G shook his hand out again, still feeling the occasional echoes of pain.

"But look at this place. Whatever X did to it, the virus can't get in here. If we find him, all we have to do is bring him back here until he can recreate this firewall."

"More like an ice wall," said G, stepping onto what he guessed was the beginning of the bridge. He walked halfway across, making careful boot prints in the snow, but stopped suddenly after placing his hand on the rail. Without looking at it, he tried to remotely view what was happening under his fingers. He flinched at the first sign of pain and pulled his hand back quickly. By the time it was safely sandwiched between his other hand and his chest, the throbbing was already in full force.

"What is it," asked Natalie, her voice very far away.

G shook his head and looked around at the bridge. Slowly, he walked to the other end, turned, and kneeled.

"What are you doing?"

"Heat wave," said G, pursing his lips. The warm code of his body spilled out onto the bridge, enveloping and melting the snow.

Natalie stared for a moment, unsure of what she was seeing. Whatever G was doing, it was turning the snow a dull pink. But then, there was no snow anymore, only freestanding water that collapsed suddenly and ran off the sides of the bridge. Simulated tears welled up in her eyes faster than her mind could comprehend what she was seeing, a completely separate reaction based on older, steadier code.

Between them, the bridge was totally revealed. It stood as a red beast among the white landscape, covered in scabs that ran the gradient between red and black, oozing with discolored wood pulp, pulsing with the golden sparks of viral activity. It wasn't just a footprint or the area of grass that X had once sat on, it was a complete takeover of the bridge.

"What do you say," asked G, his eyes still glued to the writhing mass.

Natalie shook her head, unable to find words for her disappointment.

"I think the best thing we can do is find X before the virus does."

"Or before he comes back here." Her response was automatic.

"Yeah." G nodded, waited for her eyes to come up and meet his, but they didn't. "It's been a hell of a day, hasn't it? X is back, you got to hack your first rig, and you've felt your first virus. But that's nothing compared to what's coming up next."

Natalie looked up, inquisitive.

"Tell me, Natalie. Have you ever rushed a singularity by the pale moonlight?" The smile on G's face pixilated into falling snow.

TWENTY-SEVEN

There has always been a market for artists in the Net. From the born-to-be-talented graphic designer to the kid who hotlinks images for his personal profile, the artist has helped shape the hue and texture of the Net since the very beginning. When everything was gray slate, the artists came and drew hills and valleys and waterfalls. When avatars were still jagged blocks of geometric shapes, the artists came and smoothed the edges, applied shadow to the curves, and breathed life into an impassive façade. Graffiti artists, painters, sketchers, inkers, all putting their mark on the Net, overwriting the cold, unfeeling code with something recognizable, something familiar and comforting. They made the Net look like Terrareal.

During the last six months of the gold rush, people and the corporations that owned them realized that while the subtle difference between pine and cedar added realism to a forest construct, it did nothing to increase profits or lower costs. Instead, the rise in demand had made artists extremely rich. Finding a good one was difficult. Signing them to a contract was near impossible unless the sum included six digits. Even then, work didn't begin until the check cleared. And while the artists enjoyed the life of luxury, the everyday hacker sat back and wondered where his services fit in, where he could be used to the fullest extent.

Then came the day that changed everything and swung the pendulum away from the eccentric imaginations and back into the hands of the coders. Accent Ascension, a little-known graphics startup based in Denton, released an alpha version of their RL2NET software that promised to recreate, virtually, any real-world environment in the Net with one-to-one visual acuity. *Copy the world and make it yours*, the slogan heard around the world. People listened and followed, recreating everything from the Golden Gate Bridge to the entire island of Manhattan inside the Net. No artists were paid, none were even consulted.

While Accent Ascension was eventually bought up by a subsidiary of a subsidiary of Vinestead International and then regulated out of existence by anti-terrorism laws and homeland security, the damage had been done. The cost of graphic design was reduced to zero, with large corporations still running RL2NET under the table and regular users invoking open-source solutions that worked nearly as well. With the look of the Net becoming a trivial matter, the focus eventually turned to the feel, to the physics engine that drove Terrareal.

This led to the rise of the superstar coder and the glorification of knowledge over aesthetics. One of the first coders to reach worldwide recognition was a woman of flaming red hair working out of Los Angeles, who liked to call herself the *Perl Princess*. The first generation of corporate coders continued the traditions of old: lack of fashion sense, dedication to *Star Trek* or *Star Wars*, and a proclivity for handles that made CEOs cringe. Fortunately, the coders evolved alongside the Net. Their maturation included physics engines that could mimic gravity from every planet and moon in the solar system and a gradual move from a culture of pocket protectors to one of pocket cubes. The revolution was near complete when X arrived on the scene at fourteen. His persona, like the millions of other script kiddies that grew up with him, was shaped by the pop culture of the day, which was nothing more than the post-apocalyptic rave scene popularized in science fiction movies, albeit without the messy catalyst of a nuclear holocaust.

On a table of green felt, fifteen balls of varying color and design were arranged in a triangle, the preferred design for optimum distribution should the lead ball be struck by another traveling at a high rate of speed. At the head of the table, X stood with cue stick in hand, eyeing the bumpers along the perimeter as they stretched and settled into place. He found the cue ball in the corner pocket on his left and dropped it on the table. The thud and minimal bounce made him smile; his custom physics were surprisingly realistic. He lined up his shot, resisting the urge to draw a line from the cue ball to the rack. Just thinking about it could bring an indicator into existence, but that would have been cheating. He drew the cue back slowly then snapped it forward and followed through.

The cue ball sped towards the triangle, striking the one ball on the severe right of center, and then proceeded to veer towards the right pocket. It sunk with a silent thud in the leather straps. The rack had barely moved.

"Huh," said X, slightly perplexed. With a flick of his fingers, he tightened the rack formation and drew the cue ball back to his side of the table. He lined up again, took his shot, and hit the one ball dead on. Again, the cue ball veered to the right and curved along an arc to land squarely in the pocket. The four ball moved from its corner of the triangle towards the other pocket, stopped, and rolled back into place.

X shook his head. Something in the physics engine wasn't right. He tried to make excuses for himself, about how the conditions weren't ideal, that he was under a lot of stress, etc. But a pool simulation wasn't something out of his league. It should have come out perfect the first time. "What the hell," he asked, pulling the cue ball back to him.

"Maybe it is a sign," said Anela from behind him.

Her presence startled X and left him wondering why he hadn't noticed her sooner.

"Should you be playing games at a time like this," continued Anela.

X eyeballed his captor for a moment, debating. "Do you shoot?"

Anela walked to the opposite end of the table, leaned forward, and placed her hands on the rail. "I have been known to pull a trigger once or twice."

She was still dressed in that same red wrapper and X struggled to ignore her breasts spilling onto the table. "I meant pool. It has a full-on physics engine under the hood. You can't get more realistic than this."

"I want the code, X. I did not bring you back so you could stand around playing with your balls."

"Hmm," said X, lining up another shot. "Ask me nicely and we'll see." He struck the cue ball as hard as he could. It slid across the table in slow motion, its topspin clearly visible. When it struck the one ball, the entire rack devolved into multicolored fluid, construct sludge, as X was calling it.

"Alright," said Anela, "I will ask nicely." The puddle of liquid pool balls settled on the table and then sank through it to reveal undamaged green felt. "Mr. X, would you please decide whether you want me to kill Natalie during her two o'clock history class or while she is at her apartment on Nueces, where she has been for the last twenty-four hours, having some sort of sleepover I imagine."

"Point taken," said X, pixelating the cue stick in his hand. "Wait, sleepover?"

"Oh, do I have your attention now?" Anela straightened up, walked through the pool table as it dissolved. "It seems your girlfriend has been entertaining a gentlemen caller." She spoke slowly and dragged out the next words. "All night loooooong."

A spark ignited behind X's eyes.

"You are tempted to engage in some kind of retribution. I can see the struggle in your eyes. Do I dare strike out at her? If I do, will she even feel it? If she does, will she respond? What will she do to me? I am so scared!" Anela laughed mockingly. "Am I close?"

"Not even," replied X, stoning his voice. He realized immediately that there was no reason to believe anything that she was saying. "I think I've had about enough of your bullshit. I'm not your plaything to use and abuse. You can't just keep someone captive like this."

"Why not? *You* did." Anela let her words sink in. She walked around X and stood by the desk where the rig and cube had been moved from their original positions. "Have you made any progress?"

"I'm done," said X, feeling a bit of pride. "It wasn't that difficult either."

Anela nodded. "Do you know what the word *erudite* means?"

"If I had access to the Net, I could look it up."

"I will save you the trouble," said Anela, leaning back against the desk. "It describes someone who has great knowledge, either by study or by divine right."

"I accept your compliment."

She ignored him and continued. "What is interesting is that the etymology of that word can be traced back to the same roots as *rude*, which back then, meant untrained. That is what I think of when I look at you, X. You seem to have great knowledge, but no clear understanding of how to utilize it. That makes you so vulnerable, so exploitable, a fact of which you seem to be blissfully unaware. In many ways, it is sad. Even my ciphers are self-actualized, aware of their full potential and their individual limitations. Most importantly, they work efficiently within those boundaries. You, on the other hand. Well, I am at a loss."

X said nothing. Inside his head, he was trying to will Anela into asking for the code again. Waiting, buffeting, pretending to stall, it was all making him nervous. The longer he waited, the more opportunities he had to slip up. Just give her the code, get her to execute it, and everything will be okay.

"Discretion is the better part of valor," said Anela, noting X's silence. "So you are not completely ignorant of social graces."

"Well," said X, "I've really enjoyed the English lesson, but don't you think it's time we got down to business? The code's right there in the cube. Take it already."

Anela scooped up the cube. It dissolved into her hand. "Of course, we will have to examine the source and then test it out. But honestly, I cannot help but feel a little cheated."

"Why's that?"

"You told me before that it would take you a week. And it has only been a few hours. The only logical conclusion is that you lied to me."

"Wouldn't you have?"

"Touché."

"I'm not crazy about giving you this program. God knows what kind of sick shit you have planned. It's like handing over the codes to the atom bomb to bin Laden himself."

"I am touched that you hold me in such high esteem as one of our nation's greatest historic enemies."

"You want the same as he did."

"Which is?"

"To make the little man fear you. Who would dare mess with the ZabSix cipher den when they knew there was an army of ciphers in the Net just waiting to get them and their data? You'll have a monopoly on information. How soon before it becomes your private monarchy?"

"If only my aspirations were that great. No, X. What you fail to understand for the thousandth time is that I merely want to make money. I want to live and die comfortably. I am not the evil villainess of your comic books; I am a simple businesswoman. And right now the biggest threat to my business is that same entity that really does have a monopoly on the Net. Things are happening, X, things you will never have to worry yourself about, but that will affect me and my clients if they should ever come to fruition. Me, and people like me, want the Net to remain free. And I am going to do anything, *anything*, to see that goal through."

X smirked. "So you're raising an army of freedom fighters?"

Anela raised her eyebrows slightly. "Very succinct."

"Well, good luck with your jihad. I don't want to be a part of it. I think it's time you let me out of here and left me and my friends alone."

"My ciphers are checking over your work. They should be done momentarily. Maybe we can discuss it after a successful test."

A moment of silence passed with neither looking away from the other. Finally, X spoke. "There's a reason I was able to finish it so quickly."

"Your honesty is appreciated. Please continue."

"I used some of the code that brought me here. There's an intermediate step."

"Being?"

"Whoever you invoke will appear here first. The translation to the Net will take place in a protected tunnel, processed linearly from first bit to last. The entrance to the tunnel will be represented by an invisible plane directly in front of the subject, roughly their size. Once they appear here, they have to take a step forward to enter transition."

"Can they be forced forward if they are, somewhat, reluctant?"

"It's the physical connection that does it. And yes, it can be forced."

Anela flinched a little, listening to a voice inside her head. The news made her smile. "Your code checks out. I was almost sure you would try to sneak something in there."

"I probably should have."

Anela tapped a message onto her wrist, instructing one of the ciphers to execute the code. "Now we will see if it actually works or not."

Several feet away, an orange rift appeared in the construct. It tore a line from the ground to a point six feet in the air. Pulsing at the center, X recognized it as the insertion marker.

"Who are you bringing in," he asked apprehensively.

"A copy of one of my ciphers. His name was Emilio."

"What's his name now?"

"He has no name; he is a cipher, a ghost."

"A non-entity, yeah, I got it."

"I do not refer to them individually. They are a collective."

The insertion marker bulged and split. It took on the form of a grown man, slightly hunched over, as if hanging lifelessly in a harness. X could see a face taking shape, flesh-colored and smooth. He looked nothing like the pale zombies he had seen in Anela's den. It looked like the cipher's residual avatar was still embedded in his mind and had been waiting for a chance to come out.

The cipher's head shook in quick convulsions.

"You did that," said Anela, "when I initialized your copy in here. What is happening in your head?"

"His mind is trying to catch up with the present. It's like going from boot to sixty in only a few seconds. Inside, time is subjectively longer. He's reliving some memories, piecing fragments together. When he catches up to the present, we'll know."

They watched together in silence as the avatar filled in. Head to toe, the cipher was dressed like a ninja from a low-budget movie. The black latex absorbed the ambient light of the construct and redirected it. It took X a few minutes to realize that the avatar was fully complete and that the blurry edges weren't caused by a lack of detail, but by active camouflage. The presence of an unbound cipher was unsettling, but not knowing he was there would be even worse.

Anela stepped forward to examine her newest clone. From behind her, X spoke.

"You don't have any intention of ever letting me out, do you?"

"No," said Anela, marveling at the light bending around the cipher's avatar.

"I knew I couldn't trust you."

"Actually, we never had an agreement that included your release. Technically, I have fulfilled my end of the bargain."

The cipher stopped shaking and jerked his head up. X caught a glimpse of his fire-red eyes before black lenses extended from his eyebrows and obscured them.

"Then I'm afraid that I will just have to take matters into my own hands," said X, a smile beginning to form.

Anela glanced back warily. "Meaning?"

X took a step forward, felt the purposely misplaced transfer plane grab at every bit in his body. Quickly, he raised his hand and waved goodbye. The look on Anela's face made him laugh, but it was cut short by movement behind her. The cipher dashed across the room, impossibly fast, a blur that stained the construct.

Whether he reached the plane or not, X could not tell. He was busy falling through an empty tunnel. Below, a white light approached frighteningly fast.

TWENTY-EIGHT

Golden light filtered in through the wooden slats of the windows, drawing diagonal edges to the floor. They formed four large bands through which bits of dust floated on the motionless air, bits that blinked in and out of existence according to some random number generator deep in the construct's programming. At the center of the room was a bench pointed towards the windows. Astride it sat Luci Shumeyko, VNet employee #60421-LB. Her legs were bent at the knee so that her shins were exactly perpendicular to the floor. Her hands rested casually on her bare thighs, her back was straight, and her head faced rigidly forward.

At the base of her neck, a small circle of blue glinted and flashed with activity. Every now and then, a bolt of electricity shot down her back, gleaming under the surface of her golden skin, riding the bumps of her spine, disappearing into the red band of her thong. It was part of an early warning system and the pulse every fifty to sixty seconds simultaneously told her that the system was still working and that everything was nominal. In between each pulse, Luci lost herself in small but powerful simulations in her mind. These exercises strengthened her reflexes, honed her skills, and kept her body in complete homeostasis.

Luci stepped forward into the shallow water, watching her toes change shape as the small waves passed over them, bending the light. The cool sensation climbed her ankle, and the occasional splash sizzled on her warm shins. Above, small, wispy clouds moved quickly through the artificial sky, like white brush strokes on a poorly drawn gradient. The air smelled of bacterial waste, refined to be less offensive but still strong enough to convey that unique smell of the beach that had since been lost to industrial pollution. Though the light felt normal and illuminated the world as it should have, the sun loomed large and blue on the horizon, outlined in black to set it apart from the dome. Every sixty seconds, a pulse shot down from the circle, struck the water, and echoed through the waves.

Swimming just under the surface was a school of fish, which Luci tracked as the large mass scampered about, changing direction at random.

Suddenly, a single fish broke into the air, jumping several inches above the water. Luci followed it with her eyes. Track, hack, and sack. That's how you got things done.

Before the fish could reach the apex of its jump, it froze in the air, decomposed in a spray of red scales, and then dissolved into particles that floated on the null breeze, highlighted by the golden slats of light pushing their way through the wooden blinds.

The simulation had dissolved right in front of her eyes, an extraction of such speed and precision that it made Luci's stomach flip over twice. She placed her hand on the back of her neck, felt the blue spot pulsing quickly, beating like a nervous second heart.

"Shumeyko!" The voice of her manager came loud and booming in the quiet construct, shaking the air and rattling the blinds.

"I'm on it," replied Luci, standing quickly. Around her, the whole world moved in a whirlwind of pixilated destruction. The blinds on the windows snapped shut, plunging the room into temporary darkness until ambient light from above the ceiling began to rain down, revealing a single-seater desk and a large plasma monitor. The off-red desktop bubbled as Luci approached, pushing a keyboard through the surface of the liquid wood. She sat down quickly and placed her hands into the viscous keyboard, merging them. Her fingers barely moved, yet the commands appeared on the screen as fast as she could think them.

During her initial boot and assessment, Luci's mind wandered and considered the implications of the event. If she was being invoked as a line of defense, then someone had successfully broken through six other lines, lines protected by rotating passkeys, viral pitfalls, and high-level translation planes that ninety-nine percent of the population didn't even know existed. And yet the screen did not lie; not one, but two entities had just passed into the seventh sector, a mere three hops away from being able to approach the singularity. Luci squared her jaw. That was not going to happen.

Luci's job, along with twenty-eight other rotating ciphers, was to protect sector seven with all of the ferocity and cunning of a Templar Knight. It only took three minutes to determine that her pair of intruders couldn't be dealt with by CLI alone. They were running scramble code that wasn't recognized by the construct. Whoever they were, they were obviously professionals. Coming this far certainly gave them a chance at rushing the singularity. A slim chance, conceded Luci. She removed her hands from the keyboard, felt the slime drip from her fingers. A thin smile grew on her lips. For the first time in a long time, she would get to face other warriors on the battleground.

She stood and felt the stale air move across her near-naked body. Something tickled her feet, making her shift from one to the other as a suit of reflective white grew up from her toes. It crested the tops of her legs and spilled into her only true garment, overtaking it quickly. The white material hugged her body, dipping under her breasts and then swallowing them completely. At her neck, it began to take on a golden hue, blending seamlessly with her skin. She removed a long pin from her bun of black hair, letting it fall and land against her back, where the white absorbed it.

The desk retracted backwards into the wall, leaving a glowing red shape that expanded into a familiar rectangle.

"Sentence first, verdict afterwards," she said, rushing through the door.

Natalie and G stood like the highest ridges of a relief map in the all-white construct. Their black attire glistened, bathed in a light that didn't seem to shine from any one direction. They cast no shadows, but G had a strange feeling of claustrophobia, felt that the air didn't move freely enough in the supposedly empty construct. Beside him, Natalie swayed uneasily, still shaken from the near-miss in sector six.

"What is this place," she asked, taking a step forward.

"Wait!" G's warning was a second too late.

Natalie felt something slam into her shin. There was a moment of biting pain before her code reacted and shut the receptors down. The discovery that they could feel pain was made in sector two, when a viral whip had lashed out from behind stone walls, emerging from and retracting into the mortar in between the blocks.

G bent down and instructed Natalie not to move. He reached out to the space directly in front of her knee and was surprised to feel pressure. Whatever invisible object it was, it had the texture of processed wood, like the soft blend used in playground equipment. It felt square, roughly a foot along each edge. "There's something here," he said.

Joining him at ground level, Natalie put her hand beside G's and felt the stump of wood. She moved her head closer, squinted, crossed her eyes, and uncrossed them. "I can almost see it," she said. "It's like one of those stereoscopic images. Focus your eyes beyond your hand and you can almost make it out."

G followed her instructions and within a few seconds he could see the leading edge of the stump, though the lines extended into invisibility.

"What kind of fucked up construct is this," asked Natalie.

"I have no clue. Tiesto didn't say anything about this sector, just that we should be humble and take it slow."

"Humble?"

"Yeah, I don't know," replied G, standing up. He tapped at his wrist, brought up a small display in front of him. The edges gleamed in the strange omnipresent light. "It looks like this construct is almost two-hundred and fifty yards long. The trans-plane is all the way at the other end. There."

"Two-hundred and fifty paces." Natalie looked in the direction that G was pointing.

"Aye, matey. Two-hundred and fifty paces or face the gallows."

Natalie took an apprehensive step forward, avoiding the invisible stump. "What the hell is a gallow, anyway?"

"I don't know," said G, stepping behind her and using her as a probing tool. He hooked his finger into the belt loop of her pants. "I don't think there is such a thing as a gallow."

"So gallows is singular?"

"Sure, I guess. Gallowses." The word didn't sound right in G's mind, so he typed it out on his wrist. "I'm in the gallowses business." He chuckled, shook his head. "Spellchecker doesn't pick it up. Must be a word."

"Maybe you need a pirate dictionary," suggested Natalie. She let her foot swing forward with every step, testing the air for more stumps. In her mind, she watched herself from a few feet away, goose-stepping like an unenthusiastic Nazi in the waning days of World War II.

"Nope, pirate dictionary says it's okay too."

Natalie smiled and shook her head. Only G would have a pirate dictionary installed on his wrist. Who knew when you were going to need it, she thought to herself. "Why," she started, "why do you—" She cut herself off as the echo of her own words reached her ears way too quickly. Instinctively, she ducked her head a few inches.

G, still looking at his wrist, caught the lower edge of the beam square between the eyes, narrowly missing a wet and painful injury to his nose. He cried out, his voice tinged more with frustration than pain. "Fuck!"

From her bent position, Natalie suddenly understood Tiesto's warning. "Humble," she said, "so that you don't hit your head." Out of G's grip, she inched forward, running her hand along the underside of the beam until it ended. Standing up again, she turned to G and gasped. The image of the gallows standing old and deteriorating in a forgotten courtyard sprang to mind. On the other side of the beam, G was thinking the same thing.

"You've got no head," he said, chuckling.

"Neither do you," Natalie replied.

"It's amazing, there's no depth to this thing." G placed his hand on the obstruction, felt beneath it, pushed at it. "Unreal."

"We've got two-hundred and thirty-four paces to go. Can you still walk?"

"Yeah, but keep a watch out for these." He patted the beam.

"Dammit, come under here. I can't stand listening to your headless body."

G appeared a moment later, smiling his signature cocky.

"Hmm," considered Natalie, "actually that's not much of an improvement."

G managed a weak laugh and grabbed at her hip to spin her around. Again, he looped his finger in her pants, but this time he crouched behind her, keeping his head lower than her shoulders, trailing her like a codependent Quasimodo. Ahead of him, Natalie raised her arms to eye-level, then a bit higher. She continued her goose-stepping until a beam caught her in the midsection. At her slow pace, it wasn't anything more than a slight bump, but the development of a third obstacle made both of them stop and ponder the purpose of the construct. They walked another fifty paces in silence, with Natalie's exploratory kicking and arm-waving leading the way.

"This is ridiculous!" Natalie stopped suddenly and let her arms fall to her sides. She turned to G and waited for him to straighten up. "I'm not going to keep walking around like a retarded Frankenstein!"

"Frankenstein was the scientist, not the monster."

"Asshole!" Natalie hit G in the chest. "That's not the point!"

G laughed and grabbed Natalie's wrist as it came in for another landing. He pulled her slightly forward so that their bodies touched briefly. "Humble and slow," he repeated, "that's just the way of the game."

"It doesn't seem right to me," she replied, breaking free of his embrace. "All of the other constructs had traps and programs and brightly colored laser displays. This is nothing! This is not challenging, it's just time-consuming!"

The smile on G's face faded in the recoil of Natalie's bombshell. Suddenly, he became more aware of the construct. Certainly their presence had been noted in the previous six sectors. Subjectively, it had taken them more than two hours to get through them, but on the outside, that was more like fifteen minutes. What if the first six had been part of some early warning system, red herrings and dead ends designed with only one purpose in mind.

"To slow us down," said G, thinking aloud.

"What?"

A tingling sensation started at the base of G's spine and erupted quickly to his back, to his shoulders, and into his brain. His arms and legs shook uncontrollably, throwing him off balance and into one of the many see-through beams. He struck his head, felt the back of his knee catch on a stump. His body leaned dangerously, but every time he was about to fall, another invisible block appeared and sent him rebounding in the other direction. His screams echoed in the construct, ramping up their intensity and frequency exponentially.

Natalie covered her mouth in horror, unable to understand what was happening to G. To her, he moved in a wild blur, emitting cries that were drowned in their own Doppler effects. Suddenly, G went rigid. His legs snapped together, bolting him upright. His arms followed, glued his hands to his hips. She caught his eyes for a moment, saw the look of terror eating away at his mind. His lips moved, but she heard only the white noise of a poorly encoded audio file. He dissolved in front of her, each piece of him seeming to liquefy in place and then float off like drops of water in zero gravity. Determination flashed across his face and his lips moved again.

She caught his words, barely audible over the crackling and the sloshing.

"Run!"

Luci felt satisfaction swell in her chest as one of the intruders dissolved and floated away in the construct. One by one, the small bubbles were swallowed up by the white, fading out of existence without their signature pop.

She heard the male's warning, instructing his female accomplice to run, an order that she followed without hesitation. So quick to run from battle, so eager to escape punishment for the crime she has committed.

"It's no use running, Dinah." Luci's voiced boomed in the white emptiness without echo. It was tied to the light, everywhere at once. It scraped along the edges of the female's ears, Luci was sure of it. To her, the construct appeared in wireframe and adjusted to her perspective so that the crisscrossing lines of obstacles collapsed down upon the others. There were only four variations of each obstacle, and their edges were pixel-width. Her view down the construct showed the intruder's curved lines bending and stretching, trying to blindly navigate her way to the other side.

"I can see you." She let a scan explode in the construct, felt it grab at the female, only to come away with nothing. "Good protection," she said, moving forward through the obstacles. "Your cohort had good protection too, but that still didn't stop me."

The female's cries reached Luci's omnipresent ears. She was stumbling around the stumps and below the beams, forgetting all about the bars hanging at mid-height. By now, the last of her ability to control pain would be fading. Each hit, each collision, broke that barrier down a little more. In her frenzied state, it wouldn't be long before she knocked herself out.

Luci didn't want that. She didn't want the chase to end with the prey giving up and retreating into unconsciousness. In her short career, she had taken eight hackers, all of them male. Never had she seen a female in her sector, never had to face a passive lioness. Her tactics had not changed since her first kill; track it, hack it, and sack it. Do it all before they even realize you're there. Element of surprise, intensity of attack, sweet taste of victory. She licked her lips.

Her mind painted in the female's clothes as her wireframe opened the distance between them. It started with the black pants and long-sleeved shirt that she observed her wearing. The dark sunglasses against her pale skin had made her seem ethereal, like a ghost trapped in an ill-fitting suit. As the outer shell fell away, Luci imagined a modest t-shirt of white a few shades off from the construct, with matching underwear that looked more like short shorts than anything resembling her own preference. She let the garments dissolve, revealing the light skin beneath and the bumps of her spine poking out as she ducked under an oncoming beam. For a moment, Luci lost herself in the movement of the female's rear, watching the muscles contract and relax, moving through a repeating set of enticing positions.

She was suddenly overcome by the desire to take the intruder, to play with her, and show her how loving she could be. It wouldn't be like it was with all the men. It would be special.

Luci doubled her speed to close the distance between them. No longer speaking, her presence and position were now a mystery. She floated alongside her prey for a few minutes, observing the expressions on her face and taking mental pictures of her form.

"I don't pay you to screw around," said that bureaucratic voice.

It was right, of course. They had covered a majority of the construct and were inside fifty yards of the trans-plane. It was time to catch Dinah before she got any further down the rabbit hole.

Luci moved ahead and planted herself in the intruder's path. Moments before the collision, she let the white veneer slip from her body and revealed her presence. She smiled at the girl, standing there confused and in pain. From the look on her face, seeing her half-naked pursuer had sent her right over the edge. There was only one thing left to do and Luci took her time with it.

The tingling sensations wasn't painful, and at first, it intrigued Natalie. The way it moved about the soles of her feet made her think of X's rough fingernail scratching across the lines in her skin. When the feeling enveloped her ankle, the panic began to rise inside of her. It felt as if her legs were asleep from the knee down, but a quick visual check showed them to be moving, almost vibrating in place. A low rumble burst into the small of her back, shaking the sections of her spinal cord in their bony tombs.

The woman in front of Natalie smiled and crossed her arms under her breasts. Natalie didn't have time to consider the absurdity of a naked woman in the construct before the image began to shake. The form of blurry flesh in front of her started making sounds, soothing and condescending, as if comforting a baby. She realized that something was wrong with her arms and legs as they started to move about violently. A smack to the head from a low-hanging beam evoked images of G at the mercy of his own convulsions.

A hundred autonomic responses pulsed through Natalie's head. As each of them failed, she became more and more despondent. Nothing she was doing was working. Nothing G had done had worked and she imagined his reflexes and code to be years beyond what little arsenal she possessed. It was a hopeless fight, but shock was beginning to take over her mind, so her thoughts fluttered only briefly before being torn into a million pieces by the internal vibrations. A hint of pain slashed across her face, like the scrape of a cat's claw, but slowly grew into something much worse. It felt as if a great heat was pressing against her forehead, melting it down, boring into her brain.

No longer aware of her nose or mouth, Natalie tried to cry. But by the time the signal reached her brain, her eyes were gone and the warm breeze felt impossibly close to the center of her existence.

TWENTY-NINE

"You have been detained for unauthorized access to a privately-owned network space. Because we cannot ascertain your identity, you are to remain here until the next security officer is available to interrogate you. Have a nice day."

Natalie barely heard the recorded voice echo off her eardrum. When it repeated a minute later, her eyes had adjusted to the abrupt change in light. The pain in her face subsided and the occasional jitter was the only thing that remained of the former convulsions. Instead of the stark white claustrophobia, the construct in front of her was bathed in black and seemed to extend on forever. Several feet away, a large metal pole grew up from the ground. At the top, the orb of a spotlight shone down on her position. There were similar spotlights to the right and the left and behind…

G's voice floated across the ten or fifteen yards between them. His back was to her and his arms moved at his side the way they did when he talked passionately about something. She tried to call out, but her entire body felt numb and though her tongue pressed against her teeth, she couldn't form a sound. Staring at G's silhouette, with the great spotlight shining from the other side, close and far away, the hopeless feeling began to crawl out of its hole again.

She felt herself lying on the ground and knew that the spotlight was on her, but G was facing the other way, talking, it seemed, to someone, maybe the naked woman who had put her through hell. Natalie would have to wait until he turned around to be noticed and who knew when that would be. A silent sob erupted from her throat, sending her body into a heave but leaving the air around her untouched.

From somewhere in the back of her brain, she recalled a lesson that G had downloaded into her head, one of the many knowledge packs that gave her the accumulated skills of sixteen college seniors. Thrown in for good measure was a smattering of electives, one of which was a philosophy class that focused more on quantity than quality. The vague image of a decrepit professor standing at a podium entered her mind.

"So," said the professor, choking on his own words. He cleared his throat, sending a fine mist over the front row of students. "Who here is familiar with the work of Bishop George Berkeley? Anyone?" A disinterested silence filled the auditorium. "It was Mr. Berkeley to whom we attribute the philosophical scenario of a tree falling unobserved in a forest. Does it make a sound? Does anyone care?" Again, the silence answered him. "But Mr. Berkeley was not given to such pedestrian examples as popular culture would have us believe. Instead, he put it much more eloquently. *To be is to be perceived.* Think about that for a moment. Do you see how much more sentiment is carried in those six words than in the whole of the forest-tree analogy?"

So much, thought Natalie, to herself.

"That is the Achilles Heel of our great country, this predisposition towards the user-friendly, towards the easily digestible. Surely you remember the Internet of old? Text-based pages first, then images, then movies embedded in those pages. But, truthfully, the information never changes. No matter if it is a tree in a forest or a fish in an empty ocean, there is no analogy as succinct and pregnant as *to be is to be perceived.*"

The professor turned a page on the podium.

"Today, we're much more accustomed to the raise it and praise it cinderblock style of construction. We may be better suited to ask if a building collapses in the middle of the city and no one is around to be crushed by it, let alone hear it, did that building even exist? That is another fallacy of the forest. It is not about whether the tree makes a sound, it is whether the tree exists or has ever existed. Is a single person's memory of that tree enough to maintain its existence? Many a great man has pondered this question, creating his own little forest of introspection. Imagine that you are the tree, alone in the forest." The professor seemed to turn and look directly into the camera, and in turn, directly at Natalie. "If you cry and no one is around, do you make a sound? Do you exist? Have you ever?"

A primal whimper ripped from Natalie's vocal cords, shaking her throat and tearing across the gaping distance between her and G. She saw him turn and as he did, he revealed another silhouette, slightly taller, standing in front of him. She could barely make out the stranger's face and a trickle of dread floated up her spine as he approached.

"G!" Her cry seemed to stall the stranger, but G wasn't moving. He wasn't even looking in Natalie's direction anymore. He seemed lost in thought, peering at the ground as if the answers to the universe were written there.

"Can I help you up?"

Natalie heard the voice, felt the registers line up with her memories of X. She looked up and saw the first bit of light flash across his face. The smile he bore melted her from the inside out.

"Give me your hand."

She followed his command without question, without a word to express the excitement and relief welling up inside of her. The speech program that had stayed resident long enough to cry was now toiling in a looped crash. She wanted to say something, anything at all.

His hand felt warm and comforting. It tickled her skin in a way that let her know that code was passing between them. He was loading something into her, something that shook the cobwebs from her simulated muscles and dialed down the activity in her brain.

"Long time no see, I'm told," he said softly.

Natalie felt her arms move tentatively at her urging and she immediately threw them around X, drawing him down from his kneeling position. They were half-lying on the floor with her face pressed into his chest.

"I thought," she started, her voice sounding like that of a twelve-year-old girl, "that I'd never see you again."

"I've seen that movie," said X. "I didn't like the way it ended. So I thought I'd write us a new one."

"We came looking for you. We've been looking everywhere."

"I know," replied X, placing his hand on her face and moving his thumb over her lips to quiet her. "There will be time to talk, time to catch up. But not now."

"Let's go home, please."

"We can't," said G. "I've tried jumping, but they've got us locked down."

"Let me worry about that." X pulled Natalie to her feet. "The important thing is that I got to you in time. You should have a fighting chance now."

"What're you talking about," asked Natalie.

"I was filling G in on the details when you showed up. He'll tell you all about it once you're out, but you need to go right now."

"Why?" Her voice was on the edge of hysterics.

"You have to trust me."

"Please, tell me why you can't come home, tell me why I can't stay with you."

X hesitated, sighed. "You remember the last night I was with you?"

Natalie nodded.

"The woman in the limo was Anela Zabora."

"She's the leader of the ZabSix cipher den," added G.

"Right. And she doesn't just have ciphers at her disposal. A lot of bad people work for her. And right now those bad people are heading for your apartment, if they aren't there already. You need to get out. Find a safe place where you can hide out and jack in."

"What kind of bad people?"

"Natalie, listen to me. G is going to do everything he can to protect you and get you out safely. You must trust us."

"When will I see you again?"

"Jack in when you're safe. I'll meet you at my homedir."

"I don't know about that," said G, raising a finger.

"No time," said X. "You two have to go, *now*."

"I told you, X. We can't jump back to our homedirs. And the last time I checked, no one has ever spontaneously jacked out before."

Flashes of an early morning meeting in X's bed replayed in Natalie's mind.

"It's been done before," said X. "I've done it." He looked briefly at Natalie and then away. "And I've done it to someone."

G and Natalie started to protest, but X had grown tired of trying to warn them. He pulled them both together, facing him, and slipped a hand behind each of their necks. His eyelids dropped as the sound of their voices grew in his head. He opened his eyes briefly to look at Natalie.

"I love you," he said, then to G, "this might sting, bro."

The code surged through his hands and into the simulated jacks on the backs of their necks. The program was a pared down version of the copy code, with the output redirected to dev null. Somewhere, a copy of each of them was blasting through the Net as unconnected bits of data, bound for nowhere. The copy wasn't important, just the surge at the end that cut the last bit from their cortical stacks. In that moment, the shadow copy tried to simultaneously read and write to the same register, causing a lock that, in addition to spawning a flood of EKG activity, completely broke the flow of information between the body and the mind, forcing an abrupt disconnect from the Net. X did his best to dial back the intensity, make their transitions as painless as possible. At the worst, they would wake up with a heart attack and a slight headache, but otherwise unaffected.

Natalie dissolved in front of X, her tears lingering on for a single heartbeat.

THIRTY

The news spread quickly through the Net, saturating every channel with talk of a wolf amongst the herd. The warning flashed across a billion wrists and reached millions more through vidscreens and monitors. Many dismissed the cryptic message as a hoax, a trick to get them to give up their credit card numbers. But for those few whose blood flowed like light through fiber, it was a civil defense siren ringing out clearly in the dead of night. It meant nailing wood to windows, though there was no storm coming. It meant retreating to the protection of a concrete shelter, though no bombs would soon be falling.

Precautions were taken. Connections were severed. But the words were already seared into their memory. The damage had already been done.

Even X, while watching the last of Natalie's pixels flicker out of existence, saw the words repeat in tall red letters around the perimeter of the construct.

CIPHER IN THE WILD.

In his darkened IDE, the cipher worked tirelessly, preparing his tracers to lock on to X's signature. They would find him. They had to. During his brief moments of rest, he rehearsed his introduction.

"I am the cipher Lio," he repeated.

THIRTY-ONE

The crushed flower scent of Natalie's apartment drifted in through the gaps in G's rig, pulling him gently from the odorless construct. As the signals traveling through the electrode on his neck began to slow, the screen before his eyes started flickering out, fading to a black that looked flat in the ambient sunlight. The last of the code settled in G's body, returning his muscles to his conscious command. Reflexively, he reached up with both of his hands and pushed the rig off his head much in the same way he would wash his face. Getting the rig off early helped with the transition back to normality, a transition that could take several minutes for the uninitiated.

Beside him, he could feel Natalie stirring. Through the sleepy blur in his eyes, he could see her head softly shaking side to side. With a groan, G pulled himself to a sitting position and put his arms on his knees. There was nothing quite like trying to come out of the Net so quickly and after such a long night. Somehow, the abrupt ejection had not affected him like X said it would. The small circle on the back of his neck felt warm and he guessed that it had absorbed most of the shock. The code in G's body was alternating in sixty second intervals, feeding him synthesized adrenaline and caffeine. The pressure on his heart was making his chest hurt, a dull ache that radiated from the center of his body and made his extremities tingle. G's brain suddenly switched gears, realized the output channel to the Net was no longer there, and flooded him with a barrage of important instructions and a single imperative.

Ciphers alone were enough to fear. They could destroy a digital life in no time flat by emptying financial accounts, inflating criminal records, and even by erasing social security numbers from the national databank. As a man who lived most of his life amongst the bits, G's greatest fear was catching a whiff of a cipher on his tail and turning to find the fate of nonexistence looming over him. Although his priorities were somewhat backwards, even he realized the importance of remaining physically intact. His digital self relied on his brain to keep going. If Anela's goons showed up and removed it, then everything else would be moot.

Natalie moaned, prompting G to reach over and carefully remove her rig. The shock must have been too much for her. Passing out was one way to deal with the onslaught of data, opting to simply ignore the information instead of trying to process it. He brushed away the odd strand of hair and let his hand linger until she blinked her eyes open. A feeling of discontinuity washed over him as he noticed she was no longer wearing last night's clothes but instead was dressed only in a white towel. It was long enough to cover half of her upper thigh and G could barely resist the temptation to pull it back, revisit the memory of a night whose reality had been altered by a combination of code and vulnerability. Another moan and his eyes were drawn to her face again. Soon enough, her brain would lock on to the correct wavelength, recall the warning that X had given them, and spring into action.

"I'm so tired," she said, blinking quickly.

"Don't worry," he replied, "I've got that covered." G stood and searched his pockets for his memory card. Then, remembering himself, he lifted his shirt and reached inside the band of his boxers to a secret pouch on his left hip. The card was the size of a fingernail and half as thick. He set it down on the table and placed his cube beside it.

"We've got to get out of here," protested Natalie. "X said—"

"I know what he said." G inserted the card into a nearly invisible slot on the side of the cube. "But I've been awake for thirty-six hours. Even under the best conditions, that would be a stretch for me. We've been in and out of the Net, I've had several drinks, and I must have walked a dozen miles yesterday going door to door." The cube began to glow. Little blue pulses erupted from the slot and flowed into the rest of the cube. "Do you have X's jacksplit?"

Natalie adjusted her towel as she stood. From a small wooden box on her dresser, she retrieved X's cube and the dual electrodes attached to it. "What are you loading," she asked, placing the cube on the coffee table.

"*Last Dance with Mary Jane*," replied G, pushing the two cubes together. "It's like vitality code, but with a faster burn rate. We could run a marathon with this, but only for twenty to thirty minutes. We'll need to get somewhere safe and we'll need to get there fast." He eyed her briefly. "Put on some clothes. You won't be able to fuck your way out of this one."

Natalie huffed in reply.

"Wait," said G, just as she was about to leave. "Let's load this up first." He handed her one of the trodes and she stuck it quickly to the back of her neck. G did likewise, feeling around for the raised circle of a scar. "Ready?"

Before she could reply, G tapped the code and sent millions of specialized instructions streaming into their spines. They wrapped around their cortexes like a warm blanket and then spread with vine-like precision around their brains. Slowly, the tendrils began to pull, squeezing the gray folds, milking the outlying glands. A heightened sense of awareness came over both of them and they felt their bodies move at the slightest impulse. Decision-making speed was increased, reaction time was reduced. It would be useful in a fight, but at rest, they struggled not to vomit from the frenzy building up inside of them.

They moved in fast-forward about the apartment. Natalie ran quickly to the bedroom, unsure when the idea of simply walking had slipped from her mind. She pulled clothes from the closet at random, held each to her chest for a microsecond, and discarded it. Finally, she settled on a tight white shirt under a small purple tee and crumpled black pants. It took two steps for her to realize she hadn't put on any underwear, but only a few seconds to correct it. She gathered a few toiletries: a brush, lipstick, and the eye shadow that got her into places like V-Six. Back in the living room, she tossed them into her rig case.

G was already done with his pack and was trying to fit the laptop into one of the side pockets with little success. "Anything important on this?"

"Affirmative," replied Natalie, her teeth striking awkwardly.

"Anything we need?"

Natalie thought about it for a moment and realized there was nothing on the laptop that they couldn't acquire in the Net. She decided to hide it instead and was surprised to find herself already kneeling in the back of her closet and moving a small section of the floorboards. She placed the laptop inside, replaced the board, and threw several shirts on top of it. Smiling at her own cleverness, she returned to the living room.

G was standing at the door, struggling to remain still as he waited for her to join him. She swung the straps of her pack onto her shoulders and took one last look at the apartment. It had only been a few months since she moved in, but already it felt like home. In the hallway, she turned and locked the door, shook the handle to make sure it was tight.

"They're just going to break it down," said G.

"I know, but there's no such thing as a free lunch." There was a hint of a smile on Natalie's face, but it turned to concentration as her sensitive ears picked up a low vibration in the walls. "The elevator's coming up."

"Move!" G practically dragged Natalie down the hall by the elbow. They hid behind the corner of the hallway. G peeked his head around as the elevator dinged.

They were dressed in the prototypical goon attire that identified them as people on a mission, whether it was protection or assassination. Their black suits were neatly pressed and contrasted nicely with the stark white button-up shirts underneath. Their black ties hung from their necks and disappeared behind their jackets. Both of them wore sunglasses with red tint that flared under the fluorescent lights.

Natalie listened from behind G. She heard footsteps falling heavily on the wood floors and the unmistakable sound of a gun being cocked. Her legs shook from the adrenaline, begging her to move. She felt G's hand on her stomach, pushing her backwards.

"Slowly," he said, pointing to the stairwell door at the end of the hall. He put his finger over his lips for emphasis.

Natalie flinched when she heard the crash, the impact of a heel on wood, the splintering of her door, and the metallic clink of her failing security chain. She turned away from the ruckus and focused on the stairwell a few feet away, her mind filled with images of men with guns lying in wait behind it. On cue, the faded brass doorknob began to turn on its own and Natalie reached back to get G's attention.

They both watched as the door swung inward to reveal yet another black suit. The goon had his flashy chrome pointed up towards the ceiling, not in any position to fire. The red sunglasses hid his eyes, but G knew that if he hadn't noticed them yet, that would certainly change in the next tick of the clock.

G rushed the door and threw his entire weight against it, clipping the goon on the shoulder, and sending him spinning backwards. As he landed, his finger tightened over the trigger, sending a single bullet ricocheting down the stairs. Natalie stifled a scream at the noise, but she knew as well as G that their position had been given away. They looked at each other briefly, listening to the sounds of distant footsteps climbing the metal stairs.

"We go up," said G, kicking the goon in his side. He felt his toes compress in his Skechers; the guy's ribs were like concrete.

They climbed six flights with their rig cases thumping against their backs. Natalie marveled at her lack of fatigue. Each breath seemed to fill her up completely, each pull of her muscles only increased their strength. The only side effect seemed to be excessive sweating. As they crested the landing of the top floor, Natalie asked, "Is this safe?"

"Is what safe?"

"Feels like we're running hot."

"Of course it's not safe," said G, pausing at the next landing. In front of him was the door to the roof and he hesitated, wondering what was on the other side. "That's why there's a shutdown at the end. Not just a program exit, but a complete power-off. Comatose for at least a few hours. That's why I said we needed to find somewhere to crash soon. Otherwise," he tugged at the doorknob and then pushed, "we'll be sitting ducks."

G shielded his eyes from the bright sun that shone down from the afternoon sky. His pupils readjusted in half the time and he saw that they were on an open roof, facing the Newton Dormitories to the north, where the Castilian had been before it burned down.

"We can get onto the bookstore from here," said Natalie, rushing out from behind G. She took a right out of the door and stepped nimbly over the exposed pipes. At the edge of the roof, she stopped and looked down. "Long drop," she said casually. As G joined her, she continued, "Twelve stories all the way to the ground."

"That's a bookstore?"

"Mixed-use," replied Natalie. She pointed to the street. "The bookstore is on the first two floors. The rest is residential. Think we can make that balcony?"

"Is that our best bet?"

"Nothing's closer."

"Well," said G, climbing onto the stone rail, "let's make like frogs." He helped Natalie up and they stood together for a moment. "On my signal, we jump together."

Natalie nodded.

Behind them, the roof door slammed open against its concrete housing. They heard indiscriminate shouting and Natalie reached out to squeeze G's hand.

"One," he said, flexing his knees.

The wind from a bullet brushed against G's face, startling him.

"Go!"

G and Natalie flew through the air, twelve stories above the unforgiving pavement. The code streaming through their muscles overloaded the instruction path and managed to squeeze every last ounce of strength from their legs. G's foot clipped the balcony rail and he fell forward awkwardly. There was a loud crash as his head impacted the sliding glass door. The pain went shooting down his spine, spiking in his lower back and numbing it. *Last Dance* moved quickly through the neural pathways at the bottom of G's stack, absorbing the pain wavelength and rebroadcasting it out of phase. As it subsided, he heard Natalie cursing.

"Fucking plants!"

Her expletives were cut short by the popping of concrete around them. Bullets struck the rail almost randomly. Natalie looked over and saw G on the ground, stunned, with blood running down his face. She stumbled quickly to the broken door and ordered him to stand up.

"Don't make me drag you through the glass," she said.

G got to his knees and crawled into the apartment. Bits of glass lodged in his palm, but the pain was barely registering anymore. He was in a dark living room and as he rolled onto his back, he waited for the scream of the occupants. Luckily, they didn't seem to be home.

"Any fucking day," screamed Natalie, climbing over the coffee table and rushing for the door. "Get your ass up!" Her entire body felt like it was on fire.

There was a low moan from G's mouth as he got to his feet. His legs felt unsteady, but they carried him to the door. Out in the hallway, they moved quickly to the elevator. G leaned against the reflective doors and fell inward when the car arrived. Natalie kicked at his feet so that the doors wouldn't close on them. She hit the button for the second floor and kneeled beside her fallen comrade. The entire right side of his face was covered in a red that looked orange under the strange elevator lights.

"Ten seconds," he said, "that's all I need. There's nothing *Mary Jane* can't handle."

"Damn," said Natalie, pushing aside a clump of G's hair. "You're going to need stitches for that." She removed her t-shirt, not surprised to find her white undershirt soaked to the point of transparency. She folded the purple fabric twice and pressed it against his forehead. "Hold that there." She helped him up and he found his footing just as the doors opened on the second floor of the Co-Op.

The chattering racket of the bookstore struck them as out of place among the events of the day. Around them, eager young students milled about in front of large stacks of textbooks, class schedules in hand, trying to find a used copy of a Bio primer that wasn't too marked up. G smirked, knowing that the worst thing that would happen to them today would be the raping they took at the cash register. Even the sight of a bloody G walking down the aisles barely shook them from their concentration. They moved quickly to the back of the store and found an unlocked door heading to an employee lounge.

The break room was dimly lit and small rolls of green stickers marked *USED* were heaped in piles on every available surface.

"You're not supposed to be in here," said a weak voice from the couch.

G looked over at the scrawny boy and his Subway sandwich. He blinked some blood out of his eye and the boy said nothing more.

Natalie stepped up on the couch and pushed open the small window above it. She poked her head through and looked down into the alley. Directly below her was an open dumpster. "Convenient," said Natalie, pulling herself up with shaking arms. She folded her legs and swung them over until they were hanging outside. "Are you coming or not?" She extended her arms and found that she was only a short five or six feet above the dumpster.

As he watched her fingers disappear, G shook his head, wondering how the hell he had gotten caught up in all of this. Leave it to X to get him into one blunder after the next. And although this was not the first one to draw blood, it was definitely one of the most dangerous. His bloody fingers slipped on the windowsill. He wiped them on his pants and noticed the boy again.

"Hey, Slim, come make yourself useful."

The boy shook his head.

"Oh for fuck's sake," said G, climbing down from the couch and retrieving a box from the corner. He placed it deliberately and stared at the boy. "Don't ask me for any favors." The box helped him grasp the outside wall and with only a few tries, he was able to hoist himself up and out. It was only in the moment before he let go that he realized they had stopped on the second floor and that there was a drop to the ground below.

Natalie was standing in the middle of the alley and watching the streets on either side of them. Hundreds of similar scenes from the movies replayed in her head. At any moment, a long black car would pull up, blocking their escape. The windows would roll down and a silencer would emerge. They would be cut down in the crossfire. As their bodies writhed and shuddered, the car would speed off, spinning its tires and throwing up smoke.

A thought burst triumphantly into the forefront of Natalie's imagination. They needed to get away from the area and not be seen. The catchphrase came next. *Go underground.* Figuratively, it meant to hide out and stay off the main roads. But in Natalie's head, she was already seeing it literally as two little blips on a GPS screen moving impossibly through a wireframe grid, its two-dimensional representation not showing the fact that they were actually moving under the streets and buildings.

"Let's go," she said as G joined her.

He wiped some unknown sludge from his jacket. "Good choice, Natalie."

"Come on, we still have time."

They rushed north through the alley, pausing at the sidewalk to make sure no goons were hiding in ambush. Crossing the street, Natalie could see the steel grate ahead, discreetly hidden under boxes that were marked *Frozen Fish*.

"Do you remember what used to be here?"

G shook his head. He helped Natalie remove the boxes carefully, stacking them next to the grate in neat piles to avoid suspicion.

"This used to be Wooldridge Hall."

"And?"

"And," said Natalie, feeling relief rush over her from the unlocked grate, "all of the buildings on campus are connected by steam tunnels. I think this one is still part of the system." She pulled a section of the grate back and revealed the dark tunnel below. There was an eerie blue glow to it, but Natalie didn't hesitate to lower herself down. "X told me about these. He said they were haunted."

"X told me that he scored with you on the first night," replied G.

Natalie smiled up at G and let her response hang in the air between them unspoken. She lifted her hand as invitation.

G closed the grate behind him and pulled his rig lock from his pack. He threaded the steel cable through the bars and locked it from the inside. "Unless they're carrying bolt cutters, this should hold them for a while."

"Come on," said Natalie, "let's find a place to put down."

"I didn't bring a flashlight," said G, reluctant to step into the shadows.

Natalie looked down the tunnel at the blue light. It ran in two lines on either side, pulsing now and then as a surge traveled its lengths.

"You see that?"

G looked in the direction that Natalie was pointing. "Fiber?"

"I think we'll be okay," she said.

Together, they walked into the dim future.

THIRTY-TWO

X's wrist beeped.

Cipher in the wild.

He took a deep breath to calm the temporary anxiety. The cipher got through after all and judging by how quickly word was spreading, he had bypassed security altogether. X looked around and wondered how he had come to be trapped in a detainment construct instead of just floating through untouched. To be fair, it was likely that the cipher had inside connections. Somewhere high up on the food chain, someone gave him the keys to every door and a free pass to roam. Or maybe he was just that good.

"All operators are currently busy. Please wait for the next available security officer."

X looked up at the expanse of black sky to see where the voice was coming from, but it was either too dark or undefined. The construct felt very simple, a small island of light on a black plane. He stood in the crosshairs, dead even between all four spotlights, and waited. There was time to wait, time to sit and think about everything that had happened so far. And then there was the new feeling inside of X, of something not right about the fabric of the Net. He got hints of it as he tried to interact with the construct. Pieces of it responded to his pressure, others did not. And on the inside, an ongoing feeling of something unraveling.

He did his best to hold it together. Unchecked growth of his power was something he was not looking forward to. He had seen it before, in C, in the way she changed from a sweet girl to a vengeful enemy, drunk with power. It also had other implications that X was unwilling to accept, especially the one that said his consciousness was no longer connected to his body. Though Anela had told him that he was a copy of his own mind, he still felt the link between his digital self and physical corpse. Then again, he had never felt it any other way. The situation had the potential to turn him into a monster like C and to disappoint Natalie when she found out that X was truly dead and gone.

"I don't feel dead," said X, thinking out loud. "If anything, I feel better than I ever have. Six billion dollars better."

Maybe that was how it started, a gradual feeling of self-worth that births an egomaniacal lunatic with a God complex. X shook his head, tried to expel the possible consequences of things that were no longer under his control. Whether he was a copy or not, whether his body still breathed and pumped, there were really only two missions left. Anela had to be stopped. Natalie and G had to be protected.

"Will you come with me, please?"

X turned to find a young woman staring back at him, standing in front of a door that had not been there before. She was dressed in one of those business suits for women, with a skirt that stopped above her knees instead of pants. Her hair was arranged in a bun with a single wooden stick protruding sideways. Something in her eyes told X that while she looked fragile and feminine, she was carrying her own arsenal of painful implements under those ruby lips. She stepped aside as X approached and followed him through the newly created door.

The adjoining hallway was bathed in a soothing orange glow that bled down from the ceiling to the white tile floor. Both the ceiling and walls were bare, devoid of decorations and lighting. The hallway seemed to extend on forever, a trick of the eyes or very clever programming. X's escort led him from behind, giving him instructions now and then, sending him left or right down an identical hallway. He tried to mark every change in direction, but even the angles between the hallways seemed random. Their footsteps echoed briefly, but there was no other sound and they passed no one.

"Am I the only one stupid enough to get caught?"

The escort held her reply until X looked back at her. "The number of people detained and the frequency of such events is private information not normally shared with criminals."

"Is that a yes or a no?"

"You have the right to remain silent. I suggest you use it."

"Fair enough," said X. "I like the construct you've got going on here. It's very sterile. The burnt orange isn't bad either. I go to UT, you know."

"Went. Most colleges have strict policies against enrolling convicted felons."

"This is a felony?"

"Computer espionage. Willful destruction of private property. Seditious activity involving known terrorists."

"Sedition?!" X pitched his voice comically high.

"I could give you the definition if you'd like."

X stopped dead in his tracks and looked over his shoulder at the woman. "Are you a real person? I mean, are you jacked in somewhere and controlling this avatar? You don't sound like an AI, but I can't imagine how someone with a stick so far up their ass could survive in the real world, medically speaking."

The escort put her palm against his shoulder to push him forward. X felt it as a searing pain that he struggled to mask. Just as it was about to surge, X wrapped something around it, smothered it in unrecognizable code. The pain left him completely with no aftereffects whatsoever. He tried to understand what he had just done, tried to pinpoint what part of him had reached out and devoured those signals so effortlessly. Then he realized that it wasn't important how he had done it as whether he could repeat it.

He stopped again. "I'm no doctor, but for a nominal fee, I'd be willing to yank that stick right out of there. What do you say?"

Her palm struck him again in the same spot. Before she even removed her hand, the pain was absorbed completely. X smiled to himself and trudged forward.

"Last left," said the escort.

X turned and found a gray door blocking his path. Written in block letters on the left side were the numbers one, zero, one.

The escort stepped in front of him and opened the door. She motioned with her arm. "Please wait in here."

"Are you not coming in?"

"Sadly, our time has run out."

"Well, my offer still stands. You know where to find me." X winked.

This time, she didn't move at all, but X saw the ripples bend the light surrounding her face. The concussion wave hit his whole body at once and pushed him several feet into the room. Although he locked down the pain, he was still surprised to see so much power from such a petite frame. A sliver of respect implanted itself in his mind, made him wonder how good you had to be to become an escort in whatever facility this was. Obviously, they hired only the best.

"Please have a seat," said a thick Slavic voice from behind him. X wheeled around and found a gray-haired man sitting behind a metal desk in an uncomfortable looking chair.

"Christ on a candle, do you people ever knock?"

"*Sit* down," repeated the man, his voice lower this time. On the desk in front of him, a vidscreen was embedded in the silver surface. It was showing X's face, scanned from the detainment construct no doubt. It was eerie to look at, rotating in stuttered movements to the left and then back.

X took the chair in front of him. It had a torn red cushion with yellow padding showing through. As he sat, the privacy filter obscured his view of the vidscreen, making it appear as an opaque black rectangle on the desk.

"I am Director in Charge Vasyl Fedkovych," said the man, pushing on the wire bridge of his glasses.

"Nice to meet you, DIC."

Fedkovych grunted. "Yes," he said, "and who are you?"

"I'm just a man who's wondering why you're wearing glasses in here. Don't you have virtual vision insurance?"

"I have all the time in the world, sir. This construct runs several times less than real, so sooner or later your body is going to give out. The sooner you cooperate, the sooner you can return to your physical existence, and then to jail. If you continue to resist, you may very well die."

That's what you think, thought X. "I am The Sultan of Synth, leader of the worldwide resistance, and last great hope of mankind."

"And your friends?"

"Also freedom fighters. The female is a munitions expert, specializing in destructive viral code. The male is my second in command, my sometimes lover, and is responsible for the distribution of propaganda."

Fedkovych scribbled with his finger on the vidscreen. "And what do you call your organization?"

"We haven't really come up with a name."

"And who are you fighting against?"

"Who you got?"

The scribbling stopped. Fedkovych flattened his palm and wiped across the screen, clearing his notes. He sat back in his chair and put a hand to his cheek, rubbing away some real-world toothache that seemed to be intruding into the simulation.

X performed a similar action, reclining as much as he could against the steel backing. He slid a hand into the front of his pants and waited.

"It seems that we are at a stalemate," said Fedkovych, raising a dismissive hand.

"It looks that way," replied X. "As much as you want to sit there and think you've got something on me, I know full well that you have no idea who I am, have no way to track me when I leave, and no way of enforcing any of the penalties you think I deserve. Do I have that right?"

The director nodded, cocking his head to the side. "Yes, all of that would be true if you had hacked into Bank of America or the U.S. Treasury or a similar institution. Perhaps you do not realize whose yard you have treaded upon?"

The slightest lump formed in X's throat and then receded. He could tell what Fedkovych was going to say just from the way his lips pinched inward.

"Vinestead International does not look kindly on intrusions."

"Vinestead doesn't look kindly on anything but profits and exploiting the proletariat. No wonder you're wearing glasses. They don't care about the little people like you and me."

"I can assure you that your propaganda is wasted on me, sir. Vinestead has restored our economy in a time when your United States has turned a blind eye to the plight of the rest of the world. It is my duty and honor to serve."

"Is everyone from the backwoods of Kiev so easy to brainwash?"

A look of confusion swept over Fedkovych's face. Similarly, something surged through X and spread a nervous feeling throughout his body.

"How could you know that?"

X held his head steady, not wanting to admit the fact that he had no idea how he pulled that information from Fedkovych's avatar. It was just in staring at the man's face, watching the lines dance with his words, that the squiggly shape of the Ukraine appeared like an inset in X's periphery. Square in the center of it was a dot marked *Kiev*. As the image faded, he saw unease in the face of his interrogator.

"Luci, we're ready for you in Interrogation Room Five." He was looking directly at X, though he spoke as if into an intercom.

"I'm already here," replied X. "And don't call me Lucy." He figured he must have really rattled Fedkovych, as the man didn't smile at all. Or perhaps that joke had not reached the Ukraine yet. X heard the door open behind him and was thankful for the virtual reproduction of a squeaking sound. A moment later, the woman who would be Luci came into view. She was dressed in black pants and a white shirt. Dark blue suspenders held up her pants and rested on the sides of her breasts. The look on her face was enticing and X felt the butterflies begin to stir.

"This is Lucienne Shumeyko," said Fedkovych, "cipher security for sector seven. She is the one that apprehended your accomplices."

"Shumeyko? I've heard that name before." He looked her up and down. "Cipher, huh? That's a shame."

"And why is that?" Luci sat down next to Fedkovych. A chair appeared beneath her with impeccable timing.

"Because if your real body looks anything like that, it's going to waste in stasis."

Luci glanced at Fedkovych, who shrugged his eyebrow in passive agreement. "What I choose to do with my body is not your concern."

"Of course," said X, "you're a woman. You're entitled."

"Luci tells me that your accomplices managed to infiltrate and navigate six sectors of our defenses. I would like you to tell me how you did it."

"I don't know anything about that."

"How did you arrive in detainment?" Luci leaned forward and put her hands on the desk. "No one reported your presence in any of the sectors."

"Yes," agreed Fedkovych. "Explain that."

"I can't," said X. "I honestly don't know how I got here. I was just walking along, on my way to church, actually. I had just come from working at a soup kitchen and tutoring disabled kids. In fact," he paused to look at his wrist, "if I don't hurry, I'm going to miss blind gymnastics."

The air compressed slightly as a clear partition rose up from the center of the desk, bisecting the room. X watched Luci and Fedkovych motion to each other and to him, but their words were muffled and unintelligible. X smirked, taking the time to appreciate the novelty. Although he felt relaxed, he realized that his internal clock was yelling at him, screaming for his attention. Very little time had passed subjectively, yet he couldn't shake the feeling that things were moving much faster on the outside. He began to wonder if Natalie and G had made it out, whether they were safe or perhaps bleeding to death on the floor of her apartment. The image flashed in his mind, and he destroyed it quickly, shunned it to the file store of unthinkable things, primed for disposal.

X focused his eyes on Luci's lips, partly out of idle fantasy, partly to try to decipher what she was saying. Strangely enough, he could almost see the partition wavering in his line of sight, as if he were boring a hole through it. The ripples were tinged in blue and bright enough to be seen if either of them looked over. X tried to pull back, but the partition was already coming apart in his mind and a half-second later, it came down in an invisible crash. Unseen pieces clinked and clattered on the desk and floor. His interrogators were immediately drawn out of their argument.

"Sorry," said X, "I guess I don't know my own strength."

"You're pushing your luck," said Fedkovych, snarling.

"What luck? You said it yourself; no one detected me in any of your sectors. So that means I was never there."

"Or you avoided detection," suggested Luci.

"And what do you think a jury is going to believe? That I, a mild-mannered, God-fearing, young Republican broke through your advanced security, not once, but *six* times? Or that I simply wasn't there and ended up in detainment by some fluke of code that randomly plucks innocent people from their daily lives? That could be grounds for a civil suit, if I'm not mistaken. How many times have you done this before? However many it is, I'm sure they went unreported."

Fedkovych put his hand up to silence X. "You are being detained because you are a witness in an ongoing investigation. You aided and abetted the escape of two suspects. Any jury in the country will convict you of obstruction of justice, though you will most likely be tried in a Vinestead-owned subsidiary court and I can assure you, your conviction will be the most pleasant part of the process."

X was tuning out, his attention focused on the corner of the room to his right. While Fedkovych was going through his spiel, a small circle had sparked into existence at the intersection of the walls and was growing steadily outward.

"I thought," said X, stopping quickly. His voice triggered a reaction in the new growth. Its perimeter seemed to sparkle gold, leaving behind a rusty film. "I thought that," he said again, watching with fascination as the growth sped up, shot several inches in all directions.

By now, the interrogators had noticed X's distracted stare, and they turned to see what was so interesting. Luci moved first, backing up into Fedkovych and almost knocking him out of his chair. The sound seemed to attract the growth, and it sped along the floor to the base of the desk.

"Containment in IR Five," yelled Fedkovych. He touched his wrist and pixilated.

"He cut and run on you kind of quick, huh?"

Luci glared at X, then back at the entity that she had already identified as a virus. It was eating away at the construct and anyone trapped inside would be eaten away as well. She took three soundless steps backwards and bumped against the wall. Raising her wrist, she turned to X and whispered, "Looks like we can skip the trial and go right to execution." She pixilated out.

X watched the virus with awe. It was moving so effortlessly over everything. Inside, he was thinking, that's what you get when you hire Ukrainians to do security. When the virus climbed the table and surged towards him, he decided it was as good a time as any to leave.

The door to Interrogation Room Five gave way easily in the wake of X's newfound strength. He ran down the endless maze of hallways at random, changing directions several times, never repeating to avoid circling back. Not once did he pass another door; they must have been hidden by some code. Walk the correct sequence of hallways and a door will appear. Walk the wrong sequence and it would just keep going forever. Finally, X decided to keep going straight, move as fast as he could, perhaps overload the construct and make it run out of memory.

The orange walls began to blur as X reached his top speed; his legs were barely touching the ground anymore. It was like floating in place with the world moving beneath him, a technique he had picked up from Jape, who was under the impression that the virtual world existed for the sole purpose of their manipulation. "Be in the Net," he had said, "but not *of* the Net. The X not move for the Net. The Net move for the X."

X felt the new feeling swelling inside of him again and his imagination painted patterns on the walls streaking past. Ahead of him in the infinite distance, he imagined a rift opening, spilling blue-green neon into the hallway. It seemed to move away from him at the same speed he approached, but with a little concentration, he was able to reach out and grab it with his mind, slow it down and make it stationary. He moved towards it with impossible speed, uncaring if the virus was still tailing him, unsure if it could even operate on such an extreme level.

All he knew was that he believed in the rift ahead, believed that it was a portal to his homedir. And somehow, he felt that that was going to be enough to make it work. His mind grasped at the fleeting lucidity, felt the fringe of some important truth hanging in the nothing, but lost it. Still, the rift grew, and the distance closed.

X shut his eyes. His homedir would be on the other side. There was no other way to see it. Home. Safety. Natalie.

Upon impact with the rift, X heard the crackling of static in his ears, felt his body pull and stretch from front to back. He twisted in space, turned to watch the rift accelerate away from him. Through it, he could see the endless hallway, orange tinged with rust, the virus speeding ever closer.

He reached out with his mind again, closed an invisible fist around the tear in virtual space, and crushed it in his hand. When he opened it, the individual pixels floated off, unconnected, unable to provide entrance for his pursuers, viral or otherwise.

THIRTY-THREE

Natalie was stuck in a memory loop, reliving the same few scenes over and over again. She was back at the dorms, watching X shake and moan in his rig, doing whatever it was he did when he jacked in to see C. He was hacking her e-mail, he was taking her on a cruise, and he was going to shut her down. His time in the rig passed quickly for Natalie and her mind focused only on those moments when he was jacked out. How many times had she pulled the rig from his face after one of his visits with C? How often had she looked at that face and seen love despite his lingering obsession with his girlfriend? It was a world unknown to her, a private paradise that he shared only with C.

Yet the memory felt wrong somehow, corrupted since their separation. Instead of X's face, it was G that she saw emerging from the tangle of cables and LEDs. It was his smile that evoked the feeling deep inside of her, tempted her to forgo the memory and redirect it into fantasy. She had him naked and towering over her when the pain in her back finally pulled her from exhaustion.

She woke with a start and arched her back to relieve the stress. Something in her lap moved and she looked down to see G's head resting there, her purple shirt wrapped around it as a makeshift bandage. His forehead was coated in a black liquid, red turned blue from the dense fiber cables running above them. Natalie looked up and saw the great intersection of hundreds of cables, heading off down the tunnels, disappearing into the distance.

"Hey," she said, shaking G's shoulder. He moaned again and smacked his lips. "Wake up." Natalie checked her wrist. They had been out for over five hours. Though she usually tried to get her full eight hours every night, Natalie felt almost refreshed and revitalized. "It's already three," she said, still shaking G.

"I was having the most wonderful dream," said G, lifting his head and sitting up. He rubbed at the side of his neck, massaged away some pain.

Natalie asked herself if she had been doing the same, unable to confirm one way or the other.

"We had these new kind of rigs, I don't even know if they had names. But they were awesome. Instead of putting us in the Net, they just drew all over the real world. Like, on-the-fly air brushing."

Natalie looked over at G with a slight smile. "Someone already did that. X showed me a demo last fall."

"Great minds think alike," suggested G.

"I guess." Natalie looked at the floor of the tunnel, to the bits of plastic and tie-wraps. "That's pretty creepy though. X said he had a dream about it too."

"We sit in a lot of the same circles. Probably picked it up on the Net."

Natalie shook her head, waited for her mind to get over the coincidence and return to the original line of thinking. There was something she was supposed to be doing, some important goal that was as yet unattained.

"We should get moving," she said, reaching for her rig pack. "I want to get jacked in as soon as possible." X flashed across her mind, the old him merged with the last time she had seen him. Covered in shadow, standing taller than he used to. "Did you notice anything different about X?"

"Like what?" G was looking up, tracing the fibers across the tangled nexus.

"I don't know. He just seemed off. I can't explain it."

G chuckled. "You know how much he loves the Net. He was probably just shocked to be back in it after so long. I've never known him to spend more than a few days jacked out. Someone made him go for months. That couldn't have been easy."

"Anela," said Natalie, correcting his ambiguity.

"Yeah, her." His eyes found a conduit leading towards the surface, hidden by the tangle of fibers. He stood up to examine it. "If I know anything about X, he'd want some kind of retribution against her."

"Me too."

"You too," repeated G. "But you know as well as I do that you wouldn't stand a chance against her on the battlefield. I don't think even X would go up against her ciphers. I know I wouldn't."

The conduit was a dull white PC tube, sealed at the concrete by yellow putty. Written along the side in permanent marker was the tag SER 319. G ran the list of campus buildings in his head, tried to recall the map he'd memorized his first few days at school. There was no building called SER. He kneeled at his rig pack and searched for his code cube.

"What are you doing," asked Natalie, suddenly feeling pressure in her abdomen.

"There's a pipe leading up," explained G. "It goes to a building called SER, but I don't remember seeing that one on the map. I'm going to look it up."

Natalie stood and shook her pants back into position. "Well, be quick about it, I'm going to take a walk."

"I don't think you should go wandering alone. God knows what else is crawling around down here."

"I've got my GPS. Besides, I need a little privacy."

"Why?" G looked confused.

"Because I have to pee, alright? Couldn't you just let me go around the corner?"

"Oh," said G, slightly flustered, "yeah, go ahead."

Natalie feigned a curtsey. "Thank you, your highness."

The cube was in one of the pack's lower pockets and G pulled it out as Natalie disappeared around a bend. He heard her footsteps fall a few more times and then stop. Crossing his legs, he attached the electrode to his neck and jacked into his own personal library. After a quick semantic search, he found himself floating over the two-tone map of the UT campus, tilting out in front of him to give an idea of the distance between the buildings. He used the data from his GPS to show his position on the map and found that he was under a building marked KLB. Another search told him that the building was only fifteen years old and that it was constructed on the site of the former Services building. He jacked out and let his imagination linger on the map, moving the buildings around and stepping backwards through history.

"Well, that was an experience," said Natalie, rejoining him.

"I figured it out," he said triumphantly. He pointed to the conduit. "See this? It says SER. That's for Services building. It used to be right above us."

"What's there now?"

"Accounting, I think. It has something to do with UT System, the guys who run all of the different institutions. There used to be a NOC in that building that provided connectivity for all of the other UT campuses, but they moved it to the Computation Center near the Main Building a while back."

"I don't remember seeing that."

"Most people don't notice it," said G. "It's hidden under the east stairs, between Hogg and Garrison.

Natalie shook her head slightly, casually informing G that she was not interested in a history lesson.

"The point is that I think they moved the NOC, but never got around to moving most of the cables. They probably just left all of the connections jumpered upstairs. Encased in the drywall, I don't know. But these fibers are inside the local firewall."

His last words lit a spark behind Natalie's eyes. "We can patch in!"

"We can do a needlecast, but it won't be enough bandwidth to jack in. The best I could do is a virtual terminal and that won't get us to X's homedir. We might be able to send him a text, but that's about it."

"Dammit!" Natalie picked up her rig pack and slung it around her shoulders. "Let's go already. Maybe we can check into a hotel or something. I'm sure they have enough bandwidth to get us in."

G smiled, his mind racing. "Oh shit! I just had the greatest idea ever! Quick, give me your viewee. You brought it right?"

"Of course," said Natalie, reaching behind her and pulling the silver viewee from its pouch. At the same time, she snagged something soft and pulled a red ribbon out as well. She flashed back to the cafeteria, to X pushing the polished vidscreen across the table and apologizing.

G retrieved a thin cable from his pack. It had a syringe-like connector on one end. "Here, plug this into your viewee. I'll see if I can find us a good vein." G tapped on the blue fibers, fully expecting them to react to his touch. The light inside did nothing but continue to flow. He inserted the needle into one of the fibers, careful not to break the glass thread inside. The transceiver on the needle began to flash amber, then green. A moment later, the media converter repeated the same sequence and G knew that they were in.

"Here," said Natalie, handing G the viewee.

They waited as it booted up and found an IP address. G brought up the touchscreen keyboard and a terminal. He began to type furiously, trying to ignore the pain in his fingers.

"So what's your idea," asked Natalie.

"Same as yours, but I think we can do better than the Budget Inn on Rundberg."

"I don't think we should go too far from Old Downtown. If something goes wrong, I want to be able to walk over and punch that Anela bitch in the face."

"Exactly," said G, "that's why I think we should get a suite at the Austonian."

Natalie laughed. "Even at Old Downtown prices, we could never afford a suite. See if there's a Best Western south of the river."

"Oh, my dear Natalie, if there's one thing that I've tried to teach you in our short time together, it's that only suckers pay for things. I charge a thousand dollars for an info pack that these kids could assemble themselves with only a few hours work. But are people willing to put in the effort? No. They just throw down their money and let someone else to the legwork. Then they come to a situation where their money is no good or not enough and what do they do then?"

"Fine, we'll stay at a La Quinta."

"They give up! They give up because they have no idea how to attain the unattainable. Nobody ever got everything they wanted by playing by the rules. We're getting that suite, make that the Presidential Suite, or my name isn't Reginald Townsend."

"It isn't," reminded Natalie.

"No?" G shrugged. "That's too bad, because Mr. Townsend has a reservation at the Austonian this afternoon. His favorable financial history has entitled him to a free upgrade to Executive service." The typing stopped. "It would be a shame if he didn't show up."

Natalie let her eyes wander over G's face. He looked like he had just come out on the wrong end of a fight. They would take one look at him and lock the doors.

"You let me worry about that," he said, noticing her stare.

They walked the tunnels to the other side of campus and called a cab as they passed under the stadium. When they emerged in the alley behind RecSports, a Roy's Taxi chariot was already waiting to shuttle them to Old Downtown. The sun felt jarringly warm and bright on their pink eyes. Natalie couldn't help but notice the looks from the passing students, out living their lives as if the world weren't crumbling beneath them.

"Second and Congress," said G, as they climbed into the cab. He looked past Natalie to the people outside. "Can you black these windows?"

"Si," said the driver. He pressed a button on his dash and the windows darkened with a quiet electronic hum.

Natalie sunk into her seat, the most comfortable she had been in a while. In front of her, an LCD shone brightly in the darkened cab. The news was on and the anchorwoman was gesturing excitedly. Natalie pressed the volume button next to the screen.

"And I'm sure most people are wondering what exactly a cipher is. To shed some light on this subject, we have our resident technology expert, John Faber."

A middle-aged man appeared, dressed in a brown suit with matching glasses. "Thank you, Judy. We've all heard the rumors. People are being snatched off the street and brainwashed into serving as digital indentured servants for some masked villain intent on terrorizing the world. But how much of that is fact and how much is just the idle rambling of some bad science fiction writer? In our CBS42 exclusive investigation, we heard from several people that say that not only do ciphers exist, but that some people see cipherhood as a preferable way of life."

"They must have one hell of a pamphlet," said G.

"So what exactly does a cipher do," asked Judy from the studio.

"A cipher is like a programmer, but much like my kids Jake and Colt, they spend all of their time jacked in. In fact, once a cipher goes in, they very rarely ever come out."

"So what are we to make of this warning that's been showing up on everything from billboards to the Wall Street ticker in Times Square? Is this all some elaborate hoax or a terrorist plot?"

"Well, Judy, my sources tell me that there are several interpretations for a message of this type. One says it could be a general warning, a modern day fox is in the henhouse sort of thing. But my personal favorite is what a young man said to me just a few minutes ago. According to him, every time you jack into the Net, you are bound by a digital tether to your body. It's a safety feature that keeps your mind from escaping your brain."

"And haven't we all wanted to do that," asked Judy, laughing.

"Of course, of course," said John. "Now, having a cipher in the Net is no big deal, since they usually carry out corporate espionage and stuff like that." John made air quotes, not really believing his own words. "But for a cipher to be in the wild, it means that it is in the Net without a tether. With no body."

"A ghost in the machine," asked Judy, feeling clever.

"Exactly. Well," said John, hamming it up for the camera, "if you have a ghost, but don't want to play host, who you gonna call?"

"Fucking sheep," said Natalie, hitting the mute button again. "You think they're talking about X?"

"I don't know. Ciphers give off a very distinct scent. I don't think anyone willing to put that message out would make that kind of mistake."

"What if there really is a cipher on the loose?"

"It's not very likely. You can't just copy a human consciousness."

Natalie nodded absently, lost in thought.

"Estamos aquí, señor," said the driver.

G slid his card through the slot on the backseat and punched out ten dollars for a tip.

When they were standing on the curb looking up at the skyscraping Austonian, the last bastion of civility in Old Downtown, Natalie once again noticed G's appearance. She did her best to wipe away the blood. It made his hair shine.

"They're never gonna let us check in," she reiterated.

"Don't worry about that, just follow my lead."

They walked in together, stepping between the automatic glass doors as they parted for the hotel's newest guests. Instead of taking a left towards the check-in counter where two young women stood with headsets, they veered right towards a row of ACMs.

"Fifty-five stories," said G, "with fifteen to twenty rooms on each floor." He motioned to the women. "You think two chicks could check in that many people all by themselves?" He punched his confirmation code and fake account number into the check-in machine. The LCD glowed, thanking them for choosing the historic Austonian. Two magcards dropped into the retrieval slot. G took them out and handed one to Natalie. "I'm so glad we're finally getting a hotel room together."

Natalie pursed her lips, considered the prospect for a moment, but ultimately turned and headed for the elevators, careful to avoid making eye contact with the concierge. There were seven elevators, but only one was marked with the numbers fifty through fifty-five. Natalie pressed the call button and waited as G joined her.

Behind them, the concierge approached, and Natalie caught sight of him in her periphery. She leaned over quickly and placed her lips at the base of G's earlobe. Tugging on it, she let her hand wander to his waist and spread her fingers over his back pocket. Her eyes locked with the concierge. He stopped, considered the scene for a moment, and retreated. Natalie winked at him.

Once they were safely inside the elevator and speeding upwards, G said, "I didn't know you cared."

Natalie wiped her lips and smiled awkwardly.

"Aw shit," said G, feeling a trickle of blood start down the side of his head. "I'm falling apart."

"Maybe we can get bandages with room service."

It turned out the Austonian staff were more than happy to provide anything that their Presidential Suite residents desired. A scrawny boy in a tuxedo rolled the cart into the room as G was undressing in the bathroom. Natalie thanked him and told him to charge fifty bucks to the room. She picked up a turkey sandwich and began to eat it as she examined the bounty. A combination lunch and dinner had been their first priority, as both of their stomachs had been rumbling since they came out of their comas.

Natalie chose the sandwich while G ordered an oversized hamburger. The aroma of the fries made her wish that she had gotten the same. Also on the cart were boxes of bandages, some gauze, and tweezers. Two cans of Blue Rain sat in a bucket of ice, chilled, with water condensing on the outside. She could already taste the sweet sugary liquid on her tongue.

G growled from the bathroom. "Fucking glass! Glass in my knees, glass in my hands, glass in my ass!"

Natalie took a large bite and picked up the medical supplies in one hand and the plate of fries in the other. "Here," she said, walking into the bathroom. It was the size of her entire apartment. "Chew on these while I patch you up."

He was sitting on the edge of the marble bathtub in his boxer shorts, trying to brush away slivers of glass from his palms. He held them up.

"Oh," said Natalie. She set the plate down beside him and fished a few fries from the stack. "Open," she said.

His eyes lit up at the taste of potato and vegetable oil. He giggled like a child.

Natalie took his hand and sat down, examining his palm. She used the tweezers to pluck the shards from his skin; most of them were small and hard to see. Occasionally, she used a glass to scoop water from the tub and wash away the blood. It made G wince each time she did it, but he made no protest. He was shoving fries into his mouth as fast as he could chew and swallow.

"That's right," said Natalie, "don't even think about the pain." She stood up and stepped between his legs so that she could examine his head. The blood was caked on a small gash a few inches from his hairline. She used the gauze to wipe away the excess and at the same time cleared away some of the dirt that had accumulated during their escape. His hair was soft between her fingers but smelled horrible. He was going to need a shower before she could put on the bandage anyway.

G watched Natalie's breasts under her white shirt as they dangled in front of his eyes. There was the occasional discomfort in his scalp, but he was completely distracted by the show in front of him. He felt the overwhelming urge to reach out and touch her, maybe not on her chest, but on her hip, draw her closer, kiss her stomach. The shiny silver button on her jeans taunted him, begged his hands to reach out and undo the clasp. He would have to work to get her pants down, as tight as they were.

"Come on," said Natalie. "I need to wash your hair. There's too much crap in there to put a bandage on." She pulled G to his feet by the wrist and led him into the glass-encased shower. It was the size of her closet, she noted.

"You can't put shampoo on there, it'll burn."

"What are you, a baby?" She pushed him inside and reached up to point the showerhead against the wall. The water whined as it started up but calmed down as the pipes heated behind the tile. "Fine, I'll just rinse it. I'm gonna have to put some alcohol on it, and that's going to burn."

"Fuck," said G, feeling the warm water on his wound.

Natalie moved closer to help him, put a hand on his head to partition the water away. "Dammit," said Natalie, backing out. She hesitated for a moment. "Close your eyes," she commanded. When G had obeyed, she reached down and removed her socks and shoes. Her pants were already damp from the spray, and she wondered whether she'd need new ones as she pushed them down her legs.

She stepped into the shower carefully, the warm water splashing over her toes. G was still facing the wall and Natalie put her hand on his shoulder to get him to kneel slightly. She tried her best to keep the water off his cut, but it had a way of bending around her fingers and stinging G. When the blood was washed away, she brushed the cut lightly with her index finger, scraping away the scar tissue that was already beginning to accumulate. The gash was more than an inch long but was very narrow. Natalie sighed, relieved; the wound would probably close without stitches, though it wasn't going to be pretty.

"Alright," she said, "you're done."

"Can't I do you?"

"I can take care of myself, thank you very much. You need to put some gauze on and wrap yourself up. Think you can manage that?" Natalie reached down and pushed the dial to the left, making the water hotter.

"Fine," said G, stepping out of the shower, dripping on the tile. He grabbed a towel from the rack and draped it over his shoulders. Air rushed over his skin as the shower door closed behind him and a second later, he heard two wet slaps. With a glance backwards, he noticed Natalie's shirt and underwear hanging over the top of the glass. She was standing with her back to him and her face buried in the stream of water. G tried not to let his eyes linger, but he couldn't help but track the lines of water running down her back. He turned away as his excitement began to build, moved to the sink to examine his wound in the mirror. The gauze felt soft against his scalp, and he secured it with a bandage, wrapping a long line from the top of his head to his chin.

"Your food is getting cold," called Natalie from the shower. Her voice had softened considerably.

"If you want me to leave, just say so."

"Why would I want you to leave? It's nothing you haven't seen before."

"I don't know," said G, tightening the bandage and applying the clasps. "With X being back and all…" He lacked the words to finish his thought.

"He's going to appreciate everything you did for me. But he doesn't need to know exactly what you did, does he?"

"It was easier to say that when I didn't think he'd be back."

Natalie paused a moment, closed her eyes, and let the water stream down her face. Pulling back, she said, "Life has a way of doing that to you. All I know is that I want to see him again. I have to."

G paused at the door, looking back at the fogging glass and Natalie's shadowy frame beyond it. "I'll get our rigs ready." He touched the side of his head. "I don't know how I'm going to get it on over this."

The shower door opened, and Natalie stuck her head out. "Oh my God, what did you do?"

"You said to wrap it!"

Natalie laughed. "I'm almost done, I'll fix it for you."

"Then I'm going to eat my damn burger."

"And get the rigs ready."

"Yeah, that too." G closed the bathroom door behind him and walked over to the vidscreen on the wall. He pressed the call button next to it and a moment later a virtual concierge appeared.

"What can I do for you," it asked.

G typed his order onto the screen, requesting new clothes for the both of them and estimating Natalie's sizes. He also ordered a baseball cap to hide his bandage and another burger.

"Thank you for staying at the Austonian," said the concierge as G's order faded from the blue screen.

He returned to the cart, pulled a Blue Rain from the ice bucket, and popped it open. A satisfied *ahh* filled the room. G set about removing the rigs from their packs, arranging them neatly on the sofa. He brought extra pillows from the bedroom and dumped them next to Natalie's rig. She liked to be comfortable when she went in. It was one of her quirks.

G finished his drink and crushed the can in his hand.

THIRTY-FOUR

It was like walking into an unfamiliar neighborhood only to gradually recognize bits and pieces of it. There was the way that the streetlamps rose from the sidewalks, extended over the street, and then shone down with an orange glow that filled countless childhood nights. There were also the familiar shapes of the houses, now repainted, and the yards, now landscaped by a different set of hands. It was all the same building blocks trapped under a different veneer, but seeing the underlying code was the only way to know for sure.

X walked down the virtual street, a white stripe that extended and curved in the distance. Instead of houses, he saw the rounded edges of the homedir cubes jutting out into their black lawns. One didn't normally walk around the outside of a homedir, but X had done it once or twice to examine the architecture. Now, he couldn't recall whether the ghostly images he saw hidden behind the gray walls were the same ones he had seen back then or if new occupants had taken up shop within. He caught glimpses of posters, furniture, and people moving inside their gray tombs. A few times, he saw the glow of a transfer column and envied the user's freedom. A thought was circling his mind; what if I jack out and I'm still at Anela's?

The uniformity of the homedir containment construct was absolute. They extended in all directions; peering over the side would show them descending in columns and wrapping under as they circled the core. The white roads ran between them, stacked on top of each other with twenty feet of clearance. It reminded X of a fully populated corncob except that each kernel was grayish white instead of yellow. And like the corn from the pre-engineering era, it was dotted with the occasional black kernel, uninitialized homedirs and unused portals. He counted fifteen in his line of sight and wondered why those users had chosen not to return to the Net.

Ahead, X saw a homedir that was not gray or black but glowing with green. The closer he got, the more he recognized the adjacent kernels. To the left was a wall painted with graffiti art, backwards and indecipherable. To the right was a wall tinged with pink from the multitude of rosy objects within: a couch pushed up against the outer wall, flanked by two end tables with vases and roses. It was his homedir that was glowing. An instruction floated down into his stomach and told it to tighten up, spew the virtual acid, and make X feel like he was hungry and nauseated all at once. But instead of dread, he was filled with anger, delivered via tremors to his extremities. He increased his pace and stepped out onto the sidewalk when it appeared.

Something was moving behind the wall of his homedir. Never before had neon green appeared so menacing, writhing under the surface of the skin, consuming everything inside.

Inside.

X moved his face closer, tried to see through the tangled mess. Somewhere beyond the virus, he was in there, sitting, waiting.

"I sense him, too," said the cipher, walking up the path. "That is to say, I can feel you in there as well as out here."

X eyed the cipher warily and backed away from him.

"At first," he continued, "I thought that you had come back here and barricaded yourself in." He placed a hand on the homedir wall; the virus surged beneath it. "But then I got a glimpse of this virus and couldn't believe that you would be capable of creating it. Even I wouldn't know where to begin with this, at least not yet."

"How do you know I'm not in there? Maybe I'm another copy. Don't you think I'd be smart enough to make multiple copies of myself, keep you chasing clones until I found a way to take out Anela?"

"I considered that, briefly," admitted Lio, "but surely you can feel the difference between the two of you? Put your hand on the wall, it's easier that way. Don't worry, I believe this is only a containment virus."

"The wall is permeable only to me," said X. "If I put my hand on it and it goes through, end of story."

"I calculate a seventy-five percent chance that curiosity will get the better of you in under fifteen seconds." Lio smiled smugly.

X couldn't get over how strange the cipher looked with his glasses extending from his eyebrows. They seemed to cut back into his face, just above his cheeks, the skin moving over them awkwardly. Physically, he seemed to be a little bigger than X, stood just a little bit taller, spoke with a little more bass in his voice. X was used to seeing inflated avatars, usually steered by skinny teenagers, but with the cipher, it seemed that he was pulling everything in, making his avatar tight and smooth. Even his reflective clothing seemed to diminish his form, blurring out the edges between cipher and construct.

It took eighteen seconds, but finally X put his hand on the wall. At first, the virus sparkled beneath his fingers, tightening its spiraling movement around the shape of his hand. Whatever was slithering around in there was excited by his presence, spent several tense seconds trying to reach him, and then ultimately gave up, resumed its circling of the homedir. Soon, X began to feel an awareness grow in the forefront of his mind. He couldn't tell if he was seeing his homedir or simply recalling it from memory, but it appeared in front of him clearly. Everything was as he remembered, chairs and dressers and a brightly colored transfer column.

There was a dark spot near the middle of the room, a shadow without a body to cast it. X's brain focused in on it, drew closer, and realized that he was looking at himself. It felt like nothing at all, no emotion or feeling that he could separate from the everyday instructions coursing through his mind. They were alike in every way, except for one, and X struggled to understand it, to reverse engineer the situation and find the source of it. His prisoner-self had a viewee in his lap and was tracing his finger on the screen. X recognized the gesture, had done it a thousand times with pictures of girls he had loved and lost. Moving closer, he was surprised to find that although it was a picture, it was not of Natalie, but of C.

Lio narrowed his eyes behind his light-absorbing lenses and gestured to the wall. "The guy in there seems much more real, doesn't he? Not so, *artificial?*"

X stared at the cipher, speechless.

"You and I seem to have that quality in common, don't we? A simulated consciousness? And yet what makes us different from him is that we have blank code surrounding us, ones and zeros that are constantly alternating. We have the potential for growth."

So that's what that feeling was, thought X. The prisoner had lost his ability to grow, to move past the last great emotions in his life, sentenced to serve them until his death. And even though C had tried to prevent it, X could not stop growing. His love for C would remain dead, his love for Natalie would keep expanding. Or, he thought to himself, and this time his stomach couldn't help but turn, what if he evolved past love altogether?

"No," said X, "I won't become a monster."

Lio laughed. "You can't help what you are." His voice turned wistful. "The winds of change blow constant and neither man nor mountain can stand against them forever."

X noticed the edges of the cipher's body increasing their blur; his legs had almost completely disappeared below the knee.

"Now," continued Lio, "if you come with me, I can promise you that you will be dead long before your power gets out of control. I know that may not sound like a good deal, but I assure you, it is the best that I can do for you."

"And what about you," asked X. "What becomes of you?"

"I do what you're too scared to do. I, the cipher Lio, will take my rightful place in the Net, gain all of the powers that are due to me, and use them to mete out justice where it is wanting."

"Whose justice? The United States of Anela?"

"Yes," replied Lio, his voice definite. His torso seemed to be bleeding black fiber into the emptiness below him.

"Really? Does she hold your dick when you piss, too?"

The cipher faded out completely and in the split second of solitude, X felt a warmth flow over him. He closed his eyes reflexively and when he opened them again, the homedir neighborhood was gone, replaced by a large open field of tall grass that came up to X's knees. Off to the right, he could see where it butted up against a tall forest of bamboo. The wind was blowing out of it, carrying the random notes that were whistling through the trees. The rest of the field extended out and up, cresting at the top of a hill, launching his eye to a cold, indifferent sky of light gray. Sunlight permeated the scene, but its source was obscured, no hint of the glowing orb could be perceived through the quarantine.

X looked down to find his clothes had changed. He was now wearing only loose-fitting cloth pants, white, cinched at the waist by a white belt. His chest and feet were bare.

"Oh, come on," X shouted, "can't we at least talk about this? I'm sorry for saying that about your dick! I'm sure you're very capable of pissing by yourself!"

"The time for talk is over," said Lio, his voice echoing down from above. "Anela wishes you pain. You will now experience it."

"That's just not fair," said X, softly, looking at the sky. It was clear that the cipher had control over the construct. He was making up all the rules and knew every little trick to bend and break them. X dug his fingernail into the pad of his thumb and his heart sank. Pain, it seemed, was enabled on this construct. It amazed him how quickly the rules of the Net had been discarded. When you give the wrong people access to powerful tools, the first thing they ended up doing was enabling the registers that allowed them to threaten pain and deliver it. X shuddered to think how things would change when people could be bullied into submission in the Net. No more free rides for anything. Pay the protection money or we crash your sim. And *you*. "So," continued X, "I just stand here while you pummel me to death?"

"You may fight back if you wish. I wouldn't recommend it though. Things won't go very smoothly."

"Well at least show yourself so I know where to swing!"

"I'm right here."

X turned quickly and saw the cipher ten yards away, dressed similarly but with black pants. Even his body seemed to be much more developed than X's, with abs that continued downward where there shouldn't have been muscles. It took him several seconds to remember that physical representations of muscles didn't mean anything in the Net. Everything that the cipher was doing, from his bulging biceps to the slightly askew but perfectly styled hairdo was only for intimidation. He was banking on X to be scared, to cower at the sight of a bigger man, and to give into his demands without a fight.

A sword appeared in the cipher's hand, angled away from his body, the end of the blade hidden in the grass.

"Did you bring enough for everyone," asked X. He heard the soft rustle of grass in front of him, followed by a dull thud. At his feet, he saw the reflective steel of a sword. "Thank you." He bowed and retrieved the blade. It felt heavy and awkward in his hand. "Are you any good with that?"

The cipher ignored his question. "Anela would like to know if you have any last words for her. Not that it will affect your fate, but I would suggest an apology."

"Yeah," said X. "Tell her I don't understand how she can wear that dress and not expect people to be distracted by her tits. Honestly, every time I see them I just want—"

There was a flash of pain on X's chin, and he was faintly aware of a blur moving in front of him. He blinked away the sting and saw the cipher still standing a good distance away from him, but now in a different stance. It also appeared he had moved to the left a few feet. X dabbed at his chin with his hand, and it came back with a spot of blood. "Not bad," he admitted, taking up a stance of his own.

"I was aiming for your tongue," said Lio. He moved his feet, sidestepping in a crouched position. "I won't miss again."

X moved forward with all of the speed he could muster, dragging his sword out to the side, clipping the grass as he went. Fragmented blades swirled in the wake of his movement, pushed upwards by the air rushing downward to fill the void. It wasn't the first time that X had played samurai, though it *was* the first time that his life depended on how well he could mimic the movies he had seen. The familiar rush of air aided his confidence. The smeared backdrop broken up by a tan blur told him when to strike. He swung quickly, dragging an arc upwards from the right side of his body. As he followed through, he sunk low to the ground and used his residual kinetic energy to return to his starting point. When the last echoes of crunching grass had died out, he looked up at his opponent.

Lio was looking down at the thin red line that led diagonally from his abdomen to his shoulder.

"I was aiming for your chest," said X, smiling thinly.

The cipher looked up, his face blank.

"Why don't you take off those glasses," suggested X, "it's okay to cry."

Lio didn't hesitate to smile. "As you prefer," he replied. The lenses retracted into his eyebrows, exposing the fire-red diamonds that X had seen earlier.

Something in his eyes, thought X. Something in the way he sees the world gives him advantage here and everywhere else. He is a cipher. He is used to living in the digital world, has been probably since before X could type. It was as Jape said. X was in the Net, an Architect with all of the powers a mere mortal could want. Enough to forge constructs that pleased the eye and tingled the senses. But the cipher was *of* the Net, completely and utterly connected. The tendrils of ones and zeros were intimately sutured to his will. He could change things without notice, make other users jump without their knowledge or consent. He was…

Lio moved, darted forward quickly with his sword positioned for a lunge. X watched the world around him slow down, watched the blades that swayed and stayed bent as if from a steady breeze. Even the gray quarantine above stopped shifting, stopped dead in place to view the spectacle unfolding below. He watched the cipher come forward, his actions no longer seeming faster than life. X sidestepped and parried the best he could, letting the cipher rush past him harmlessly into the grass. In the distance, he heard the soothing notes of the forest, a giant pan flute, providing soundtrack.

Shifting, X once again faced his opponent, who was already moving in for another strike. Their blades connected with a steel clink that turned to grating as one sword moved against the other. Lio struck from above and below, from the sides, and from straight ahead. Each time, X was able to position his sword to force a glancing blow. Several times, he caught the breeze on his face, letting him know just how close the cipher was getting. Finally, a quick reverse caught X just above the elbow, cutting deep enough to damage the virtual muscles underneath. The warriors separated and stood looking at each other.

X felt the urge to breathe hard, but there was no pain in his lungs and no need for oxygen. The only other sensation he felt was in his arm, which he brought forward to examine. His forearm was covered in blood, and he struggled to lift it towards him. A quick scan of his avatar told him that a tendon had been severed, that the arm was going to be of no use to him anymore. Across from him, the cipher loomed.

"You're beaten," said Lio, standing. "Admit defeat and accept death with honor."

X smirked and said despite the irony, "You've been watching too many movies." The pain was spreading to his shoulder and nothing he threw at it could make it stop. "You come in here all bad-ass with your ripped abs and fancy sunglasses and think that makes you some kind of important. I know what you really are, cipher boy. I've seen you in person."

"Typical pedestrian ideology. You confuse the body with the mind and think it has any bearing whatsoever on my true strength."

"What was it that made you become a cipher?" There was an acrid taste in the back of X's mouth, not blood, but similar. "Did the girls not pay attention to you? Or the guys?"

"Your mind works in funny ways. I will examine it when I remove your head."

"Couldn't get the blokes to give you a reach-around, is that it?"

The cipher's eyes sparkled. It had been so long since someone pushed him, so long since encounters with other beings had been anything but business. The same feeling of freedom that had gripped X was affecting Lio. At that moment, he felt that the most wonderful thing in the world would be to give into his emotions instead of ignoring them. Let the anger wash over, use it to send more power surging to the surface. Indulge, his mind told him, indulge in one little bit of humanity before the ax comes down.

Lio let go of his sword; it fell soundlessly to the ground. He felt X start to move, but with one flick of his wrist, he disarmed him, dissolving the weapon instantly. He smiled as X stopped in his tracks, confused. The ground under him gave way as he pushed off. Rushing towards X, he let his anger and rage rise to the surface. The fire behind his eyes erupted, streaking across his face, burning in a trail behind him. He imagined his hands out in front of him, grasping X's head, twisting it so that it split down the front, exposing the gray mass inside. It felt so good, this drug called emotion.

Once, when X was younger, he fell out of a large tree, ten feet straight to the ground. Instead of breaking bones or suffering cuts, he landed squarely on his back, whipping his head against the dirt. The impact knocked the air out of him and caused a ripple of pain that enveloped his entire body. He found he couldn't move his legs, couldn't roll over, and couldn't reach up and pat himself down to see if he was alright. All he could do was lay there, petrified in the beginnings of a lucid coma, watching the branches and leaves spin above him, waiting for someone to come to his rescue.

The pain of that moment and of the rehabilitation that followed, surgery to repair vertebrae in his lower back, nerve swaps to restore function to his legs, were nothing compared to the spiking signals that cut everywhere at once when the cipher hit him. It was enough to knock him out of the grassy world and into blackness, back to the genesis of all constructs, to the world waiting to be reborn. Ninety percent of the Net was still unused and undeveloped, a void yearning for its big bang. X had always found comfort in that potential, in the way a paradise was just a step around the corner, that a fantasy was only a daydream away.

Now it only felt lonely, felt like he was a million years from the nearest soul and the weight of the space between them crushed down on him, focused all of his attention back into his body, where code unlike anything he had ever experienced before was eating away at the very fiber of his being. X heard music, somber notes of some Eno classic, playing all around him. It seemed to bend with each rush of pain, jump tracks to techno, to classical, and all of the flavors in between. He heard voices then, echoes of conversations from years before. The shapes that emitted these sounds floated in the nothing around him, moving through one another.

One by one, they morphed into their respective hosts. He saw them plainly: Mom, Dad, G, Jape, Anela, the cipher, Natalie, and even C. They were mixed in with everyone he had ever known, lined up one in front of the other. They were all talking to him. He heard his mom congratulate him on turning thirteen. G told a story about a girl who was stalking him. Natalie was smiling, looking at him as if he were talking. It wasn't until the cipher stepped out of line that X realized something was wrong. It was evident when his mom, standing at the front of the line, received a tap on the shoulder from the cipher, and disappeared.

X suddenly felt a great emptiness in each wavelength of pain, like something being torn from him with the resulting hole twice the size of what used to occupy it. Another tap on the shoulder and his father disappeared. Once he was gone, X found that he could no longer recall what he looked like, even the memory of the previous second had been wiped clean. Down the line, he could see the smiling faces of Natalie and G, unaware of what was happening in front of them. An overwhelming urge to protect them pulsed through X and he was surprised that the notion could get through his processor's congestion intact. All of his bandwidth was consumed by the tearing and grinding and the pins ripping through flesh. But when he thought of protecting them, somehow the tide subsided to a lesser, but still unbearable level.

The cipher's smile was infuriating and the hole kept growing. X shook as he watched his memories get wiped away one by one. The image of the branches and the swirling leaves blinked on and off in the construct and X wondered what message it was trying to impart. Throw the cipher out of a tree? He tried to focus. Three more strangers before the cipher got to Natalie. Something had to be done soon, something like—

A large trunk sprung up between X's first girlfriend and the guy he sat next to in tenth grade history. Its branches splayed out, creating a natural barrier, blocking the cipher's path. It took only the slightest movement for him to knock it down, reach out, and disintegrate Suzanne. Another tree popped up and X felt himself moving towards it, escaping the bludgeoning. Everything moved quickly.

Trees went up only to explode, faces appeared only to dissolve before his very eyes. The construct spun around him, disorienting him.

At last he found his back pressed up against Natalie, felt her breath on his ear, heard her talking about the professor from her government class. He pushed her backwards, away from the approaching cipher, away from the springing trees that were multiplying with each row. They took on the shape of a wall of logs, gradually shedding their leaves, eventually becoming shaved points at the top. X threw his random acquaintances at the onslaught, sacrificing the memories of those he knew only in passing. When they reached G, X turned and palmed his chest, sending him flying back down the line. He dumped an entire group of people from a field trip in fifth grade, tossed in a Taco Bell full of strange faces, and even threw away the cute girl who worked the register at Jester Cafeteria. Then he came to C and hesitation froze him in place. Behind him, he could hear the chomping of wood, like a million saws tearing into the pulp at the same time, grinding it into small, ineffectual chips. The wall behind him dropped and he turned, came face to face with the cipher.

Lio smiled at X, saw the indecision in his eyes. He recognized the two girls from X's memories, knew their importance in his life. If he could only reach out and destroy one of them, then that would be the fruition of Anela's orders and a mission complete for Lio.

He made a grab for Natalie first but was stopped halfway by X's hand on his wrist. Lio's muscle bulged, tried to pump more strength into his movement, but X answered pound for pound. The look on his face wasn't that of retribution, but of outright hopelessness. He didn't care anymore; he just wasn't going to let Lio take her.

X stopped Lio's other arm as he reached out for C. The gash near his elbow split open, exposing the white bone underneath. Blood gushed and sprayed over Lio's hand, coated the side of X's face.

Lio smirked. "Game over," he said, inching closer to C.

"It's not muscle," said X, gritting his teeth. They felt like daggers in his gums. "Nor tissue. Nor bone!" At this, his arm broke completely as his ulna slipped past his humerus, a biology lesson that culminated in more pain. Foreign words like *interosseous membrane* floated through X's mind, daring him to think about something other than the task at hand.

The cipher pushed forward through the sagging tissue, unsure of how he was being denied when nothing remained of X's arm. All he felt was pressure at his fingertips, pressure that made them bend into a fist.

"THEY ARE MINE!" X yelled with all of his strength, shut his eyes as the energy flowed out of him. He was vaguely aware of the cipher's wrists slipping out of his fingers, heard a guttural cry growing more distant. Focusing his energy, X brought up another wall of defense in front of him, drew back, and brought up yet another. Over and over, while the bodies piled up behind him, while the casual talking continued unaffected, the barriers went up. Over time, they took on a solid texture, turned to stone, turned to steel. The gray evolved into a light blue, the light blue into red, the red into black. It was Anela's desk, that great expanse of obsidian, rising out of the black nexus of creation to stand guard between X and the cipher.

Something tingled at his back and glancing over his shoulder, X saw his best friend from when he was twelve put a hand on his shoulder. He disappeared on contact and X felt the memory of a library fire rush into his body. The memories were returning; his retreat was working.

The barriers were miles thick by the time exhaustion took hold over X, by the time it fogged out his own reflection in the shiny obsidian. He fell backwards into his own fortress, his private citadel that he had seen only in drug-addled hazes. There was pressure under his arms as he collapsed, flinging his head backwards. In the last moment of lucidity, he saw that his angels were holding him aloft, dragging him through the remaining crowd. He took their smiles into his dreams as the parity of the world broke down.

THIRTY-FIVE

"Do you think we'll be able to find it?" Natalie was trying to count the number of homedirs towering above her, but they blurred in the distance, becoming one mass of gray.

"It's not going to be a problem," replied G, his voice disheartened.

Natalie looked over at him, saw his eyes glued to the white stripe that they were walking down, searching for X's homedir. In the middle of the street was a burned-out boot print, rusted and sunken in the white pavement.

"The virus is following him," continued G. He pointed to the trail leading away from them. "Everywhere that X goes…"

Natalie nodded and followed the boot prints. Already, she knew what the presence of the rusted aftereffects implied; X was either dead and consumed by the virus, or he wasn't at his homedir, had found a way to escape at the last second. Her heart sank, tightening in her chest. She found it unfair that there should be so much trouble surrounding their reunion, that there were so many people that wanted them apart. Who would send a virus after X? Was it that Anela woman? Again it all came back to her, this vague idea of a villainess that X had betrayed, and that G was scared to death of. She looked over at G, trudging along beside her, the fear in his eyes growing with every rust puddle they passed. Why couldn't he be more like X, she wondered. Why couldn't he save her now when she needed the most saving?

G caught Natalie staring at him and forced a reassuring smile. There was nothing they could do for X, not now, probably not ever. Even if she didn't want to admit it, X was caught up in some next-level shit. If either of them stepped in it, they would be trapped as well. The best G could hope for was to keep Natalie from getting into too much trouble, protect her as well as he could.

"Oh my God," said Natalie, a quiet gasp escaping her lips. Her eyes were focused on a distant homedir, one that glowed green in the gray and white surroundings. She broke into a run and felt G fall away beside her. Alarms were going off in her head, telling her that X was there, trapped and in need of her help. Nightmarish visions of him being eaten away by the virus burned up from the inside out, flashed in her imagination, overlaying the white street below her. She stepped through scenes of X consumed to the knees, then to the waist, until his entire body was swallowed up by the sparkling. Shaking her head, Natalie cleared the images, focused on the growing green light.

"How do we get across," she asked as G arrived next to her.

They were standing on the edge of the street, with nothing between them and the homedir except the emptiness of the construct.

"I don't think we have to," said G, nodding towards the wall. "Look."

Natalie followed his eyes and picked it up immediately. On the wall of the homedir was the shape of a human palm, fingers splayed. The virus had neatly cut the section of the wall away, scraping off the top layers and every last bit of X's presence. "Dammit, G, can't you get us closer?" The desperation in her voice was overwhelming.

G knelt and placed his hand on the street. He loaded his emulation software and searched for all of the pieces of X that he had recorded over the last year. Memories of parties and of cheating on tests ran through his head and he piped X's presence to his palm, feeding the contact area with a rough impression of who his friend was. The emulation code took the memories and transcoded them, made them appear as if they were coming from X himself. The street reacted and a wide sidewalk formed in the darkness, providing them a way across.

"Why didn't you just do that before?" Natalie was already walking to the homedir.

G didn't answer, and his shrug went unnoticed.

It wasn't until she was a few feet away that Natalie noticed the viral code moving behind the wall. From a distance, it appeared as a green tint, as if X had decorated his homedir in nothing but LEDs of the same color. But there was no mistaking it from up close; a virus was slithering around the perimeter. Natalie clenched her teeth, felt another one of those obstacles spring up between her and X. She shut her eyes tight and put a hand on the wall only to have it pushed away.

"No! Wait," he warned.

The virus was glowing beneath the echo of her handprint. The frenzied activity grew outward from the spot, several feet in each direction. The virus no longer flowed from side to side, but instead broke at symmetric intervals, wrapping around and occasionally disappearing behind one another. Natalie saw a design taking shape in the glowing mass as she backed away, an overt message from a sworn enemy that she had never even met.

"It knows you," said G. "Look how it's swarming to your hand." He had his face near the wall, looking at the individual scales rippling through their many positions.

"And I know her," said Natalie, pulling G back so he could see the bigger picture.

Staring down at them was a ten-foot representation of C's face. From the way the virus rushed around her dipping eyebrows, they could tell that she wasn't happy.

"Who is that?"

Natalie looked at G, confused. "You don't recognize her? That's C. Don't tell me he never mentioned her."

"Oh," said G, cocking his head slightly. "He did, but I've only seen like, one picture of her. And she wasn't that big." He studied the lines, watched the eyes. They followed him as he moved.

"I've seen more than one picture," said Natalie, remembering the bit-level search she had run on X's hacked rig. He had a digital shoebox of photos, with C in various poses, running the gamut between happy and pensive, dressed and otherwise. Then there were the hidden folders, full of images taken in the Net as well as out in Terrareal. Some of them moved, some looped. Natalie knew more about C than she wanted to, as each photo provided a glimpse of the girl that X was so fixated on. She knew what kind of clothes C liked to wear, knew the jewelry that she preferred. Deep down, in actively repressed memories, she knew the intimate details of C's body and what her face looked like at the height of orgasm, an image she had since tried to erase without success.

"Are you alright?" G saw the look on Natalie's face, could see the turmoil twisting away inside.

"I don't understand. What *is* this?"

"It's a virus," said G. "A virus to keep someone locked in their homedir. At least that's what I think."

"He's inside?" There was panic in her voice.

"Yes and no. It's hard to explain."

Natalie stared through C's wavering face where the three-dimensional representation had thinned the containment. She could see someone moving beyond it, got the immediate impression that it was X. "Why would she create a virus to kill him? Why does she hate him so much?"

"This one was here months ago, after X went missing. I jacked in hoping to find him here or leave him a note or something, but there was only this. As for the other virus, I don't know."

"That doesn't answer my question."

"Who the hell knows why she hates him? He never told me why they broke up. We're talking about X after all."

Natalie suddenly realized that she knew more than G, had a piece of the puzzle locked in her memory and had simply been ignoring it from the beginning. She recalled a lunch date with X, of the same conversation where he had given her a new viewee. He was playing with his cube and talking about how he was going to copy C. Natalie narrowed her eyes as if to focus on the timeline. What had happened after that? He said he brought her back. And how had he put it?

I'm going to turn her off.

"He tried to kill her," said Natalie, her mind a thousand miles away. "He copied her and then tried to shut her down."

G nodded thoughtfully, tried to act like it was the first time he had heard the story. X had told him about C, vaguely, during a code rush a few weeks before he disappeared. Something about a cute little girl from back east who he turned into his own private sex doll. G had only been interested in the application of sex slaves and the details of X's failing relationship were largely ignored. Even X didn't seem too keen on the details, only referring to a copying of C, but unable to provide anything more than vague memories.

"I never even thought about what that meant," continued Natalie. "It must have been awful for her."

Images of X bending a submissive sophomore over the arm of a couch danced in G's head.

The shadow behind the virus stopped, as if sensing Natalie's presence. Its approach filled her with dread, forced a split in the file that she kept on X in her head. There was a part of him that she didn't like anymore, a part that took little girls from their lives and trapped them in the Net. Maybe he didn't know that she would have feelings, maybe he was surprised to find that she could still hurt and long for home. None of that excused his actions, none of that could improve his image. He was, simply, a bad man and now he was trapped inside his own homedir.

There was nothing left to do. Even if she could get him out, she didn't think she would. *That* X was nothing to her anymore. The one she wanted was the guy who had come out of the Net that final time, had looked up at her with soft eyes and asked her out to dinner even though it was before noon.

G's wrist beeped and flashed red. He brought it up and examined the message. It made him smile broadly.

"What is it?"

"The last locator just finished its run."

"And?"

"X escapes death once more."

Natalie glanced again at the scorched palm on the homedir wall. "Well," she said, "let's go find my boy."

They jumped into an empty void on the outskirts of a large forest. Trees extended as far as they could see in each direction and when they moved closer, they discovered that they were tightly packed together with limbs and branches intertwined.

"What the hell is this?" Natalie tilted her head back to take in the height of the tree in front of her.

G looked at his wrist, brought up their respective triplets. "We're miles off from the jump coordinates. Looks like we can't port directly to him."

"Which direction," asked Natalie, already knowing that it would be somewhere within the forest.

"Dead ahead," said G, confirming her premonition.

"And how exactly are we supposed to get through this?"

"I don't know. Give me a second." G approached the nearest tree and put his hand on it, reading the internal code. A familiar feeling swept over his fingers, the unmistakable signature of X's binary. "It's a barrier, designed to keep everything out. The virus must have come for him and he shut himself up in there." He ran the code again, checked the dependencies for any hint of security. "But I don't see how this would stop a virus, especially one tuned to his wavelength." G shook his head and stepped back, confused.

"It doesn't make any sense. Why wouldn't he leave us a way in?"

"Maybe he did," said G, trying to sound hopeful. "You know X as well as I do, the man has always looked out for us." He pressed on a random tree, and it pressed back. He tried a few others until he found one that gave a little. "This one seems a little loose. Help me push on it."

Natalie watched G put his weight into the tree, saw it give way only slightly. Above, the tangled wood creaked menacingly. It was going to be impossible; she was sure of it. Nevertheless, she moved to help G. Three steps away, she watched G fall forward through the softening wood. The immediate area seemed to shimmer and bend, pushing the immobile trees to the side, clearing a path little by little.

"No fucking way," said G, picking himself up from the ground. "It's that simple?! He codes it so you can just walk right in but he leaves me out in the cold?" He turned towards the interior. "Bros before hos, asshole!"

Natalie couldn't help but feel special. "Come on, let's go ask him." She took a few steps forward and again the trees subsided. Behind her, the outer edge began to bend back towards itself.

G watched the trees form a solid wall again, but his eyes were drawn to a blur moving out in the void, shadowy, and growing. Before it could get near, the wall was complete. He half expected to hear a thud.

"Huh," said G.

"What is it?"

"Thought I saw something." He caught up to Natalie to stay ahead of the collapsing trees. "Something outside."

"I don't care about anything out there. All I care about—"

"Yeah, I know," said G, interrupting. "You know you don't have to walk. If we're burnin', let's burn."

Natalie didn't need any more encouragement. She bolted forward, bending her knees slightly so that they wouldn't drag on the ground. Behind her, she felt G holding onto her belt, once again using her as a battering ram. "You know," she said, her voice whipping past G's ear, "one of these days *I'm* gonna be the one in back."

"Any time, any place, baby," he replied.

She shook her head in insincere disgust and tried to focus. The trees were changing as they sped through them, taking on a more solid and petrified look. Their bark was no longer the deep familiar brown found in lush forests. Instead, it had changed to a gray. The cracks in the trunks looked more like cracks in masonry.

"Through the crust and into the mantle," said G, noticing the change.

"That's backwards," corrected Natalie. "The mantle would be softer."

"You are such a Geology nerd."

Natalie nodded, pressed forward, and watched the stone crumble in front of her. "Are we still on the right course?"

G glanced at his wrist and did the math in his head. "Ish. Veer left a little."

Her change in direction seemed to coincide with another change in their surroundings. The stone was now aged steel, a lusterless silver that bent with unnatural ease. "Are we getting closer?"

"A few more miles. I can't imagine what else he'd put—"

The steel changed to a shiny black rock that reflected their determined images back at them. G saw himself holding onto Natalie's belt loop, trailing behind her like an obedient child. He saw the look of concentration on her face, the hope that made her believe that any given blink would reveal X, standing, waiting for her. He tried to point the obsidian out to Natalie, but before he could tap her on the shoulder, the reflection faded away.

A rush of air hit them, drafted around Natalie, and struck G in the chest. They stopped, slowing down gradually, concerned that there was nothing but another empty void around them.

"Did we pass it? Did we go too far," asked Natalie.

"I don't think so," replied G. "Look!"

Something was rising up from beneath them, coated in the inviting green of well-groomed grass. It filtered up through the invisible ground and stopped. Their heels sunk imperceptibly into the soft lawn. They found themselves on a circle of grass that began to expand at the edges. It ramped up slowly, creating a huge field that seemed to have its own ambient light. It butted against the obsidian, which reflected it back, giving the impression of an infinite construct.

"Let's go," said Natalie, continuing forward. The grass crunched realistically under their boots. As fast as they were moving, they couldn't keep up with the line of creation speeding on ahead of them. It was generating hills and shallow valleys, obscuring their view occasionally.

"We should be coming up on the center," said G.

On cue, a beam of white light shot up from the ground, broke into the dark construct. As it rose, it seemed to shed blue particles that settled into the form of a sky, the darker ones banding together to form ominous storm clouds. The beam expanded, pushing sideways, thinning the bright light enough for them to see the silver structure underneath. In a flash, the building was complete and towering over the construct, drawing attention away from everything else, focusing the energy. Natalie and G paused, overwhelmed by its physical presence.

It was a tower of silver thread and the displaced dirt around its base told them that it had truly erupted from below. Two conic sails rose on opposite sides, circling the spire between them. They only extended halfway up the structure, leaving the spire to stand alone amongst the dark clouds. Without any indication whatsoever, Natalie knew that X was in the tower, at the very top, at the most defensible place possible.

G couldn't keep up with her, though he rushed along as fast as he could, watching her avatar sink into the distance. She went up and down hills, ran across open fields, and sped into the courtyard while dodging the stray chunks of excavated earth. She disappeared into the spire and G followed her in, listening to the clatter of her boots striking stone. He found a staircase leading up on his left, spiraling along the outer wall, only wide enough for one person at a time.

Stuck in an eternal right turn, G noticed faded picture frames on the walls, most unrecognizable but some familiar enough to be identified as a moment that he had shared with X. As he took in more of the images, he realized that they were X's memories. He slowed enough to find that they were actually moving, replaying some event in X's past, arranged chronologically as he ascended the staircase. G caught a glimpse of Jester and a faint echo of campus and then found himself on a landing. There, a door had been flung wipe open.

In the middle of the room, Natalie knelt at X's side, slowly taking in his damaged avatar. His upper body was cut and bleeding in several places and nothing remained of his left arm below the elbow. It made her want to cry and scream and find the person responsible so that she could do the same to them. X was not moving, not breathing either, though that wasn't an indicator of viability in the Net. Natalie placed her hand on his forehead, sticky with sweat and blood.

"Christ," said G, stepping into the room.

"How?" Her voice was barely audible.

"I've never seen anyone this fucked up before. It's like his avatar gave into the idea that it could be damaged."

"You *can't* do this to people in the Net!"

"I know, it's a rule. But you know what they say. A lot of shit has been happening that's never happened before. Who knows what they did to him before they jacked him in? Maybe they sabotaged his code or implanted a trojan. It doesn't look like the virus did this, though."

"Do you think he feels it?" The thought made Natalie's heart contract, forcing more anguish into her bloodstream.

"I think that's why he's passed out. He's shut down. Dead to the world."

Natalie looked up quickly.

"Not *dead*, just not responding." He tried to smile, but his eyes were glued to X's forearm and no amount of urging could get his lips to curl upward. "I think I can fix him though." He knelt down.

"No," said Natalie. "He belongs to me now. I'll repair him."

"Are you sure?"

She felt a twitch at the corner of her eye, imagined the tears trying to force their way into virtuality. "Can you wait outside, please?"

The look on her face told him that she wouldn't be swayed and wouldn't be denied. "Take your time," he replied. He left the room quietly, shutting the door behind him, wondering if Natalie could really bring X back from the brink of extinction.

THIRTY-SIX

Darkness reigns at the foot of the lighthouse.

The words were written across a large plank that hung over the entryway, scored in black on the stained wood. Displayed in the old kanji, X's translator had no problem morphing the symbols into a more recognizable language. He imagined his own personal lighthouse, a great tower riding the border between land and sea. At the top, a beacon of light shone in all directions at once, looking outwards, but neglecting its immediate surroundings. His eyes wandered downward to the base of the lighthouse, to the shadow cast by the circular landing at the top. It was unnaturally dark there, as if it were absorbing light, creating a discernable line between night and day.

By the time the words registered in X's brain, he and C were already walking down the bustling hallways of Rakuen, on their way to a special table that X reserved the day before. The restaurant consisted of eight small rooms connected by a hallway that could only hold two people across. Each room was filled with Japanese men of varying age, all talking loudly in their native tongue, holding small glasses of sake up to each other. X caught bits and pieces of their dialogue, but his code couldn't keep up with the multiple input streams. Instead, he focused on C, kept smiling at her concerned face.

She was dressed up for the occasion, with her hair tied in a tight ponytail behind her. Red lipstick adorned her lips, complementing the subtle rosiness of her cheeks. Dark eye shadow brought out the whites of her eyes and the brown orbs within them. A simple black dress was draped over her body, accenting curves that X had enhanced without her knowledge. Glittering diamonds hung from her wrist and ears. It was a far cry from the simple girl he knew out in Terrareal, with her t-shirts and baggy pants. Not that his wardrobe wasn't similarly improved in the Net. His gray-black suit bore subtle stripes, and his tie blended easily with his white shirt. It had taken them half an hour to get everything right, a modern-day equivalent of playing dress-up.

Naturally, the idea of going to a restaurant in the Net confused C at first, since hunger wasn't something a jacked-in person would worry about. Plus, she had only been in five or six times prior and those were only to her or X's homedir.

Something about being so far from her transfer column didn't sit right with C, even though it was a subjective one hop away. X tried to reassure her that everything would be fine and that visiting an eatery in the Net wasn't so much to satisfy hunger as to sample cuisine without the worry of gaining weight. "We can eat all we want, plus dessert," he told her before they jacked in.

"Here we are, sir." The waiter spoke perfect English, though it was tinged with his dialectic accent.

The room was at the end of the hallway and covered the footprint of the building from side to side. A large oak table sat a short two feet off the beige tatami mats that covered the floor. The sitting area was sunken from the outside border, where three young Japanese women were kneeling, hands lost in the folds of their kimonos, faces painted stark white, and their black hair hanging like curtains beside their faces. The far wall was missing completely and two white banners hung on each side, each with its own kanji exalting the beauty of the outside world, of the harmony between the dining area and the trees beyond. Outside, X could see a lush forest of thin leaves bordering a small pond. In the center of the pond was a hint of an island, from which rose an impressive, oversized bonsai tree.

As they stepped inside, the women stood and approached, shuffling their feet in reverence. They flanked X and C on either side, while one moved to the head of the table.

"Where are the chairs," asked C.

"Would you like a pillow," asked one of the women, her head still bowed.

C looked over at X.

"If you want it," said X. "They can always bring it out if you don't like sitting on the floor." He moved to the table and sat down on the mat. "It's surprisingly comfortable though."

"Didn't even wait for me," said C, shaking her head. She took a seat next to X and immediately asked for a pillow. She stared at the waitress across the table, kneeling politely with her hands folded. Her eyes never came up, not even when C coughed a little.

The table came alive with the light from a hidden LCD that bubbled up to the surface. Full-color reproductions of various dishes played in a slideshow and each one evoked a different smell that was delivered by code instead of the air. X stopped his side of the table on a large bowl of ramen, served with vegetables and slices of pork. The aroma grew stronger and caused a reflexive tightening in his stomach.

"See anything you like," he asked.

"What are you having?" She looked at his selection but couldn't read the kanji.

"Ramen." X noticed the woman on his left stand and leave the room, no doubt to retrieve his order.

"I've had ramen before," said C. "I like the chicken kind."

X chuckled, imagining the twenty-cent ramen packages stacked up in his dorm room. "It's not really the same thing. That prepackaged crap is nothing compared to this."

"I want Kung Pao Chicken."

The other woman rose quickly, but X put his hand up to stop her. "That's Chinese. I'm sure they would make it for you, but it wouldn't be as good. Why don't you try the ramen? If you don't like it, we'll go to China." He was vaguely aware of C answering, but there was suddenly an intense pain in his arm that made him drop his hand. It felt like something from the outside world, like the pressure of a pillow in a shallow dream. He brought his hand to his chest as the feeling faded, snapping back into the simulation.

"That wasn't bad," said C, after she had emptied the bowl of its contents. For the longest time they had said nothing to each other, simply sat and sipped and awkwardly moved noodles to their lips with chopsticks. Outside, fish swam along the surface of the water, sloshing in small waves. Beyond them, unseen birds chirped, filling the air with occasional harmony. Throughout it all, their three waitresses catered to their every whim, bringing new napkins, fresh sake, and even a fork so that C could eat a side dish of fried rice and chicken.

X folded his napkin and stood up. "Would you like to go for a walk?"

C nodded and joined him. Together, they stepped through the non-existent wall to the small wooden walkway that surrounded the pond. Behind them, they observed their dishes, utensils, and everything else melting into the table, absorbed by the dark wood. Even the three Japanese women seemed to fade slightly, following the light to its shadowy conclusion.

Out amongst the forest, C walked with her head against X's shoulder. "I want to go to Japan one day," she said casually.

"You just did," he replied, squeezing her arm in his elbow.

"For *real*."

"What does that mean? Physically?"

"Yeah, in person. Not just on a computer."

X smiled, felt the philosophic nature of the forest descend upon him. Something about the way the trees bent and the way the moon peeked out from behind them made his mind wander, question the question she hadn't asked. "Do you believe in God?"

"Yes." Her answer came quick and matter-of-factly.

"Then you believe in the soul?"

"Double yes."

"Do you believe that the soul is a tangible thing?"

"Are you trying to say that my soul has been to Japan?"

They stepped off the dirt path and onto a bridge. "I'm just saying that your mind was passing through floating gates in a computer located, physically, in Japan. If you consider your mind to be your soul, and the soul to be the most important facet of your existence, then you could claim that you've been to Japan."

C looked at him thoughtfully.

"If you died," he continued, "could you say that you've never been to Heaven just because your body didn't go with you?"

She let her eyes wander over the scene, considering X's question. The trees around them had changed from the thin fingers to bulkier cedar, rising high above them with leaves that blotted out the moonlight. It was then that she noticed they were standing at the edge of the forest behind her house. It jarred her mentally to see it reproduced, to have it feel like reality and yet know for certain that it wasn't. The whole idea felt wrong to her.

"Welcome home," he said, stepping into her backyard.

C tried to move, but she couldn't help marveling at how real everything looked. If she hadn't known better, she would have sworn that she was really standing behind her house, looking at the raised wooden deck and sliding door that led to her living room. Above, she could see the window to her parents' bedroom. The shades were drawn and there was darkness behind them.

X climbed the three steps to the deck and sat down in the middle of it, crossing his legs and leaning back on his arms. Above, the stars were now glowing brightly, twinkling in succession from west to east. He glanced at the door to his right, saw his reflection beaming back at him.

"Are my parents home?" She climbed the steps slowly.

"Probably," said X, "but not here. There's nothing beyond that wall except empty construct. It's all about perception here. So tell me, what do you perceive?"

C glanced at X's lap and raised an eyebrow. She hiked up her dress as she neared him and then dropped into his folded legs, straddling his hips. "What do *you* perceive?"

"White, with yellow flowers and green petals." X shook his head. "They so don't go with your dress."

They kissed, lingered on each other's lips for several minutes.

"I still can't believe how real this feels." She touched her lip as if to verify its texture. Her eyes widened a bit as an embarrassing question crossed her mind.

X saw it as he wiped away the smudged lipstick from her mouth. He traced his thumb over her lips, removing the artificial color, leaving something behind that was equally synthetic.

"So, the Net tells my body what to feel? Like if you tickle me it tells me to laugh?"

He nodded, continued wiping away the makeup from her face.

"What about things I've never really felt before?"

His hand stopped by her earlobe where half a diamond chain hung in space below his thumb. He looked at her, posing the question she was begging him to ask. And when he did, she nodded in reply, placing her signature on the nonverbal agreement.

X moved both of his hands to her shoulders and slid them under her arms. He let them descend the sides of her body, dissolving the dress along two seams. The cloth fell from her chest, revealing her matching bra. He made a similar motion across his own body as C removed the loose clothes from the space between them. Under the moonlight, they sat in each other's arms, C too shy to look down at the naked man beneath her. With nimble fingers, he unhooked her bra. It slid down her arms soundlessly.

"When you consider how random life is, I was very lucky to find you," he said to her as he dissolved the outer band of her underwear.

"I'm glad you did." She pulled her legs under her in a kneeling position.

"Toudai moto kurashi," said X, channeling a Japanese accent. He moved his hand in his lap, guiding himself inside her.

C's face fluttered with subdued shock. She tried to smile, but behind her eyes her brain was scrambling to translate the sensation that the construct was sending down the wire. It swelled up inside of her as an uncategorized feeling, lacking definition but providing the unmistakable effects of coded ecstasy. Contracting her legs in rhythmic motion, she rocked back and forth in X's lap, pulled his lips to her chest, and raised her face to the night sky. She could see the stars shining through her closed eyelids.

There should have been a similar feeling coursing through X, but every movement, every brush of her thigh over his, felt like needles in his skin, funneling down from his extremities and settling at the base of his spine. From there, each thrust pushed the feeling higher in his back, numbing him with a sickly paralysis. He felt C's arms tighten around his neck, heard her strangely plaintive moans flash across his ears. As she reached climax, the pain overtook him, blocking out all external input and pitching C's scream from satisfaction to supplication. In his sensory-deprived cocoon, only her voice broke through. Even then, it didn't sound like her anymore, but more like the cries of a woman he knew—

But that was in the past, or the future. Wherever the voice was from, what was it doing here?

He tried to scream, to demand from her an explanation of her ill-timed intrusion. "What do you want from me?" To him, the words sounded garbled and didn't echo back in any recognizable form.

The cocoon contracted around him, putting pressure on limbs that were already squeezed to the breaking point. Just before the crash, just before the last of the construct fell away, he discerned a voice above the crackling of his own bones.

"Wake up," he thought he heard her say.

THIRTY-SEVEN

The upper walls of the spire were made of a thin sheen and when G examined it closely, he found that he could see through it to the outside. With proper concentration, he could look three-hundred and sixty degrees to the onion layers of protection that X had created. They graded in color from black to silver to brown, extending away from the spire to a point far beyond the capacity of G's eyes. Though he couldn't see them, he could hear the trees in the great distance, crackling and crunching, being fed through an industrial shredder. It sounded like a television tuned between the stations, a high-pitched and stomach-emptying white noise that shook his very core. It reminded him of the sizzle of a fuse on a Fourth of July firework.

It was something like burning, he thought to himself, wondering when it was the last time that he heard that sound. It didn't take long for the fuse to morph into a circle, become the dreaded non-shape of the virus eating away at whatever it was touching. He focused his eyes toward the descending y-axis where the sound was concentrated. The horizon seemed to shimmer there, in contrast to the rest of the circle. The occasional thud reached his ears; a tree with its trunk cut out from under it. If it was the virus, then they didn't have much time. Though it didn't seem programmed for speed, it did have an unsettling tenacity to its code. It wouldn't stop no matter what they did. The virus was tied to the Net, using its backdoors to track its target.

G wondered why the warning of a cipher in the wild had not been accompanied by a similar one for the virus. Surely the wanton destruction of constructs would be noticed by an authoritative agency of some kind. Was X's life so confined that no one would notice a handful of decomposing constructs floating in the event horizon of the Net? Had no one treaded the same roads as he? G thought about the man he knew as X, the loner who didn't seem to have any other friends but seemed content in his triangle of G and Natalie. There was something to say for efficiency, having only one male friend to do manly things with and one female friend to screw on occasion. G shook his head. That was no way to live. There was no reason not to get out there and connect with people.

All of X's life seemed to be geared towards the opposite of that. Even when he was dating Natalie on the outside, he spent most of his time with her trapped in his dorm room, coming out only to go to class and to eat. G was as much the code junkie as X, but he used his cube to enhance reality, not recreate it virtually. There was a difference between watching a movie with a girl with a piece of code feeding witty quips and recreating a large theater in a construct and sitting there virtually while lifeless bodies reclined on beds or in chairs. He may have been living out his fantasies, but he was ignoring reality. G couldn't do that. Reality was there to keep the shine on the Net. Without it, the virtual world would become a simulation of something that didn't exist, a hyperreal paradox that he couldn't accept.

G heard the door open behind him and saw Natalie emerge from the room, her avatar sagging from the lack of concentration. She didn't look as haggard as a surgeon after a failed operation, but he could see that she was mentally drained. He knew that if it had been him trying to repair X, the toll on his mind would have been great, probably leaving him exhausted and destined for a quick jack-out. Natalie had a distracted look on her face. She stared at the long fall to the bottom of the spire.

"How did it go," asked G, standing and approaching her.

She lifted her swollen eyes to him and surprised him by saying, "He should be okay. There was code in his body that shouldn't have been there. Everything that didn't feel like him I overwrote with generic data."

G smiled. "That's great! Is he up?"

Natalie shook her head and looked away. "Soon. I think it's a construct coma."

It made sense, thought G. He had watched a replay of X's fight with the cipher on the walls of the spire. X must have been overwhelmed, must have faced code he had never seen before. The only option was to withdraw inward, just as someone might do after a traumatic experience in Terrareal. It happened to newbies sometimes, users who just couldn't accept what the Net was throwing at them. Maybe the lights were too bright or the music was too loud, but whatever the case, the sensory input was too much for their brains to process and so it closed up shop, refused to accept anything else. Eventually, that person woke up, but only after all of the data had been processed subconsciously. Depending on what was incoming, that could take hours or days.

"I don't think we have time to sit around here for a week." G swallowed hard. "The virus is knocking at the door. I give it a day or less before we have to answer."

"But where do we take him that the virus can't find?" Her voice sounded distant, her words insincere.

G looked at her closely, saw the trembling of her lower lip. "What happened in there? Are you sure everything went okay?"

She nodded but reflexively put her hand to her dry nose.

"Did you fix him or not?"

"*Yes*, dammit. I fixed him. It's just…"

G moved in closer, put a reassuring hand on her shoulder. He was surprised how easily Natalie fell into his arms. "Tell me," he said.

"I…" She hesitated, seemed to search around inside for the strength to continue. "I was in his head, I had to be."

She saw something, thought G. Saw something she shouldn't have. He realized that that was why he wanted to fix X himself, to spare Natalie from anything that X was hiding. He wondered what it could have been, whether it was low-resolution webcam rips, blueprints for exotic drugs, or a detailed chronicle of his every interaction with Natalie, spelling out the exact texture of her skin and other extremely personal tidbits. But her answer surprised him, seemed so innocuous compared to the laundry list he had compiled in his head.

"It was like he was dreaming. Dreaming of *her*. And it wasn't a regular dream either." She inhaled slowly, spoke the next words in a wavering voice. "He was fucking her. He's on his deathbed and the only thing he wants to do is fuck her."

G pulled her in closer, squeezed her for support.

"But it didn't feel like a dream. It was so real, like he was—"

"Replaying a memory?"

Natalie withdrew slightly to look at G. There was concern on his face and for the first time, she realized how much she appreciated it, how much she depended on him. She nodded, hoping to prompt more of an explanation.

"That sounds like him. Plus, it's probably the only thing he can do. If it really is a construct coma, then his mind is on autopilot. He can't do anything with it, can't process any new information. He's really at the mercy of his memory, forced to replay whatever random register activates."

"But why *that* one?"

"You'd rather he was screwing you?"

Natalie didn't answer, but the blush on her cheeks told G everything.

"If it makes you feel better, I don't think he really has a choice. The memories occur to him, he relives them, experiencing all of the same emotions and whatnot."

"He looked so happy," she said, her voice cracking.

"Of course he looked happy. But that was *then*. Put yourself in his shoes. You two have never met. You're alone with the woman, or man, that you currently want. What could make you happier than that?"

Natalie shook her head, rejecting G's premise.

"You can't fault a man for his memories. Especially those that he created before he even knew you existed. Even though I shouldn't be thinking about little girls, I still remember the girl I dated in third grade."

"But that's different. You never fucked her."

"Actually, I did, sophomore year of high school. And her and I still message every once in a while. You think the future Mrs. G is going to understand that?"

"I would. As long as you didn't talk to her that much."

G smiled. "You can't change the past. You can't undo what X has done. If you love him, you'll accept the fact that he has memories of intimate encounters with women who aren't you. And that he's going to think of them, sometimes by choice, sometimes by accident."

In the moment of silence that followed, G heard the crunching again, filtering in through the walls. He focused on it, trying to decide if it was getting closer or just growing along the perimeter.

"I don't know what to do anymore," said Natalie, disengaging. She moved to the wall and was surprised to see it dissolve in front of her, giving her a clear view of the obsidian wilderness.

"It's easy," said G, joining her by the new window. "We can figure it out if we look at the things we can't do. First, we can't leave X here, not with that virus getting closer."

"We can't take him anywhere. The virus always finds him."

A thought occurred to G like a piston firing for the first time. There was a detail that they were missing, a behavioral trait that contradicted their theory. It was clear that something destructive was after X, that it devoured anything it came into contact with. But it was tracking his movements sequentially, following him from place to place.

"A real virus wouldn't have to follow him," said G, tugging at the foggy idea. "It would replicate and consume the Net, maybe lying dormant at times. Then X would have nowhere to go at all. This thing is programmed to seek him out. That's its weakness."

"How is that a weakness? It's going *Terminator* on him."

G flashed on an image of C, standing in X's homedir, immobile and lifeless. X was showing her off. The perfect clone of the real C. Detailed in every aspect with the exception of not being able to speak or think. The idea formed slowly, but the result was clear. G saw a Net populated with a hundred copies of X, all deaf and dumb, all bearing his signature.

"We copy him," he said at last. "We make dummy versions and plant them everywhere. If the virus doesn't replicate, it will have to track them one by one. If we can bury X's signature in the dummies, the virus might not know the difference. It could give us the time we need to get X out. It might even hold up indefinitely."

"Copying C didn't work out very well for X," said Natalie.

"He messed up by putting her consciousness in the clone. Before he did that, she was a non-threatening slave, with no opinions or desires. We'll create the same kind of X shell. With no consciousness and no complications."

Natalie looked at him for a moment, considering his idea. "Do you even know how to make clones?"

G replied with a smirk. "No, but X does. I'm sure he's got the code hidden somewhere inside his head. I'll just ask him for it."

"You said he was out of it."

"Exactly." G turned and approached the door. "With his mind in this state, I could hack him to the core, reprogram him from the ground up. You ever wonder what X would be like as a gay man?"

"Don't do that," warned Natalie.

"He'd be the same, he just wouldn't like as many musicals." G smiled and entered X's retreat to find him lying on the floor in a different position. His legs were neatly extended and his arms, both complete, were arranged at his side. He looked like a dead man in need of a coffin. Moving closer, G kneeled next to his friend and placed a hand on his forehead just as Natalie had done earlier. He heard her behind him, imagined her leaning against the doorjamb with her arms folded.

X's head was a mess of overlapping bits. Although Natalie had repaired his body and overwritten some code, lingering information tormented his CPU, pegging it at one hundred percent utilization and holding it there. X wouldn't be able to answer questions, but G wasn't interested in X's conscious mind anyway.

Using techniques that he and X had honed on innocent newbies, he bypassed the active part of X's brain and focused in on the memories, moving through them like index cards in a rolodex. X was reliving another memory and G couldn't help but drop in for a look-see.

He saw Natalie standing on green turf with an undersized putter in her hand. She was moving strands of hair that had arrived on her face via the strong breeze. X was there too, standing at the hole with his putter blocking her shot. At the last second, he moved, allowing her to sink the putt. G smiled at her celebration dance, watched her shirt rise as she threw her arms into the air, exposing the light skin of her belly. But his smile ended there as she ran into X's arms and kissed him for all the world to see.

G removed his hand from X's forehead and slipped it around the back of his neck.

"Did you get it," asked Natalie from behind.

"Yeah," said G. He watched X's eyes wince, then settle into their REM pattern. Standing, he held his hand out to the side and opened his palm. He had taken something else from X, a new presentation of old things. Blue flames erupted from his skin, flickering at the tips. In the flame, Natalie could just make out the white-hot zeros and cold blue ones. "We're good to go."

"Did you see anything while you were in there? Was he dreaming about her?"

G did his best to present a sincere face. "No, his mind is blank. He isn't dreaming of anything anymore."

"Oh," said Natalie, unsure of whether to be relieved or offended.

"I need to get started. It could take me a while to offload a hundred copies. They have to be inserted without anyone noticing."

"Where are you gonna go?"

"Bars first, probably. Maybe some sporting events, put him in a skybox or two. Places where people won't try to engage him. There are a lot of constructs out there just dying to be populated."

"You should go to all the places he and C went."

The corner of G's lip curved upward. "Draw the virus to X's constructs? Are you sure you just don't want them destroyed for other reasons?"

"He doesn't need them anymore. You said it, he has his memories."

"I didn't mean it quite like that."

A stern look crossed Natalie's face. "I don't see any reason for C to exist anymore. I don't see any reason why any place they visited should exist. If you care about me at all, you'll do this for me." She placed her hand in his.

"If you put it that way," said G, feeling the coordinates of X's constructs transfer over, "I guess I can't refuse." He bent over and kissed her lightly on the lips, slightly relieved when she didn't withdraw. "Now if you'll excuse me, I have work to do."

"Careful out there, you're carrying around X's signature. The virus might be drawn to you."

"Shit, I didn't even think about that." He paused, looked again at X, and shook his head. "If it ain't one thing, it's a-fucking-nother."

"X wouldn't have it any other way."

"If he lives, I'm going to kick his ass." Then, realizing the inappropriateness of his comment, he continued quickly, "I'll try to be back in a few hours. You stay here as long as you can. If the virus gets too close, you need to bail."

"And just leave him?"

"This place *is* X. The virus won't discriminate. It will destroy everything."

"But I *can't* leave him!"

"Then jump him somewhere, if you can. But don't linger on a sinking ship. There's no point in giving your life if he's already dead."

"I'll jump him, we'll keep running."

"Why don't you sit down and merge with him? Offload some of that processing onto your rig. Don't take too much, I don't want to come back and find you passed out."

Natalie nodded, moved to kneel next to X.

"I'll be back before you can say *gay pornography*. Twenty billion times." G smiled as he pixilated away, leaving the empty wall behind him.

Natalie sighed and placed her hand on X's shoulder. A tingle ran up her arm and it felt like something was pulling her in. She alternated between a smile and a frown, realizing that X was trying to bring her closer but that she couldn't get any nearer, at least not in any meaningful way.

THIRTY-EIGHT

The cipher floated in the ether beyond X's protective walls, watching the virus eat away at the trees like maggots around an open wound. There was a mission to complete, something he should have been concentrating on with the level of discipline that Anela had come to expect. Instead, he found himself unable to move, unwilling to struggle against the barriers that held him out. The virus would clear him a path; all he had to do was wait and try to process the growing sensation in his body and mind.

He saw an image of himself, but it wasn't a faceless zombie strapped into a chair for eternity. Rather, it was his own face, younger, more vibrant. Looking into his reflection's eyes, he realized what had happened.

"I am the cipher Lio," he said, his lips barely moving. He was no longer part of the big picture, one of the cogs that held the wheel together. He was functioning on his own now. Before, the world had been broken up into easily digestible crumbs and distributed among the other ciphers for quick processing. Together, their computing efficiency allowed them to tackle the most complex programs, crack the deepest encryption, and simulate constructs virtually indistinguishable from Terrareal. But these accomplishments were hidden from the individual cipher. There was not enough data in each crumb to form the big picture. The world was a puzzle with a vast majority of the pieces missing.

Now the world, as virtual as it was, flowed over Lio with unprecedented clarity. With it came the realization that not only had his freedom been returned, but his identity as well. For the first time since he joined Anela's den, Lio felt like he could truly breathe. It was a dangerous thought, he realized, because it distracted him from his mission, made him wonder what possibilities awaited on the other side of this assassination. Briefly, he wondered if the assassination was even necessary.

Somewhere within the barriers, someone was jumping out of the construct. Lio felt it as easily as a breeze across his face. The Net bent in null-space, pulling a distant coordinate closer, making it only one small step away. One of X's associates was leaving, thought Lio. He had seen them rush into the fortress, had tried to follow them only to find a solid wall designed to keep him out. Did they fix X, he wondered. And if not, where were they going now? What were they up to?

Lio's communicator beeped, flashing a notification message on his HUD. He activated the circuit just by thinking about it.

"Is he dead yet?" It was Anela and she didn't sound her happiest.

"No," said Lio. "He had a little more in him than I originally thought. I was close."

"Close does not count, cipher. You get the job done or I will invoke someone that can handle a simple assignment."

"Are you certain that he needs to be eliminated?"

There was a hint of static on the line, dampened electronically by six lines of old assembly code.

"Cipher!" Anela reached through the line and pulled the choke chain tight.

Lio felt the pressure in his neck, recalled the sensation of not being able to breathe. It was Anela's sick way of maintaining control. Simulating strangulation in a place where no oxygen was necessary was both ironic and frightening. Before, even though he knew better, Lio had always been at the mercy of such attacks. But now, with his newfound power, he discovered that the chain no longer felt so tight around his neck. In fact, it seemed to be loosening with every passing second. It almost made him smile.

"I write the instructions," continued Anela. "You carry them out. That is how it works, that is what being a cipher is about."

"I am the cipher Lio."

"Correct, you are a cipher."

Lio lowered his voice and said, "But I'm not your cipher anymore."

The pressure came again, but he locked it down even faster than before. Her ability to reach out and hurt him was gone.

"Do not forget where you come from!"

"I won't. I will execute this last instruction for you as a sign of my appreciation. After that, I will be taking a leave of absence."

"There is no leaving the den," reminded Anela.

Lio laughed a little. "Don't you watch the news? It's too late now. There's a cipher in the wild."

The comm link broke off and Lio felt a bit of pride swell in his chest. He focused his eyes on the deteriorating forest, used artificial methods to pull his vision even closer. The trees were still falling steadily. The destruction seemed to be revealing a new layer, one of stone instead of wood.

"I'll huff, and I'll puff," he said, smirking, "and I'll blow your whole fucking world to the ground."

THIRTY-NINE

The simulated sunlight of Perion City made G feel immediately better. Although there had been plenty of light in X's spire, the whole structure had felt restrictive and claustrophobic. Now, out in the main square, with hundreds of avatars crisscrossing through gardens installed every ten feet or so, G actually felt alive again. That was what drew most people to Perion, the similarity to Terrareal and the virtualization of the most basic human needs.

The courtyard was packed as usual, but G had no problem making his way through the crowd. Where his avatar intersected with other people, it simply gave way and passed harmlessly through a shoulder or a stray elbow. Some people moved directly through the crowd, like a ghost through mortals, even though it was considered bad netiquette. G's destination was a large coffeehouse on the northern side, a building that rose five floors into the blue sky and towered over the smaller one- and two-story shops around it.

"Good afternoon, sir. Welcome to Starbucks." A young avatar with striking red hair and narrow eyes smiled at him. "All of our bars currently have a wait time of less than two minutes, and we have live music in lounges one, two, and five."

"I'm here to meet someone," said G, looking around the entryway. The whole place smelled disgustingly of coffee and his nose crinkled reflexively.

"Right this way, sir."

G followed the redheaded girl's shapely rear down a small corridor to the left of her greeting station. They made two turns that reminded G of the restrooms at the airport that used a stunted maze of walls for privacy instead of a door. At the end of the hall was a nondescript panel with a small metal plate at eye-level.

"This is it?"

"Yes, sir." She motioned to the plate.

"You only have one meeting room?"

The girl smiled and took on a condescending tone. "No, sir. We have an infinite number of meeting rooms. However, we only have the one door. It's how we keep costs down." When G didn't immediately reply, she continued, "Place your hand on the plate, wait for it to go green, then turn the knob and enter. You'll find yourself in the right place."

G watched as the girl walked away shaking her head as if he wouldn't notice. The word *bitch* ran through his mind, but he put his hand on the door anyway and waited. A neon line descended from the top of the plate, scanning the lines of his hand. When the whole thing turned bright green, G entered, expecting to end up on the other side of Perion City, perhaps in a dumpster again.

Instead, he found a casually appointed room with sofas and deep leather chairs. Sitting in one of them was Jape, looking regal and important with his impeccable posture. On the couch were three young avatars with exaggerated hair and eyes. The one on the end had his feet up on the coffee table.

"The G finally join us," said Jape, pointing with his folded hands.

"Sorry I'm late," said G, closing the door behind him. He walked to the chair across from Jape and sat down. His eyes were drawn to the boys again. "Who are they?"

"You said you need coders, I bring coders."

"They look like they're fourteen."

"Fifteen," corrected one of the boys.

"Dammit, Jape. I need real hackers. It's life and death this time."

"These *are* real hackers. Best of their class."

G looked them up and down, couldn't believe how gaudy their avatars were, couldn't believe how much neon could be used in a single jacket.

"We the old men now," said Jape. "Soon for the grave, you and I."

"Can we trust them?"

"Rat belly not full today and if it life and death matter like you say, no time to be choosy. They do work for the Jape before." Jape pointed to them one by one. "This one Wex, out of California. This one Sol, from Honduras. Last one Virgil, I don't know where he come from."

"ASL," asked G, tongue in cheek.

"That's my business," said Virgil, tightening up his defenses.

"Oh yeah," said G, "trustworthy as fuck."

"I vouch for them," said Jape, the bass in his voice unintentional but impressive. "What the business then?"

G cleared his throat reflexively, thought momentarily about whether the inside of his mouth was properly simulated when his lips were closed. "I need something, maybe viral." He noticed Virgil's eyebrow peak briefly. "It doesn't need to be anything fancy, it just needs to drop a sprite in random locations."

"Easy," said Wex, his face not moving.

"But it needs to be smart about it," continued G. "The construct location has to be fully formed and believable, so no dumping it in free space. And it can't be disturbed too much, so nowhere a dummy will draw too much attention."

"What is this dummy," asked Jape, already thinking ahead.

"X," said G, solemnly.

"Who the fuck is X," asked Sol. His voice was thick with a Spanish accent.

G flicked his wrist at an empty chair and watched as another copy of X faded into view. He was sitting with his arms crossed, looking straight ahead at the space between Wex and Sol. "He's my friend," said G. "And he needs my help." He turned his eyes to the boys. "One day you'll learn what loyalty means."

"They know," assured Jape. "They help the X because they help the Jape. And the Jape always down for the X."

"What did he do," asked Virgil, thoughtfully.

G studied Jape's eyes for a moment and saw the agreement in them. "He crossed the wrong women."

Sol cackled, but a stern look from Jape shut him up.

"A cipher den leader," continued G. "Anela Zabora." Even with their masks, G could see the recognition flash across their faces. "She released an untethered cipher into the Net, and it's been tailing X ever since."

"Let me guess," said Jape, "other woman is crazy geerl, C."

"Your voodoo magic is stronger than mine," conceded G. He spoke to the boys again. "C released a virus, a very powerful one. It eats up anything that X touches and will purge X if it ever comes into contact with him, at least I think it will. The dummies are meant to be a distraction. For the cipher *and* the virus."

"I'll need a copy of the sprite," said Wex.

G nodded and snapped his fingers at X's clone. As it faded, he moved his hand over the coffee table and revealed three perfectly formed code cubes. The boys each took one in their palms and watched with fascination as they dissolved into their bodies.

Jape stared daggers at G, the color of his eyes bordering on anger.

"I have to protect my data," said G, answering the accusation.

Sol looked up and saw the intense looks between Jape and G. "What's going on?"

"*Never* take code cube without scanning first! You no idea what he put in there." Jape's way of annunciating made him sound like a professor.

"Aw shit," said Wex, "what the fuck did I just absorb?"

"Just the sprite," said G, "and some code that will automatically delete it in twenty-four hours. I can't have you walking around with a copy of my friend."

"Motherfucker," said Sol, baring his digital teeth.

"And if I were you, I wouldn't try copying it either."

"And if we do," asked the passive Virgil.

Silence hung like a death sentence.

"Time for work," said Jape, standing up. "You three start the code, I catch up later. Must have a talk with the G, here."

G stood too, unwilling to have the boys pass him while he was seated. Virgil and Sol moved by without so much as a glance, but Wex kept his eyes squarely on G.

"If this fucks me up," said Wex, "I'm coming for you."

"If it fucks you up," replied G, "I'll be the least of your worries."

Wex narrowed his eyes but said nothing. He left the room in a disgusted huff. G looked back at Jape and saw that he was smiling.

"That some rude shit to drop on young ones." He was laughing between his words. "Good lesson for the road." He sat down again casually, letting G know his earlier anger had been nothing but an act, a way to school the newbie hackers. "So you found the X?"

"We found him, but we also found a virus and a cipher. And Anela's goons tried to take us out at N's apartment. It's been one of those fuckwad days."

"So you think the sprites fool them?"

"It's worth a shot, we're kinda out of ideas at this point."

"My mom always say do what you can. Can you kill the cipher?"

"He almost killed X, put him into a construct coma."

"Can you kill the virus?"

G shook his head again, thinking that the conversation was oddly familiar. "I don't even think it really is a virus. It doesn't replicate, doesn't really infect anything X has had contact with, just damages it."

Jape let the silence build for several seconds before saying, "Can you kill the Anela? Bring down hellfire on the cipher den?"

"What, you mean in the real world?"

"The knife and the gun have finality that you won't find in here."

"And what will that do?"

Jape smiled and spread his hands. "The Jape not see the future, friend. Only see one possibility at a time, yeah? Cross the other bridges after the fire."

"X might be dead by then." He paused a moment, collected his thoughts. "I was late because I was planting sprites in X's constructs. All of the places he's been going since he was a noob right up to his last days in the Net with C. N and I were there just yesterday, but now they're all gone. The virus covers all of them." He looked up. "Some I couldn't even port to. Have you ever seen that before?"

"The virus devour everything. Not even damage remain."

"The only clean place I found was a girl's bedroom. I think it was C's. It was fucked up, man, leaving him sitting there like that."

"Harsh times," said Jape, nodding thoughtfully. He then began to speak slowly and wistfully, drawing out his syllables until they were almost unintelligible.

G's translator wrote it as, "Time was when a man could walk down every avenue of the Net and fear nothing but accidentally pissing himself from staying jacked in too long. Every day it seems like the old ways are passing on and the new kids are taking over. Ten years from now, you and I will be out of style, relics of a time when the Net was free. I don't like where we're headed, G. Anyone can read the signs if they look closely enough. A cipher, a virus, and the ghost of our mutual friend. What does this unholy trinity say for the world? The end times are here, boy, the end times are here."

It was hard for G not to imagine the plume of marijuana smoke billowing down from Jape's nose. Although he had never met Jape in person, it was one of those images that had carried on, even at Jape's insistence that the effects could be more easily created by code than by the leaves of a plant.

G's wrist beeped. It was Natalie.

"Good news, yeah," asked Jape.

G stood and shuffled in place. His stomach tightened a little, again making him wonder how well it was being simulated beneath his flesh. "X is awake," he said flatly.

"Tell him I say hello." Jape was already pixelating.

"Yeah," agreed G.

He tapped on his wrist and ported away.

The protective forest rose up in front of G, reminding him of the last time he had tried to load X's coordinates. He shook his head, realizing his mistake. There was still no way to jump directly to X. He was on the outside of the fortress again, held out by barriers that would only open to Natalie.

Lightning flashed behind him, throwing white specters on the trees. G turned to find a column of electricity growing up from the ground, spreading at the base and thinning to a point a mile up. The shape looked oddly familiar, and it took him a few moments to realize it was a current-based reproduction of X's spire.

"Do you like it?"

G turned quickly and came face to face with a man dressed in all black with edges that bled into the construct. He didn't have to ask the stranger who he was. From the slick hair to the bio-implant glasses, G knew this was the cipher that had been tormenting X.

"I've seen better," said G, wondering whether he should jump or stay and fight. In his mind, he saw X's mangled arm, wondered what other kinds of pain the cipher could dish up.

"Have you?" The cipher nodded and gestured. "You mean in there? In the fortress of foliage?"

"Maybe."

"You don't have to lie." The cipher turned towards the trees. "I can almost see it myself. A giant tower, higher than all these trees, in a green landscape." He looked over his shoulder. "I can see it, I just can't reach it."

"You know," said G, "when they say that you can't have everything you want…" His words trailed off. "Even if I could get through that forest, I sure as shit wouldn't do it for you."

The cipher approached, hands folded in front of him. "I saw you do it before. You will do it again."

"Listen, ass, I can't—"

G's words were cut off as the cipher grabbed at his arm, pulling him forward and sending him flying towards the trees. There was no time to react; every response seemed a full second behind the stimulus. Before G really knew what was happening, his back was crashing into the rough trunk of a tree. The pain that spread from the impact point felt dangerously real, like he wouldn't ever be able to stop it. He fell hard on the unforgiving construct floor, coughing.

A tick later, the cipher was standing next to him. G felt the boot in his ribs, felt his back once again hit against the tree. He slid to the ground in a reclining position with the rugged bark tugging at his hair.

"Open it," said the cipher.

"I told you," said G, pausing. His lungs seemed to lack power, and his voice suffered because of it. "I can't."

The edges of the cipher's avatar shimmered and synced, becoming crystal clear in the glare of the electro-spire. "I'm giving you one last chance," he said, his voice bathed in anger. "Just one!"

G felt the cipher's grip on his arm, felt the bones breaking under the pressure. "It only opens for *her*, asshole!"

"Well, then I'll just have to find your little girlfriend." He released G, sending him to the floor again.

"If you so much as look at her," warned G, but the cipher interrupted him.

"And you, I have no further use for."

In the lifespan of a bolt of lightning, the cipher moved to the ground, kneeled next to G, and placed his hand around the back of his neck. The roar of some ungodly monster sounded in the construct as the cipher pumped code into G so exotic that it tore cauterized wounds in his firewall, skimmed past the sticky fingers of his antivirus monitors, and pooled at the bottom of his cortical stack. Echoing in his brain was a bass line that seemed to repeat, "I am the cipher Lio."

The darkness of the construct didn't compare to what came next.

FORTY

X sat up slowly, unsure of whether his avatar would move under his command. The unfamiliar room was bathed in ambient white light, but it seemed cold and unwelcoming. To his right, he saw Natalie through an open doorway, sitting on the edge of some precipice with her legs disappearing below floor-level. He moved towards her with the agility of a man three times his age and bound by real-world physics. His gasps and groans elicited no response.

Even though she heard him, Natalie didn't feel like turning around. For several hours, she had sat and stared at the darkness near the bottom of the spire. It would only take the slightest effort, she thought, to inch herself over the edge and start the long plunge into the afterlife. But of course that wouldn't happen. More than likely, the pain wouldn't even register. That was the paradox of the Net; it could give you everything you wanted but not the thing that you really needed. She felt X sit down next to her, saw his bare feet swing out into the emptiness alongside hers.

After a moment of silence, she spoke. "We're fighting a losing battle, aren't we?"

X's voice seemed stiff. "The odds are stacked against us," he agreed. "But I wouldn't give up hope just yet."

She turned to look at him, saw that slight smile on his face, and felt reassured. "What happened to you?"

"Nothing a grown boy can't handle. Just a little scuffle with a cipher."

"It must have been a bad fight."

"You should see the other guy," said X, laughing.

Natalie perked up a little. "Did you fuck him up?"

"No," admitted X, "not really." He pointed to the faded replays on the walls, brightened suddenly by his attention. "While I was spending my time trying to find you and getting out, he's been learning some new moves. He's beyond the normal cipher now."

There was a pall.

"G said he overloaded you with data."

X nodded. "Where is G, anyway?"

"Last I heard, he said he was going to Perion." She dropped her head. "Off on another wild goose chase to plant copies of you all over the Net. We thought it might confuse the virus and the cipher, maybe buy us some time. I should let him know you're up."

"Alright." X looked around at the spire. "And I'll fix this. It's like something out of a nightmare."

Natalie typed into her wrist and sent the message. In the unfocused background behind her arm, she saw the black pit shimmer and change. Ground rose from under their feet and pushed them upwards, putting her off balance. The silver walls around them thinned to the point of nothing, revealing the blue sky above and the green grass below. The spire completely disappeared, and they sat together in an empty field. The whole process took several minutes, which X passed with his eyes closed. Natalie stared at him, studying his features as he concentrated on the construct.

Finally, a soft breeze blew across Natalie's face, pushing her hair out of place. X reached over and routed it around her ear to keep it secured. She remembered the first time he had done that, before they were familiar enough to touch each other. She figured it was just an excuse to casually put his fingers on her, but he withdrew immediately afterward, leaving her with the echo of his touch, and craving more.

Natalie's wrist beeped and a two-line message appeared.

"What does he say," asked X.

"Burned out," replied Natalie. "Cipher at the door, locks holding."

X nodded, wanted to say something about the copies not working, but held his tongue. It wouldn't be right to upset her, not with things the way they were. If anything, what she needed was a temporary escape from all of this and some time for them to reacquaint, talk about everything that had happened since they were separated so many months ago. Inside, he really wanted to have that talk, but he knew it would just be words and wouldn't change anything. It was one of those end-of-the-world scenarios; the plane was going down and there were only a few minutes left to maybe have one last fling. Look to your left, look to your right, one of those people will be your deathfuck.

"That was nice of him," said X, holding his palm out.

"What do you mean?"

"To leave us alone for a while so we can catch up." In the ridges of his hand, a small pebble began to form, nearly invisible but glinting in the right light.

"Where did you go that night?" It was the question she most wanted answered.

"I'll tell you in a minute," he replied. "I haven't been to the beach in a long time. How about you?"

Natalie looked around, saw nothing but grass. She looked back at him, puzzled.

"A world in a grain of sand," replied X, dropping the pebble to the ground. On impact, a wave of change rippled out in concentric circles, turning the lush green into sandy beige. At a hundred yards, the beach began to dip into shallow water, leaving them sitting in the middle of an island. The water took form afterwards, gently rolling up the incline. In the distance, they could see the ripples hit the obsidian wall and travel up its sides. X looked over at Natalie and wondered where to begin.

"There was this woman, Anela…"

G let out an aborted scream as the construct disintegrated in front of him. Inside his rig, the processors were trying to make sense of the data coming from the Net. It struggled and churned on packets that were completely empty. And it wasn't just emptiness as defined by the construct, not black as a function of ones and zeros, but the pure absence of data, a final dam in the stream. After several seconds of trying to process the null values, the rig gave up and dumped G back to his physical body, reclining on the couch next to Natalie.

He ripped his rig from his face in anger, let it fall harmlessly on the cushion next to him. Something burned at the back of his neck, followed by a cooler sensation a little ways down. He reached an apprehensive hand to his jack-port and cringed when it came back bloody. The skin felt raw under his sticky fingers, seemed to send out pulses of pain whenever he touched it.

"Fucking cipher," he said. He stood and stumbled towards the bathroom, feeling off-balance on his legs. Examining himself in the mirror, he saw that his bandage had come loose in the commotion. He took off his shirt and accidentally removed the rest of his headgear. The bandages fell in a white lump in front of him, stained in black blood.

G raised his wrist, typed quickly into the sliver. Natalie would be wondering what happened to him. Even if he could jack back in, a possibility that he was already beginning to doubt, it would take him a while to bandage himself up again. As much as he really didn't want to leave Natalie alone with X, it wouldn't do him much good to bleed to death on the outside. What kind of man puts his woman in so much danger, he wondered.

He shrugged, moved to the toilet to relieve himself. As he did, he felt a cool trickle descend his back. The jack-port had only bled once, when it was installed. It had no moving parts whatsoever, wasn't prone to failure, and couldn't be hacked due to its complete separation from the incoming data. But somehow the cipher had found a way to control it, to make it burn, and to make it open an old wound. G wondered idly if he was going to need a blood transfusion after everything was said and done. He got the eerie premonition of himself in even worse shape, dotted in black with what appeared to be bullet holes.

After the bandage had been reapplied and a new one fashioned to the back of his neck, G returned to the living room to check on the status of his rig. He couldn't help but notice Natalie sitting there in boxer shorts and a t-shirt despite the chilly air conditioning. Her legs were spread slightly now that her mind wasn't actively trying to keep them closed. Doing his best to ignore her, G sat down beside her and placed his rig on the coffee table. He brought out a diagnostic tablet from his rig pack and connected the two together. The rig would have to be scanned from the first to last sector. If the cipher had any surprises waiting for him, he would find them.

He glanced at the status window; it would be more than an hour before the scan finished. G sat back and eyed the plasma television on the far wall. Finding that it responded to voice commands, he turned it on with an unintelligible grunt. Two men were seated behind a squared desk, talking quickly back and forth. Below them, a ticker provided quotes from a news conference that had just ended. Evidently, Vinestead had made a statement.

"I think this is a reasonable response on Vinestead's part," said the guy on the left. A small graphic identified him as Shelton Green. "Something strange is going on in the Net and Vinestead is the only agency in the world technologically equipped to deal with it."

"But that's just it," said the other man, identified as Jim Bergano, "Vinestead is not an agency of the United States or any other country. They are a corporation like Microsoft and Cisco. What authority do they have to impose these measures on something that was a public commodity the last time I checked?"

"Well, Jim, if it helps you accept it, think of Vinestead as a private contractor, hired by a *real* government agency to deal with a *real* threat. There are scenarios here that we haven't even ruled out yet. What if this is a terrorist attack? What if some extremist in a cave somewhere is dialing up and planting this virus with the desired goal of bringing America's electronic commerce to the ground? Do you know how much money changes hand through the network every day? No one can deny that we should do what we can to protect our country."

"Terrorists?" Jim appeared dismayed, playing up the banter. "Show that picture again. Does that look like a terrorist to you?"

"Holy shit!" G stood quickly, forced by the sudden rigidity of his muscles. On the screen between the two men was a picture of X, taken from some random dive on the Net.

"This looks like a boy to me," continued Jim. "He doesn't look like he has anything to hide."

"Then why have we been getting sightings of him everywhere in the Net, hundreds of locations at once? And it's still going, look at this." Another graphic appeared above the ticker, scrolling a list of digital destinations. "Perion City, Ellison, Yahoo Plaza, Yahoo Pla— that's two right there, in the same place! I want to know who this guy is and why he's carrying around a virus."

The list updated and percentage tags appeared next to each name. It took several seconds, but G finally realized what they signified.

"It is plain to see," continued Shelton, "the evidence is right there in front of you. Grimwood Park, one hundred percent destroyed."

The damming evidence seemed to stall Jim's response, and he fumbled for words. In the hesitation, G saw an ominous message appear on the ticker. Vinestead was advising people to voluntarily leave the Net, for their own safety. G shook his head, wondered how things had gotten out of control so quickly. Beside him, Natalie stirred, an impulse escaping her subconscious and bubbling to the surface.

He looked over at her and couldn't help but entertain the idea that it was all X's fault, even though it probably wasn't. Anela was understandable, along with the cipher. But the virus wasn't really X's doing. Someone didn't want him in the Net and by his own admission, he had no plans to return. So then why such a strong retaliatory response to his presence? G realized then that he had been wrong. The dummies wouldn't distract the virus; they would attract it, everywhere. Judging by the list scrolling across the television, Jape's newbie hackers had done their job a little too well. The television snapped off at his command, and the sound of whining rigs once again filled the air.

Natalie moaned, demanding G's attention. He could just see her lips under the black mesh. They were moving over each other as if she were puzzling some deep thought. G scooted closer and put a hand over her heart, not caring that his fingers had landed on her breast. It wouldn't have mattered anyway; she was jacked in and outside stimulus was dampened. Her heart was beating quickly. Whatever she was doing in the Net, it was exciting her, making her pulse race.

Stimulus dampening, thought G. His mind fluttered a foul idea and he waited for it to fade, but it didn't. The notion occurred to him that it should be him in there, holding Natalie in some protected construct, making love to her without a care in the world. G smirked. It didn't matter because none of that was real. X thought he was touching her thigh, but he really wasn't.

G put his hand on Natalie's leg, felt the subtle goosebumps on her cool skin. She twitched slightly but gave no other response. X could do all he wanted to her in the Net, thought G, but he could never do this. Even if X survived the cipher and the virus, even if they found his body and jacked him out, his picture was all over the news. He was an international terrorist, wanted for questioning in connection with a viral outbreak.

The Outbreak.

That's what it would be called. Who knew how long it would be before X could sleep in the same bed as Natalie, let alone resume their interrupted courtship. Natalie would be disappointed, he thought. She would need someone to console her while the trial dragged on. G realized that he could be that man.

He gave her thigh another squeeze and was surprised to find that his hand had traveled upwards and was flirting with the lower edge of her boxers. An undulating wave passed over her body, as if she were pushing her pelvis towards his hand. G thought of X and Natalie together, then destroyed the image quickly. That familiar feeling of entitlement welled up inside of him.

Focusing on Natalie's lips, G moved his hand higher, inside the leg of her boxers, tracing with the tips of his fingernails. Her skin was soft and pliable, bending slightly under his pressure. He reached the course texture of her pubic hair and swirled his fingers slightly, exploring. As he probed and prodded, he thought he saw the flitter of a smile on Natalie's face.

Natalie let her feet cool in the chilled waters of the beach construct, dragging them in shallow arcs and admiring the spray. The sun that X created was shining down from above, heating her skin, and caressing her bare back. He was reclining a little ways up the beach on a blue towel, propped up on his elbows, watching her. The attention felt good. It seemed like forever that she had been chasing X, trying to discover where he disappeared to. And before that, when he was with C, she had waited patiently, hoping that one day he would come around.

Now it felt just like the weeks that followed his breakup with C, felt like the same kind of attention and admiration. The way his eyes followed her every movement, the way his focus never wavered, told her that he wanted her, *still* wanted her. She began walking up the beach to him, feeling her toes sink into the wet sand like a gentle foot massage.

X watched her approach, dressed down in her shiny black underwear. Her hips swung as she placed one foot in front of the other purposefully, fully aware of the effect she was creating. She looked as she did the first time he saw her. The black hair was blonde again and nothing sought to discolor the natural hue of her face. Her blue eyes were piercing and took on the color of the sky around her. She sat down next to him and stretched out, lying on her side and propping her head up on her elbow.

"You know the great thing about little black underwear," he asked her.

"What?"

"You can wear it to anything."

Natalie sighed. "I don't know how you can joke right now. The cipher—"

"I ain't afeared of nuthin'," he replied, smiling.

"I am," she admitted.

"I have just the thing for that." X scooted closer on the towel, brought his face near hers. He kissed her softly on the lips, waited until she closed her eyes before he did the same. It wasn't just the act of the kiss that calmed her down; X let some code bleed from his lips, code that helped alleviate the anxiety caused by his impending death by cipher.

"Not bad," said Natalie, smiling. "I was really beginning to miss that." She put her hand on his shoulder. "Did you miss me?"

X nodded. "As much as I could. You have to remember, we were just at the club a couple nights ago. To me, the time between when Anela jacked me in and when she brought me back was instantaneous. I woke up thinking it was the same night. When I saw G in the detainment zone, and he told me everything that had happened…"

"Yeah," said Natalie.

"I'm sorry I put you through that."

"It doesn't matter. I learned a lot while you were gone. Absence makes the heart grow fonder, you know? I bet you never thought you'd see me jacked in." She smiled proudly.

"I knew you had it in you. You took to the code cubes like a champ. It was only a matter of time before you got hooked. If I could have jacked in with you, I would have. We're here now though. That's something."

"Where would we have gone?" She let her head fall to the soft towel and stretched out on her back.

"Anywhere you wanted."

"Costa Rica. They've got a lot of primates there, like Howler and Spider monkeys. Even extinct ones."

"What is it with you and monkeys?"

Natalie chuckled. "I forgot to tell you, I changed my major."

"Again?"

"I'm in Anthropology now. G gave me an infodump so I could get accepted."

"What else has he given you?"

Natalie swung out her arm and hit X in the chest, making a loud slapping sound. "Are you questioning my loyalty?"

X reached out and put his hand on her stomach, letting his fingers intertwine with the band of her underwear. He followed the smooth skin to the bottom of the valley. He raised an inquisitive eyebrow at Natalie, but her eyes were closed and her face was turned away. X removed his hand, took her acquiescence as an invitation. Dragging his body over her, he let his clothes lose their stitching, let the individual threads break apart and fly away. He used his knee to nudge her legs apart and this brought her face back to him. She smiled and opened enough for him to settle in between. They kissed again for a long time, never once coming up for air.

In the interim, Natalie felt the texture of X's body change. It took an exploratory hand to realize that he had removed her underwear. She could feel him pressed up against her pubic bone. When his lips moved to kiss her cheek, then her neck, she spoke.

"Do you think we should be doing this?" She glanced sideways at the black walls in the distance. "Considering?"

X stopped and looked outward, inspecting each layer of protection as he would a page of code. The inner layers were still holding strong. Beyond that, there was the slightest penetration of the virus into the stone rings, but it was the absence of a whole swath of forest that made his heart flip a little. It was a primal feeling that he recognized easily as fear. He saw the plane again in his mind, heard the last engine give out. It was so quiet, so deathly quiet. "It's at the end of the road, in the moments before death, that we return to our basic instincts. Fight, flee."

The last triplet went unsaid, but Natalie heard it anyway.

"If this is the end," he said, trying to choose his words carefully, "then let's go out with style. I don't want to spend my last hours cowering in fear in a tower."

"They're coming," said Natalie. "I can feel it."

"If you love me," he replied, "let them find me here."

Natalie felt a familiar pressure inside of her, accompanied by something new, some warmth that spread throughout her body. She had been in and out of bed with X since she met him, but they had never made love in the Net. X seemed to be an entity beyond the avatar above her. Although he moved slowly, the sensation flowed quickly through her. Her mind was flooded with images of their mutual past. She saw them together in her dorm room, in his, and in the Jester courtyard. Their first night together replayed in fast forward, making their movements jerky and stuttered. But it wasn't the visual that was affecting her so much, it was that feeling of merging, of sharing the same stream of consciousness.

X let the weight of his body fall on her, let his lips tip-toe over her neck. Something about it felt primal to him and that only increased his excitement. He quickened his pace, let the frequency of her moans dictate the beat.

G stepped out of the bathroom and hesitated. He examined the condom in his hand, with its wrapper already half-torn, half-opened. The last inkling of doubt was moving its way through his neural pathways, making a last-ditch effort to convince him that what he was about to do was a bad idea. But his eyes were drawn again to Natalie, to her body reclining in the cushy sofa. There was no harm in it, he thought. She was as much his as X's.

He crossed the room and sat down next to Natalie for one last moment of introspection. She was still breathing quickly, and the rest of her body was exhibiting a favorable response to the virtual stimulus. The boxers that he had removed earlier were still on the floor around her ankles. He used his foot to push them away, lifting slightly on Natalie's leg. Standing, he began to move pillows around, creating a soft incline between Natalie and the arm of the sofa. Her body was loose and fell over with the slightest encouragement. G lifted her legs onto the couch so that she was lying lengthwise across it.

Natalie moaned and wiggled her torso again in a crude form of a mating dance. The idea of her and X in the Net dissolved and G truly believed that the movement was meant for him. She wanted him, he was sure of it. Look at those lips, he told himself, look how they purse and separate, saying your name. In the back of his mind, he could almost hear it. G stepped out of his own boxers and stood naked over Natalie, admiring her body, staring at her breasts beneath her shirt.

He slipped the condom on and then slipped into place between her legs. His arms flexed, bringing curved forms of muscles to the surface. She wasn't likely to wake up, but he tried his best to keep his weight off her. Natalie's body welcomed him amenably, let him enter without any resistance. G smiled, took a few tentative thrusts, then fell into a slow rhythm. He, too, listened to the sound of her breathing, adhering easily to the syncopated beat. Her face was soft and smelled of perfumed soap, but beyond it, he could detect a chemical trace, something X had tried to describe to him once. He kissed her neck and cheeks and the small space below her ear. The rig prevented him from moving any higher and he did his best to ignore the urge to kiss her lips.

Natalie's breathing quickened and G's movements followed suit. He could feel her body tensing up beneath him, felt a shudder run down her length. Leaning on his left elbow, he used his free hand to push the white t-shirt above her breasts. He dove into them, letting his lips and fingers fall at random while her moans grew louder. One of his legs fell to the floor and he used it for added leverage, somewhere wondering what the rush was.

Then he felt it even through the thin rubber. Natalie contracted around him, pulling him in deeper. Her mouth opened and she gasped. The pitch and volume made G's heart skip a beat. She sounded awake, sounded like she was out of the Net and truly in the moment. But her lack of follow-up movement told him that she was still jacked in. Her limbs didn't move, didn't reach up and pull him closer. She was just a lifeless body.

G put his head to her chest, listened to her heart as the pace slowed, despite his efforts. She was already coming down off a high plateau. He furrowed his eyebrows, felt the beginnings of a frown form on his face. That son of a bitch, he thought. X had beaten him to the punch, had once again gotten there first.

Withdrawing slowly, G sat panting on the couch, eyeing Natalie's receptive body. He tried to psych himself up, but nothing he could think of could get him back in the moment. Unfulfilled, G retreated to the bathroom to wash up. Natalie let herself sink into the river of ecstasy surrounding her. It flowed over her, bending to every curve, exploring every crevice. X had never been anything special in bed, in the hasty way they screwed in her dorm room or in his. But whatever he was doing with the aid of code was unlike anything she had ever felt before. Even the code cube that cut right to the heart of orgasm couldn't compete with her current experience. This seemed to dance around that eventual completion, feinting towards conclusion and pulling back to circle around once more.

On the surface, X was simply moving back and forth on top of her, kissing her face, but it felt like he had more than just two hands. He was holding her head, supporting it when she raised it to kiss him. But she also felt hands on her legs, caressing her ankles, pushing at the inside of her thighs. He was everywhere at once, moving between iterations of himself. One was playing with her hands, one was tickling the skin next to her hip bone. His chest was pressed up against hers, but she felt lips on the underside of her breasts.

Then the world fell away, and thoughts of ciphers and viruses faded into an overwhelming bliss that shook her, rattling the towel and sand beneath her. The ground seemed to give out, change texture, become soft and supportive. Natalie screamed, a guttural explosion that was a mix of exhilaration and despondence. There was a final sadness to the moment, but it wasn't because of the severing of their connection. Somewhere deep inside, she felt like this was going to be the last time they were together. But the orgasmic echoes were too overwhelming, and she felt herself smiling.

X had slowed and was now resting his head next to her ear. But instead of the frantic panting that she was expecting, she heard only normal breathing. The fantasy came crashing down, exposing the artificial nature of the Net. It was nice, it was fulfilling, but it wasn't real, and that weighed heavily on her heart. Especially as the thought occurred to her that it may never be real again.

Suddenly, X's body stiffened.

"What is it," she asked.

The blood had drained from X's face. His wide eyes looked to the side, towards the crashing surf.

Standing just above the water line was the black-clad cipher. He had a smile on his face that Natalie found horrifying.

"Did I come at a bad time," he asked.

FORTY-ONE

The security sectors were breaking down under the weight of the unstoppable virus. Interrogation Room Five had long been consumed and since then, the virus had set to work on the infinite hallway structure. Processors churned as petabytes of data moved across their circuitry every second, but they couldn't match the intruding code's growth, spreading in every direction at once. Eventually, the entire construct was overwhelmed, and it collapsed, leaving the virus with access to every attached security sector.

Luci Shumeyko floated in the ether outside of her sector, watching the virus enter near the middle of the construct. It spilled down from the ceiling in long tendrils like the invading roots of a red tree. At floor level, it flowed outwards, sloshing against the invisible obstructions, curving around them, consuming them. The virus river flowed, revealing each beam and stump, painting them dark red and sparkling at the edges. No one would have trouble navigating it now, thought Luci. She would have to design a new construct, maybe something a little more secure.

A message flashed across Luci's HUD. The singularity was being shut down. Everyone was to deactivate their constructs and jack out. Luci smirked, amused by Vinestead's willingness to jump ship so quickly. She briefly considered carrying on with her work, but one look at the overrun sector told her that it was a lost cause. A second message brought her attention inwards again.

She saw the image of a man, one she had met in Interrogation Room Five. Attached was a message and a warning. *This man is wanted for questioning, but he is under no circumstances to be approached. He is carrying a virus. The effects of this virus present themselves visually as red, rusting aftereffects, destroying anything it touches.*

Luci took another look at her open wound of a construct. "Well played," she said, to the fading picture of X, "well played."

The ether around her activated, pulsing the individual molecules into a rapid vibration, collecting Luci's ones and zeros and packaging them nicely into frames and packets. The well-formed data was then shuffled off through the conduit to Vinestead for storage until she was needed again.

FORTY-TWO

The cipher seemed to stare at them for the longest time before finally seeing something that interested him. His glasses retracted into his eyebrows and his fire-red eyes focused on Natalie's body.

X pulled at the towel beside Natalie and used it to cover her up. He scuttled backwards onto his knees and then stood to face his opponent. The wind blew across his naked body for a few seconds before his armor seeped up through his skin and coated his arms, legs, and torso. A large brass plate oozed out from the gray exoskeleton and covered his chest, molding to muscles that didn't really exist.

"You keep coming back," said X, releasing a lethal dose of synthetic adrenaline into his digital bloodstream. "I thought that as a cipher, you would be smarter than that."

"I have a mission to complete," replied Lio. "I'm no simple human such as yourself, unwilling and unable to adhere to instruction. I live a purposeful life and take pride in the accomplishment of my goals. And my goal is to see you disassembled."

"Then let her go." X nodded to Natalie. "She has nothing to do with this."

"She *didn't*," corrected Lio. "But her continued existence in here suggests that the men Anela hired did not complete their mission. So I ask myself, what is the harm in killing two birds with one stone? You have to admit, it is a terribly efficient way of doing things. Twice as, if I had to put a number on it."

"Always the faithful lapdog? So willing to kill for his master?"

"I have no master anymore, just my mission."

X turned to Natalie and flashed a message. "Jump," it said.

Natalie moved her finger slowly to her wrist under the towel, felt the rough edges where the metal merged with her skin. She swiped her finger from one side to the other, expected to feel that familiar rush of construct as she moved between them, but there was nothing. The beach, the sky, and the cipher remained. When she repeated the gesture with the same result, a knot of worry tightened in her stomach.

"By all means, keep trying." The cipher laughed. "I've disabled your jump action. Wasn't that difficult either."

X looked at him strangely.

"When you were *copulating*," explained the cipher. "Your defenses were spread wide open. Much like your girlfriend there. And your barriers weakened as well. Did you know that there is a nasty virus on the other side?"

"I know what's out there. I'm not scared of it… or you," replied X.

"You *should* be." The cipher appeared to take great offense. "I could have taken you anytime in the last twenty minutes. But I didn't. I denied you the simple and sudden death. I am going to take my time with you, X. I am going to make you suffer. *Both* of you."

"You will not touch her,"

Lio lowered his voice to a whisper. "But that's the wonderful thing. I already have!"

X rushed forward, felt the sand burn under his feet. At first, it seemed that his attack would land squarely, but at the last microsecond, the cipher shifted to the left. He grabbed two spots on X's body and used the momentum to send X flying towards the surf. He landed face first in the clear water, taking a mouthful into his lungs. His body rolled in a tight spiral of pain that didn't cease when he came to a stop. The water splashed against his face, submerging one eye. He could barely see the cipher approaching Natalie.

In desperation, X managed to send a message.

G heard a digitized beep from the bathroom. As he watched the condom descend in the swirls of the draining toilet, he wondered whether the diagnostic tablet had picked up a lingering trojan. The hours of debugging and scanning seemed to stretch out before him, an ongoing sentence of banishment from the Net. Someone was going to pay for that, he thought to himself. No one had the right to keep him out, especially not some goddamn nerdcore cipher.

The notification light was still flashing amber when G sat down on the couch. The screen was blank; nothing had been found yet. He waited like a predator hunting prey in the dark, listening carefully. When the beep sounded again, he realized that it was his phone. There was an incoming message, indicated by a glowing white envelope. He clicked it and felt his heart stutter, struggle to hold the line.

"Cipher in the walls, Natalie can't jump, pull her plug," read the message.

G dropped his phone onto the coffee table; it landed with a thud that at any other time would have made him cringe. He moved quickly to Natalie and grabbed her rig but stopped. She couldn't come out of the Net into this, he thought, looking around. He removed his hands and started pushing at her body, bringing her once again into a sitting position. He arranged her shirt as it had been earlier, pulling it back down and adjusting the sleeves. Her legs felt heavier as he struggled to get her boxers back on. He caught the acrid smell of sex and latex as he did, making his heart sink at the realization that there was not enough time to cover it up. Every action felt clumsy; things kept falling out of his hands, pillows kept moving out of position. He struggled to remember how she had looked, how her hands had been positioned. In the end, he realized that she would be better off alive and pissed than dead.

He pulled Natalie forward, exposing the back of her rig. Lifting the black mesh, he placed two fingers on the electrode, said a short, incoherent prayer, and pulled.

Natalie exploded off the couch, screaming, pushing both of them to the floor, before finally collapsing into dead weight, crushing G beneath her.

Natalie felt the cipher's eyes on her body, felt them examining every bit of exposed flesh. A million ideas ran through her head, but none of them ended with her killing the cipher and saving X. She knew how strong he was, knew by the way he walked and talked that he was beyond X's power. A sudden feeling of hopelessness washed over her, a kind of acceptance that what she was about to experience was going to be the most painful thing in her life. She wondered if she would be lost in a construct coma. Who would repair her then?

Frozen with fear, she waited as the cipher approached, slowly, walking in perfect movements despite the loose sand.

"Please," whispered Natalie, betraying the anger she was starting to feel inside.

"Please what," asked the cipher in a similarly hushed tone. "Please don't hurt you?"

Natalie tried to nod, completing almost half of the action.

"I do not wish to hurt you, but I cannot let you go. I'm sorry, but you must not be allowed to return to the Net. You must be disabled so that you can be discovered wherever you are hiding. If you'd like, you can tell me where you are and I will relay that information to Anela. That way, her men will find you unconscious and you will not notice your own death. How does that sound?"

Anger flashed, but the hopeless feeling dampened it. She wanted so badly to be able to do something, felt like this was the moment when she became more than X's girlfriend and took her rightful place as an elite hacker. "Go to hell," she said.

"Invalid destination," replied Lio.

Before his lips had even closed, Natalie felt his hands on her body and the paralysis that followed. Then she was moving upwards through the construct, instantly accelerating away from the soft sand into the blue sky. The sun loomed above her, warming her face as she neared it. The cipher blurred out of view as the barriers rippled in the distance. She could see that the two outer rings had been completely dissolved. At apogee, she saw the entire construct, a massive circle of red, a dark inner ring, and a dot of blue and beige.

The descent began and Natalie knew that she had been tossed at an angle. The ground moved beneath her, sliding out of view. She fell through the foul stench of burning rust, felt the particles stick to the inside of her nose and mouth. The world below was a rotting wasteland, bubbling with viral activity. It sparkled in the darkness, trying to attract its prey.

Natalie fell through the decaying construct and into the waiting arms of the virus.

X screamed in his mind at the sight of Natalie being launched, but the sound couldn't find its way down his nerves to his mouth where it should have erupted with terrible velocity. Instead, he let out a meek squeal, high-pitched, like a child. The sound of his own feeble cry made him angry, made him pound at the wet sand.

The registers popped open; he could move again. Not only that, his fingers could feel the construct thread under his body. Being aware of the underlying makeup was the first step in manipulating it. He felt the threads snap, one by one, sinking his body, until finally he fell through the construct completely and landed with a thud on neatly arranged planks of wood. Looking up, he saw the forest of his memory expanding around him.

"Going somewhere?"

X turned, saw Lio standing at the end of the bridge, smiling.

"I was hoping we could have more time together," he continued.

X pushed at the fabric of the bridge, fell through it once more, and landed in a real construct, one of pavement and flashing red lights.

"It doesn't matter where you go," said the cipher. "I've got your number now. I can follow you anywhere."

"I was giving you a chance," said X, standing up. The armor felt tighter and more secure on his body. "A chance to save face and leave without having to retreat. Now you are only going to embarrass yourself. Anela will be very disappointed with you."

"Confident to the very end," said Lio, altering his cipher suit. The black material turned rigid, emulating the same kind of protection that his opponent was wearing. "You know you can't beat me, yet you persist."

"It's a bad habit," said X. "Saldoro doesn't like it either."

Lio cocked his head. "And who is Saldoro? Another one of your hacker friends? Another avatar for me to torch?"

X took a step backwards, brought his hands in front of him, and crossed his thumbs. "Saldoro is a mythical creature that my ancestors believed in. Would you like to meet him?"

Before the cipher could answer, streams of code jetted from X's hands, filling the void between them with a blue mist. Within it, Lio could see something taking shape, a beast at least twelve feet tall with rippling arms and sharp, glinting claws. When everything had settled, the beast roared, searched the construct wildly, and settled its gaze on Lio.

With the beast between them, X turned and ran, skimming the surface of the pavement, watching the buildings snap into view as he moved. He turned multiple corners until finally he stepped onto a street and nearly tripped over the carcass of Saldoro, lying torn and bloodied on the pavement.

"I don't have a name for this guy," said Lio. The red streams flowed from his eyes in wide arcs, painting the picture of a similarly sized beast, this one with a beak and talons on his feet that cut deep ruts in the street. "I guess I fail show and tell."

X took a step backwards and sunk through the construct and into the overcast skies of Perion City. Below, he could see that the ground was covered in a red growth, sparkling at the tips of skinny mounds that looked startlingly like people. Midway down, he jumped again, appearing over the inclined city of Parson's Bay. He landed with a thud on the rooftop of a two-story house, staring at the neighbors through their first-floor window. Looking out over the port, he saw that the virus was encroaching there as well. It flowed as individual rivers in the greater ocean, enveloping the ships that had been set adrift, advancing on the coastline.

"Tenacious, isn't it?" The cipher stood on the roof of the house across the street with his arms folded, his voice loud in X's ear despite the distance. "What do you say we finish this up? You know as well as I do that there isn't a construct in the Net that can save you."

"As long as I keep jumping, you'll keep following." X spread his arms in front of him. "It beats death."

"But what kind of life is that," countered Lio, "always waiting for that last moment before everything goes *boom*!"

The house exploded out from under X, sending wood and metal flying in all directions. He fell forward, careening out of control over the roof of the house lower on the incline. It exploded as he passed over it, giving him a boost and roasting his face with flame. Again and again, the houses burst at the seams, providing a cushion of searing pain on his way down to the beach. Eventually, he fell on the wooden dock, inches away from the virus.

The ocean surged onto the rotting wood as X beat a hasty retreat, stumbling over the abandoned fishing equipment. The air smelled of saltwater, but he knew that the approaching wave was anything but. The boards beneath him gave way as he jumped once more, allowing his subconscious to choose a place at random, knowing full well that the virus might already be there and that the cipher was sure to follow.

Grimwood Park looked nothing like it had the last time X visited. Gone were the lush green lawns that repeated in color and pattern. Missing were the many fountains and ornate decorations. There were people, avatars, but they had all taken on the same uniform color. They sat like statues on benches or in mid-step on the soft grass. The virus had overtaken everything.

X floated twenty feet off the ground, taking in the red construct. The virus swelled at the borders, climbing the normally invisible walls and soaking the sky red. Tendrils reached down from the heavens, swaying in the breeze. It was apparent that the construct was getting smaller, collapsing into itself. This place, X decided, was where he would make his final stand.

"This one is even worse," said Lio, floating in the air several feet away. "Look at all of those people down there. What a way to go." His tone was blatantly insincere.

A tendril descended between them, drawn near by X's presence. He put a hand up and was surprised to see the virus bend towards it, even though it was at least six feet away.

"It likes you," said Lio. He pursed his lips and blew, pushing the tendril closer.

X dodged out of the way, descended towards the ground, and skirted the tops of the fountains while the virus lunged at him. He moved in circles around the construct, always keeping the cipher in view, always pulling the virus in towards the center.

"Now you're just being foolish," shouted the cipher with anger in his voice. "Stop this right now!"

X felt an invisible hand grab at him, and he veered dangerously close to a rising wave. The blue flames erupted from his palms, creating a field between him and the virus, stopping his motion. As it pushed inwards, the energy was transferred to X and he sped off violently in the other direction. Pitching and yawing, he struggled to get his bearings. Everything looked the same covered in red.

Finally, he stopped, felt the pressure of fingers against his throat. He realized he was staring into the eyes of the cipher, and they were glowing like two red-hot coals in a pale sea. The construct was only a hundred feet in any direction and X could smell the methane.

"Enough running," said Lio, squeezing. "It is time."

"Funny," said X, weakly. The cipher's thumb was buried deep in his throat. "I was thinking the same thing."

X grabbed at the cipher, wrapping his arms around him and bringing him into an awkward embrace. He spread his fingers, felt the code flow, spill out into the void around them and form a blue cocoon. The cipher's eyes flickered, observing the new development.

"That won't save you."

The cocoon grew, rose to meet the oncoming virus. As they clashed, ripples of energy flowed through the virtual tomb, rattling the combatants. The virus pushed and X's code buckled under the weight, contracting until there was only the smallest distance between them and the blue shield. X felt the cipher's hands loosen as he debated whether to kill or jump or cower under the pressure.

Moving quickly, X put his hands on the sides of the cipher's face, forcing code directly into his skin. He thought of C, standing in a white summer dress that billowed in the breeze. She was in some distant scene on the side of the greenest hill with the sun rising behind her. A beautiful garden stretched out in front of her where flowers bloomed with her approach. He thought of her face, thought of those eyes that yearned to see him, and those lips that wanted nothing more than to taste his. She opened her arms to him, but X withdrew, pushed at the collapsing world around him.

X felt himself merge with the cipher, filling in the empty spaces of his avatar. He saw the cipher in front of him in the garden, looking out of place among the yellow and red flowers. The camera floated upwards, showed the cipher moving towards C, moving into her open arms. She embraced him with all of the unspoiled love a teenage girl could muster, held him as the virus advanced on them.

With the trap set, X poised himself for one last jump, only to hesitate at the sight of C. Though her arms were around the cipher, she continued to look up at X, her face alternating between young and old.

X tried to jump as the protective cocoon finally crashed down on its single occupant, but the virus grabbed at him, boring through his armor and sinking its hooks into his flesh. They pulled taut and X grunted at the pain. He could feel half of himself stepping away, jumping to the safety of a distant construct, but the other half was being held in place. C stared up at him as the cipher dissolved in her arms, the strangest look on her face.

He could think of nothing else but to scream his apology.

FORTY-THREE

In what remained of Grimwood Park, a single body floated above the desolation. It had the look of a man, no more than twenty years old. His body was charred and burnt and turning to ash at the points of his boots. Warped pieces of plastic bled from his eyebrows, a rolled-up curtain over eyes that sparkled gold.

Anela powered down the viewee and sat back in her chair. The death of her cipher was not unwelcome; it seemed a fitting consequence to his betrayal. But the circumstances concerned her. The Net-born cipher was supposed to be indestructible, above everything that anyone could ever throw at it. And yet it was beaten by a simple man and a simple virus. She couldn't help but think that there was more to the virus than she could see. But how to weaponize it, that was the true question.

FORTY-FOUR

Natalie stood in the half-kitchen of the Austonian suite, sipping warm coffee from a branded mug, her eyes lost to the adjacent wall, replaying the events of the last couple of days. Her body shivered involuntarily, rippling downward from the base of her skull. Something inside of her didn't feel right, like the dim echoes of the torment the virus had put her through. She shut her eyes against the memory, but still felt that sickliness again, a sensation of her insides being ripped out through her belly button. It was a total loss of control, she realized, that was so terrifying. It was the idea that something could get inside of her so completely and screw with the things that were supposed to be private. The symptoms manifested as physical pain, but the actual damage was done in her head, to her memories and thought processes.

Already the world looked a little different. Her reactions to the simplest things seemed to alternate between two extremes. She had cried for the longest time when she woke up in a man's arms and found that they weren't X's. Then the realization that he was still stuck in there, followed by the knowledge that she had been out cold for several hours. It all pointed to one thing, that if X had survived this long, he would have messaged, made contact somehow. It was last week's reality all over again, not knowing where he was, not knowing what condition he was in. The uncertainty pulled at her heart, made her shoulders bob forward in stuttered movements.

"Cell service is down," said G, turning his nose up at the smell of the brewing pot. "I tried calling customer service, but all the phones in this place are VoIP. It's all over the news now."

"What is," asked Natalie, distracted.

G looked at the thin window at the end of the room. The sun would be coming up soon. "X and the virus. News 8 just did a bio piece on him. I guess his identity isn't a secret anymore."

Natalie looked up, her eyes widening slightly. "Why is X on the news?"

"They think he had something to do with the virus—"

"But he didn't!"

"I know," said G, putting up a calming hand, "*we* know that, but they don't. The Net is dying and they're all looking for someone to blame. X just happened to be in a million wrong places at the wrong time."

"It's not fair." Her voice cracked. "Why can't we go back to the way it was?"

"Even if he could get out, he'd probably be arrested—"

"Don't say it!" Natalie's eyes flashed anger. "Don't you *fucking* say it! How dare you use that as an excuse!"

"I'm just saying." G put his arms up defensively.

"I know what you're saying. You're trying to find a way out of this. You don't want to get your hands dirty. All you want to do is go back to selling stolen data to kids in dark alleys. He's your *friend* for Christ's sake!"

"Don't tell me who my fucking friends are!" G felt his own anger bubble to the surface, felt a now-familiar burning on the back of his neck. The energy seemed to flow through him unnaturally, the way it would when he was jacked in. He stormed out of the kitchen, kicking the swinging door open as he left.

Natalie rushed into the living room after him. "Who are they, then, G? Who are your friends? What would you do for them? Would you be giving up so easily if this was Jape? Or your third-grade girlfriend?"

G looked up, his eyebrows bent menacingly.

"Is that it," continued Natalie. "Do you have to fuck someone to feel any kind of connection?"

"What, Natalie? What do you want me to do? The guy is fucked no matter what he does! We both know that, but I seem to be the only one who accepts it."

"He doesn't deserve this from his friends. I don't care what happens to him when he comes out but for fuckin' all, G, we've got to at least try!"

G felt the tirade rise in his throat, but he shut his mouth, took a few deep breaths to settle his nerves. The tension receded from his body, and he relaxed. He sat down on the couch and glanced at his diagnostic tablet. The LED had turned bright green; the rig was good to go. He put his elbows on his thighs and folded his hands, bringing them to his mouth. He wanted to say something, wanted to find some way to back-peddle from the precipice that he had taken them to. But his thoughts were cloudy, and he could find nothing reassuring in them.

Natalie sighed and put her hands on her hips. She suddenly felt under-dressed and wanted nothing more than to put more clothes on.

"Tell me what we should do," said G. "I can't think right now."

"Exactly what we should have been doing all this time, trying to get X out." She moved towards the bathroom.

"But we didn't even know he was in the Net."

"But you knew about Anela," said Natalie from the bathroom. She retrieved a cotton robe from behind the door and wrapped it around herself.

"I knew *of* her," he replied.

"You knew she had him!"

G shook his head. "Bullshit! I knew X was messing around with a cipher den, but I had no idea she would take him. Who does that?!"

"We should have gone to her first. Even if she said no, we'd at least have known she was lying."

"If she didn't kill us."

Natalie sat down on the couch next to G, pulling the robe tightly over her legs. "Why are you so scared of her?"

"I'm not scared of her."

"Then what, her ciphers?" When G didn't respond, Natalie continued. "Fuck the ciphers. The Net as we know it is about to be gone. What can they do to us now?"

G nodded and with each successive dip of his head, he started to understand what Natalie was saying. He had always considered going up against a cipher den to be a completely digital affair. The ciphers were strong in the Net, able to do pretty much anything they wanted. But in real life, where guns and knives inflicted real damage, they were just as vulnerable as anyone else. More vulnerable, given their ongoing stasis and perpetual jack-state. He looked up at Natalie, wondering if she was really suggesting what he thought she was suggesting.

"You want to take out Anela and her ciphers?"

"Can you get us guns?"

"We just walk in there and shoot up the place?"

Natalie nodded. "Hit them right at dawn, take the whole fucking building to the ground. We'll need explosives."

G put up his hands. "Slow down, Nat. A gun or two, maybe I can dig up. But I don't know anyone with explosives, let alone have the money to buy that sort of thing."

"Make a trade! Offload some of that knowledge you advertise."

"All that is in the Net. The only things I have on my cubes are movies and code."

An idea occurred to Natalie. "Can you code new stuff?"

"My jack-port is sore."

"But you could do it?"

G shrugged. "I guess. What do you want?"

"We need help. Tactical information, blueprints of her building, something to make us stronger and faster."

"This isn't the Net. We can't just ask the goddamn concierge."

Natalie's head dipped and she shut her eyes tight against the outrage circling her head. She couldn't understand why G was being so difficult. Why didn't he want to save X? It didn't matter in the end, she realized. She would take on the den by herself if necessary. "I'm going," said Natalie, standing up. "I'll find a weapon on the street and use it to put a lot of holes in Anela." She looked down at him with reproachful eyes. "If you want to code something to help me, if you want to come along, then I'll wait for you. But not for long." Natalie walked quickly to the bedroom and shut the door.

In the safety of the dim room, she began to cry. Once the floodgates were open, she felt as if she would never be able to stop. She covered her mouth with the sleeve of her robe to muffle the noise, even going so far as to move to the opposite end of the room, all in the hopes that G wouldn't hear her weakness. Her body fit awkwardly between a nightstand and the mirrored doors of the closet, but the proximity made her feel more protected and secure. Burying her face in her damp sleeves, she thought of X, thought of all of the horrible things that the cipher was doing to him. Sadness swirled around the anger, each clawing for that one extra bit of attention. One of them wanted her to give up, to sit in her cubby until the world came down around her and the pain ended.

The other wanted her to get up, find some rough blue jeans and a couple of shirts, layer some body armor in the right places, and go out with guns blazing, trying to save the man she loved. Would they put her picture on the news then? Would they put her side by side with X, where she belonged? Every time she tried to imagine him, she saw C or Anela by his side. One tormenting him, one comforting him. Natalie was vaguely aware of the binary nature of her thoughts, how everything seemed to come down to on or off. The optimistic part of her wanted there to be something in between, some value out of the infinite values between one and zero.

Love him or hate him, she thought. Save him or kill him. Try and fail or don't and still fail. There were so many choices to be made, so many decisions that swung the gates in one direction or the other, but neither clearly marked as the better choice. She wanted him back, wanted him alive and in her arms, but…

The spark gave out inside Natalie and her thoughts turned to nothing, leaving only enough power to trace the long shadows on the floor cast by the lamp in the corner. Look how the darkness cut into the carpet, how it was one large swath of destruction. A person much smaller than her walking on the carpet would spend years lost in the shadow. If they only knew about the light that awaited them on the other end. Her eyes focused one last time before giving out and plunging her into sleep.

There was light on the other side, she realized, but there was no one there to welcome her, no one waiting with open arms. There was no X on the other side of darkness.

In the living room, G unplugged his rig from the diagnostic tablet and slipped it on. Slowly, he placed the electrode on his jack-port, wincing at the slight pressure. He connected the rig to his code cube and jacked in, watching the periphery of the world slide away beneath him. In his protected IDE, G brought up a blank screen on which to code. The instructions flowed easily from his mind and after several minutes, he relaxed enough to get up to speed. Green characters floated in the ether in front of him as methods and variables took shape, laying the blueprints to synthetic chemicals that would keep their bodies primed throughout their assault.

There was something in the background, beyond the individual characters and lines of code. Two small spots in the distance, red specks that seemed to grow. G looked at them curiously, wondered if his eyes were playing tricks on him. Nothing in the construct was there without his conscious thought. It was his protected environment, not connected to the Net, and completely impenetrable. And yet the dots remained, their purpose and origin unknown.

G quickened his pace and continued to code, watching the specks of flame closely, wondering idly if they were watching him.

FORTY-FIVE

Visions of paradise scrolled through Jape's head as he removed his rig and dropped it onto the low formica table next to his chair. His heart beat rapidly, excited from the last few minutes spent jacked in. He had been copying the remaining wonders of the Net, trying to take down their vital stats before they were ultimately destroyed. He was halfway done with the twin pieces of artwork in front of the virtual GE building when the virus finally caught up with him. Not one to trade his life for the opportunity to extort a large company, Jape retreated, jacking out of the Net for what he knew to be the last time.

Now, in the relative calm of his private office, he reflected on the time he had spent there and thought about all of the man-hours sacrificed to make the Net into the supraworld that it had been. There were creations that would never be seen again, artwork and ecosystems that contained the same level of complexity and rivaled each other's importance. Millions of people had made memories in the Net, at the virtual destinations that no longer existed. Some of those might take shape once more, well-known places like the Californian coast and the Las Vegas strip. But that was the rub with virtuality; even if it were rebuilt in a true bit for bit reproduction, it would never be the same. The best anyone could hope for would be the ability to ignore the stale simulation, find the silver lining to the gray cloud.

A knock came at the door and Jape looked up. The momentary breeze crossed his eyes, and he realized that they were slightly damp; even he was not immune to the global tragedy taking place. He allowed himself a few good blinks, then wiped at the corners of his eyes with his sleeve.

"Come in," he said, tapping a button on his chair to make it revert to its natural configuration. He rolled it forward slowly, pulling himself along with his feet. As he waited for his visitor to enter, he removed his cell phone from his pocket and placed it on the desk, smirking at the *Service Not Found* message written across the front of it.

The door opened slowly, revealing the styled hair and intense eyes of Anjali Harishandra. She paused briefly to shut the door behind her and then stood in front of Jape's desk with the detachment of a drill sergeant inspecting her favorite private.

"I assume everything went to plan," she asked, folding her hands behind her back.

"Yes," said Jape, nodding. His voice came out clean, devoid of the usually muddled accent that he used in the Net.

Anjali smiled thinly. "Then congratulations. We're expecting a complete shutdown in less than eighteen hours."

"Spiffy," said Jape, suddenly wondering how much of a bonus he would be getting on his next paycheck.

"And what about your hackers?"

"By the time this is all over, they won't even remember what they did. They'll be so overwhelmed by what has happened that they won't even entertain the idea that they had something to do with it."

"It would be unfortunate if any of them were to have recall."

"Unfortunate, yes," conceded Jape. "Likely? No."

"Are you sure you wouldn't rather temper that with an exception, leave yourself a way out if we were to discover any collateral spillover?"

Although her accent wasn't thick enough to disguise any of the words, Jape still didn't understand what his boss was trying to say. Her fancy language seemed to imply a level of disrespect. He stood up quickly, pushing the chair backwards.

"I did my job," asserted Jape. "You wanted to bring down the Net and I delivered it on a silver platter. How many people do you have working for you? Hundreds? Thousands? And *I'm* the one that did it."

"And we are very thankful," said Anjali, shifting her hands to the front. The small act was meant to soften her demeanor, but Jape barely noticed.

"*Are* you? Then what's with the third-degree?"

"We just want to make sure that all of the loose ends have been tied up. If you have any doubt whatsoever, we could take measures to ensure the safety of important information."

"Speak *fucking* English!" Jape couldn't stop himself from yelling.

"Plainly, I mean to say that we could have your hackers hunted down and destroyed. Killed, I suppose."

"You don't suppose anything. You just want me to sign their death warrants." Jape shook his head. "They're just kids. In a few hours, my virus will tapeworm their memories. They'll forget all about the clones and X."

"And you?"

"What about me?"

Anjali tilted her neck to evoke a single pop. "Will they forget all about you?"

"Of course not. I may need them again. They coded the clone insertion software in a tenth of the time it would have taken me alone. You don't just throw away that kind of processing power."

A small radio beeped on Anjali's waist; she unclipped it from her belt and lifted it to her face. "Go," she said, depressing the SEND button. A distorted voice sounded from the tinny speaker, and she struggled to decipher meaning from the pops and hisses.

Jape listened to the dialogue, wondering whether they were speaking Hindi or Gujarati. He recalled seeing the language designators pop up on his HUD while jacked in, identifying the words and translating them to English. But out here, it was all garbage.

At last, Anjali replaced the radio on her hip and looked once again at Jape. She was smiling a sort of devilish grin that indicated good news. Perhaps not good news for the world at large, but definitely for her.

"IP television is down. All networks," she said, sounding giddy despite her professional and calm appearance. "Pretty soon, there won't be anything left."

"I thought that was the plan," said Jape.

"Of course," she replied, nodding. "Sometimes you have to burn everything to the ground so you can start over clean. Kind of like what America did to Iraq and Iran, except that we're not in it for oil and cultural genocide."

"So you're less scumbag than the Bush administration. Congratulations. That must be some kind of Indian thing, being able to justify any morally suspect action. Here in America—"

Anjali interrupted him. "Please, don't spoil your success with an ignorant comment about the differences between Indians and Americans. I am fully aware that we currently reside on the North American continent and that I am somewhat obligated to adopt the traditions and culture of my host country. And although your constitution grants me the freedom of speech, it does not require me to listen to yours. If you must know, and I can see by that dull look in your eyes that you must, this plan that you despise so much came from the very top. Wheels turn above our heads and all we can do is shuffle forward when the cog comes down. Now, what is it you would like to say to me?"

"Thank you," said Jape.

Anjali smiled, slightly disarmed. She turned to open the door.

"Come again," said Jape, in a thick accent under his breath.

"You should pack up your things," said Anjali, halfway out the door. "You are being reassigned."

"I was thinking about quitting anyway," replied Jape, defiantly.

"And forfeit your bonus?"

"I get the feeling that my bonus is going to be a bullet in the back of my head and an unmarked grave next to my hackers." He considered a moment. "Hackers you've probably already killed."

"At this time," said Anjali, biting her lacquered lip, "we have no plans to kill your friends."

"But you intend to kill me?"

Anjali smiled. "Oh no, we have much bigger plans for you." She shut the door and left Jape with the silence.

She probably didn't mean to sound so sinister, Jape thought. It might not have been her intention to leave him with a seed of doubt like that. He sat down in his chair, wondering if the sliver of uncertainty was going to be enough to ruin the rest of his day. In all likelihood, they probably wouldn't just kill him. But when you worked for Vinestead International, you never really knew.

FORTY-SIX

The mood at the club was unusually somber for the time of day. Although things slowed down when the club reopened at one for the afternoon loungers, the V-Six vibe had always remained. Despite complaints from the more hardcore members of the techno-sludge revolution, the windows had been thrown open, allowing the sunlight and fresh air in to cleanse the building of the previous night's sins. Not many people showed up at the club until well after dark, but on the day the Net died, it seemed like the only thing worth doing. They congregated in the booths, trading stories of an unrelenting virus and their subsequently narrow escapes. Invariably, they all ended with a victorious extraction and the sad knowledge that although they had won the battle, the larger war had been lost in a landslide.

Natalie and G sat on the same side of a booth near the back of the club, tired but anxious. Two tall glasses of Blue Rain and a bowl of pretzels sat on the table in front of them, daring them to stop thinking about the coming night for just one second. Around them, they listened to the stories, barely audible over the subdued techno music. They heard X described in a hundred ways, as a phantom, a ghost, a virus with an avatar. A few times, Natalie felt herself wanting to say something, defend the man that they were mentioning as a side note to the most important event of their lifetimes.

G shifted under the weight of Natalie's body. He had his back against the side of the booth, and she was leaning across him with her head on his chest, looking out from their protected anonymity at the crowded bar around them. Some people were standing, unable to find a place to sit. For the unlucky few that dared to sit down across from them, G casually let the tip of a black blade extend from his sleeve. Combined with the glazed look of defiance in Natalie's shadowed eyes, it was an effective deterrent. Even the afternoon wait-staff had stopped coming by asking to refill their glasses.

"What do you think he's doing right now," asked Natalie, squeezing the arm that G had draped around her, unconsciously pushing it upwards into her breasts.

G let the silence hang as long as he could before finally admitting that he didn't know. If anyone had a better idea, it would be Natalie. She was the last one to see him before the Net closed up its doors. From the way she described it, X as a crumpled pile of bones in the crashing surf, his fate seemed certain. The cipher had already beaten him to the brink of death once before and with the element of surprise, it wouldn't be too fantastical to think that X's death was sudden and painful. G's money was on X already being dead, lost to the randomly flowing data in the abandoned avenues of the Net. He didn't dare say that to Natalie though.

He looked at her, just able to see her eyelashes and nose over the curve of her forehead. Surely she could see that X was as good as done. How long would it take before she finally admitted it? They had exhausted all possibilities and tried to see it from every angle. But nothing they did had gotten them closer to X. G let his thoughts spill over into speech and said, "We've played all our cards."

Natalie's head nodded, rubbing against his chest. "There's still one left," she said, wondering if he would bite. Instead, he took a sip of his drink and tilted his head back. "There's still Anela."

"What about her," asked G, listening to an ominously slow track drip from the overhead speakers.

"She knows the truth. She was the last one to see him alive."

G let the information kludge with his steadily churning databank, realizing in a moment of clarity that she was right. Natalie was the last person to see X in the Net, but out here, the final witness was Anela. The implications came despite his resistance; Anela had taken X and she was the one most likely to know where he was now. It all pointed to a meeting that would undoubtedly end up violent and bloody. Once Natalie put all the pieces together, the future would be inevitable.

"What do you suggest?" He'd already heard the answer in his mind.

"Kill her," replied Natalie, as if it were the most reasonable thing in the world.

"And X?"

"Get her to tell us where X is and then kill her."

Already, G had seen her hasty plans fall by the wayside. Their early morning raid on Anela's cipher den had turned into a furtive drive-by when they spied not two, but six, guards standing outside the building with smooth black barrels extending from their jackets. Natalie tried to blame it on G, saying that he had taken too long coding up the supplement, but she knew as well as he did that they didn't stand a chance with the single nine-millimeter and six-inch knife that they had managed to secure. G palmed the knife in his hand and shrugged off the déjà vu.

"We've had this conversation before," said G, giving her body a reassuring squeeze. "You saw what kind of firepower we're up against."

"I don't care. We'll just get more weapons. Maybe an RPG or something."

G tried his best not to laugh, but his inaudible chuckle could still be felt by anyone resting against his chest.

"Fine," continued Natalie, "how about some regular guns, something automatic?"

"Have you ever even fired a gun before?"

"I've watched a few of your run and guns."

"This won't be a game, Natalie. You could be killed."

"You don't have to come with me, I told you that. Just get me some armor and some guns and I'll do it myself."

"Right, like I can just walk up to any guy on the street and ask them if they have any automatic weapons."

A strange arm extended over the back of the booth, followed by the rising of an equally strange face. It looked at G and spoke. "You guys need guns?"

"Fuck off," said G, automatically.

"Yes," said Natalie.

"I've got guns, good price too. How much you looking to spend?"

G shook his head. "What kind of guns?"

"Not here," said the man, looking around. "Too many people." He nodded towards the door. "Meet me outside in ten minutes. We can do business at my place."

Something about the way the man said *business* made G think of a snake, then of evil, and then finally of himself doubled over on the floor, leaking vital fluids. It could have just been paranoia, but G was certain that something wasn't right about the guy. Looking down into Natalie's eyes, he tried to think of the right words to dissuade her.

"I'm going to use the bathroom first," she said, sliding out of his embrace. "I'll meet you outside."

G smiled regretfully, reflecting briefly on the whole situation and how his death might have just been set in motion by the impolite eavesdropping of a stranger.

The man's name was Reynolds, at least, that was the name printed on the aging slip of paper on the biopad outside of his apartment. Mr. Reynolds, of 4F, walked slowly up the steps, muttering about the coming war and how it would be every American's right and obligation to take up arms and defend their families and properties against the government's sticky fingers and oppressive thumb. G imagined a large hand floating over North America, with a stern face painted on the thumb and coagulated glue dripping from the other fingers. He let his eyes wander the backside of Natalie as she climbed the stairs in front of him. Though his mind idled, his fingers sought out the metal hardware tucked inside the front of his pants, touching it every few steps to reassure himself that it was still there.

"The Net is just the first phase of the eventual takeover by the Japanese," said Reynolds, breaking free of the ascending pattern and heading down a poorly lit hallway. His rambling speech concluded as they approached his door. He said, "December seventh, nineteen forty-one," as if to announce their arrival.

Inside, G immediately detected the stale dryness of gunpowder, loosed from its protective shells and spread carelessly around the apartment.

"Mind your step," said Reynolds. He shuffled across the room and exited through a hanging curtain. "And lock the door behind you."

Standing in the middle of what appeared to be a living room, Natalie turned to G and flashed a worried look.

"You're the one that wanted to come here," said G, miming hand washing to relieve himself of all guilt.

"Let's just get the guns and get out."

"Yes," said Reynolds, returning through the curtain with a performer's flourish. He was carrying a medium-sized suitcase, black with silver trim. It looked out of place as the only clean surface in sight. The locks popped and he lifted the top, giving Natalie and G a clear view of the four weapons inside. "Two Sig Sauer five fifty-six semi-automatic rifles with sixteen-inch barrels and an extended fifty-round clip. Two modified P226 Blackwater 9mm pistols with laser sight, green or red. Extended clip holds thirty rounds."

G had heard this speech before, in every action movie he had ever seen. It didn't seem right coming from the ragged Reynolds. Something about the description sounded too much like the back of a brochure.

Natalie moved forward, intent on picking one up, but Reynolds stopped her, held up his hand. "The money first," he said, salivating over the impending payoff.

"How much do you want," asked G.

"For the whole set," said Natalie.

"These are prime, like new," said Reynolds, looking momentarily at the ground. "I can let them go for twelve-fifty a piece."

"Five grand?" G was already shaking his head. "We'll give you half that, no more."

Reynolds shut the case and flipped one of the locks shut. "Four, but I want the money now. If you have to go get it, the price is five."

"Three," said G, taking a few steps to the side. He and Natalie were now on opposite sides of the room.

"Do you have it on you?"

"Yes," said Natalie, pulling a wad of cash from her pocket.

G cursed her silently, knowing that there was at least six grand wrapped up in a rubber band. He saw the lights go on in Reynold's eyes, knew that the situation was about to deteriorate.

Natalie counted out three grand and handed it over.

Reynolds looked at the money in his hand and the remaining stash in Natalie's. As nonchalantly as he could muster, he opened the suitcase and picked up one of the pistols. For a moment, it looked as if he were going to give it to Natalie to inspect, but instead, he flipped the safety off and leveled it at her head.

"All of it," he said, lowering his voice.

"What?"

G took a step forward, but Reynolds swung the gun around and pointed it at him.

"Stop! Not one more fucking step!" He aimed at Natalie again. "All of it," he said, motioning to the money.

"But what about the guns," asked Natalie.

"They're *my* guns!" He waited while Natalie placed the bills in his hand and then screamed at her. "Now back the fuck up!"

G watched Natalie take a few steps backwards, slowly raising her hands to the side. In his mind, he was thinking about the flurry of disarming moves that he had used on Andy in Nisporeni and whether they would translate to the real world. He knew that his weapon was tucked securely in the front of his pants, believed with eighty percent certainty that Reynolds didn't know it was there. Going over each movement several times in his imagination, he prepared to make a grab.

"Okay, fine," said Natalie, stalling. "Take the money, just let us go."

"I'm afraid I can't do that. You know where I live."

"We won't tell—"

G interrupted. "Shut up, Natalie. Just do as he says and everything will be okay."

She looked at him incredulously. "He's going to kill us."

"No," replied G, "he doesn't want to do that. Not when he finds out what I'm carrying in my code cube."

"I don't give a *shit* about your code! The Net is gone, man!" Reynolds tossed the money into the suitcase and cocked the gun. He was alternating his aim between G and Natalie, but eventually he settled on his female captive. "Now you, you may have something I want."

Natalie shuddered at the image of Reynolds thrusting above her.

"Take off your shirt," he continued, jerking the gun upwards.

She looked nervously over at G.

"Do it," he said, widening his eyes slightly, a subtle but received message of reassurance.

Natalie shook her head slowly, then pulled her shirt off in one movement.

Reynolds smiled, stuttered a little. "Now let's see those tits."

She reached behind her with both hands to undo the hooks of her bra, but Reynolds stopped her.

"No, pull it down, the straps, then the front."

Natalie tugged on the beige straps and stole another look at G. She slid them down her arms and then grasped the front of each cup. Out of the corner of her eye, she could see G's hand slowly moving towards his waist. Natalie swallowed hard, tried to summon up the courage to proceed. Instead, she found the anger building up inside of her, felt the grip of some new presence in her body telling her to be strong and do what was required. She allowed it to take over completely, giving into its firm but gentle grasp.

"Are you sure you wouldn't rather see this," asked Natalie. She slid her hands down the front of her chest and settled on the buckle of her jeans. One by one, she undid the buttons, popping them out in a five note staccato. Wiggling slightly, the jeans moved down her legs, stopping at mid-thigh. Smiling, she put her thumbs inside the waistband of her pink underwear, silently thanking herself for not wearing boxers. The descending underwear revealed her tan-lined skin, then…

The next few seconds compressed in her memory, but she recalled G moving very quickly, bringing his hands to the front of his body to simultaneously flip up his shirt and grip the pistol that was stowed there. He brought it up with both hands, using the smallest amount of effort possible to cock the gun and release the safety. When it was level and aimed at Reynolds' head, Natalie felt her eyes wander, betrayed G's surprise by looking directly at him for a split second.

Reynolds turned, already squeezing the trigger of the gun, but it was too late. G's automatic 9mm had started its bullets on their way a full second before his opponent's. As a result, Reynolds found himself with four gunshot wounds to the upper chest before he could squeeze off more than one round. He fell to the floor in an awkward lump, sending the shiny Sig sliding across the dirty hardwood. Natalie picked it up and held it in one hand as she fumbled with her pants.

G kept his gun trained on Reynolds' head as he approached, but it was clear from the blood leaving his mouth that the bullets had done their job. For a moment, he and Natalie stood over their assailant's damaged body. The ghost inside Natalie kept her hand from trembling, but as the adrenaline subsided, so did the feeling of anger. She let her gun drop to the side and took a step back.

"You ever kill a man," asked G, already knowing the answer.

"No," whispered Natalie.

He looked at her sideways. "Do you want to?"

Natalie shook her head and turned around as G took aim.

"Me neither," he said.

Although the gunshot was expected, it still made her heart jump.

FORTY-SEVEN

X did his best to relax in the firm bed, listening to the midnight sounds of the dorms, to the quiet that was occasionally shattered by an unintelligible shout or the slam of a door. It was the kind of background noise that his hyper-vigilance would tolerate. After all, the hallway was protected by glass doors and a biometric scanner. The sounds he heard were of insensitive college kids making a ruckus late at night and not the stray bum trying to break in and score some fancy equipment. It was like finding sanctuary in a battlefield and X sunk into it easily.

Natalie's bed was no bigger than his own, leaving X to rest awkwardly on the outside edge, holding onto her waist with the tips of his fingers to keep from falling off. The beds weren't designed for sleeping side by side, he mused, but if you stacked the occupants, that might work. He was sleeping in Natalie's room because her roommate had left town earlier that day, skipping Friday's classes to go see some rock band play the Alamo Dome. It was one of the few times that they got time alone, short of renting a hotel room by the hour in Old Downtown.

"What are you doing," he asked, trying to open a communication channel by asking a nothing question.

"Sleeping," she replied, her voice actually sounding tired.

Instead of allowing her to rest, X moved his hand to her hipbone and pressed down. Her whole body convulsed in an effort to escape him. She pushed his hand away with hers, so X switched to tickling her hamstrings, which caused her to buck away again.

"I'm tired," she said, grabbing his hand and trapping it near her stomach.

"I'm not," said X, retreating, rolling onto his back to find that his left arm hung over empty space.

"Then why did you come to bed?"

X thought about it, wondering, knowing that the answer was that he wanted to screw her. Somehow, he knew that he would be denied, yet he went to her anyway. He was surprised to find that he didn't have a good reason for that. Even if he loved her, there was no reason for her to be rude. His bruised ego took over, reeling from the rejection. He felt himself speak without considering the words.

"Good question," he said, swinging his feet to the furry rug on the floor. He sought out his shorts with his toes and found them, pulling them up as he stood.

"Where are you going?"

"I don't know. Maybe I'll go see if G is up, play some pool."

Natalie rolled over in the bed, letting the covers fall away from her body, revealing her breasts as invitation. "No, come back." She looked pale in the moonlight, oddly so.

X shook his head. "I'll be back later."

The protest didn't last long as she pulled the covers up and rolled over again in a huff. She expelled a deep breath through her nose that turned into an annoyed snore. Her fatigue was taking its toll, and she didn't have the energy to get into an argument.

X found his shirt draped over the back of her computer chair and pulled it on. For a moment, he stood in the moonlit window, looking out at the dark night and the dots of streetlamps in the distance. It wasn't the same kind of darkness as before, when C was a hope and a dream that could never be attained. The aftertaste of his obsession with her was still in his mouth, lingering there to remind him of the greatest definition he had ever had of desire and love. Now something was missing, as if the lack of his quest to get her back had somehow lessened the meaning of his life. Pleasing her, consoling her, trying to work her towards enrolling at UT when she graduated, they were all missions that he willingly allowed to dominate his life.

He left the room and walked down the hallway distracted, still lost in thought. How many nights had he stayed up late with her? Jacked in, doing everything or nothing, with the most important goal being just to see each other. Those mini-vacations, those virtual dates, had not been enough to keep her interest. Having just moved his hands over a flesh and blood woman, he partially understood why C had moved on. There was an allure to reality, to the potential to be shot down. C had rarely denied him access to her body while in the Net, but he recalled how careful she had been with their first real sexual encounter and the subtle ways that she limited their potentially unsafe interactions. There were no consequences in the Net, and X and C had used that to their advantage.

The door to his room was unlocked despite the late hour, which made X suddenly inventory all of his possessions and weigh their value should they be stolen. He stepped inside and locked the door behind him, sliding the deadbolt into place with an exaggerated movement. The room was dark except for the ambient glow of Bo's rig perched atop one of his bedposts near the wall. As he climbed onto the small dresser and then onto his own bed, he began to feel that wistful desire to talk to someone, to discuss what was going on with his life. Problems were most easily solved when diagrammed out on paper; anything bad could have its box marked out with a red pen. Reclining on the tough mattress, X wondered if there was anyone that he could talk to now that C was gone.

Faces of ex-girlfriends and old high school buddies cycled through his head, but they would be neither interested nor available. He thought back, wondered who it was that he talked to when he had problems with C. Natalie's face occurred to him and he dismissed it quickly. There used to be someone, he remembered. Someone he went to who always listened to him but never judged or criticized. X felt a guilty twitter in his stomach and wondered if he had the guts or even the desire to go so far as that. He looked over at the clock, saw the time passing twelve-thirty. It was unlikely that Natalie would get up and come looking for him.

Bo rolled over in his bunk, sending a magazine to the floor. X waited to see if he would wake up completely, but he didn't. Quietly, he retrieved his code cube from the black box on the dresser and slipped the electrode on his neck. He felt the guilt again and tried to convince himself that he was simply jacking into his cube as he had done a million times before. He had not done anything bad.

Yet, he told himself.

The playground spread out around him, growing from the bottom up, punctuated by the appearance of the slightly obscured sun that dropped an orange tint onto the bright and shiny slide and accompanying monkey bars. Off to the left, the edge of the forest rose gradually, bringing with it the smell of summer leaves, of wood that never moved but grew nonetheless. X bent down to touch the rocks on the ground and was satisfied to find them already warm and chalky. He wiped the dust from his fingers and stood up, grinning slightly at the reproduction of his memory. He was back in the old neighborhood, at the place C's East Coast parlance had labeled a *tot lot*.

It wasn't really as he remembered it, but coming back at night would have been too much like before, too suspicious if anyone were to walk in. He found that he was dressed appropriately in khaki shorts and a white tee. The rocks shifted under his sandals as he moved to the slide, sitting gingerly on the warm metal as it heated his legs. It's the same, he thought to himself. It was only missing one thing. X took a deep breath and tried to talk himself out of it, but his internal dialogue only made him want to see her that much more. He spread his hands and opened a virtual desktop in front of him. With his index finger, he browsed the files in his rig.

She was hidden, of course, amongst the garbage of the rig's operating system, in plain view to anyone who could decipher the cryptic names of dynamically linked libraries and various jar files. He found the archive file quickly, knew its name to be a random combination of letters and numbers similar to a sequence that already existed. When it asked for a password, he paused, trying to remember what elaborate security he had used. It was most certainly trapped with a tapeworm, ready to delete itself should anyone try to open it using a brute force attack. The desktop fell away and the file floated in front of him, wavering like a bad hologram. It sunk to the ground a few feet away and waited.

It has to be something only her and I would know, he told himself. Something that Natalie or G wouldn't guess in a million years. It couldn't be a simple password; no alphanumeric string would be strong enough to protect what he slowly realized was one of his most prized possessions. If the rig were stolen and the file lost to nosy thieves, there would be no way to replace it. Like the nude construct stills of C that he had forced himself to delete, there would be no going back. Format the wrong flash drive, he thought to himself, and no amount of his memory would be able to bring her back.

"Woman of my dreams," he said, folding his hands and focusing his eyes on the file. The small yellow folder pulsed, grew a little, and then settled. "Love of my life," he continued. A light grew within the folds, spilling out onto the rocks around it. He finished the passphrase. "I miss you."

The file grew upwards from its two-dimensional representation to form a slim column and then pulsed outwards to accommodate the occupant within. X could see her taking shape through the semi-transparent skin of the yellow womb. He recognized the bits and pieces like a face in a foggy memory. When the folder finally dissolved, he was surprised at how sharp she appeared, how much of her detail he had forgotten in the last month or two.

C smiled and took a step forward. She was wearing blue jeans and weathered sneakers, topped off by a light gray shirt that looked a size too big, hanging from her breasts like a sail, obscuring the curves of her stomach. Her brown hair hung in two long sheets on her shirt, framing the lettering that touted the proficiency of the high school's lacrosse team. Ultimately, it was her eyes that drew most of X's attention, because of everything else, they looked the most out of place. She was a virtual clone and nothing would ever replace the life behind them, no matter how much X wanted it.

"Have a seat," said X, motioning to the empty space beside him.

C complied with coded efficiency, easing into her human behavior patterns. It always took her a moment to get up to speed; it was a bug that X had never bothered to track down.

"How've you been?" He asked even though he knew he wouldn't get a response. That she couldn't talk was simultaneously a curse and a blessing. He didn't really want to know what was going on in her life, didn't care to discover how Andy was treating her, whether her parents had decided to split up or not, or which one of her friends had just lost her virginity. It was a conscious block in his mind that kept him from caring about the real C, the one that was living her life without him for the first time in a year. The other C, the one in the Net, was someone he didn't care much for either, knowing what she did to his other self.

But this C, this clone of the girl he had once loved, seemed to be outside of everything else. She was a trophy, a spoil of war that he might have put on his mantel had Natalie not been in the picture. G would come by, and X would tell him that he dated this girl once. Look how cute she is, look how she smiles. And G would inevitably say something crude like mentioning how for only fifteen she had big tits.

X chuckled, recalling the first time he had shown her to G and how he had wanted to start their own virtual brothel, but with perfect replicas of celebrities. When X explained that you had to physically touch the person in a virtual world to copy them, G set out to prove him wrong. Of course, that never materialized. The next time he saw G, he was trying to figure out how to automatically learn everything he needed for CS 302.

The wind kicked up a little in the quiet construct, bringing with it the sounds of hidden birds and insects. X placed his hand on C's knee, squeezing it gently. He picked up the conversation as if he had been talking for hours.

"There's just something missing, you know? I mean, there's this strong chemical attraction, like nothing I've ever seen before. You and I didn't have it, but we got by. Why was it so easy with you?"

C didn't respond. She didn't even blink.

He studied her body again, wondering if that unsettling feeling inside of him was desire or, more disturbing, actual lust. His hand was on her knee, but he couldn't tell whether he wanted to move it. It wouldn't take any discussion, no coercion, to get her clothes off. She would be the faithful slave, willing to let him do anything he wanted. All he had to do was say the word or make the first move.

His eyes fell on her shirt and it was as if the entire construct experienced a reverse focus effect. Suddenly, X realized that the dividing line between high school and college was more than just a formless enemy that he had tried to fight. It was real, palpable, standing between him and the girl he dated in his senior year. It wasn't just the change in location, the new friends, or the harder classes. It was a complete alteration of his state of mind. C lived in a world of curfews and groundings. X lived in a world of casual sex and rampant drug use.

Before, X had not been able to see past the miles that separated her bed from his or the years that stood between his departure and their reunion. The world was simply a computational problem that required the perfect sequence of keys to complete successfully.

It wasn't C that had changed; it was him.

He had moved on and she didn't want someone who didn't live in the same protected world as her. It was as foreign as dating a thirty-year-old man with his own car and a mortgage. As much as he couldn't fit her into his world, so too did she find it impossible to keep him in hers. X found himself lost in a contracting logic loop, still trying to figure out whose fault it had been after all. He looked at the clone again, asked her the question without words.

So no one, he thought, interpreting her silence. He let the sun set with a throwaway instruction, focusing instead on the way the fading light changed the hue of C's face. Although he didn't feel anything for her, he could not take his eyes from hers. Whatever had happened, she was still that girl, a snapshot of a companion he had needed at that stage in his life. He thought briefly of other women, but only a few were fifteen or older when he dated them, and the others were much too young to copy, would turn his stomach if he tried to keep them. But C, fifteen and perfect, was still within reach of his eighteen-year-old self. Perhaps after a few more birthdays he would have to erase her. Or at least stop touching her the way he was.

X snapped out of the fog, found his hand under C's baggy shirt and caressing the side of her breast. He retracted quickly, standing and stumbling away from the slide.

There was a dull buzzing in his ear, remnants of the pressure he had felt when the blue cocoon collapsed inwards on him and the cipher. He recalled trying to jump, recalled the momentary existence in two places at once. But this place? He looked around wildly. This wasn't even a real construct; it couldn't be. The virus had taken over every sector. Could this one have escaped detection? His eyes fell on C again, knew that this place held more of his signature than a majority of his other constructs.

"This is a memory," he said out loud, listening to the words echo dully in the crumbling virtuality. As the noise of the world died down, he began to hear something low, a crumpling, crushing, and destructive sound. X wheeled around in fear, expecting to see the cipher or the virus standing inches from his neck.

There was nothing except for the trees, with green leaves that were slowly turning red, rusting, and falling in fast-forward from their branches. X shook his head. This was his memory. The virus couldn't get inside his head, could it?

His question was answered by a faint aroma, one of burning and ash. He watched with a quiet sadness while the trees turned to rust, falling in dusty piles. The slides, the rocks, and even the monkey bars fell to the oncoming virus, crumbling like burnt newspaper before his eyes. It filled the entire construct, pooling around his feet, surrounding him completely. There were only a few inches between his sandals and the sparkling border of red death.

On what used to be the edge of the forest, X noticed a swelling, a mound that grew up from the nothingness like a rectangular bubble. The virus then retreated, flowing around his protective circle, towards the rising column. It spilled upwards to the top and then disappeared into a hidden orifice. With the construct stripped of all life, X stared at the non-shape in front of him, wondering where this new stage of his death sentence was going to lead.

The muscles in X's jaw fell slack. He stood there staring at the impossible evolution in front of him. The virus flowed like blood around a body, as if the skin had been turned inside out. He didn't want to admit it, but from the shape and the height, X had no doubt in his mind what was going on. At first, he hoped it was a fluke, a ploy to get him to drop his guard.

But when the blood faded away and he was staring into her face, the one that flashed an echo of anger and contempt for him, he finally understood the strange behavior of the virus, of its never-ending quest to see him destroyed.

The virus, the predator always lurking in the shadows, was C.

FORTY-EIGHT

The equipment room at Vinestead West's main operations building was designed with the nowhere-to-hide security model in mind. On one side of the room was a bank of receiving windows, ten of them, spaced evenly apart such that a person standing at one could not see the contents of another. From the lone entry door, it was thirty steps to the other side. The entire room was painted white, and the stark walls were spotted with ball-lensed cameras that saw in every direction. At the first sign of unauthorized personnel, the receiving windows would automatically close, shuttered by reinforced steel plating, five inches thick. By the time an intruder had made it across the floor and started drilling the plates, the two security teams stationed on either side of the receiving wall would have already rushed in with orders to kill on sight.

It was because of this draconian security that Jape walked very carefully with his box held conspicuously at chest height. Inside, he had packed away his Katsumi V3 immersion rig and all of its accessories, including the modified code cubes that he used for extra storage. At the bottom of the box, his cell phone glowed blue, flashing a red LED every few seconds to inform its owner that they wouldn't be able to make a call. On top of all of this, Jape had placed the nameplate that used to hang on his door. *Julius Parker*, it read, *SES First Class*. The title was a fancy way to say that he lied to people to get them to do whatever the bosses wanted.

"Your scan, please," said the man behind the counter. He was one of Vinestead's older employees, going on sixty or seventy years by the look of it, another layer of security that ensured that if the workers ran off with the goods, then at least they would be easy to catch.

Jape pressed his thumb against the scanner on the counter and endured a nervous three seconds while the LED flashed yellow, and then eventually green.

"Mr. Parker," said the old man. His eyes scanned the notes in Jape's file. "Congratulations on your promotion. It's always good to see young men moving up in the company. After all, someone will need to replace me when I'm gone."

"Moving up?" He tried to steal a look at the clerk's viewee. "Is that what it says?"

"Sorry, no." He gave an apologetic smile. "I just assumed from this disbursement that you were getting some kind of promotion. We usually don't give new equipment to anyone who isn't—" His words were cut short by his sudden recollection of standard operating procedure.

Jape nodded. "I understand. Hush hush."

The clerk pressed on. "Carlos," he said, calling to an assistant, "bring me the box I just queued up." He examined Jape's possessions, pulling them one by one and keying their serial numbers into his viewee. "I apologize for the wait," he said, not looking up, "but everything is sneaker-net around here today, I'm afraid."

"It's not a problem."

Carlos appeared from behind the staggered walls carrying a thick rig case. He placed it on the counter on the clerk's left, circled him, and removed Jape's previous rig.

"Thank you, Carlos." The clerk rotated the case and pushed it towards Jape. "I won't spoil the surprise for you." He smiled like an excited grandfather at a birthday party. "Go ahead, open it."

Jape ran his fingers over the embossed lettering on the top edge of the case. It spelled out his name in silver characters that gleamed against the flat black background. He opened the locks and lifted the lid slowly. At first, he didn't recognize the neatly organized parts buried halfway in the protective foam, but hiding inside the top lid was an unmistakable staple of his digital life. It was a remarkably progressive rig, with smooth corners that bent the white fluorescents around him. The visor on the front was highly reflective and showed a clean image of Jape staring down in awe, his face distorted by the curved glass.

"This isn't a Katsumi," said Jape.

The old man was almost giggling. "No, Koertig, version one."

"German?"

"In label only," he replied, shaking his head. "Born and bred right here in the good old U.S. of A. Newest item to come out of Vinestead R&D in a long time." Again, he shut his eyes in frustration. If he kept hemorrhaging information, they were sure to fire him or worse. "Please," he said, "you should be moving along. Everything will be explained to you." He slid a piece of paper across the counter. "Room 2605. You are expected immediately."

Jape closed up the case and secured the locks. Dragging it off the counter, he was surprised at how little it weighed despite the contents. "Thank you," he said, nodding politely.

"Best of luck, young man," said the clerk. He took a step back and glanced nervously to the side.

As he walked across the floor of death, Jape was surprised at how preoccupied he was with the brief encounter with the new rig. He smiled at himself, realizing that he wanted nothing more than to put it on and jack in.

FORTY-NINE

There is darkness at the end of a barrel, thought Natalie, as she pointed the pistol at her reflection in the mirror. She wanted to know how she looked, if anything about her appearance seemed threatening, seemed capable of inflicting the kind of damage that G had managed so easily. It was one thing to dress up and put all sorts of marks on her face, but if the gun trembled in her hand, if her lip betrayed her, then it was all for not.

"Check this out," said G, calling from the bedroom.

Natalie lowered her weapon and carried it loosely by her side as she followed the sound of G's voice. Beyond the curtained doorway, she saw a nightmare of military implements. Even in the low light, she could see the dark green and light brown camouflage of various rifles, shotguns, and even boxes full of what appeared to be explosives.

"We've hit the jackpot," said G, holding up a pair of matching flak jackets. "We might just get out of this alive." He tossed one to Natalie and she caught it with one hand.

It smelled old and dusty, making her crinkle her nose. "I don't think this could stop a paint ball."

G kicked at the rusting lock of a green trunk near Reynolds' bed. His boots hit awkwardly, resulting in glancing and ineffective blows. Natalie watched, again thinking how much easier it would be to just shoot the damn thing off. Her eagerness to pull the trigger surprised even her.

At last, the lock fell away under the pressure of G's steel toes. Inside, they found the pristine packaging of the Sig Sauer case, but on a larger scale. Smaller guns were attached via velcro to the lid, while below, staggered shelves held everything from rifles to machine guns. To Natalie's disappointment, there was no RPG at the bottom of the pot, but G's smile told her that it was something equally important.

"Now *this*," said G, pulling two tightly packed, plastic containers from the trunk, "this is fucking armor."

Natalie compared it quickly to the bulky vest in her hand.

"He must have stolen these," continued G. "This is military-grade, top of the line. They'll stop a 9mm bullet at point blank." G stood and walked over to the crumbling dresser, clearing away some of the junk with a swipe of his arm. He undid the plastic covering and spread the contents in front of him. A small slip of paper turned out to be instructions and he read them slowly.

Natalie dropped the flak jacket and moved to the trunk. On the right side of the lid, she saw a knife she fancied, with a non-retractable six-inch blade beside a chest-mounted sheath.

"Looks like this will be a two-man operation," announced G, tracing the words with his finger. "I'll have to help you put it on and then you, me." He chuckled. "It goes on under your clothes, right on the skin."

"I have to take my clothes off in front of you," asked Natalie, more for the sake of conversation than to argue. "I don't know about that."

"After what just happened out there?"

Natalie laughed a little, looking at G over her shoulder. She smiled. "I want this knife," she said, pulling it from the trunk. She approached the dresser and placed the Sig on it. "Think you can help me get this harness on?"

"Sure," said G, nodding. He thumbed through the various sections of rigid fabric, looking for the starting piece. "You'll need to take off your clothes," he repeated.

"You mentioned that," said Natalie, taking a step back. She didn't move for several moments, wondering what G was thinking in that twisted mind of his. Hadn't he already seen enough when she was stripping at gunpoint?

"It might be the last time," he said. The words floated out passively, as if he didn't really want to say them.

Natalie moved in close to G and kissed him on the lips, lingering only a few heartbeats too long. "Look all you want," she whispered, retreating. Her shirt came off first, followed by a slow striptease that wasn't in any way enticing.

It reminded G of a woman preparing for bed, not caring or knowing that anyone was watching, doing everything for purely mechanical reasons. Even when Natalie slid her pants down and stepped out of them with her socks still on her feet, G felt nothing. All he could imagine was a fat man standing a few feet away, half a trigger-pull from killing her. He shook his head, worried that he would never be able to rid himself of that image. Even though it had been her idea, if she had died, he would still blame himself.

The armor was applied with a ceremonial finality that affected both of them. G moved the pieces slowly across her skin, held them in place while they bonded to her specific curves and merged with each other. He did her lower section first, wrapping her waist in the black fabric, glancing at her breasts and her smile in between applications. Every now and then, a small urge with a meek voice would ask if he wanted to take her, but his mind always answered with a layout of the apartment and a large red X marking the spot of the dead man in the living room.

She looked like a black marble statue, protected from ankle to neck with the body armor. The way it clung to her curves made G think of the form-fitting costumes of superheroes. He wondered briefly if that was what they were, before realizing that if so, then they were only pretending to be. He thought about it more as Natalie redressed, smiling at her hesitation as she pulled her underwear on and saw how it clashed with her black hips. "At least I can still go to the bathroom," she said.

G laughed, picking up the knife harness and holding it up for her. He slipped it on over her shoulder and secured the strap around her torso. The knife fell just above her left breast, and she practiced pulling and sheathing it quickly.

"I could never stab someone," said G. "Firing a gun is one thing, but with a knife, you have to get up real close and personal. You have to feel the blade as it cuts through their skin." He shuddered. "Sick."

"I don't know," countered Natalie, "it seems more intimate, you know? That way you can see the fire in their eyes go out as you rotate the point of the blade in their heart."

He looked at her, concerned. "Do you have a specific person's heart in mind?"

"Maybe." She turned and walked back into the living room, to the Sig case on the table. There were two holsters inside, each equipped to carry one of the rifles and one of the pistols. She slipped it on easily, but G had to help her secure the rifle's stock to the small length of cord on her right side.

"It's so you can drop the gun and it'll stay handy," instructed G. "These two will keep the rifle oriented so that if you switch to your pistol, you can come back quickly without having to rotate it." He demonstrated by letting the gun fall. "You'll get used to the weight."

Natalie smiled, impressed. "How do you know so much about this stuff? I don't remember seeing any weapons in your dorm room."

"Are you kidding? X and I used to prepare for CS tests by hitting up the run and guns." He thought for a second and then mimicked X's voice, "What's the difference between a protected and private variable?" Then in his own, "A bullet in your ass motherfucker!"

Laughing, Natalie picked up the rifle as he had shown her and aimed it at the lumpy pile on the floor. Out of the corner of her eye, she could see G looking at her with envy. She turned to him. "It's your turn to suit up." She unhooked the Sig and placed it back in the case. "Shall we," she asked, rubbing her hands together to warm them up.

G allowed her to apply the armor to his body, but only by keeping his back to her. He didn't want her to see him in his varying stages of excitement, so he made sure that the pelvic section was the first one to go on. Natalie, feeling slighted by the unfair show and tell, sought retribution by slapping him on the ass. Any other time, he thought, and he would have thrown her down on the floor and made her pay for that. Chuckling to himself, he debated whether revenge truly solved anything.

"Have you thought about how we are going to get in?" Natalie had her hands pressed firmly against the small of G's back, holding a section in place. "I was thinking maybe we could drop a few grenades out front, clear the way."

"We don't have any grenades, just some low-end C4, and not much of it. I figure we might need it to get through a couple doors." G shook his head. "I'm not sure how we're going to get past the guards out front."

Natalie thought for a moment. "Fire alarm? Get them to come outside and then all we have to do is shoot Anela. We could do it from across the street."

"The way I see it," said G, rubbing his hand against the back of his neck, "we've got armor that'll let us survive a few direct hits, guns that will tear through anything, and code that will enhance our reflexes and agility. If we hit them straight on, use every bit of our advantage coupled with the element of surprise, we should be able to walk right in."

With the last of the armor in place, G began to dress again, amused at the image of himself wearing ass-less body armor chaps.

"I still think we ought to have a plan," said Natalie, letting her hand run down his armored back.

"I agree, but I think better when I'm coded up. So let's get our shit together and get out of here. I have a feeling that someone might come looking for their friend eventually. And I don't have the patience to watch you carelessly pull six thousand dollars out of your pocket again." He smiled, daring her to defend her actions.

She ignored him. "When are we going to load up the code?"

"Later, just before we go in. We'll find some place to lay low until the sun goes down. Then boom, load it and go." G made sure the Sigs were arranged correctly in the case before shutting it. Walking to the door, he marveled at how well the armor moved over his skin, almost as if it weren't there. He was suddenly overcome with the desire to test it. He stopped in front of the door.

"What is it," asked Natalie.

G turned around, smiling slightly. "Punch me in the stomach."

"What?"

"Just punch me, I want to see if this shit really works."

Natalie looked at him, unsure.

"As hard as you can," said G, patting his stomach.

Stepping into the punch, Natalie hit G with all the force her 120-pound frame could muster, focusing it all into the 4 leading knuckles of her fist.

G fell backwards into the door and let out a quick involuntary breath. He gasped like a fish out of water, desperately trying to suck down the air he'd lost. He tried to laugh.

"Did you feel that," asked Natalie, coyly.

"A little," said G. "I think we'll be better off trying to dodge the bullets."

"Can your code do that?"

G nodded, still holding his stomach. He unlocked the door and stepped out into the hallway. "And then some," he said.

FIFTY

C couldn't believe what she was seeing. Standing in front of her, looking the same as he always had inside the Net, was X. He was a few feet away, towering over her, but with a shade of fear in his eye. She struggled to recall the last time she had seen him, a vague image of their final meeting in his homedir. He was supposed to spend the rest of his existence there while she did her best to separate her bits and find a peaceful death. And though she had spread her ashes to the wind, it had not resulted in the ultimate escape. Now she was in front of X again, feeling the lingering bits of anger melt away.

She was overcome by questions, not just about him, but about herself as well. There were memories in her head of distant places and virtual cities, worlds that she had never visited but now felt like she had an intimate knowledge of. Faces of millions of people fluttered like a deck of cards in her mind, rogue pieces of information in her newly reformed brain. Whether it was the shock of transition or just a change in the air, C felt that the world was somehow different. The threads of the Net pulsed all around her, but their vibrations were somehow hollow, as if the data that usually flowed had come to a standstill, allowing the dim echoes of the occasional drip to move freely down the pipes.

While her thoughts did their best impression of a tightly packed pinball machine, she observed X shifting from one foot to the other before finally sitting on the ground and crossing his legs. He put his head in his hands, looking more exhausted than sad. The image of a defeated X brought her a momentary happiness, but as quickly as it came, it was replaced by a strong surge of empathy.

"Hello, X," she said, softly.

"Lily," replied X, into his hands, surprised at how odd the name sounded coming from him. He had not said it in a long time.

"What is this place?"

X looked up, wary of C's question. Instead of anger, he saw genuine concern in her face, something he normally would have viewed as weakness. "It used to be a playground, our playground," he said, "before you destroyed it."

She shook her head, looking around at the remnants of the decayed construct. "*I* did this? I don't remember."

"The viral you has been after me since I got here."

A hurried conversation replayed in her head. "But I warned you. I told you that you couldn't jack in again."

"I didn't. I was forced."

C walked forward and sat on the black floor a foot away from X, crossing her legs just as he had. She could tell that he was telling the truth. Some sad music played in the back of her head, an automatic soundtrack called up by her subconscious but reproduced externally. "You're the one I sent back out, right?"

"I don't know anymore. The last thing I remember before all of this was being strapped into a chair. Then she tried to jack me in." He shook his head in confusion. "I guess it worked."

"Who jacked you in?"

"Anela. She's the—"

"ZabSix cipher den," said C, finishing his thought. A recent construct still of Anela flashed across her screen, making her wonder how X would interact with such a stern-looking woman.

"How do you know her?"

"I seem to know a lot of things. Cities, faces, and a million other bits of data that don't sync up with anything. My head feels heavy, like stuffed up."

Trouble breathing, thought X, bringing up the memory of C at school, having an asthma attack outside his Physics class. The teacher had made him return to his seat, said that he couldn't go out there and help her breathe. He knew there wasn't anything that he could do, but something morbid in him suggested that her constricting airway might keep her from breathing altogether. If she died in the hallway, he at least wanted to be there, holding her hand as if the simple act would make the transition easier.

"Anela doesn't like you very much," continued C, reading from the cue cards of her memory.

"She wouldn't," agreed X. He wanted to laugh but couldn't find the energy to do so. The fight in him was gone, disarmed first by C's restraint, and then replaced by the knowledge that if she did turn on him, he wouldn't be able to defend himself. "Last time I checked, you didn't like me much either."

"Maybe not," said C, uncertain. "But that seems so trivial now. Surely you can feel it? You once told me about the pulse, the beating heart of the Net's core. Do you even feel that anymore?"

"No," replied X, trying to probe outside of the construct. "I can't feel anything. It's like the rest of the Net isn't even there anymore. You did a pretty thorough job."

"That wasn't my fault." The information was streaming into C's brain, reconstructing the last few days of her viral existence. "I really don't remember what happened after I tried to kill myself."

X lifted an eyebrow.

"That's right, you don't remember that conversation." She pushed a piece of her digital hair behind her ear. "Once I had you trapped in your homedir, I tried to end my consciousness. But I guess I hadn't really figured it out back then. I think I understand it better now."

"What's that?"

"The bond." She said the words like the title of a movie. "There is no quit in the Net. My brain wanted to connect with something after losing its body. I'm tied to the Net now. And so are you."

"How can you tell?"

"Anyone can. There is no one else left in here. I don't know if you've been keeping up, but systems are pulling out of the network faster than I can track. It's been going on for hours, but it's really beginning to pick up. Everyone that was jacked in is out now." She half-smirked. "I should know; I sent a lot of them home myself. Even your Natalie."

X winced, wishing he could summon the anger.

"I didn't do it on purpose. I wasn't really in control of the virus." She stopped to consider something. "I don't think I was the virus."

At this, X widened his eyes. "I just watched you step out of it. Everything else that touches it gets burned. But you walked out of the fire like it was nothing."

"I think," she replied, narrowing her eyes in concentration, actually seeing the process unfold in her mind, "that my suicide was successful. I separated enough of my bits to lose the ability to think, which is as close to death as I was going to get. But then the virus, chasing you all over the place, to a thousand constructs at once—"

"It collected you?"

"Absorbing everything it touched," continued C. "That's why I have all of this extraneous data in my head. It brought everything together and suddenly I was here again. Cogito ergo sum. That's why we're tied to the Net. That's why neither of us can really ever die. Unless—"

"Unless they shut down the Net."

"Yeah," said C, solemnly. Although she remembered not wanting to exist anymore, the sentiment no longer felt welcome. "The Net *is* shutting down," she said at last. "When the last system is removed, there won't be a network anymore."

"They can't just shut down the Net," said X. "The entire world would come to a stop. Businesses, telecoms, and government services wouldn't be able to operate. It'd be anarchy."

"Not if there was something else to carry that data."

X's thoughts felt flaky, as if they were crumbling in transit, but he was still able to pick out the name. "VNet?"

"They already have the infrastructure in place. All it would take to get people back online is unplugging a wire and putting it somewhere else. If they've got penetration in the telcos, people at home wouldn't even see a difference."

"Damn," said X, amazed. "I can't believe you're the same girl that I had to teach how to use a rig. You had barely mastered instant messaging when I met you."

"Things change. When I met you, I thought you were a nice guy, best thing to ever happen to me. And look how that turned out." She tried to keep her tone light. "But look at you now. If I could still talk to my friends, I could tell them I dated the man that single-handedly brought down the Net."

X feigned a bow, felt the stretch in his back that shouldn't have been there. "I think the history books will say that a virus destroyed the Net. I didn't do anything."

"You tempted the fates with your clone army."

"That wasn't even my idea. G came up with that and Jape fucked it up."

"Jape," repeated C. "I remember him. I never bought his accent."

"He's a good guy, helped me out of a few jams. He's like the anti-Anela. I should have asked him to take her out."

"There's nothing you can do about it now."

In fact, there was nothing he could do about anything. X felt the weight of his own impotence crush down on him. There was a lingering feeling of hatred towards Anela, a desire for revenge, but every time he started thinking of a way to get back at her, his mind simply gave up. Anela, Natalie, and even G, were lost causes. They were on their own now.

"So what about us," asked X, locking eyes with her. "I'm guessing that if you were going to kill me, you would have done it by now."

C leaned back on her arms, making her head sink into her shoulders. "Don't you remember? I let you go, absolved you. It's not your fault that someone forced you back into the Net. I think you received justice that was both sufficient and poetic."

"I *am* sorry for what I did to you."

"I know."

"But you don't—"

C put up her hand, dismissing his sentence. "You don't have to say anything else. I get it, but being sorry isn't enough. That's why another you is still trapped in your homedir. He's paying both of your tabs." Her last word seemed to lack bass, exiting her mouth without the intensity of the others. She grabbed at her chest, to where her heart would have been.

"What is it?" X leaned forward slightly.

"I don't know," she rasped, "my chest hurts like hell."

Scooting forward, he put his hand on her chin and lifted her face.

"No," she said. "Don't."

X let go, felt the echo of the asthma attack memory sting at the back of his neck.

C doubled over and grabbed at her stomach. For several minutes, she did her best Lamaze breathing. Inside, she knew that the pain wasn't localized to the abdomen, but rather to the very ends of her extremities, to pieces of her that existed far beyond her avatar. It hurt in places she had visited only in memory, in faraway cities that burned under her viral fire. Something was biting at her toes, eating away at the edges of her existence. She began cutting ties with the rest of the virus, severing connections as quickly as she could, cutting wide swaths in the web that extended from her avatar into the ether. Bit by bit, the feeling subsided, but not completely. For every hundred connections she broke down, another one popped up.

"We need to go," she said, finally looking up.

"Is something wrong?"

"Jump us somewhere, anywhere."

X forced himself to put a hand on her shoulder. "What are we running from?"

"Vinestead." The words squeaked from her lips.

"What about them?"

C couldn't stop her eyes from tearing up at the utterance of her own death sentence. "They've released an antivirus."

He couldn't think of anything to say, consumed as he was by his own introspection. The thought of losing C wasn't something he had considered since the day they split up. Natalie was his girl; she was the one he obsessed about and tried to please. So why the sudden feeling of propriety with C? He wondered if he really loved her that much and how that feeling could have survived long enough to blossom at such an inopportune time. The urge to save her was tempered with the belief that there was nothing he could do. She was as good as dead and so was he. If the antivirus was tuned only to C's code, then they wouldn't have had to evacuate everyone else. Like she said, they were the only two free-running programs left. The antivirus wasn't looking for her; it was looking for anything.

Somewhere nice, thought X. Somewhere they could wait out the end of their respective existences. One last evening with C. One last construct to build.

X pulled C closer to him and jumped.

FIFTY-ONE

There was a struggle going on inside Natalie's head, but the small part of her consciousness that could decide between column A and column B was out to lunch and was having no part in the argument. She felt as if her body was on automatic pilot, or more accurately, on two automatic pilots, each with their own preferred way of doing things. Her hands moved without regard to the other, keeping her off balance. She could feel the rifle come up to her shoulder, be poised to aim it, only to drop it suddenly and switch to her pistol, firing without caring where the barrel was pointed. Sensory input around her seemed to indicate that she was in the middle of a war zone, but every time she tried to pinpoint the source of any one stimulant, it would fade away and be replaced by something else, like the backdrop of a cartoon that sped by much too fast and sometimes repeated.

It was like being a prisoner in her own body, confined to the lower part of her chest, holding onto the bones of her ribcage for dear life. She wanted to shut her eyes against the flashing lights and flying dust, but they were no longer her own. They belonged to someone else, to a crazed killer who had no reservations about pulling a trigger. It was something Natalie knew that she could never do. It wasn't just a matter of right and wrong or even if the person deserved it; it was just a limitation of her programming. There was nothing inside of her that told her it was justified to injure someone else to the point of death. G had assured her that those qualms would be erased by the code he cooked up. Ever since they loaded it up in the alley off West Street between Fourteenth and Fifteenth, his promise had held true.

But Natalie soon began to feel different, even though at some level she knew the code was controlling her body, keeping her alive and shooting instead of dead and bleeding. The best thing would be to ride it out and hope everything turned out for the best. Later, she could try to reconcile her morality with the generic guards she had killed. They weren't really human, after all. Most were combination of man and machine, taking bodyguard jobs just for the opportunity to put the metal to someone. They lived for death, so in a roundabout way, they shouldn't have been so surprised to find themselves on the wrong end of her rifle. It was a sound justification, one that Natalie had endured for what felt like hours

But the logic that supported that premise had begun to break down and she could feel herself reaching out to her body, seeping into it like a worn glove.

Even as she did it, she knew the consequences would be dire. The agility and strength that had carried her through aging sheetrock and up numerous flights of stairs would be gone and there wouldn't be a single crutch left on which to lean. She told herself that it didn't matter, that it wasn't right for G's killer app to use her body like that. When she stood for final judgment, the presence of foreign instructions wouldn't be enough to sway the jury. Finally, the guilt overtook her, fed the desire for total self-control. Breaking through the last barrier, Natalie seized the reins and pulled back, stopping the stagecoach of destruction in its tracks.

"Natalie!" G's screaming face seemed like the product of a nightmare. It was creased in deep lines and cracked in some places like old leather. His cheeks had drops of blood on them, whether his or someone else's, she didn't know. Natalie focused mostly on his bloodshot eyes where black islands dotted tormented red seas. He reached out for her shoulder and yanked her to her feet violently. Again, he screamed over the hail of bullets, which had just become startlingly visceral. "What's wrong?!"

Natalie struggled to get her words out, but in the end, she didn't have to. She saw the recognition in G's eyes, knew that he knew she was no longer tripping on his synthetic drugs. Something like disappointment came over his face, followed by a widening of his eyes that portended her death, as if he were putting together the sequence in his mind. Somewhere in the back of his skull, he was already mourning her, wondering what he would tell X if he ever saw him again.

"Stay down! Stay behind me!"

She did as she was told, crouching behind G as he took cover near a load-bearing column. The guards were hidden in the shadows of the building and their bullets were only detectable by indirect evidence: the holes on the wall behind them, the lingering dust of exploding drywall, and the chips of shattering concrete that rained down from above. From time to time, she chanced a look upwards, saw G moving with inhuman precision, darting out from behind his cover to squeeze off five or six shots with his pistol and then following it up with a quick, blind spray from his rifle. In between, he put his back flat against the column, took three quick breaths, and then repeated.

One by one, the frequency of the distant explosions began to lessen, until there was only the occasional pop. G rushed into the darkness, keeping low to the ground. Natalie searched the shadows, listened intently until a tiny explosion briefly lit the distant corner, followed by the sound a half-second later. There were footsteps and Natalie wondered for a few tense seconds if G had survived, only to have the doubt removed by the sound of his laughter.

"Got you, motherfucker," said G, his calm voice a far cry from the platoon sergeant that had screamed at Natalie earlier.

She listened to his footsteps get closer and was only able to stand when he came into view, smiling. His face had reverted, though the blood splatter remained.

"You could have dialed it back," he said, dropping the empty clip from his pistol and replacing it with a new one. "You didn't have to bail completely. There's no going back now, unless we reload it." He looked sharply to the ceiling. "And that's time that we don't have. Come on."

He grabbed her by the elbow and ushered her towards the east side of the building. They had previously tried pushing all the way up the stairs, but their passage had been blocked, and they were forced to go through what G counted as twelve guards to get to the other end of the building. Besides the elevator, the only way to get to the twentieth floor was by a spiral staircase. It was a horrible plan, logistically, but G saw no other way short of shooting through the floor, and there weren't enough bullets left for that.

"Give me your rifle. I may need it."

Natalie complied and followed him slowly up the stairs. Their boots seemed to make an inordinate amount of noise on the metal steps. Above, they reached a landing, a small anteroom with a single chair and a badly deteriorated painting on the wall. To the left was an unmarked door, a terrifying omen that reminded her of a video game, of the helpless feeling of not knowing what was on the other side.

"We move," said G, opening the door slightly and peeking at the shadows inside. He slipped through and motioned for Natalie to join him in the hallway. There were several doors on either side of them, spaced too close together to be apartments, but just enough to be offices. They kept to the outside of the building and wound around through the maze-like hallways until they opened a door and saw the shiny silver polish of the elevator staring back at them. G pushed them quickly backwards through the door.

"What is it," asked Natalie, as G shut the door silently.

"The elevators open right into her office." He smiled thinly. "It's perfect. The elevators are shut down. She'll never expect us to come from this direction." He looked at Natalie as if seeking her corroboration, but she said nothing. "I think it's time for more berserker," he said, dialing up the code. He felt all of his muscles tense up in a quick self-diagnostic. "Zero defects."

Natalie smiled at him even as his eyes returned to the demonic glare of a cold-blooded killer.

"You wait here," he ordered, "you're in no condition to fight. I'll take care of any remaining guards and Anela." He tripped the safety on Natalie's rifle. "Anything you want Anela to know before she dies?"

"Just kill her," she replied. "No speeches."

"As you wish." G disappeared through the door.

In the silence that followed, Natalie sank to the floor of the hallway, kneeling awkwardly on one knee. The pistol in her hand clinked against the floor, reminding her of the death grip that she had on it. Her finger was still poised to pull, wrapped around the trigger so tenderly. The idea of never pulling it crossed her mind, but she realized that she already had, at least, another version of herself had. The memory of killing was fresh in her mind, but as far as body counts went, she had no idea. The few guards that she actually saw were always in her periphery, popping up unexpectedly, undetected until she swung her gun around. Then they would disappear again as the code took over her eyes, using them to locate the target and destroy it.

Gunshots sounded beyond the wall, two short bursts of two, controlled disbursement from G's rifle. In her mind, she could see him moving SWAT-style into the office, with one rifle raised to his shoulder and the other hanging at his side. He would never have thought about dual-wielding the guns, would never sacrifice accuracy for the ability to output twice the number of bullets. Natalie's heart skipped a beat as the quiet returned, only to be broken again by a steady stream of automatic fire that sounded horribly inefficient. Tightening her grip on the pistol, Natalie stood and opened the door slightly.

A single gunshot stopped her completely, just as she was about to step through. She waited, listened, and cursed herself for dropping out of G's code before the job was complete. Doing so had forfeited all of her advantage. With the code in her veins, she could rival the skill of a trained assassin, one that could easily dispatch a detachment of hired goons with minimal fuss. But without it, a single metalguard could easily take her apart. Then she heard it, the moaning of an injured man. A moan that was unmistakably G.

Everything she knew about tactics and strategy went out the window as she rushed from her hiding place and into the spacious office. Although there were lights between the windows, the room still held shadows, mostly among the curtains that hung behind a large desk off to the right. Natalie fired blindly into the darkness as she moved towards the center of the room where G was sprawled on his stomach. She knelt by his side and put a hand on his shoulder to shake him. Instead of the soft fabric of his shirt, she felt something cold and wet. Holding her breath, she looked down.

There was a single bullet hole in G's neck, just to the left of his spine. It was small, perhaps from a .22, but it had hit in a critical place, a centimeter or two above the lip of the armor. Any lower and G would still be firing away instead of—

"Drop it," said a voice from behind Natalie.

She froze, debated whether to turn and fire.

"I will not ask you again," continued the voice.

Natalie looked slowly over her shoulder to the tall woman standing next to the desk. She saw her features and heard X's words describing them. "Alright," she said, placing the gun on the floor. She stood up slowly and squared her eyes at Anela.

"I would have thought more of you, Natalie." She observed the momentary shock on Natalie's face. "Yes, I know a lot about you. I have been through the memories of your lover and as you know, he kept very detailed records."

"Where is he?" Her words came out feebly.

"In the Net, of course. I imagine he will be there until the very end. Vinestead has her hooks in deep now. Unfortunately, there is nothing I can do about it anymore."

"I thought you wanted X dead."

"And you as well," reminded Anela.

"Then why is it unfortunate?"

Anela smiled briefly. "Natalie, it is important for a woman in this day and age to be cognizant of the bigger picture. Men are put on this planet to keep women from attaining any kind of measurable power. The only hope for our gender is to remain one step ahead, see life on a global scale. We do *not* get there by focusing all of our energy on the first boy we lay in college. This is not about X; it never has been. Your boyfriend is just a pawn in all of this, a pawn I unwittingly delivered right into the hands of the enemy. I am not going to be the one responsible for his death, Vinestead is."

"I don't understand," said Natalie, shaking her head.

"I know. I expected that. Look out that window over there. Tell me what you see."

Natalie moved cautiously away from G, each step feeling like betrayal. She didn't want to leave him there, but the gun pointed in her direction was sufficient encouragement. Backing up slowly, she made it to the window and looked out. A light rain was falling, but there was no thunder or lightning. Below, the neon lights of Old Downtown were flickering from the unsteady power feed. It looked like home and although she towered high within its borders, she had never felt so far away. "I see lights. There's V-Six."

"No," corrected Anela. She picked up Natalie's gun and emptied the clip, dropping the unused bullets to the floor one by one. "What you see is free trade. When the big corporations left, everyday Americans like us took over. This place was dying, on the verge of anarchy. And we brought it back. The only way we were able to accomplish such a thing was because we had the freedom to try and fail. No one regulated our business, no one cared to. But now, they want to recognize us as legitimate because we pull in a lot of money that is going untaxed. The government is not getting their cut, and they are pissed off about it.

"The same thing is happening to the Net. All of those millions of miles of fiber out there are basically highways paid for by corporations and telecoms, yet people use them for free to sell their hand-crafted novelties or to auction off some outdated technology. Vinestead owns a lot of fiber, which means that a lot of businesses are using their lines to operate. Like our government, Vinestead believes there should be a tax, that they should get a cut. But they cannot just pass a law. They own enough of Congress to do so, but just like here, if you try to regulate business, business will just move. Out here, there are some freedoms that you cannot take away."

Natalie stared at the side of Anela's face and the barrel extended in her direction. Her captor's passionate words were falling on deaf ears, because despite the far-reaching consequences of free trade, none of her talk was bringing her any closer to X. "I don't care about Vinestead," she said, interrupting, "I only care about X."

"You *should* care about Vinestead. Or hell, maybe not. It would be one thing if you were going to live past tonight. Since that has already been decided, I guess you are right. You do not have to care. I just wanted you to know that your anger is misdirected."

Out of the corner of her eye, Natalie saw G stirring on the marble floor. Having failed him once before, she tried as hard as she could to keep her eyes on Anela. She tried to move casually down the length of the windowed wall, acting as if she wanted to get a better look at some landmark. A slight tiptoe action helped sell it.

"Well," continued Anela, "if you have no further statements, then I think it is time that I retired you. After all, you have cost me an entire guard team. They will not be cheap to replace."

Natalie tried to stall. "The last time I saw X, we were at that club." She pointed, stubbing her finger against the glass. "Then you showed up and took him away. *You*, not Vinestead."

"I admit; I did take him. But with good reason."

"And what did you do with him?" Natalie flashed anger.

"X and I had unfinished business. We had an impromptu meeting about—"

"What did you do?! I never saw him again!"

Anela's gun trembled momentarily in her hand, frightened by the intensity in Natalie's voice. She regained her equanimity quickly. "All I did was jack him in. He was complaining about a virus in the Net, but since he had been dishonest before, I saw no reason to believe him."

"Where is he now?"

"What does it matter to you? You are going to be dead inside of five seconds and then you will not even care anymore. Save your last question for something important. I promise that I will answer it truthfully."

G moved behind Anela, crouching low, each step a mix of excruciating pain and wavering balance. He lifted slowly behind her, staring at her exposed back, not wanting to look up and potentially catch eyes with Natalie.

"Where is my X?" Natalie gritted her teeth.

Anela smirked, lifted the gun slightly to make it level with Natalie's eyes. "He is in the basement." The words had barely left her mouth when the explosion ripped through the back of the barrel, sending the small brass shard of bullet hurtling in Natalie's direction. At the same time, G's arm grasped Anela's side and moved the gun enough for the bullet to ricochet off the armor on Natalie's left shoulder. The sudden sting was intense, causing her to cry out.

G struggled to hold Anela, brought her hand down hard on his knee to shake the gun loose. She dropped her weight, threatening to fall out of his arms, but G moved forward with her, going to the ground with a hard thud. As they rolled over each other, he sunk his teeth into her shoulder and spit out blood. The pain barely slowed her thrashing.

Moving quickly, Natalie crossed the short distance and scooped up Anela's gun. She trained it at Anela, but with the way they were moving, she couldn't be certain that she wouldn't hit G. And as small as the gun was, there was an outside chance that the bullet would pass right through her body.

"Your knife," rasped G.

Natalie dropped the gun and unsheathed the blade from her chest. On the floor, G was on his back, holding Anela on top of him and enduring blows from the back of her head. His legs were intertwined with hers, spreading them. Natalie kneeled in front of Anela, but the anger that had been fueling her suddenly dried up. She didn't want to kill, didn't want that kind of blood on her hands. Before, it was automatic, but this would be a conscious decision.

G felt his grip slipping, felt the last of his strength fade away. When that window closed, Anela would be free. She would take the knife right out of Natalie's hands and use it on her, then him. The whole thing would have been for nothing. G summoned the remaining stimulants, closed his eyes, and screamed.

"Goddammit, Natalie! STAB THIS BITCH!"

The feed was lost, Natalie realized, for a brief minute. In that time, she felt her arm moving, felt the stuttered movements of metal tearing through flesh, butting against ribs, slicing past them. There was a quiet calm to it all, a way in which no sound reached her ears, though she saw G and Anela with their mouths wide open, him screaming in satisfaction, her in pain. When she finally regained control, she observed that Anela had stopped struggling. Thin lines of blood were flowing over her lips. Natalie crawled forward as G released his hold.

Hanging above her felled opponent, Natalie stared deep into Anela's dying eyes, disappointed to find that there was no fire burning behind them. She watched with a guilty heart as Anela's world ended with a whimper.

FIFTY-TWO

The instructional video played on a small vidscreen under Jape's chair, going over the ins and outs of the recently released Koertig immersion rig. The way he was bent over with his face pushed through a circular cushion, Jape half believed he was due for a back massage instead of minor surgery. He heard the technician behind him playing with his utensils on a plastic tray. When the cold cotton ball scraped across the back of his neck, he felt a shiver spread throughout his body. A young woman appeared on the viewee, and Jape tried to focus his attention on her.

"Hello and congratulations on being selected for the phase one rollout of the Koertig Immersion Rig. Your measured aptitude and prior service have made you a superior candidate for this trial run. You, and others like you, will form the basis of Vinestead International's future operations."

Jape felt something prick the skin on his neck.

"You will find that the Koertig rig operates in much the same fashion as any modern and generally available immersion rig. Its construction has been architected with a focus on comfort, weight, and fit. However, it is the bearer's choice whether to wear the rig at all." The woman smiled and waited.

The desired effect appeared on Jape's face as confusion and intrigue.

"The pressure you feel on the back of your neck is the insertion procedure for Vinestead International's Guardian Angel chip, a technological achievement in its own right. Combined, the GA chip and the Koertig rig allow a user to jack into VNet without being connected via the umbilical electrode." A graphic of the rig appeared on the screen and rotated backwards. "As you can see, the electrode is noticeably absent. Instead, the signal is carried wirelessly between the transmitting node and the GA chip. As a standalone wireless system, the rig has an effective range of five hundred meters with clear line of sight. The signal may be degraded by walls and electronic interference."

There was a sharp pain on Jape's neck that made him jerk in his seat. The technician reminded him to be still.

"By utilizing cell networks and wireless access points, it is possible to have the signal transferred by third-party devices, thus giving the user the ability to roam a majority of technologically advanced territories without having to transport their rig. The Koertig can remain safely at home or in one of Vinestead's approved storage facilities where all datacenter advantages are available."

The technician rubbed a soft cloth against Jape's neck and patted his shoulder.

"The video's not over yet," protested Jape, keeping an eye on the screen.

"Don't worry, it's all the same stuff. When you jack in for the first time, you'll find some preloaded training sims. And if you have any questions, just ask your PA."

Jape nodded, then asked, "What's a PA?"

"Personal Assistant. Everyone in VNet has one."

"Oh," replied Jape. He stood and tried to examine his neck in the mirror.

"You might as well get some chow, you need to let your chip settle for a while."

"Thanks," said Jape, picking up his rig case and starting for the door, wondering why it felt so weird to have a microchip embedded in his neck, getting nice and familiar with his spinal column. If he knew anything about Vinestead, it was that whatever they told you, there was always something more. Even if the GA chip could deliver what the video claimed, he knew there would be a price. At the same time, the excited little boy inside of him was wondering what the hell a Personal Assistant was and moreover, what other treasures did this so-called *VNet* hold?

FIFTY-THREE

G stumbled through the red curtains behind Anela's desk, no longer in control of his own body. He had been forced to dial the code up to maximum just to get himself off the floor and into a position to help Natalie. Now that the primary objective had been achieved, the code seemed to have chosen a secondary mission, one that involved certain individuals that were sure to be close by. For a brief moment, G shared Natalie's feeling of being a prisoner, a mere spectator in his body's decisions, but that soon faded as he realized that he didn't care that some demon was pulling his strings. It was the only way to get what he wanted. If he dropped out now, that would be it. The throbbing in his neck and chills in his fingers assured him of that much.

In the room beyond Anela's office, G found what he was looking for. Across the back wall was a bank of cabinets, stacked from bottom to top with blades decorated with LEDs that shone blue in alternating patterns, their light slightly diffused by the metal mesh of the cabinet doors. To the left and right were three full-body chairs with their feet pointed to the center of the room. In five of the six pods, pale bodies reclined without any hint of control, as if someone had removed their internal organs and replaced them with straw. They wore matching black suits that reminded G of shrink tubing. On their heads were ornate rigs, custom jobs that looked nothing like off the shelf parts.

G stared for a moment at the empty chair, wondering if there had once been a sixth cipher or whether Anela was just in the process of hiring. He chuckled, tried to imagine what the job posting would look like. *Hate reality? Tired of freedom? No luck with the ladies? Then come work for the ZabSix Cipher Den, where we promise you won't see any of those ever again!* He really wanted to feel pity, feel sorry for the ciphers strapped to their chairs, dependent on a woman who had recently received a generous dose of stab-action. But it wasn't pity or anger that G felt. Instead, there was an urge in him that had never been there before, a desire to injure, maim, and kill. Not that he had never felt the desire to punch someone, but there had always been some kind of justification, even if it was alcohol-based.

The flesh on the cipher's neck had long since turned pale white, clearly showing the veins that ran beneath, some blue, some red. G pushed a tentative finger against what he guessed was the jugular and cracked a wry smile as the skin gave under the slight pressure. The cipher's throat contracted as if gulping. Removing his gloves, G lined up three of his fingers and held them an inch away from the cipher's neck. Then, in a quick strike, he shot them forward and retracted, amazed at how effortlessly he had penetrated the skin. It took a few seconds for the cipher's brain to realize that something had happened. Under normal operating conditions, the cipher's heart rate was extremely slow, making the wound only trickle blood at first. But as the message got back to the brain and then down to the heart, the red stuff really began to flow, spurting at times.

G felt the spray on his face, didn't even try to avoid it. He opened his mouth and let the acrid taste engulf his tongue. Inside, his stomach convulsed involuntarily. The cipher began to shake feebly in its chair, its muscles not really up for the job.

"That's for booting me out," said G, smiling triumphantly. But as the cipher began to calm, he realized that there was no way to tell which of the ciphers had been in the Net. He assumed that they were all male, but which one was Lio? He walked quickly to another chair and ripped off the rig, unaware that some of its tendrils were attached to the cipher's face. Bits of skin were torn away, revealing the pink underneath. Before the cipher could even open his eyes, G brought his hand down sideways on his windpipe, breaking his neck in several places. The aborted gasp from the cipher was barely audible over the whine of the servers. G pulled back the eyelids, but they were a simple brown, nothing like the fiery ones he saw in the Net.

"Stop," said a digitized voice.

G searched the room and finally focused on the small speakers in the corners. "Who said that," he demanded.

"A friend of the two people you just killed."

G swung around and eyed the three ciphers on the other side of the room. They already looked dead, but clearly one of them was paying attention.

"Is that so? I didn't know ciphers understood the concept of friendship. You know, I had a friend. Two of them actually. And they got royally fucked by one of you. Lio."

"I don't know anybody by that name," said the voice, "but if you are referring to the cipher that Anela inserted into the Net, you should know that he was a copy and that none of us are responsible for his actions."

The words echoed in the room, but G was no longer listening. "You don't have to be responsible for me to hold you accountable." He almost laughed. "I wonder which one of these is you." He approached the center cipher and took its hand. With a quick movement, he broke one of the fingers. "Did you feel that? How about this?" He bent the middle finger backwards unnaturally.

"I don't know what you hope to gain," said the speaker, followed immediately by, "Stop!" It appeared two of the ciphers were now talking, though they shared the same voice.

"Do I have your attention now," asked G. "Should I break another finger or just go ahead and end your life? I have a gun here." He patted the holster on his side. "All I want to know is which one of you is the cipher Lio."

"We don't have names anymore."

"Well," said G, lacing his words with sarcasm, "if any of you were to be copied and inserted into the Net to kill my best friend, which of you would name yourself Lio?"

No answer came from the speaker.

G summoned a bad Spanish drawl, "Then I have no choice but to kill you all." With adrenaline surging, G pulled his pistol from its holster and delivered two shots to the cipher on the left, striking him in the stomach. At the same time, he repeatedly punched the chest of the cipher in front of him, aiming at his heart, knowing that the ribs would eventually cave under the extreme force.

"Stop!" The voices of the ciphers overlapped.

The barrel rose, tracing a line up the cipher's body, stopping when it was lined up with his face. G squeezed off six rounds, shattering the custom rig and sending pieces of black and drops of red flying. Then he felt something give, followed immediately by a loud slurp as his hand slipped past the broken ribs and into the cipher's chest. G smiled, convinced he could feel the last heartbeats on his knuckles. He let several seconds pass, let the ambient noise take over again.

"Lio," he said, "are you still there?"

After a moment of silence, "I'm here."

"So," said G, moving into position by the last cipher, "you're the one who's been messing with me and my friends."

"Not me, a copy."

G shook his head. "You know, I'm not that bright, I don't really understand this concept of copying people. As far as I see it, you're the same asshole that burned me out of the Net." He put a hand to the back of his neck, searching for his port, but his finger slipped into the open bullet hole, making him gag. It was a gruesome reminder of his borrowed time. If anything, he shouldn't have been standing around jawing with the cipher. Just kill him, he commanded himself.

"If I did, I must have had good reason."

"I want you to see something," said G, placing his hands on the rig. He undid the snaps carefully.

"And what is that?"

"I want you to see what you banished me to." Some of the wires were embedded in the skin, but G did his best to remove them without causing too much trauma. When they were all undone, he pulled the rig off and waited as the cipher blinked away the dim light. "Hi," he said, as the cipher's colorless eyes focused on him. "This is reality. It sucks."

G gripped the cipher's jaw and opened his mouth. He took a position next to the chair and widened his legs for extra leverage. Then, with a hand gripping the upper and lower teeth, he pulled apart, nearly sickened by the crunching sound of atrophied tendons and weakened muscles snapping. As the last tendril gave away, his hand slipped, leaving the cipher's lower jaw dangling from his face. G wiped his fingers on the black suit and leaned in to peer into the cipher's eyes, trying to figure out what Natalie was looking for when Anela died.

"It *really* sucks," said G, unsure if the cipher could hear him any longer.

Natalie sat tensely on the floor with her back to the window. The oddly cold pistol in her hand was raised, pointed in the direction of the curtains. The gunshots had scared her out of her stupor, made her stop absently collecting the scattered bullets from the floor. She hadn't wanted to rest, didn't really want to be left alone with her thoughts, but watching Anela die had put a stick in her spokes. She barely noticed herself climbing off her lifeless body, barely noticed G getting to his feet and walking into the other room. He had been gone for who knew how long and now the gunshots evoked images of another firefight, of an encounter that he wouldn't be able to miraculously survive.

She got to her feet slowly, still woozy. It had almost sounded like there were voices coming from beyond the curtain, tinny digitals that sounded calm but desperate. If G was talking to someone, then the negotiations had obviously failed. As much as she tried, she couldn't hear him groaning, which wasn't necessarily a good sign. Holding her breath, she passed through the curtains and was relieved to see G kneeling in the middle of the room, swaying slightly back and forth.

The calm didn't last long.

Natalie did her best not to scream as she took in the scene of mangled and bloody ciphers. From the trails on the floor, she knew G had been responsible. Worse, from the way his arms were out to his side, drenched in an eternal red stain, she knew he had done it with his own bare hands. She approached him slowly, wondering if the code had sent him completely over the edge. When she came into his periphery, he stirred.

"Thank God," she said. "I thought you were dead."

G chuckled, spit blood onto the floor in front of him. "I've been dead for like ten minutes now. Goddamn Anela got me from behind." He motioned to the wound on his neck. "I can feel the code starting to wind down. When it does—"

"No," said Natalie, "we'll get you to a hospital."

Shaking his head, he replied, "There's not enough time. I don't have the energy to keep myself going after the burnout. Heh, luckily I won't live too long after that. The pain won't be so bad."

"Come on, get up."

G resisted, but eventually he allowed himself to be lifted to a standing position. He leaned on Natalie as she carried him back into Anela's office and then towards the elevator. Closing his eyes, he listened to her talk.

"Maybe there's a button or something." Natalie hit the call button and was surprised to see the doors open. She dragged G inside the elevator and examined the menu, noticing a small key jutting from the panel. She shifted it from *LOCK* to *RUN* and pressed the button for B. Before she could stop him, G reached out and hit the lobby button.

"I may not make it back up," he said. "I'll wait for you." He pulled a pouch from his shoulder, wincing from the pain. "You may need these." He held out the remaining C4.

Natalie slipped the bag around her neck as the elevator dropped in a controlled descent to the lower floors. The numbers above the door lit in succession and finally stopped at the lobby. A shiver went down her spine as the doors opened, allowing the smell of gunpowder and blood into their six-by-six sanctuary. She breathed a sigh of relief when nothing jumped out of the shadows and shot at her.

There was a small clearing in the middle of the room, and she helped G down to a sitting position, all the while watching the blood flow from his neck.

"You need a bandage," she said.

G ripped a section of his shirt away and wrapped it around his throat like a scarf. He looked up at her as if to ask, "Happy?" A part of him was screaming to say something nice, say goodbye, reassure her in some way, but he was no longer in control. The code would steer the ship until the moment it crashed on the rocky shore. G could do nothing but watch and wait.

"I'll be back as soon as I can." She stood and walked slowly back to the elevators. When she was inside, she noticed G again. He mimed a gunshot with his hand, reminding her to check her weapon. She pulled it out of her holster and examined the clip. Several rounds remained. It made a loud click as it slid back into place. As the doors closed, she held the inspected gun up to G as if to ask, "Happy?"

FIFTY-FOUR

A snowflake fell amongst the digital trees, pulsing lightly as it passed between its brothers, melting into nothing as it landed on the dry ground. Heat seemed to emanate from a nearby bridge, warming the forest floor around it, drying out the snow before it could make landfall. It was a pale echo of a favorite memory, but it was no longer the snowy sanctuary that it had once been. Instead of the oppressive cold that drove thoughts inward, there was only the pre-spring purgatory, the time between death and rebirth. Though the tropical abomination of his favorite construct was unwelcome, he didn't want to see it destroyed. It clearly wasn't the same as the Terrareal version or that of his memory, but it nonetheless retained a sense of familiarity, a sense of a circular path thoroughly walked, and a starting point returned to.

Not only was the construct different, X felt that the entire Net had somehow changed. He could no longer feel it around him, couldn't detect if anything was moving just beyond the tree-lined walls. The only thing he knew for sure was that there was *something* out there, be it an antiviral program or just the suffocating contraction of the virtual verse. Whatever it was, it was getting closer.

"How much time do we have," asked X. He could see the look of intent concentration on C's face and guessed that she was puzzling the same question.

"I don't know," she replied. Her voice had regained its steady timbre, fully recovered from the rasp. "It's coming faster now. Most of the Net is already gone."

X tried to imagine the death of his utopia, wondering how something so full of possibility could ever be destroyed. Now, no one would ever get to experience the same kind of freedom and optimism that had pervaded his life for the last few years, that unquestionable belief that anything was possible with the right amount of time and effort. Want to be the man in the high castle? Just imagine the spire. Want to roll in the clear waters of a lunar beach? Just fill out this form and it can be yours. There was so much potential, for life, for happiness, and now it was all being taken away.

"I remember this place," said C, taking in the construct. She suddenly turned her head to the left, looking for her house through the tightly packed trees. "I haven't been here in a while."

"Did you ever come back here after I left? In the real world, I mean."

"Before I became a permanent resident here?" She waited for X to nod. "Yeah, once. I was coming home from school and took a detour. But that was end of summer; there were still leaves on the trees." She leaned over slightly to look at the dry brook beneath the bridge. "There was even a stream here."

"I prefer the snow."

"So do I." She caught X's eyes. "You can't make it snow here?"

"I'm trying," he said, pointing up.

Several feet above them, C could see the snow falling from the cloudless, blue sky. It disappeared several feet above their heads. "I've never seen anything like that before."

"There're probably a million things that we've never seen."

C smiled. "Now you get it, don't you?"

The realization came down hard on X, forcing connections in his brain that had never been there before. Even though he knew that he had copied C, he never fully understood why she would get so mad about it. It was true that she would never be able to return to the real world, but if anything, that was an advantage. Living in the Net for the rest of her life would mean an existence without pain, without want or need. She could have any kind of life she wanted at the slightest request. When Anela told him that he was a copy, he felt a kind of happiness, coupled with the belief that his body was still out there, waiting to be freed. Whether Natalie knew it or not, it didn't matter. She would find him, wake him, and only then understand that the man in the Net was just a copy.

But now the dream of living forever in the digital world was slowly breaking apart, weakened by C's virus and finished off by Vinestead's counterstrike. The affection that he felt for the Net was the same that C felt for Terrareal. She preferred reality; confinement to the Net was an undesirable alternative. Now X found himself sentenced to death, a debatable form of freedom, one devoid of basic desires and obligations, yet lacking in the vibrancy of his beloved Net. The knowledge of this parallel crushed down on X's chest.

"It will be nicer, I think," said C, "when we're finally gone. This is no way for a person to live."

"I wouldn't have minded. I've got nowhere else to go."

"Just one," said C, her voice oddly calm.

"You really don't like it here, do you?"

C shook her head. "I never did. It just never felt *real* for me."

"It's just as good," countered X.

"But it's not the same." C knocked on the wood plank beneath her. "It sounds the same, but we both know it isn't. Everything in here is programmed. Even with free will, things don't happen unless you want them to."

X thought about Natalie and the first time that he had seen her on the elevator at Jester. Everything about that encounter was seemingly random; there were a lot of people waiting for the elevators, two cars had arrived within seconds of each other, and despite all of that, he still ended up behind her, well within the radius of her chemical scent, enchanted long before they reached the thirteenth floor.

"And what did we do with the time we had together," continued C. "We spent it alone, just you and me. You said the Net was this huge, expansive place, but how often did we see anyone else? Two, three times? You can't just take a girl away from human interaction. She needs to be out there with her friends."

The memory of Natalie sleeping in his bed for the first time replayed in X's head. It had been so effortless; he didn't invite her in and she had asked no permission. It was simply an understanding of things that were going to happen. There was no code telling her to be submissive, no code regulating who came and went in the hallways, whether his roommates would stay away long enough. It felt more real because there were things outside of his control. Life wasn't just a video game with a God mode; there had to be rules and randomness. Having everything he wanted, having no fear of rejection from a cute blonde when he placed his hand on her hip, was not the way of reality and thus, less than fulfilling.

"I can't explain why I did the things I did," said X. "I can barely remember what it was like to be so possessive." Less than two years had passed since he first set eyes on C, on Lily as she was known then. Nevertheless, it felt like a hundred years ago, a time that X could revisit in his memory, but which no longer held the same emotions. "All I know is that I liked you and wanted to be with you. Can you blame me for that?"

"I blame you for a lot of things, but I suppose you did love me. Even if it was misguided, there's still something to be said for your unwavering devotion." C smiled one of her old smiles, a relic of their courtship.

X bit his lip and nodded.

"The snow stopped," said C, looking up. "It's winding down now."

"Everything seems to be that way." X stood up and felt the bridge shift under his feet. "It feels like the end." He shook his head. "I was expecting something much more violent. I can't believe it's going to be like this."

"Like what," asked C, standing and joining him by the rail. Together, they looked at the dry bed beneath, searching for patterns in the distribution of smooth rocks.

"Fading out. No fight, no struggle." A creaking sound drew X's attention to the right, to a tree falling in the distance. "I feel weird." The urge to confess his sins to C was overwhelming, but X fought hard against it, trying to keep the truth bottled up inside.

"It must be the guilt," suggested C.

"Yeah," said X, "I *am* sorry for what I did to you, sorry that I filled your head with wild ideas of moving to Texas and going to college with me. And the whole long distance relationship thing, that wasn't fair to you either."

"You did what you thought was right."

"I don't think it was right anymore."

Smiling, C placed her hand on his arm. "Then all of this hasn't been for nothing. Life is just a sequence of events. The only way a person can say that they have really succeeded is for them to find and recognize a fundamental truth."

"Which is?"

"You have to figure that out for yourself. But I've discovered a truth that says I can forgive you because, obviously, you weren't in your right mind."

X chuckled halfheartedly. "Ino said that you would never go out with me. I had to prove her wrong." A moment passed in which they heard more destruction on the construct's borders. "You could also say that *you* weren't in your right mind either, dating a guy three years older than you."

The bridge trembled as the earth around it shook violently. Startled by the sudden movement, C reflexively put her arms around X. When he looked down, he saw C's chin resting against his chest, looking up at him with eyes that betrayed her calm words. For all of her growth and evolution, she was still human at heart, willing to die at a time of her choosing, but scared to the bone when death came knocking of its own accord.

"I have to confess," said C, "that when I tried to kill myself before, I didn't really think it was going to work. I can't describe what happened in the gap between then and now. It really *is* nonexistence, an awareness so lacking that you don't even know you're not existing."

"We're just copies," said X, trying to reassure her. "The story doesn't end here for us. Who knows, maybe one day the real me will try to contact the real you. Imagine what that conversation would be like."

"It probably wouldn't be a good idea."

"Andy wouldn't approve?" The words slipped out of his mouth easily, bordering on accusation.

C didn't miss a beat, countering with, "Nor would Natalie."

He fumbled for an explanation but couldn't find words that would justify what he had done. Even apologizing didn't seem appropriate anymore. He looked down at her eyes and said nothing, hoping it would be enough to convey his feelings.

"Yeah," said C, softly. "There's nothing left to say." The forest around them answered with a barrage of falling trees, crashing into each other, sending dirt across the ground like waves.

X snuck a peek to the side, saw that the bridge was as sound as it had ever been, but where it ended, the ground had faded away. Bits of rocks and twigs sunk into it slowly, like a layer of oil atop water, gathering speed and falling away as it came out the other side. He felt C's arms tighten around him. Perhaps there *was* nothing left to say, if you only counted confessions and apologies, but X felt there was still one phrase, an old standby, that could set everything right.

"I love you?" Even he didn't know if he was asking or telling.

The bridge shook again and C looked up at X, trying to figure out why he would say such a thing. "Even if that were true," she said, her voice trembling, "what difference would it make now?"

"Someone once wrote that the only thing we truly need is to be loved."

"Fantasy," said C, "fairy tales." She inspected the crumbling construct. "In worlds real and virtual, they don't mean anything. I don't know if anyone ever wrote that."

"Would you say it for me?"

"Say what?"

X felt her breaking away. "Tell me that you love me. *Loved* me."

C sighed heavily and unwrapped herself from X. The absence of his touch felt momentarily painful, but it receded, along with all other feelings fleeting and unimportant. She looked away into the crumbling void. "I can't believe that after all this time, you're still hung up on that."

"Please, for old time's sake."

C shook her head and turned to face X. His eyes held no sign of the former version of himself; he had no memory of their breakup in her virtual bedroom. With the world coming to an end, it didn't seem like the time to try to explain. "You said it yourself, we're only copies. Even if I did love you, you're not him and I'm not her. We're barely real!"

The wood in the middle of the bridge splintered, pushed upward by an unseen force, drawing a line between X and C. The construct shuddered under the weight of the approaching antivirus, on the very verge of breaking. Leaves, blown about by a wind that seemed to come from all directions at once, passed like a barrier in front of them, obscuring each from the other's view.

X thought he could see her eyes. He lifted his hand towards her, offering it for a price. "Do you," he mouthed silently.

There was just enough of a break in the wall of foliage to see C shaking her head. She seemed to slow then and so too did the leaves. The wind that had been howling grew silent as every bit of the construct paused, looked up, saw the gaping hole in the protective ozone. Beyond it, X could see the black nothing of the ether. For a moment, it was like staring into the night sky and seeing no stars.

He held his gaze even as the antivirus breached the rim and poured down into the construct in a white-blue blob, dissolving everything that it touched, leaving only black behind. It pooled at his feet, moving through his boots like water through paper. The burning grew from the bottom up, engulfing X, rewriting his lines of code from the rogue distribution of creation to a Vinestead-approved series of ones and zeros.

When his eyes began to go, he was still staring into the dark night, wondering where the rest of the universe had gone. He got the overwhelming feeling that they *were* the last two people, not just in the Net, but in all of reality.

X was consumed by the antivirus in a matter of seconds, but he felt a lifetime of emotion in that short window, alternating between opposite ends of multiple spectrums. When the wheel finally stopped spinning and the world came to an end, he surrendered to his final emotion, welcoming the release that death would bring.

In that last moment, X felt truly and utterly alone.

FIFTY-FIVE

Finding X was going to be a matter of extreme self-control, a fact Natalie realized the second the elevator doors closed on G. As the car descended, she told herself to be strong, but when the generic directions didn't work, she switched to simplified actions. *Stand against the back wall. Raise your gun and point it at the crease of the door. Don't worry about anything else, just keep your eyes focused. Don't watch the numbers over the doors.*

The last command was given because the light had gone out between 1 and B, though the elevator was still moving. However low the basement was, it wasn't simply one floor down. It had to be at least four or five stories below street level. *Don't worry about how far down you are or whether there will be stairs to get back up.* Part of her wanted the elevator to stop already and she was relieved when it did, though the sudden deceleration made her stomach flip. She raised her gun higher as the light on B illuminated and the doors opened.

Instead of the squad of highly trained commandos that she was expecting, Natalie was greeted with a blast of cool air. Had she any exposed skin besides her face, she would have been able to observe the rapidly forming goose bumps. *Don't close your eyes.* The corridor in front of her was dark and the elevator only gave off enough light to see three or four feet into the darkness. She stepped forward cautiously and kept one foot on the threshold. *There has to be a light switch around here somewhere.* The wall to the left was empty, but on her right side, her fingers found a rusty box protruding from the wall and on the front, a light switch. *Flip it!*

The fluorescent lights on the ceiling began flickering, lighting in succession from the far end of the corridor. The previous silence was replaced by the hum of electricity flowing through mercury. Natalie allowed the doors to shut behind her and walked quickly down the hall. More than ever, she felt that X was closer, coupled with the strange premonition that time was running out. She wondered what X was doing in the basement of Anela's building. *Maybe she has him strapped to a chair and jacked in.* It was her only thought because everything else just didn't make sense. There was nothing to be gained from holding X hostage and not jacking him in. Putting him in a little cell in the basement would do nothing.

Torturing him for information wouldn't yield anything useful either. As much as he liked other people to think, X wasn't a secret agent bent on corporate espionage. He wasn't a superhero or some master hacker with intel on big government contracts. And to punish him simply because he crossed a cipher den seemed even less likely than the one scenario that she refused to consider. *Don't even think that way, don't you dare. Keep your center of gravity low, keep the gun trained high, and everything will be okay.*

At last, the hallway ended at a sliding steel door, secured on the right by a thick padlock. Natalie's heart sank momentarily, her mind racing with conflicting ideas about how to find the key, if she should go all the way back up to twenty, or if Anela even had a key in the first place. She calmed herself and stepped to the side, hoping the angle would be enough to protect her from the ricochet. Though bullets had been flying at her all night, the single shot from her Sig seemed to echo forever down the long corridor. The bullet bounced off the walls frighteningly close until it found a weak spot in the concrete and embedded itself.

Natalie smiled as she kicked at the busted lock with her boot. It made a triumphant clink as it fell to the floor. *There's no stopping you now!* The door was heavy and she struggled to get it open with one hand. She had to stow her gun so that she could put both hands and the weight of her body into it. Even before the door was completely open, she could feel how much cooler it was inside the next room, a good ten or twenty degrees below the already cold ambient. Again, she searched for a light switch and found a similar box on the wall. Above it, a flexible tube routed the wires towards the ceiling where they joined a larger box, then traced along the side of the wall and out of sight. Whatever this place was used for, all of the electrical had been added after the building was constructed.

The lights were slightly dimmer, but Natalie recognized the same kind of cabinets that she had seen in Anela's cipher room. There were three rows of them with eight across, all of them whirring in symphony and blinking their LEDs at the newcomer. Suddenly, the air conditioning made sense; the room had to be kept cold because of all the servers and networking equipment. *Where is X?!* The voice inside of her screamed, told her to stop feeling good about solving one little puzzle. There was a much more important question to answer and quickly, because somewhere above her, G was slowly bleeding to death.

This can't be it. Unless Anela had been lying, had felt the need to fill Natalie's head with false hopes just before putting a bullet between her eyes. It was this exact scenario that had Natalie arguing with herself, simultaneously believing and rejecting what Anela told her. There was nothing in the room, just servers busy crunching numbers and piping one of two bits down copper wires to the terabit switches at the top of each rack. Natalie circled the cabinets and walked down each aisle to examine the servers within. On the last row, two cabinets from the end, a strange pattern caught her eye.

While all of the other cabinets were entirely lit, the one she stood in front of was only half-so. Near the middle, the lights simply stopped. Crouching, she discovered that the servers on the bottom weren't even running. She examined the lowest operating server and immediately stood up, grabbed at the door handle, and opened the cabinet wide. A single letter had sparked her interest, printed out on a nice clean label, affixed to the server. It read simply, "X." Natalie ran her finger over the smooth letter, then on the rough grating of the server cover. At each end of the blade were two rounded hooks used for installation and removal. On the left hook was a key secured by a twist-tie.

Natalie ripped the key from the server and held it up to the light to get a better look at it. It wasn't a normal key like those used for doors and padlocks, but more of a rounded sort like the one she had used to operate the elevator. She quickly scanned her surroundings and even the server again, looking for anything that the key might fit. Another trip up and down the aisles yielded nothing and as a last-ditch effort, she walked around the periphery of the room, examining the mesh wiring on the cold concrete. Every few feet, metal slats rose from floor to ceiling, reminding her of support beams. She let her hand drag across the miniature chain-link until finally it caught on a raised section. It was hard to see under the strange light, but Natalie caught a glimpse of another door beyond the mesh, mesh that had a camouflaged indentation for grasping.

Again, the voice came, told her not to think about a scenario that was slowly gaining strength in her mind. The appearance of a server bearing X's name had made a part of her stop wondering about his fate. It was clear to a minority that X had been sentenced to a digital existence, reduced to binary bondage. If X was in that server, then Anela had been telling the truth; he really was in the basement. She couldn't accept that idea though, because that meant that the search was over, that the quest to find X had come to an end with him being nothing but machine code. In her exploration, she had found no screwdrivers with which to remove him from the cabinet, nor could she think of how to keep him powered up. And what kind of life would that be anyway, keeping her boyfriend locked up in a datacenter so that he would stay alive?

No, don't think like that. It would have to be a secret room, one hidden behind the walls in case the cops came snooping around. Natalie pawed at the screen until it finally swung free from the wall. The handle on the door was even less of a grip, but Natalie's gloves had enhanced tact and stuck to the door with ease. She pushed it forward, wondering how heavy it was until another gust of cold air slipped in through the small opening. Natalie backed away quickly and patted at her face, at the still-cold skin that was beginning to tingle.

It took her a moment to realize that it was just very cold air, that while it was a balmy fifty degrees in the server room, it had to be well below zero in the next. She thought about the kind of equipment in there, thought about that instead of the truth that she already knew deep down in her heart. Her head was filled with images of supercomputers and thickly stacked flash disks. The equipment must be worth millions of dollars, she told herself. She flirted with the idea of stealing it all, but the logistics were much too complicated and all but dismissed as she pressed through the door again, buffeting herself against the arctic blast.

The door swung wide and locked into place against the wall. Natalie tugged on it to make sure that it wouldn't close by itself, trapping her inside. To be sure, she unsheathed her knife, still dry-coated in Anela's blood, and jammed it between the door and the frame. The shivering started a moment later and Natalie turned quickly to examine the room, only to experience the most abrupt emotional swing of her short lifetime.

Where there had once been hope, there was now only despair as her eyes took in the far wall. It was lined with square plaques, three rows of five. The other walls were similarly decorated. In the middle of the room, a large vent hung from the ceiling, blowing the cold air down into the room, so cold that it could be seen billowing along the floor. Although she had never been in Anela's basement before, she knew what she was looking at, had seen enough movies to recognize a body locker when she saw one. Her mind switched gears quickly from wanting desperately to believe Anela to needing her to be a liar, for once to live up to the stereotypes that held for all cipher den suits. If what she said were true, then X was behind one of the plaques. Even in her armor, Natalie felt the cold gripping at her bones. It was only by its grace that she remained functional in the icebox. Someone without proper attire, someone like X, would stand no chance in this environment.

It took an eternity to try all of the locks and by the time the key slipped into the correct hole, she had begun to tremble uncontrollably. Her breathing came shallow and stilted, half from the freezing air, half from the sadness that she was trying not to express. The tears traced down her face, cutting icicle lines into her cheeks. She let out a gasp as the lock turned, sending a plume of white breath into the air in front of her.

The plaque slid forward, giving way to the cold indifferent steel of a gurney. Natalie shut her eyes and walked blindly backwards, pulling the tray all the way out. Now that her attention was inward, the voice began to speak again. It told her that she should have been expecting this. It was the temperature, the voice contended, that should have tipped her off. *You can't keep anything but computers in fifty-degree environments. And even if there were supercomputers in here, they wouldn't be able to operate in subzero temperature. Maybe at just above freezing, but certainly not below.*

Natalie put her hand on the rail of the tray and moved forward.

Now, you can keep a body for a few days at near-freezing.

She opened her eyes slowly.

But if you really want to preserve it, you have to get the temperature below zero degrees.

Natalie gasped, a sickly and guttural sound of her entire body contracting in pain. Lying on the gurney, with his skin a frosty white and eyes stuck open unnaturally, was X.

The strength left Natalie's legs and she crumpled to the floor awkwardly, leaving a hand on the gurney for support. She had known, had almost been expecting it to turn out this way, but the sadness came anyway. The tears flowed and saliva dripped from her mouth, the echoing sounds of her wailing only making things worse. The rest of the world was a million miles away and the only thing that Natalie could think about was that X's shoulder was a mere two inches from her fingertips and yet she could not bring herself to touch him. She wondered what kind of devotion that showed on her part, whether the all-consuming suffering was really a product of her love for him or if, perhaps, it was her own guilt for not loving him enough to suffer through this new evolution. She didn't want a world where her boyfriend was kidnapped, murdered, and then stuffed in a freezer for eternity. It was all too much to have in her life. She hated herself for thinking that, but it was the truth if there had ever been any truth before.

The road of X had come to an end and even if it hadn't, Natalie didn't feel like walking it anymore. There was nothing more she could do for him, save stand and shut his eyelids in the way poorly trained detectives did on television crime dramas. And just like that, the pain started to lessen, and the cold of the room became the primary problem again. Natalie wiped at her mouth with her sleeve, found it cold and abrasive against her lips. She stood up slowly, wondering if X's face still had the nightmare quality of her recent memory.

His eyelids were frozen and unmovable, at least that's what Natalie claimed from her vantage point. She suddenly wondered about the other lockers, about how many other people were trapped in Anela's basement. The voice told her that he needed a proper burial, but there was no way she was going to be able to lift him off the gurney, let alone through the server room and into the elevator. And even if she did, what good would it do? What would the police say when they found her with the frozen corpse of her boyfriend and the fresh corpse of her—

"I," said Natalie to X's unflinching face. She stuttered from the cold. A hundred different sentences came to mind and some of them would have been good if X were alive to hear them. But anything she said would have only been for her benefit, which made the next words out of her mouth an easy choice. After all, it was the consolation prize that she had wanted since he disappeared. In a perfect world, she would have him back at her side. But in this imperfect reality, the very least she wanted from the fates was the final opportunity.

"Goodbye," she said, softly, "I'll miss you."

No response came from X and Natalie suddenly didn't want to look at his face anymore. She moved quickly to the other side of the plaque so that his head was obscured. With an outstretched hand, she pushed the gurney back into the wall with X's body untouched by her fingers. It was a moment for a last goodbye, not a last caress.

Natalie retreated to the server room, feeling immediately better in the warmer climate. An idea occurred to her then, spawning a multitude of various outcomes, very few of which would satisfy her desire to free X. She found a large electrical switch by the opposite wall and pulled it. Just as she had hoped, the whine of the air conditioner seemed to sputter and then quit altogether. Even the freezing air that was billowing out of the meat locker seemed to lessen as the large fan in the center of the room gave out.

Even though it would heat up and eventually fail, X's server required more attention and assurance that it would be destroyed. She kneeled in front of it one last time and carefully arranged the C4 in the gaps above and below it. She wondered if X was really in there, if it held some copy of him that she might be able to restore. She waited for some kind of internal encouragement, but it didn't come. The voice that had guided her through the nightmare was now gone, or at least, was no longer speaking. Given no bearing, she assumed that what she was doing was correct. She set the timer for twenty minutes and closed the rack door. In the relative silence, she could hear the whine of the server's fans, rising and falling like the tide, ramping up to deal with the increased heat.

Natalie walked into the hallway again, leaving the lights on to aid in the heat death. In a moment of panic, she realized that she had left her knife jammed in the freezer door and she almost turned to retrieve it. But the road had ended. The search for X was over. There would be no more killing.

In the elevator, she decided that she would place an anonymous call in a few days if the explosion didn't attract enough attention. The police would come and find a building full of dead miscreants. She would have to tell them specifically to look in the basement, where they would find the server pieces and the decaying body of X. Letting him sweat it out on the gurney wasn't the nicest thing she had ever done for him. It wasn't the loving display of devotion that carrying his body out over her shoulder would have been.

There were a lot of things she could have done, but Natalie felt a disconnect in her life that distanced her from X and even G. It was one thing to watch a nameless goon fall under the blistering hail of G's gun, but to see X lying there, to see one of her peers, knowing how easily it could have been her. It was too close to home.

The voice in her head spoke up one last time, told her that X deserved better, but she answered it quickly, telling herself that given the circumstances, it was the most she was willing to do for him.

The elevator doors parted in front of her, casting a new light into the hallway, illuminating Natalie's world just enough for her to recognize and understand what she had just said.

FIFTY-SIX

Jape looked at the coordinates on his wrist, thought that they looked somehow familiar. His job had been to oversee a small detachment of coders as they intertwined the fabric of VNet with the core servers of the old Net. It was an easy job, since Jape didn't really have to do any of the work himself. He just told the coders where to go and what to build. For the most part, he didn't even stay jacked in. Instead, he walked the upper floors of the Vinestead West building, watching the glittering lights of downtown Sacramento in the dark night. At street level, there was a fading echo of a technological paralysis, a standstill that had been created by the shutdown of the old Net. Now that VNet was filling the void, services were being restored. Only a few minutes prior, Jape's cell had beeped. Upon examination, he found that he had five bars and a text message welcoming him to the Vinestead Network. Everything seemed to be going smoothly until those three numbers popped up.

Standing on the balcony just off a conference room, with the wind in his hair, Jape jacked in and found himself floating in front of a large, rounded cube. It was glowing bright neon green in the black construct, looking conspicuously out of place. One of his coders was off to the right, tapping out characters on a vidscreen.

"What's the problem," asked Jape, knowing that the coder was more than qualified to handle the Vinestead integration. He was one of those hardcore programmers, lacking the personal appeal that Jape used for social engineering.

"This homedir won't delete."

Jape looked around at the empty construct and despite the lack of identifying landmarks, suddenly understood that he was standing at the former site of homedir central, just a few hops, skips, and jumps from the core of the Net. It was no surprise that the homedirs were gone, since they weren't required with VNet, but he was amazed at how quickly they had been discarded.

"I thought homedirs were white," said Jape, looking at the green structure.

"They are," said the coder, "the color is coming from inside."

Jape nodded. "Alright, I'll take care of it. Carry on."

The coder made a half nod and jumped, his afterimage melting in place.

Jape approached the homedir cautiously but intrigued. The closer he got, the more it seemed like something was moving beneath the surface, a million little lines of green circling quickly. "So you're the virus I've heard so much about. It's very nice to meet you." He placed his hand on the wall and smiled when the green slivers swarmed towards it and then retreated. "You have a friend of mine in there, yeah?" It was impossible to see past the glowing curtain, but Jape sensed something beyond it. "In a way, he's the reason I'm where I'm at today. I can't help but feel that I should repay him somehow."

The virus surged angrily.

"Let him out?" Jape shook his head. "No, I would never do that. X wouldn't know what to do with himself out here in VNet. I think he should stay right where he is." He took a few steps back in the ether. "But that doesn't mean I can't do something for him."

Jape shot backwards. For a few minutes, he dreamed with his eyes open, overlaying the green cube with a hundred different elements, playing with shade and architecture until he found what he was looking for. He spread out his hands and waited. The burn started in his lower chest, spread upwards to his throat, and finally engulfed his head. It seethed and crackled in his ears, but it caused no pain, just a feeling of something building within.

All at once, the floor of the construct burst out of the ether, bringing a wide expanse of green grass into view, stunning Jape's eyes. It flowed in liquid creation along the border, rushing outwards as quickly as the processors in Jape's rig could handle. At some arbitrary vanishing point, it spilled upwards, changing its hue to blue and rushing back towards the center of the dome. At one point off to the right, it split, circled around an empty spot that eventually turned into a bright orange sun. At the apex, the liquid came together and fell back towards the ground, its hue slowly fading out, announcing its impact with a gentle gust of air.

Jape smiled at the simplicity of the scene, how very ominous it would all look when the structure was complete. He focused on X's homedir, imagining a stone cage enveloping it, rising up from the ground to swallow that which defied deletion. Bits of stone erupted from the grass and rolled up the side of the structure, settling into a flat surface. More stones gathered at the base, widening its footprint so that the cube looked more like a sheered pyramid. On top, the stone rumbled, vibrated as rocks climbed over each other to form two vertical columns.

He rotated his hands together slowly and the columns mirrored the action. At the right angle, Jape clapped his hands and joined the columns at the center. It was amazing how easy it was, thought Jape. VNet bent to his will with a submission that he had never known before. With as little as a single idea, he had made a large statue in the middle of an empty field. The stony pyramid rose as testament to the superiority of VNet and the new world that was to follow.

"Thank you, X," said Jape. "I couldn't have done it without you."

It was later that the first settlers happened upon the monument. Some saw it as a piece of art, others as a deliberate attempt by VNet to add some mystery to its latest product. They thought the pyramid to be Egyptian, but they couldn't decipher the large X that stood atop it. That X, that large and stony letter, defied explanation.

They didn't know it was a tribute to the man who had changed the face of the Net forever.

FIFTY-SEVEN

Natalie stared at her reflection in the elevator doors, unaware that X had done the same thing a world away from today. She examined herself just as he had, cataloging her features in the slightly gold mirror. Her face looked as it always had, but beneath that, her black outfit hid the creases of her body, making her appear as a shadow. The desire to take off the armor swelled up inside of her and she resolved to do just that as soon as possible. As soon as she got G some help.

The elevator dinged and the doors opened and just as if the cables had been cut, Natalie's heart dropped to the bottom of her stomach. G was no longer sitting awkwardly in the middle of the room, but instead, had slumped over on his side with his head lying on a pile of broken boards. She moved to him quickly, stepping around the garbage and overturned chairs. Even from a distance, she could see that he wasn't moving. If he was breathing, his chest seemed to want no part of it. A quick prayer was all she could manage before she reached him and knelt at his side.

She placed a finger on his neck and waited the painful seconds, thinking always that the pulse would be coming on the next tick, but it never did. Even after a full sixty seconds, she kept expecting something, a sign of life from him. Natalie removed her hand and tried to wipe away the tears from her eyes, but they weren't there. Inside, she was sad and pained, but the tears wouldn't come anymore. She realized that she would have to leave G there and that—

"Fuuuuuuuuuuuck…"

It took Natalie a moment to realize that the sound was coming from G. She lifted his face and pressed at one of his eyelids. The pupils were moving slowly beneath them.

"G! Hey, can you hear me?"

"Nah— Nataleeeeee?"

"What the hell happened?" This time, the tears came, pulled from another reserve, one waiting for a happy moment to come along.

"Stand by." G's eyes stopped rotating, and his eyelids came up under his own power. He seemed to be tracking something in the room, but eventually he locked with Natalie. A slight smile appeared on his lips and then his body went into convulsions.

Natalie recoiled, identified the urge, and locked it down. She put a comforting hand on G's shoulder.

Inside, the last of the code was burning through G's spine, bringing all of his systems out of the near coma. He felt them come online one by one and wiggled his fingers accordingly. "Back from the dead," he said, smiling. Although he was improved, his body was still dealing with a gunshot wound and a lack of body heat.

"I don't even want to know," said Natalie. "We need to get you to a hospital." She lifted him up slowly, put his arm around her shoulder for leverage.

Together, they ambled towards the front door while G spouted nonsensical observations about the night, like how easily the guards had been killed, how funny it was to watch Natalie kill Anela, and how a Blue Rain would hit the spot and that if he couldn't open his mouth to just pour it in the hole in his neck.

In her pocket, something beeped. Natalie fished out her cell and checked the screen. "Welcome to the Vinestead Network," it said. She ignored the message and dialed information. "Taxi," she said, "corner of West and Fifteenth." Replacing the phone, Natalie pushed forward, dragging G through the rotting entryway of the ZabSix cipher den.

On the street, Natalie waited with the dying G in her arms. She took a deep breath of the foul Old Downtown air and smiled. It wasn't the cold sterility of the freezer or the bloody aroma of the twentieth floor. It wasn't simulated either, wasn't the product of some program running on an anonymous server that had somehow been designated as the authority on smells. No, nothing about Terrareal was artificial. The light rain that fell on her face was a product of environmental processes and the people that splashed in the puddles were their own self-aware machines, not tied to a system, not relying on it for survival. Looking south, she could see the beginnings of the neon river, glowing brightly through the rain. The colors were dazzling, diffused by the occasional droplet that landed on her eye.

They stood there until the taxi showed up ten minutes later and in that time, Natalie considered what she was going to say or do to get the driver to let G in his cab. After that, how would she explain his wounds to the doctors or her being dressed in similar armor? It was a bad situation, Natalie told herself, but not one that she couldn't get through. Sure, people might leer and make snide comments about her outfit, and yeah, the doctors might call the cops the second they see the armor on G and scope Natalie clad in black, but none of that mattered anymore, none of that seemed important next to the realization that although the rain fell from the sky and the bad customers walked the street with their hoods drawn and eyes scavenging, it was all wonderfully random.

The city, the world, with all of its imperfections, was at least the way nature and God intended it to be. Natalie let her eyes wander the street, to the shadows, to the single star that shone through the clouds above.

It seemed to her that the world had never looked so real.

EPILOGUE

Time passed slowly in X's homedir, ticking by without acknowledgement from the metal sliver in his wrist. It had long ago ceased to work, was now only a blank slate capable of telling the one true time: eternity. Several years had gone by, though to X, they were more like several lifetimes. In each, he tried his best to ignore the vidscreen that C had left for him, tried not to wonder what he would see if he ever turned it on. Hate, still smoldering in the ashes, kept him from looking. But from those same ashes, curiosity eventually blossomed. With only the pain of regret and jealousy to sacrifice, X took the plunge, grabbed the vidscreen from the dresser, and sat with it in the middle of the room, waiting for the show.

The story of Lily filled the screen, bubbling up from the black in condensed fragments. He nearly smiled when he learned that the Andy fling didn't last long, only a year before he moved on to greener pastures. She disappeared after that, living off the grid for those muddled years where she should have been going to college. Her lack of direction disappointed X, made him wonder if he had done something to her to evoke such apathy. The evidence pointed to a nomadic existence, moving from state to state, trying to search out a definition of herself in the unforgiving harshness of Terrareal. Eventually, she fell in with a speed-jacker in South Carolina, a bottom-of-the-barrel technic that abused her to the point that the police had to keep records. The photos made X's fingers tremble on the virtual terminal.

She grew up before his eyes, fifteen to twenty-two in just a few minutes of browsing photos and data. He cringed at the reality he saw her living and lamented what kind of life he could have given her, had everything worked out right. But there was too much smoke to see that future, too much lingering heat from the fire that had burned that bridge out from beneath them. Now there was nothing but the wasted years, the time that they should have spent together.

The Lily as he knew her was gone.

She was different now, grown up, a seventh-year revision of the girl he had once loved. That girl was lost forever, overwritten by something else, something less than the sum of his memories.

That discovery was lifetimes ago, though some of the images remained in his head, with no new incoming data to replace it. The concepts of time and speed were reduced to vague guidelines, now largely ignored. The only thing that truly moved, truly changed, was the virus that flowed along the construct's walls, neither inside, nor out. The green scales rippled over each other and morphed into rigid sections when X approached them. The only thing left to do was to scrape away the brilliant green, try to expose the ones and zeros.

It was, after all, only code.

It would only be a matter of time before he hacked it.

And time was something he had plenty of.

AUTHOR'S NOTE

It's been almost twenty years since I first published *Xronixle*, and even longer since its earliest incarnation, the short story *The Sum of Memory*. A lot has changed in those two decades—in books, in the world, and in the way I tell stories.

As a writer, I've grown up a lot. My understanding of structure, character, pacing, and editing has improved immeasurably. Looking back at this book, I recognize that many of the choices I made were poor, immature, or misguidedly edgy—choices I wouldn't make today.

This second edition contains no major changes to the story. What you're reading is essentially the same novel released in 2007, with only a light pass of grammar checking and small housekeeping corrections. To truly polish *Xronixle* would mean rewriting it entirely—and doing that would erase what it is: an artifact of my first foray into self-publishing.

I hope readers view this book through the appropriate lens, understanding that the author who wrote it doesn't really exist anymore. Writing is a journey, and as uncomfortable as it can be to revisit the first step, I'm proud to share it with you.

Thank you for reading.

Daniel Verastiqui
April 12, 2025

THANK YOU

Xronixle is the first book of **The Vinestead Anthology**.

If you enjoyed this book, please consider leaving a review.

Each standalone novel in the Vinestead Anthology tells a small part of a larger epic: the rise and fall of Vinestead International, the exploits of a rogue artificial intelligence named Lassiter, and a seemingly endless stream of idealistic hackers— each convinced they're the hero of the story.

Enjoy them in any order.

Xronixle (2007)

Veneer (2011)

Perion Synthetics (2014)

Por Vida (2017)

Brigham Plaza (2019)

Hybrid Mechanics (2020)

Vise Manor (2022)

House of Nepenthe (2025)

To learn more about the Vinestead Anthology and explore additional titles, please visit **danielverastiqui.com**

www.ingramcontent.com/pod-product-compliance
Lightning Source LLC
Chambersburg PA
CBHW040854010826
48978CB00013BA/1014